MW01170607

Lady of the Mist

ISBN: 9798360064015

Imprint: Independently published

Lady of the Mist

By S.L. Thorne

Book 1 of the Gryphon's Rest

Dedication

For Jack, Tré and Laura, and Chris.
You know what you did.

And for my daughter, who put up with 'Do not
disturb' signs and 'Stop reading over my
shoulder!'

And for Stanley, who never lived to see this but
none-the-less, never doubted I'd do it.

1

The woman they called the 'lady of the mist' leaned on the parapet rail, drinking in the early morning air. She smiled softly as she watched the fey sun rise, wildly colouring the sky and beginning to burn off the morning fog. The two guards on the wall with her stood at opposite ends of the walk between two small towers and politely ignored her, keeping their watch in silence.

She was not what anyone would call 'beautiful'. She had an unremarkable Irish face. Her complexion alone was enviable, fair but with a light gilding from the sun. Her eyes were a faded silvery-green, nothing at all striking about them. Her hair flowed down her back in waves of mousy brown and stopped just short of the bottom of her ribs, teased just now by the fresh dawn wind. Compared to the willowy elven women she dealt with daily, she was short and thick, though in truth, she was neither. Back home she was considered tall for a girl, but not rangy. Her attire was like everything else about her: modest, only hinting at the figure beneath the front-laced bodice.

Her clothes were good elven plain cloth cut in old Celtic style. A full-length peasant skirt that just brushed the lower laces of her short boots in a rich evergreen that matched the bodice. Her white blouse was the finest thing on her, cobweb linen and embroidered at its high throat and wrists with some fey flowering vine hiding tiny owls and dragonflies picked out in white threads. The little princess had embroidered it for her with her own hands, and it was precious to her.

The sky slowly eased out of its gaudy splendour and the sun began to dimple the forest floor through gem-like dewdrops. She cast her eye past the great oak and over the jewelled forest and decided that today was an excellent one for wood-lore. Reaching up, she gathered her hair and wound it into a bun at the nape of her neck, securing it with a twisted pin she pulled from a pocket. Satisfied, she turned and left the wall for the tower door, her boot heels clicking softly in her wake.

The two guards watched her go without turning. The senior of them smiled, taking a deep breath. The newer of the two actually turned his head to catch the last swirl of dark green skirt and black boot heel as the door closed behind her. "Bit of a starling, that one." He did not mean it as a compliment. "I think that's the least severe I've ever seen the Governess."

The older man's smile only half faded. "Aye, the only time you'll catch her with her hair down, in any sense. But I'd not write her off just because she can't hold a candle to fey women."

"Oh, she's country pretty, I guess," he interjected.

The other man brushed off his compatriot's rudeness. "Never be fooled by a pretty face, lad, nor a plain one either. Deep as a well, that one. Sure, you kin fall in and maybe drown," he shrugged, then his eye took on a hungry glint, "but you'll ne'er die o' thirst, if ye ken."
Apparently, the younger man did not 'ken', and shrugged, turning back to watching the sky and the wood before him.

She was every inch a governess as she entered the children's rooms. The suite began with a large, comfortable room that served as playroom,

2

sitting room, and schoolroom all in one. From that chamber radiated three smaller ones belonging, respectively, to the Lion Prince- the eldest, and eleven by all appearances; the Eagle Princess- an introspective eight; and finally the youngest prince- a small, thoughtful boy of five. At her entrance, the three attendants straightening the room snapped to attention and ran into their respective charges' apartments to wake and dress them for the day.

She moved to arrange things on her desk and gather the materials she would need in the woods for a lesson decent enough to justify the picnic she had requested in the kitchens. As a mortal girl serving governess to fey children, she often had her hands full. Human children can be playful and unconsciously cruel at times. But fey children can be puckish; pulling pranks that are dangerous to any but themselves and twenty times more difficult to control. They had magics at their command she could not begin to fathom or reign in, but while she could not teach them how to use them, she taught them how to apply them responsibly. Over the first few decades, she had developed methods of disciplining them with disapproval, as she could not very well lay a hand on them. They were more than just fey; they were royal fey, gentry, and rare as water in the desert. And she loved them.

Though she had been just sixteen when she had accepted the position a century and a half ago, she looked barely over twenty. The children had not aged a day in all that time, in either appearance or manner. They learned, though, like all children. They soaked up all she could teach them, like the sponges that children are, and asked for more. She had exhausted her own skills and knowledge after the first decade and had been forced to continually educate herself to keep apace.

The keeper of the library had given her a marvellous bracelet to celebrate her first quarter-century when it became obvious she was going to stay for the long haul. It allowed her to absorb in all the information she could on any given subject until she no longer needed it to teach them and let it slip away again to make room for other things. It seemed that human minds can only hold so much, while fey ones are infinite wells so long as they are young. She found that the adult gentry seemed to lack the ability to take in new information if it was too complex. That, or remembering too much was hard. Oh, they could remember everything that happened to them personally, and sometimes gossip of people they knew, (especially where it affected themselves,) but remembering words of a new language that did not fascinate them, or, say: the pertinent facts of the process of experimentation... these things slipped from their minds like sand through an hourglass.

It was not long at all before the children began to filter in from their rooms. The youngest was first, trotting in with his fingers in his mouth and an arm around a huge, armoured teddy bear. He grinned broadly at the sight of her and ran over, pulling his fingers out of his mouth long enough to cry "Nan!" and throw his arms around her skirts. She bent to return the hug and laughed when Teddy winked at her and shrugged an apology when he was crushed against her as well. She gave his ear a tweak to straighten it and caressed him fondly before standing at the princess's entrance.

The princess was far more formal than her brother. She curtsied when she saw the governess had noticed her and chirruped a polite, "Morning, miss."

She noticed that, although she had not told the servants her plans for the day, they had nonetheless prepared them appropriately. The princess was in a heavier cloth than her usual embroidered silks, much the stuff her elders wore hunting, though still finer of cloth and cut than that of kings in the world of men. It was cut suitably for a day in the wood: a shorter skirt that was not over-full and stopped mid-shin, a pair of ruffled pantaloons beneath for modesty and soft leather boots with no heels. Even her heel-length fall of golden hair had been drawn back from her face. The intricate braids were gathered and pinned up with flowers and one or two live butterflies so that they seemed to form a crown above her sharply perceiving, steely eyes. It brought the length of it up to the middle of her back, which was practical.

Not far behind her was the eldest. His features were strikingly handsome and his hair fell about his face and shoulder like a rippling mane of red-gold no matter what was attempted to tame it. His eyes were a jewelled blue and his mischievous smile could charm frightened birds to his hands and maidens into swoons. He was outright dressed for hunting. He smiled at her as he reached out to slide a stray braid from his sister's shoulder. "Teacher," he purred.

Names were things of power here and long ago she had accepted the loss of her own. She was merely what she was, even as the children were what they were. They were called by their titles, even as the King was called by his.

They watched her, waiting. They seemed to suspect something out of the ordinary was in the offing. She smiled, taking down a large book on wood-lore. "I thought that today would be a good one for a picnic..."

She braced herself just in time as the youngest threw himself at her legs again, then began dancing with his Teddy. She smiled indulgently. "Teddy can't come, darling." The boy stopped, frowning. "Teddy will get dirty, for one, and he has been up all night watching you. He needs his rest."

The prince looked at his bear, only a little shorter than he. Teddy nodded solemnly and made a big deal of yawning. The prince sighed and hugged him. "Night-night, sleep tight," he said.

Teddy saluted the governess and marched back to the bedroom. The moment the door closed on him, the prince regained his excitement about the trip. "Where we going?"

She smiled. "A mile or so out. There's a nice glen near the river we haven't explored, and there are plenty of berries and other things I need to teach you about."

The young prince frowned. "I thought it was a picnic, not a lesson."

The governess laughed. "No reason it can't be both. And if you ever go hunting and lose your party, then what I will teach you will help you survive until you find help or your way home. Besides, you should know every inch of your kingdom." She held the book out to the eldest, "Would you carry that for me, Your Highness?"

He bowed and accepted the book, flashing her his winning smile.

The governess turned for the door, "Now, if we are ready, we just have to stop in at the kitchen for the basket and we can go."

2

The glen was now dappled with the early afternoon sunlight, and the remains of their picnic lay spread out on the blanket in the centre. The princess sat on one corner with a lap full of flowers, carefully weaving them into a wreath as she named each of them off with their properties and meanings. The governess looked on from where she sat nibbling the berries the youngest had brought her. It had been a successful outing. The High Prince was beside her, comparing a small twig of leaves with the ones in the book that they had brought, trying to identify the tree they had come from.

"Is this it? The Hawthorn?" he asked.

She glanced over. "Aye. Very good, your highness. Now, what is it good for?"

He read through the page. "It says it's called the bread and cheese tree, cause you can eat the leaves and it's just like eating a plate of bread and cheese. It keeps you from being hungry," he read, a little surprised.

"Good in a pinch. You can make a tea from the leaves for tummy troubles, too. And the flowers are quite tasty in salads. You can cook with the leaves, the berries are good for the blood..."

"All in all, a good tree to find when you're lost in the woods," he concluded. "You can eat everything but the wood."

She nodded. "Aye. 'Tis a good hardwood that, if it is inclined to carving ye be."

He laughed. "Maybe. Does the wood smoke a lot?"

She smiled, admiring where his mind went. "Why don't you look in the book and see?"

She leaned her head back against the tree, closing her eyes for a brief moment in the shifting glints from the overhead sun. She opened them quickly when the glittering shafts of light suddenly stopped piercing through her closed lids. She scanned the sky through the thin canopy and thought a cloud had passed overhead. Then she saw the shape of the cloud and that it was not alone.

She was on her feet in an instant, her eyes locating each of the three children without a thought. The princess was aware there was danger but not in a panic; The eldest prince was beside her, dropping both book and hawthorn twig and drawing a stick he had shaped for an earlier sword fight with his brother; but the youngest was well out of her reach, about a hundred yards downstream by the river chasing a small boat his brother had made him. What was worse, he was being stalked.

Without tearing her eyes from his brother, the governess addressed the eldest prince. Her accent slipping from her soft lilt into a clipped, no-nonsense one that told him he was to obey without question. "Lion, change yourself and your sister and get into the trees. Hide yourselves. Head back to the castle once I've drawn them off. Do not fly." With that, she ran for the river and the unsuspecting princeling.

The creature creeping up on the child could only be described as a thing. Unlike the makar in the sky above them, which were hideous mockeries of gryphons, it had no wings. Its fore-body was vaguely cat-like, maybe a tiger but dark of fur; its back legs were more insect and had an extra set of talons sticking out and up from its main body for snatching and carrying. Its head was vaguely serpentine, and slightly equine, with sunken eyes and long fangs. It saw her just a little too late, putting on a burst of speed that brought it to the river steps behind her.

She snatched the boy up and spun towards the river, tossing the little prince over the rushing water as if he were no more than a doll. "River! Take him to safety!" she commanded the torrent, as the creature swiped at her unprotected back in frustrated rage.

It felt as if she had been set on fire, but she turned to face the creature, unarmed, watching the cold yellow eyes as they swayed in front of her, trying to figure her out. She knew not to run. She had repeatedly told the children that unless something is chasing you, never run. It will only attract its attention.

From the glen, there came a shrill cry from Eagle and the thing's head whipped around, interest peaked. Lion was bending over his sister, trying to draw her away when she had seen the attack on her brother and screamed.

The thing took a step in their direction and the governess did the only thing she could. She ran.

Its head swung her way, then back, uncertain which to choose. But there was only a squirrel with an acorn in his mouth on the blanket and a large, juicy human doe running from it... It chose the doe.

Commander Skye stood at the edge of the muster field, watching his troops training. Raw recruits, fresh from God knows where and God knows when, still trying to get used to altered bodies and increased strengths. A couple were still trying to adjust to the language and the concept of where they were. One, a newly eagle-eyed red-head was complaining in rough Irish, a language less and less recruits came in speaking. "I was promised a ride home, sir. This isna home and I've folk countin' on me," he insisted.

"Aye, ye were," Skye responded, glancing at the small silver leaf gracing the shoulder of his chain shirt. "But ye promised ten year o' service in exchange. And now ye'll serve." His soft Scottish burr stood in stark contrast to the brogues around him, affecting even the Irish he spoke.

"But I meant after I had time t' put me affairs in order!"

"Ya were the dead dobber who followed some red-haired fanny into a wood. What she'd have done to ya, ah've seen and ah've killed. Ya were rescued, an' ya accepted the price. Think on it this way, when yer done ye'll be better equipped to take care o' those dependin' on ya."

The recruit opened his mouth again, but anything he said was drowned out by the horns. "What's that mean?" he managed in between the long blasts.

Skye waited, counting until they were done. "Three. Tha' means makar," he ground.

"What th' hell are makar?" the recruit stammered.

"Ye'll foind oot soon enuff, laddy-buck!" Skye snapped, then turned to the field and bellowed, "Groun' troops t' ballistae an' prepare t' finish off th' fallen fliers! Let's pluck us some wee crow!"

His men began to stream from the field headed towards the ballistae on the far side to provide support for those manning the artillery even as a flight of black, half-panther, half-crow things flew overhead. Bowmen loosed arrows into the sky and he started to run to join them, prepared to deal with the vicious creatures once they had been downed. Then he heard the scream from the woods. He hesitated a bare moment. Out of the corner of his eye, he saw a small, laughing figure bobbing in the river that sped through the camp. The river tossed the figure out and into the arms of one of the washerwomen, trying to gather her laundry in before fleeing. In a flash, he saw that it was the young prince, and knew who was screaming in the woods and that the attack here was merely a diversion. He drew a gleaming claymore from an unseen sheath at his back and turned from the field to run into the woods, away from the ballistae and the main fight.

The last three of his men, the higher ranks whose responsibility it was to see to the raw recruits, saw their commander heading away from the fight. They looked at each other, and in unspoken agreement the leanest and fastest of them darted off after the men to report and send further assistance, while the other two fled after their commander, trusting his instincts to the fullest.

She ran faster than she ever had in her life, deliberately not keeping to a straight path, dashing through narrow gaps in the trees. She was trying not to follow the river but, just when she thought she was well away, she would hear it again. She swerved behind a dead-fall, away from the sound of water. Feeling her skirts tear through branches, she spared a glance back. It was closer than she had thought and it hissed and spat at her, spraying her face with some acidic poison. She screamed as her eyes burned away in her sockets and the creature bulled past her.

She hit the ground, rolled over and tried to press her back against something, anything to give herself a chance. Her hands found a tree, and she pressed herself as far into it as she could, hoping beyond hope that it was a dryad tree and she would be snatched to safety within the trunk, but it was not. She only felt a single, white-hot claw rake her leg as she scrambled and then it withdrew. There was something or someone in front of her, between them; something large and armed. No longer needing to fend off her attacker, she clawed at her face, trying to pull off the gooey substance that felt like it was melting her eyes.

The smell of blood filled her senses, flavoured by the vomitous stench on her face and now her hands. She could hear steel singing through the air and the slicing of flesh. Her rescuer made no grunts of pain or discomfort, even when she was sure the thing had to have clawed him. He gave only a growling shout that served for battle-cry, causing the thing to lurch backwards and hiss.

She remembered that sound, cried out a warning, "Spits poison!" and just in time from the sound of it. There was a shifting of feet and then a hissing off to the right with the rising stench of leaves beginning to dissolve. There were more sounds of sword cleaving flesh and the paring off chitinous carapace. Then the creature was the one screaming, as it fell to the earth with a heavy thud and lay still.

Her defender knelt beside her, a large but gentle hand on her arm, the other firmly on her thigh to staunch the bleeding. His words were soothing, the voice a deep, warm baritone. "'Tis gone, ma'm. No more trouble to ya."

Others approached in a hurry, clanging in armour, and she guessed where they had come from. "The Prince?" she gasped.

"The wee royal bairn's safe as houses," he said. "Right noo we havta attend yer own."

She grabbed his arm, her fingers locked on the band of iron that was his bicep. "The other two... they're... glen. Look for... squirrel. ...don't forget the a...corn...." She had been holding on for word of her charges. That done, the world slipped from her grasp and she mercifully fainted dead away.

The world remained dark as everything else swam into focus. She was aware she was lying on a cot of rough linen; covered by a sheet and in fresh clothes. The pain in her back and leg had eased off and were now only a dull throb of fading ache: a memory of pain. Even her face only held the ghost of a burn. She brought her hand to her cheek, felt only smooth flesh when she had expected a melted mess, but she also felt a bandage over her eyes.

There were voices on the other side of a canvas wall and she surmised she was in a tent. One of them was a deep bass; familiar and comforting, though it was angry and frustrated. The other was lighter, feminine, afraid and concerned. "...the damage?" came the deeper voice, the King's.

"I've healed the body as best I can. There will not even be a scar, but the eyes... they melted away. There is nothing to repair. Is there anyth...."

The voices drifted out again as the information sank into her brain. Blind. Her eyes were gone. How would she teach? How would she protect? She was now a burden on everyone she knew. She heard snips of other words, drifting through her mind without context: "...Boon ... Not her job and yet ... That harridan will pay for this ... It's for the best ... can't risk ... compensate ... one way or another...."

And then His presence filled the tent; a mild, spicy warmth that soothed her more than any drug. Her first question was as always: "The children?"

"Safe, and worried about you."

"The attack?"

"Is over. They are finishing the last of it now." She sighed at that and seemed to sink into herself. His hand, large and cool, and yet beautiful in a masculine way, slipped into hers and pressed gently. "What you did... I cannot repay." The sound of his voice told her, even if she had not known him as she had, how much that weighed upon him. "The best I can do is grant you a boon. Anything your heart desires within my command."

"My eyes," she said softly.

He took a deep breath. "That I cannot give."

Her decision was simple then. "I do not wish to be a burden to my king. Send me home."

"Your home is not as it was," he warned. There was something in his voice she had not the skill or experience to unravel. "Time... passes, and there was not much to hold you there, if you still remember."

"Aye, I do... mostly. And I know. I've met others more recent to yer service, My King. But I'll manage somehow. I canna watch them any longer, or protect them, or read to learn new things to teach them, though, after a century and a half, I am running out of things to teach them," she added with a rueful chuckle. "I love them, Sire. I love you. I love this place and will always consider it home, but... I'll not be a burden to ye. I will take my chances, and if life is hard out there, it was not always easy here. I regret nothing but that I can no longer serve. We both know they will seek me out if I remain here, and that will not serve them well."

She felt what she hoped was only a tear trickle from beneath the bandage. She felt his other hand reach up and brush it away.

His voice was serious and deeply moved when he spoke again. "Again, you serve my house beyond what is asked. I did not choose poorly, and I will ..."

She knew he would not truly mourn her leaving. She was only mortal, and it was not in him to miss her long. She was grateful that he did not lie to her, though he had tried, and she was grateful for that, too. The children were another matter, and they both knew that. "May I tell them?"

"I will make the arrangements."

"I want to...." she stopped herself. One did not thank the Tuatha De Danann. "My life was good."

She did not need to see his face to know there was a smile. She could feel it in his hand. When he took it from hers, it felt cold and empty, but such was the way of the Sidhe. One could not help but love them.

As his presence left the tent, it was suddenly filled with the lively and unhappy voices of the children. The first thing she could coherently understand was the youngest's, "I should have brought Teddy."

She sat up and pulled him onto her lap. "Nonsense. He would have had the stuffing torn out of him and then who would guard your dreams?"

He shook his head, "Teddy not guard dreams. Guard body while I dream."

She smiled, fighting back tears. "Still, he was not built to fight fomoire or makar."

He sighed and gave in, leaning his head against her.

"It wasn't a makar," the eldest said. "And I'm fairly certain not a fomoire, either. I'm not sure what that was. The ones above, those were makar. The general and her men made short, bloody work of them." His tone told her that he wished he had been with them on the field.

She reached out for his hand and gave him a reassuring squeeze when he set it in hers. "You will be out there soon enough, I expect. It seems to me that should be the next step of your training. Something I could never have taught you." She had slipped into a more formal manner of speaking without a thought.

He bowed over her hand, and she felt his forehead touch the back of it. The gesture moved her deeply. He had never done that before, to anyone that she knew of. "I will never forget what you have taught me," he said, in a tone that told her he understood what she was trying to tell him. He sounded... older.

She gave a dry laugh. "Best not. I spent near two centuries trying to teach it to you." She was rewarded with an answering chuckle.

The princess's frown was evident in her voice. "How will I choose what to study with you gone?"

The young prince's head came off her shoulder at that.

"Simply find something you do not know and look it up in the library. Start from one end and work your way to the other; read everything. Talk to the new people who come here, find out what they

14

know that you do not, investigate. How do you think I kept up with you all these years? In a single year, you three exhausted what I knew in as many years as I had been alive when I came here. You are as prepared as I can make you."

"You leaving?" the youngest growled. "NO. You not 'llowed."

His sister stepped in even as the governess took a breath to answer. "We had her longer than Father promised us. She was only supposed to be ours for a little while until she taught us all she knew. Because she found a way around her own lack, we got to keep her longer than we should have. Got to be children longer than any other Sidhe. You can't complain."

"Can too. Will too. Won't let go," he snapped stubbornly, crossing his arms.

The governess and the princess both sighed, and she guessed the eldest had rolled his eyes. The young prince rarely had tantrums or demanded anything, but when he did... the world would bend first.

Surprisingly, it was Lion who had the answer for this one. His voice was suddenly part his father's, in the deepness of timbre and the words he chose, but the tone itself was the governess's own: the disapproval and disappointment that had worked so well for so long, especially with the little one.

"Would you be Unseelie then? Like *Her*? To keep her prisoner to your will?"

This stopped the young prince. "N...no... but I want..."

"And what about what Nan wants?" the princess asked softly, using the child's name for the governess.

She could feel the child turn his head to her. "You... you *want* to leave?"

She sighed. This was breaking her heart. "No. But I have to. You can't depend on me anymore."

"Why not?"

"I'm blind. I can't watch you, or protect you, or read to know what to teach you. I cannot check to see if you have things right..."

"Not blind. ...What is blind?"

Reluctantly, but realising it was the only way to convince him, she unbound the bandage on her eyes. The princess gave a tiny gasp, as things were clearly worse than she had expected. The eldest tightened his fist on something leathery at his hip and growled low. The youngest surprised her. He just looked, fingers in his mouth as he thought.

"That's not right. Should be something there."

She smiled. "Even with something there, I could not see. The healer said there was nothing she could do, and if there was, she would know."

"Shouldn't look scary, should look nice," he insisted. "She shouldn't take that from you. Should be something there."

His wet fingers danced lightly over her eyelids and she could feel something cool begin to fill the empty sockets, give her eyelids something to cover and not sink into. She felt less uncomfortable. She gave him a kiss, neither knowing nor caring what he had done. He sighed and curled up in her embrace again. "Better," he mumbled. "Not right, but... something."

From outside the tent, on the edges of the camp, there came a commotion that silenced everyone inside. She heard canvas move, but she paid it little mind. She strained her ears to hear what everyone else was shouting about. A few moments later, the flap opened again, and the prince said breathlessly, "A makar landed under a sign of truce. There's talk of a parley."

"Will father...," the princess began.

"No. The general is walking to the emissary now." He crossed to the bed. "Teacher, can you walk? I think this is something you will want to be hearing. We all will."

"I agree," the princess replied, taking her brother from the governess's lap despite his protests.

The governess swung her legs off the side of the bed, testing them. Hands took her arms as the two eldest helped her to her feet. She took a few tentative steps forward, felt more confident about her ability to walk, and nodded. "If ye lead, I can walk."

Lion tenderly placed her right hand upon his shoulder and began to slowly walk out of the tent. Eagle held the flap open for them, then took the governess's elbow gently, holding her little brother's hand in the other.

As they approached the command tent, they were stopped by a guard. "I am sorry your highnesses, my lady, but the king does not want you four seen. The emissary is coming. Get yourselves somewhere hidden."

Lion turned left and led the little band around several tents. At first, they seemed to go away from their original destination but, after getting her thoroughly turned around and lost, they came up behind the royal pavilion just in time for the audience with the makar and what was apparently its rider.

The king's voice filled the air as the four of them crouched behind the wall where a throne had been set up. "How dare you come here after what you and your men just tried?"

The emissary's voice was feminine and mocking, a little birdlike herself. "You cannot blame Her for trying."

"Yes. I can." The words were cold.

Pressed against the governess's legs, the young prince suddenly jumped, turned, then threw his arms around something shorter than he with a whispered exclamation of, "Teddy!"

The bear returned the embrace and quietly shushed him.

Skye stood at attention, just off to the left of the throne, beside his general. He knew why he was here. True, the king was surrounded by his own personal guard, but he and a handful of his own men were an added buffer. The king's guard was trained to fight men and assassins, not makar, and this one filled the pavilion with its foul stench. Its raven front end strutted forward with unwarranted pride as its panther tail lashed against its sleek, black-furred hindquarters, transmitting its irritation. Two gryphons and a pair of hippogriffs formed a rough gauntlet in the room, with the gryphons closest to the throne and the few courtiers and the allowed soldiers gathered behind them. The makar seemed a little itchy about it, but its rider was completely unfazed. There was something too cocky in her smile.

"She offers you a deal. A duel, actually," she said.

The dark hair that fell just past her shoulders had the slicked-back look of feathers instead of hair, but that might have been a trick of the light. Skye kept his eye on her and her posture, her hands especially, looking for any hint of a signal from her to her mount. That in and of itself was unusual. He had never seen one with a rider in all the years he had fought them.

17

"For what?" the king asked.

"The children. Get this ove...."

"Never. She is a fool to ask."

"One of them?" she countered. Her body language said she couldn't care less either way.

"None. You have overstayed your welcome."

Even Skye knew the colder that voice got, the more likely there was to be bloodshed. And when their king was angered, all the gryphons in the realm tended to be a little unruly. Something in the messenger's body caught his attention. This was what she was truly after: her real target. The first request had been meant to make the real one seem reasonable.

"Fine. Your finest against our finest, winner takes the loser."

He felt a stream of ice water run down his spine as the rider looked in his direction when she said that. Even his general noticed this.

"And why would I be fool enough to run this risk? What would I want with one of her poisoned minions?" the king demanded.

The emissary sighed. She had apparently been prepared for this eventuality, but ordered to it as a last resort. "We'll cease all attacks on your borders for three moons."

"You will cease all attempts on my children forever."

She actually laughed at that. "The borders for a year and a day."

"Leave us. You will be summoned when we have decided."

That quickly the makarin was dismissed and the subject open for discussion. The action surprised Skye and seemed to have taken the woman unprepared as well. The rider turned to her mount and led him outside, followed by five soldiers.

Not a word was spoken until the fifth soldier returned, bowing to the king, and took up sentry just inside the tent flaps, which closed behind him. Assured the enemy was out of earshot, the king turned to his three generals who came to stand before the throne.

"There is something going on here I do not see. Explain who can. This is not like the bitch."

Skye's general, the commander of ground forces, spoke. "I think I understand, Sire. She made a play for the children, yes. And the makarin is right, she had to try. But I don't think she cared that she failed this time. I don't think they were the targets. She is trying to weaken your forces."

"But why risk a cessation of hostilities or losing her own best man?"

asked the flight general, a russet gryphon, his beak making the words somewhat clipped.

The other general, a willowy Sidhe with a bow at his back who was in charge of the ballistae, spoke in an almost tired voice, as if stating the obvious. "If she wins, she gains one of our best and weakens us. If she loses, she doesn't really lose. She has to stop attacking for a year and a day, how perfect! She can build and reinforce her army without being molested. She loses her best soldier, so what? You really think he won't still be working for her, even if he takes oaths to us? His very presence will demoralise our men and weaken their ability to concentrate, fearing betrayal at every turn."

"Won't she fear that of our man?" the gryphon asked.

Skye's general shook her head. "Nay. Sire, we have in your infantry a man who has never been defeated. Men have fallen all around him, men we've been able to resurrect, to remake to fight again. He has never had to be remade. I chose him well and for good reason. It is this man she wants. If she loses, all the things Archer said are true. If she wins... she knows he's our best and she'll expect him to be the man on the field. She'll cry foul if he is not. If she wins... his honour is such that he will fight for her, to protect your honour. But... our men will be reluctant to kill him, or they will feel so betrayed they'll be ineffective. It will break the backbone of your infantry and your cavalry."

Finally, the king spoke. "And why is this? Why does one man have this kind of influence over my own army?"

She held his eyes. "Because he's trained most of them."

Skye's hands tightened on the hilt of the sword he held point down in front of him. He resisted the urge to look.

"And why has this man not been brought to my attention before?"

This was a question Skye wanted an answer to himself.

At this, she lowered her head. "Selfish reasons, Sire. One, you would have taken him up the ranks and out of the place he is most useful. Two... he is... of my line."

At this Skye turned, the news an abject shock.

"Explain," the king demanded.

She took a deep breath. "Before the borders closed, before they stopped believing, I left for a time and took a mortal lover in Dunvegan.

He is of that line and bears all the marks of my favour. I've watched him 'til he was ripe and brought him here. The moment he crossed over, the sword came to him and I knew. I... kept him for myself, Sire, and I beg your forgiveness. But... more importantly, I beg you to protect him. She knows... somehow... and how much it would vex me to know she has taken him for herself."

The king was silent for a long moment. He looked Skye over briefly, surveyed those in the room, then turned to his other two generals. "Will we be served well by this respite?"

The gryphon and the archer conferred. Skye's ancestress did not even try to join. Finally, they brought their heads up. "If we win," the gryphon began, "it will serve us very well. If we lose, for all the reasons Tania has said," his wing waved to encompass Skye's general, "...it will devastate us."

The king nodded, and all eyes turned to him.

"Then my decision is clear. It is a risk we shall have to take."

Tania cried out. "The bitch will find a way to cheat! You know she will!"

"However," he said, cutting off any further protest. "We shall still manage, win or lose, to defeat her purpose. Commander Skye, before me," he commanded.

Skye obeyed, taking small comfort in the tinge of warmth that was returning to the king's voice. It was the warmth of silk, still cool, but not the hard frost it had been a breath ago. The gryphon stepped back to make room, and Skye turned, standing in front of the gryphon to kneel before the Gryphon King. "My Liege," he managed, his sword's hilt barely visible above his shoulder.

"You have served me well, I am to understand." The King looked to the collar of his hastily donned shirt to see no pin there marking his contracted time.

"Ah'm pleased ya feel so, Sire," he intoned, being very careful with his words. The last time he had stood before the king thus had been the first time, fresh from training and in full plate. He felt decidedly under-dressed now, in only his kilt and shirt with its tiny gryphons embroidered at the hems. "How might ah continue t'serve?"

"By leaving."

Again Tania made a sound of protest, quickly shut off as she realised what this meant.

"He has undertaken no contract for a period of service," the king said, looking at her. "Therefore, it would not be... cheating... to let him go. Though I wonder why that is." He turned his great blue eyes on Skye, seeing in the man's own steely orbs the stamp of the beautiful Sidhe general. "Were you offered a contract?"

Skye raised his head a little, but not enough to meet the king's eyes. "Nay, Sire. She came t' me and said she needed me. Ah went," he shrugged. "Still nae sure why. But there ye go. Niver asked fer how long. Ah'm good at what ah do an' ah like it. Nae much opportunity fer th' s'ard back home."

The King nodded, as if this explained something or satisfied him somehow. "I have a last mission for you." He turned to the nearest page. "Fetch the governess and the things I asked to be prepared." The page bobbed and was gone.

He turned back to Skye. "Commander, one of my vassals has been gravely injured and is in need of an escort back to the world of men. I need you to do more than just take her to the gate, I need her brought to safety on the far side. She is dear to me and mine and served us better than she knows. I'll not throw her to the wolves I know live on the far side without some... protection."

The Lion Prince did not wait for the page to find them, but stood and guided his teacher around to the front of the pavilion and brought her in himself.

She clung to his shoulder, uncertain of the situation. She heard the other three fall in behind her. It surprised her that she could feel the presence of the gathered court on either side of her; hear the difference between outside and the interior of the massive pavilion. She stopped when the prince did and removed her hand from his shoulder, felt him step away from her as she bowed deeply before her king. "My Liege," she said softly, feeling love and loyalty burning fiercely, threatening to overwhelm her. She steeled herself, understanding formality and too well-trained not to remain controlled.

"Rise, my faithful one," the King said, his voice full of the warmth she had always known and loved and which, for the first time, threatened to fill her eyes with tears. "You have served me and my children better than any of us expected. You risked your own life to guard theirs, taking wounds meant for them upon yourself. Though I deeply regret the need for such things, you have asked to return to your own world, even knowing it is no longer the world you knew. I respect this. Arrangements have been made. You will leave presently, but not alone." He turned, "Commander Skye."

Skye turned from observing the slip of a girl to stand at full attention before the king.

"This woman is my treasure. You will guard her with your own life and honour and bring her from my kingdom unto the world of men, where you will see to her safety." He waved his hand and the page trotting into the tent brought a small rucksack which he handed to Skye. "Take this in keeping for her until you reach your destination."

Skye bowed, accepting the pack and slinging its slight weight onto his back.

At a nod from the king, the little party began to break up. Tania crossed to Skye, began fussing with lapels and in general behaving as far from the superior officer he had come to know as possible. "Be well. I... didn't want to give you up so soon."

"Ya coulda told me," he said flatly, unable to trust any emotions right now.

"Would it have changed anything?" she asked in her musical voice.

"Nae way to ken."

"I'll... keep an eye on you."

"The s'ard," he began, not wanting to give it up, knowing he probably could not take it with him.

She shook her head. "'Tis yours 'til death, when it will return here to wait for its heir. I'll... look after them, too. Take care of her," she warned. "She is precious to him... and to them," she nodded towards the three children who had swarmed the governess. Even the teddy bear was hugging a leg.

"I will keep my charge," he said stiffly. "I know my duty. It is all I know."

"Thanks to me," she said almost bitterly. "But you'll find more than that out there. I know." Her cool hand caressed his cheek. "You remind

22

me of him, you know. My Dunvegan man. Not enough to mistake you," she smiled reassuringly when he looked worried. "Too much in between for that. But... you're like him, in breadth and eye... and manner."

The children nearly smothered the governess. She felt her tears threaten her more strongly, but she held them back for their sakes. She whispered to each of them, to remember what she'd taught them, not just the book things, but the life lessons too. "I'll miss ye sore," she promised. "And who knows, mayhap I'll be able to leave something for ye near the forts or at a mound on Bealtaine and Samhain."

The eldest set his hand at her neck, already of a height to her, though she could not remember him being so tall. He stepped back with a regal grace, taking her hand in his, and bowed over it. Painfully, she felt his hand then slip from hers as he moved away. The princess rose on her toes and pressed her cheek to hers in a manner a bit older than her apparent eight years and whispered, "I shall forget nothing. Neither kindness nor debt."

With that, she stepped away, and the governess felt another pang of regret and loss, and filled with pride and guilt as she realised that one of the gentry had just admitted to being in her debt.

The youngest clung to her, his face buried in her skirts, crying silent and stubborn tears. She bent to hug him. "You must be brave, my little prince," she said softly. "I cannot stay and you cannot come. I have given you all you need. Make me proud?"

He lifted his head, sniffling, but could only bring himself to nod. She tenderly kissed his forehead. She felt a tug at her other side and turned to the armoured teddy bear who took her hand in one paw and placed it on his right, helped her to feel him raise it to his forehead in salute. Smiling, she returned it. Then suddenly, Teddy was pulling the young prince off her skirts and after a second he stopped resisting.

She felt the king's presence before he spoke or touched her, the looming warmth and comforting smell of him. The Tuatha king of the gryphons was not himself a gryphon, but smelled a little like them, like fur and sunshine and the fresh air beneath their wings. She felt his perfectly formed fingers touch her chin and turn her face to his. A rumble of pleasure in his voice. "I like those. Well done, my son."

She smiled, missing him already, heartbroken at being sent away from this paradise. But she had asked and knew without a doubt it was the right thing. "May I return?" she asked timidly. "When...," she couldn't say it.

She could feel his smile. "Yes, daughter. Tír na nÓg will be your final rest. You have earned it, as few others have in recent years. But one last gift and go with Our blessing."

She waited patiently, wanting to defer, to say it wasn't necessary and not daring. He said nothing more, but placed a kiss upon her forehead that filled her with the warmth of the sun. His palms slid down her arms to her hands and then set her right into the left of her escort. A nod to the commander and she was led away, a stately procession. She could feel the eyes of the remaining court on her. She held her composure until they reached the edge of the pavilion when she heard the young prince's complaint:

"I don't want to grow up."

And Teddy's soft, rarely heard voice, "But you have to."

A single tear raced down her cheek.

Skye saw the tear. In a strange burst of compassion, he felt for her, and squeezed her hand. It seemed to have been enough as she wiped her cheek and, taking a deep breath, followed him out of the camp.

3

The walk itself was not unpleasant. An knew it to be beautiful country; nonetheless she found the journey nerve-wracking. She could hear the wood and life all around her, but see nothing. The wind in the trees made strange noises and she found it hard to maintain her bearings. The emotional torment of knowing she would never see these things again did not help at all. She thought, perhaps, that, in a small way, not seeing might be a blessing on the other end. She would not compare every tree and lawn to the ones here and find them lacking. She promised herself she would not pine away for Faery as so many like her who had crossed the borders and returned. She clung to her guide's arm, having no choice but to trust his footing with her own.

Skye was partly relaxed. He knew it to be mostly peaceful on this end of things. With no border between the red-haired bitch's realm and this one, there was nothing to squabble over except the gate itself, and she had others. There should be no threat, though he still kept his eye out. The grass was soft and vivid green here, and the people they passed few.

Here and there he spied them watching, some with interest, some sadness, still others with hope. Even one of the great stags stood at the edge of the path and watched them pass fearlessly.

There were guards near the edge of the kingdom, and he could see them ahead. They were elves he did not know, but then, those like him, taken from the other world, were never given solitary border duty. The elves nodded to him as they approached. There were methods of communication among them that baffled him, so it did not surprise him that they seemed to know his errand. He paused before them. It was just as well that the girl is blind, he thought, from the looks of pity the elves gave her. If he read her character aright she would have found it unbearable.

"Be well, Mistress, Commander," the left one said. He was as fair and bright as any Tuatha Skye had ever met. "The way is clear."

The right one, dark as raven wings, with pale skin and vivid eyes, pointed down the path. "The way twists and winds a half league more, then falls straight as an arrow to the gate. If you remember nothing else in the next hour, remember to stay on the path."

Skye frowned, confused as to why he would say such a thing. Of course he would remember to stay on the path. Before he could respond, a distant horn rang out through the territory. Beside him, the woman tensed, turning her head every which way, trying to locate it. His hand over hers on his arm did not soothe her, especially not when the fair one touched his shoulder and said, "Tread swiftly."

"And swifter still," the dark one added as a second blast sounded, nearer, coming from outside of the kingdom and headed for the path. Skye glanced down at the grass of the road, watched it turn a darker green verging on black. "'Tis the Wild Hunt. The bitch couldn't ride her own trod, she has to taint ours," he spat, his dark hair falling in his pale face as he unsheathed his blade.

"She's thumbing her nose at the King," the bright one said and pushed Skye down the path. "Run with your sword in hand and don't stop. We'll try and hold her off or divert her."

Skye needed no second urging. As a child, he had once heard the Wild Hunt tearing across the moors one Samhain, the hellish hounds baying as they sought and pursued whatever they came across. The fear of it had chilled him to the core and he propelled himself and the woman down the darkening trod towards the distant gate.

The sound of the horn and the baying hounds frightened the governess more than the beast that had taken her eyes. She supposed it was that now she was the one in danger, not the children, but that was no comfort. She made herself run, fearing to stumble on something she could not see. Not that she had a choice. She supposed the Commander would have dragged her, or hauled her, undignified, over his shoulder. That thought alone made her try to keep up with him. She turned all her concentration on him, and focused on the slightest movement of his body to tell her if the next step was deeper than the last or higher, trying to read the road through him. It helped with the fear, if nothing else, and she still stumbled from time to time. She wondered why he had not drawn his sword as he had been warned.

Behind them, they could hear the sudden contact of the two elves with the enemy. They ran, the conflict already beyond bends in the road and unseen but vividly heard. Skye wondered how long she could maintain this pace, tried to keep her as steady as he could while not sacrificing speed. It seemed they had been running for twenty long minutes, but he knew better. And now he could hear the baying of hounds back along the road.

He kept his ear to it, gauging their proximity. He had to get her to the gate, or at least to the straight-away. The hounds were getting closer. Then the two of them rounded the last corner and he could see the gate looming a few hundred yards distant at the end of a gentle, downward slope.

Skye clenched his fist and the claymore melted into it. It flashed through his mind to wonder if it would still do that, come to his hand when he thought of it, when he stepped into the real world. He took her arm from his, holding her just above the elbow. "Run, straight as th' arrow an' don' stop 'til the world feels ...less. I'm right ahind ye." With that he gave her a little push in the right direction and turned to face the beasts as they skidded around the bend, hot on their heels.

She staggered a moment, heard the sudden snarling and slavering and his Scottish battle cry, and ran. She tried her best to keep to a straight line but couldn't be sure she had. She felt very uncertain suddenly, terrified, but kept running. The sounds behind her were terrible, the ones before her only the wind in the grass and too soft to be heard over the fight. She kept her hands out in front of her to keep from running into the gate itself, not knowing what it looked like or if it was a literal gate at all. Her hands met foliage: small bladed leaves, sharp, short twiggy branches, growing taller even as her hands touched them. Panic beat at her breast as it seemed they were endless, deep, her arms reaching through them and being drawn in. The commander had said nothing about a hedge.

From the sound of things, one of the hounds had either slipped past her escort or killed and survived him. Something enormous was pounding the grass behind her, slavering, snarling, baying. She felt like screaming, but nothing would come out.

Suddenly, hands closed on her wrists and pulled her through the hedge almost violently. Then warm arms wrapped around her, pulling her into a crouch, and a hand covered her mouth. There was a snuffling on the other side of the bushes, an angry growling, the sound of haphazard digging. Then the war cry again and a yelp followed by the sound of more hounds, more demonic sounding than the last. The hands that held her drew her up, said something to her she did not understand, and drew her away from the wall of green and the spilling of blood.

They did not run, they walked, and she knew why. Those were the hounds of the Immortal Hunt. She had run before because she had already been seen and targeted. But now there was another target for them, and it would not be wise to attract their attention.

The unknown person took her through a twisting pathway and more hedges, a maze perhaps, walking for several minutes before the world just felt... different. It was warmer, for one, almost unbearably hot. The smell of flowers was everywhere and there was a different type of noise, many voices doing many things, laughter and music. She could hear a fire somewhere and a pipe, a harp... and the world just felt less... intense, less real. He drew her forward several paces, saying something else in that language she felt she should know but didn't, and then let go of her.

She wracked her brain, trying to remember what was off about things, what she was doing standing... wherever she was, surrounded by people she didn't know and couldn't understand. Her memory was spilling out of her like a punctured wineskin and there was nothing she could do to stop it. People came up to her, spoke their gibberish. Someone touched her, and she jerked back with a gasp and they did not try again.

She could tell they were trying to be soothing, but she was moment-arily incapable of reason. Something vital was draining from her and she felt bereft and lost and confused and ...too many things to put a label to. It was all just too much. "*Where am I and who are you? Why am I here?*" she asked in Gaelic.

Several of the voices professed confusion; but someone stepped up, said a few scattered words in very poor Irish, "*Midsummer's eve. Celebration. Safety. You stop now, rest. Go take freshness?*"

She turned her head to the voice. It was feminine, young, from a tall source. She tipped her head up, trying to decipher what the child had meant.

Others spoke around her, some of the voices sounding shocked, one or two knowing, as if whatever they were saying explained everything, and most of them withdrew. She decided whatever was going on, it was safer than what she had fled, and allowed the girl to take her hand and lead her down a path and up a few shallow steps to a quieter area to sit.

She perched in the chair, prim and proper, ankles crossed, hands in her lap as she listened intently to what was going on around her. The girl pressed a glass into her hand and An sniffed it. It was cold, but smelled vaguely of tea. She sipped at it, found it far too sweet and held it back out, "*I thank ye, but... I'm fine.*"

"*You name? I Kellain O'Leary,*" the girl said.

She tried to remember. There had been a name. A long time ago. She hadn't liked it, but it had been hers. Then there was the name the others called her, though what those others were eluded her for the nonce. "*They called me lady of the mists,*" she answered softly.

The girl's Irish was poor indeed. What she took from the simple sentence was not what had been said. "Anne Kayoburn, *nice.*"

She sighed, let her go. Anne was as good a name as any, and hearing it... warmed her somehow. She let the girl talk, rattling on in her imperfect Irish, understanding only the gist of her speech. She talked about the Queen of the Green and someone new and a coming fight between the Holly King and the Oak King. Typical Midsummer festival activities. She was beginning to tune the girl out when she heard sounds just beyond the wall she sensed behind her, loud male voices. One of them spoke the strange words, but with a lilt that was music to her ears and salted well with words she understood, embarrassing though one of those words was.

"What the bloody hell has that *Sasanach* done this time? I'll string him up by his *magairlí* if he interrupts ma daughter's crownin'," the voice growled in a fair Cork accent.

She turned to face the direction the voices came from as the others with him said more unintelligible words. The voices started to fade deeper into the building, and she was suddenly desperate to meet the source of that voice. There was something familiar in its fluid warmth and the easy pronunciation of words her current minder would have stumbled over. Not that she held it against the child. Even in her day, many children grew up ignorant of their native tongue thanks to the 'bloody *Sassenach*', as the man had said. Desperate, she shouted the first thing that came to her mind, "*Éirinn go Brách!*"

The voices stopped. She heard the sound of turning, but not really the sound of feet. A door was passed, and a man stood before her. There was an exchange between him and the girl, and all she understood was "Anne Kayoburn."

"Ahn," she corrected firmly in Irish. "*'Tis pronounced* ahn." She then turned to the man and held out her hand. "*I don't know rightly what my name is. They called me the lady of the mists; at least most did, though that is all I can remember at the moment.*" Her expression went dreamy and wistful at that, though she could not for the life of her understand the reason for the emotion.

"*I can see why,*" came the voice, liquid gold.

"An Ceobhrán *is as good a name as any for now.*"

"*She no say who she out of,*" the girl injected.

"*Like as not, she doesna yet remember. But she need not. I know whence. I can smell Him on her.*" His hand reached out and took hers. She felt the distinct shape of eagle's talons against her palm, *and something clicked between the sound and the smell of him. Something familiar and comforting that she could cling to. 'I am Ian 'the gryphon' O'Keefe. Patriarch of the O'Keefe clan and this ...motlied mess a' refugees. 'Tis glad I am to welcome another Irish expatriate to my home. Welcome to the gryphon's Rest. I've more than a few responsibilities this Midsummer's eve, but I'll make time enough for ye after."*

"I thank ye. I'd not interrupt for the world. I'll await yer pleasure, chieftain. Might I ask where I am afore ye be going?"

"Florida, in the Americas. A long way from home. 'Tis the twenty-first century, the first day of May in the year of our Lord two thousand an' ten."

He started to walk away, then paused. *"Might I ask... why'd ye cry out 'Ireland forever'?"*

She smiled shyly, blushed slightly. *"Well, ye were the first clearly Irish voice I've heard, I speak not a word o' the Sassenach tongue... or I don't remember it, and there was a touch o' the familiar about ye. Ye were walkin' away. I knew no true son o' Ireland would let that call go unanswered."*

He laughed, warm and leonine.

"D'ye by chance remember a monarch or... a battle, some marker t' tell me how long ye been gone?"

She thought a brief moment, knowing his time was precious and could tell by the anxiously shifting feet behind him that his aide needed him badly. *"I believe I'm from County Clare, and I've only seen the monarch on coin, and ...I've no love for the English. I am sorry."*

He set a comforting hand on her shoulder. *"No matter, lass. We'll sort ye out soon enough. Kelly, go find young Bet'any to escort her around. Her Irish is better and she'll need a fairer translator. Chances are she'll remember more that way. ...All right, Reggie, I'll go and deal with that pansy-waisted* coenobite."

As he walked away, An turned to Kellain as she rose. *"He has an issue with an English monk?"* she asked.

"Monk?" the girl asked, confused.

"The 'coenobite'? *It means a celibate."*

"Is what means? Chatham not monk but live one. Stay. I get Bethany."

An remained where she was, listening to the sounds around her. There were games being played, wrestling in some places, music in others. There were a lot of people here, so it did not surprise her that it took a while before Kellain returned, breathless, with another girl in tow. The new girl strode right up to An without preamble and picked up her hand, pressing it into her own in introduction. *"I'm Bethany O'Keefe. I'll be yer tour guide t'night."*

An breathed a sigh of relief as she clasped the hand. The girl's Irish was good, though a little... off somehow. An suspected it was more modern, but far more understandable than Kellain's. "An Ceobhrán."

She felt the girl's head tip sideways, having not yet released her hand. "*Yer name is Of? Or am I mistranslatin' somethin'?*"

Behind her, Kellain muttered a farewell and ran off to join some boys calling her name.

An blushed a little. "*All I can remember being called was 'Lady of the Mist'. And it seems inappropriate to call me Lady.*"

Bethany let go of her hand and sank into the chair next to her. "*We could just call ye Mist. Mist in English, by the by. Or Misty?*"

An frowned at the English word. "*I don't like the sound of Misty. Too hissy, sounds... too much like a pet name for a spoiled noble.*"

Bethany laughed, open and free. "*Aye, that it do. Well, I suppose those who don't speak a proper tongue will simply take it for a twisted pronouncing of Anne. If you're all right with it?*" An nodded. "*I'll take you around if you like, let you get a feel of things. Things're a little bit bedlam tonight, but it's not always.*"

"*It's Midsummer's eve,*" she smiled. "*I expect nothing less than shenanigans.*"

"*You talk like a schoolteacher.*"

An could not tell from her voice if that was a compliment or not. "*I was. Governess, actually. For.... I can't remember and I want to.*"

"*Well, there will be plenty of time for that later. Now, I've a blind friend at school, so I've some idea what I'm doing. You shouldn't have too much trouble.*"

"*Good,*" An injected. "*You can teach me what I need to know.*"

The girl, on her way to standing, paused. "*You... haven't been blind long?*"

An's fingers drifted up to her eyes, touched the empty sockets and felt the faint, damp swirl of fog within them. "*This is... new, aye.*"

"*I... I am so sorry. With the name... I thought that was why.... I feel like an ass.*"

"*Don't,*" she smiled indulgently. "*There is no way of knowin', and,*" she said, standing, "*I've not been to a proper Midsummer in forever. The Gentry, I don't think, celebrate quite the same.*"

The smile on the girl's face was easily heard in her voice as she took An's hand and hooked it around her own elbow. "*Then let's get to it, shall we? Now watch the porch steps, all right?*"

She found herself brought expertly around the rather large estate, from group to group and introduced, with everything described to her with care and detail. Some things, Bethany found, had to be explained further than mere appearances, mostly the modern things. At one point, she led An to the carriage house to let her run her hands along the cars before she explained them.

"*They ride awfully low. Where do ye hitch the horses? And aren't they heavy for yer standard team?*"

Bethany laughed. "*The horses are under the hood.*"

An turned, "*Magic? But ye said these were a mundane thing.*"

"'*Tis a machine. Yer familiar with machines, aye?*"

She thought a moment, an image pressing into her mind from her only visit to Dublin. "*They're trains?*"

"*Like. No tracks, though. A lot cheaper, too. Not a steam engine, though a similar principle.*"

"*If there are books, I'd like to read about them... only,*" her face fell as she remembered. "*Ah, I think that is the part I am going to hate most.*"

Bethany brightened as she led An out of the carriage house and back toward the festivities. "*Well, you have two options there. One, I could read to you.*"

"*I'd hate to impose. I used to read a lot.*"

Beth laughed. "*Or, you can learn* braille."

"Braille?"

"*They have this way of writing the letters in raised bumps. Ingenious, actually. You read with your fingers. I'm sure Uncle Ian can hook you up with a primer or a teacher.*"

She perked up at that. "*If that will not put him out, I would like that very much. So... he is your father's brother?*"

Bethany laughed. "*Nah. The relations' a little more distant than that. He's the chief, everyone calls him 'uncle'. Beats the hell out of 'godfather'.*" She laughed at her own joke, one An did not understand, but politely said nothing. "*Only people who don't call him uncle are his daughter and non-O'Keefe's.*"

An smiled shyly, "*There are a lot of you.*"

"*Just as many not. Though a good chunk of us do live out here at the Rest. And he adopts. But he'll explain the reason for that later.*" She began to draw her off in a different direction. "*Ooo, the Bard's here!*"

"*You have a Bard?*" An gasped, her skin tingling. She had rarely been in the presence of an actual Bard. They had been rare in her day.... She paused at that thought, but the explanation refused to come. And after... after was a blank.

Bethany drew her to the back of a sizeable crowd where she could quietly translate the English words of the storyteller without disturbing the others around them.

An heard every word Bethany poured in her ear, her agile mind pairing the English words with the Gaelic like puzzle pieces snapping into place. But she was locked on the voice of the Bard. It was a beautiful voice telling the story of Midsummer, why it was celebrated, and how. Warning of the Northern Gentry Lady, the Unseelie Queen, who chose this night to ride with her hounds through the mortal realms and the precautions they took every year, the hedge they made to grow on the far side of the gate to keep her in. As his silk-on-snow voice flowed through a tale of the Wild Hunt, she found herself trembling without understanding why.

It was a pleasant shock when she realised the voice had fallen silent, and the crowd had lessened. Cool fingers drifted across her brow to catch stray locks of her hair that had fallen in front of her face and tucked them tenderly behind her ear. "*Now why would such a fresh Irish rose be all a tremble on a night like this?*" His voice still held that smooth quality, soft but clear, almost scintillating; its coolness welcome in the warm air, the accent so light and lilting. She suppressed a shiver at his touch. No one had touched her like that since her mother, so very long ago. Certainly no man. She was melting and it just wouldn't do.

"*I... am not rightly certain why your tale disturbed me. I remember... something, but nothing clear. I've...*" she struggled with the memory, almost able to see through the veil.

His tone changed as he settled himself on something near, a tense understanding, a sad kinship. "*...been chased. By the Hunt itself unless I miss my guess.*"

Inexplicably, she nodded, not really knowing why she did. But he was right. "*Something else...*," she replied, fighting for the memory, her fingers drifting up to her cheek to her foggy sockets. "*My eyes... Why can't I remember?!*" she exclaimed softly in frustration. It was not like her to forget anything.

His hand caressed her cheek as he murmured, and she felt a chill followed by a dangerous heat blaze through her body. She clamped down on her reaction immediately.

"*'Tis not unusual, not fresh out. Something happens between there and here, especially when we've put up the hedge. It's made t' confuse the Gentry. Human minds hold no chance. It takes time. If yer lucky. Or not,*" she could hear the rueful smile in his voice. "*Manners, however, are not one of those things. I am Jonny Sorrow.*"

"An... Ceobhrán," she responded, felt embarrassed of the name for the first time after a hundred introductions. "*Over there... they called me lady of the mist. I don't remember anything else.*"

"Ceobhránach," he said, the word falling from his lips like a deathbed sigh. She could not suppress the shiver.

She did not know how she knew he had lifted his head, looking off and away from where they sat by the smaller fire, but she knew he had. The subtle change in his voice confirmed it, as he began to speak while still looking, but turned back to her mid-sentence. "*As delightful as this conversation might become, I believe they are about to crown the Queen of the Greenwood, and I do not think it something ye should miss. We haven't had a new queen in... at least a decade. Maybe two.*"

He rose, stood in front of her a moment before she realised he was holding his hand out to her. As she tentatively reached up for it, she understood how she had known it was there. She found it in the air by the chill. He was a source of delicious cool in the hot night. His fingers were long and smooth, callused at the tips but not at the palms, and strong. He was a harpist, then.

Nervous and painfully shy, she allowed the Bard to guide her to her feet and across the lawn between the two main bonfires where everyone seemed to be gathering. Bethany fell into step behind them, saying little. He made certain they were comfortably seated, out of the way but with an apparently good view from Bethany's exclamation of delight. He sat the two women together and stood behind them.

Skye had followed the small, fiery-headed man through the gateway and out of the knoll which rose in the dark behind him. He let his sword go, felt it return to his back, half visible but fully felt. It was still a part of him. It did not interfere with the rucksack on his back. His mind tried to unravel the knots it was trying to bind itself into, to remember what was so important about that pack, or why he was concerned about the sword; all the while taking in the sweeping lawns filled with people around an open area between two monstrous bonfires. In the distance was a great house, antebellum style, painted in some colour other than white. In the firelight it looked a dark gold, with the windows glittering like living things when the fire caught them right. There was a large covered veranda which at the moment stood empty, as everyone had dropped everything to come watch... whatever was about to happen.

The crowd had found places to stand surrounding the area in between the fires, leaving an opening at either end. The little man brought Skye near one end where a tall, broad individual stood with his arms crossed, dressed in green. Over his brow was a wreath of oak leaves and around and through it, his mid-brown hair stuck out at odd angles that reminded him of eagle feathers. The nose stretched almost beak-like from between piercing brown eyes. He was laughing as they approached.

"'Bout bloody time, Fox," the man said to Skye's fiery companion. "Was beginning to worry you were going to miss the crownin'. Hedge up?"

Fox looked somehow even smaller next to the other man, answered excitedly, "Yeah, got it up just in time, too. The bitch was already on the hunt. I pulled a frightened little bit out earlier, snatched her out of a hound's jaws," he laughed, his adrenaline still pumping. "I dropped her off before going back for this one."

"Aye, I've met the other one," Ian frowned. "Yeh left a blind girl with no English standing alone in the middle of a crowd of strangers."

"Blind?" he exclaimed. It came out almost a fox's yap. "Shit, Ian. Didn't know that. But I had to go back for this one," he said, pointed over his shoulder at Skye. "Turns out I didn't have to. ...Well, I had to to lead him through the hedge, but... would you believe the bastard took on at least five of the bitch's hounds and survived?!" He howled his excitement. "You should have seen him, Ian! This great monstrosity of a sword and yet he ripped one's jaws apart Samson style! He's one of yours, anyway."

An eyebrow went up. The man called Ian turned to Skye. "Do yeh remember yer name, lad?"

"Th' only name they called me by were Skye, sair."

The second eyebrow joined the first, and the man laughed. "That's not an Irishman, Fox. That's all Scot."

"Hey, you all sound the same to me!" he growled, grinning.

Ian took a swing at Fox, which missed, but he did not seem to expect to connect. "Now hesh up da bot' o' yeh. M'daughter's comin'."

Skye stepped back obediently and turned.

The music changed, became a more stately promenade as Ian stepped forward to the centre of the clearing. Suddenly, he seemed more imposing, more kingly. On his head was a shining crown of oak branches, leaves a verdant green and subtle hints of mistletoe interwoven with sprays of acorns.

From the left side came an older woman, her head high and a smile on her face. Her hair was short and greying though once a dark auburn, and she wore a flower trimmed gown in gold and red silk with a crown of evergreen on her head. She crossed the open sward and stopped a few feet from where the Oak King stood.

The music changed again, became more sprightly and springlike. From the opposite direction came another woman, a younger one, who fairly danced down the path, her bare feet hardly seeming to touch the ground. Merry green eyes glittered from beneath locks of rich red, which bounced about her shoulders in unruly curls unwilling to be bound. She was breath-taking in that elven way, but voluptuous in ways that Tuatha women never are.

Skye could not take his eyes off her. She almost floated up the path to stand opposite the older woman. They closed the distance to each other and reached out their hands. The older drew the younger closer, kissed both her cheeks and smiled as they turned to face the Oak King and knelt. He said words that Skye did not hear, solemn and even, as he took the evergreen crown from the older one's head. Skye's eyes and all his attention were on the new queen, watching her quiver with anticipation as the crown neared her hair, as if she could not wait to flit away and dance into the night. As the crown hovered over her head, it changed. The needles fell out in a shower around her shoulders and the branches shifted to vine and grew, twisting into a more pointed crown with a higher centre peak. The moment it touched her shining brow it burst into bloom, a riot of colours and petals, with no colour coordination at all. They were the wild flowers of a meadow in full summer.

The Oak King drew her to her feet and the old queen rose and backed away, smiling almost with relief. He turned to present the girl to the crowd. "I, Ian gryphon O'Keefe, the Oak King, give you Liberty Merribelle O'Keefe, your new Queen of the Greenwood and Bride of the Coming Year!"

There were cheers all around, though there were murmurs of dissent growing on the opposite side. There was a thudding of hooves as the far crowd parted, allowing through a tall man who looked every inch the stag god, Cernunnos. He was tall and lean, well-muscled, naked to the waist. From there down he had the legs of a stag, a simple white loin cloth draping his hips. His hair was long and a little shaggy, a deep brown and crowned by a huge rack of antlers draped in holly.

"I've come fer m'bride, Green Man!"

While Skye had never seen such rites before, it was obvious to him there was going to be a ritual battle. Behind him the crowd began to twitch in that way they do just before a riot starts. Skye went on edge, hand flexing in readiness to receive his sword, unsure exactly what was about to happen.

"Yeh dare to challenge fer the Queen of Love and Beauty?"

"Aye, and plan t' make her ma Queen o'Winter. More dan dat, I challenge ye fer sovereignty. I, Henry James O'Keefe, de Holly King, challenge ye. De days grow short an' cold and yer time on dis earth is done. Lay aside yer crown or I'll tear it from yer head."

Beside him, Fox suddenly bumped Skye, shocking him from the battle mode he was slipping into. "Hey, you weren't given the option, but choose your side quick or stand out. No weapons, but you can wale on whoever you like on the other side. Watch for non-coms, though. Sometimes they don't get out of the way quick enough."

Skye forced himself to relax his hand and looked around, his blood up for more of a rammy brawl, something he hadn't enjoyed in... he had no idea how many years.

The two kings were now facing off against each other, with the new queen being held behind the Oak King. Skye spared a second or two to view the battlefield. Both sides were arraying themselves about twenty feet from where the kings stood, flexing muscles, stretching, rolling up sleeves and grinning like madmen. The 'squishies' were moving further back from the field, removing themselves from danger.

His eye was caught by a specific movement to the left of the Oak side: a honey-brown head in a fine white blouse, long-sleeved in this heat, and kelly-green vest being led with unusual care from the field by a willowy male figure with long white hair past his waist. He had to force himself to look back at the field, not a hundred percent certain why that scene bothered him.

When two burly young men stepped out of the crowd on his side and took the young queen to the back of their army, he understood why Fox said what he had. When this crowd had gathered, they had already chosen their sides and stood with them. He was standing on the Oak side and it felt right. He glanced around. There was something about most of the combatants that struck him odd, like the two kings and Fox beside him with his flaming hair, that marked them touched by Faery. Once he had seen it, he couldn't *not* see it. But there were men among them who were untouched, dimmer somehow. On either side of him, he watched people shifting forms, taking on more bestial aspects, growing larger or smaller, skins changing. They remained human...ish, but they were obviously not human, and that made the brave humans among them far more obvious.

The Holly King suddenly looked more stag like; the antlers on his head fitting the elongating face and his body bulking out, his hands becoming harder but not quite hooves, fine fur sprouting across his chest and arms. The Oak King had likewise shifted, and Skye understood what it was that felt right here. He had a tail and a massive beak, and the hands and arms he held out ready to attack were eagle talons, without question. The Oak King was called 'the gryphon' because he *was* one.

Beside him, Fox lit up, his body becoming that of an anthropo-morphic fox-man made entirely of fire.

Skye looked down, "Ah thought ye said no weapons."

Fox laughed. "It's not a weapon."

Then the gryphon roared and attacked and the two armies rushed together with Skye's army yelling "Save the Queen!", the enemy bellowing "Take the Queen!" and his blood singing in his ears.

Skye surged forth, making a concerted effort to not allow his sword to fall into his hand. He lowered himself into the charge, his body falling into old patterns he had forgotten it knew. He ducked under the first swing coming for him and shouldered the tree-like man in front of him, chucking him over and behind into the sea of others where he went down with a crack. He plunged forward swinging, his fists connecting with a satisfying thunk into the cheek of a shark-faced man.

The main combatants were avoided as their armies dealt with each other gleefully. The Oak King's forces were determined to maintain hold of the Queen and the Holly King's army was just as determined to steal her. It was absolute bedlam, and it seemed to go on for ages, but Skye knew better. It was likely no more than five minutes or so.

He ploughed his way through, taking the occasional hits and tossing some of the fighters aside rather than engaging, making them someone else's problem. He had just put down a mortal with a strong left hook when something came out of nowhere and cracked him upside the skull, sending an electric shock through his system. He jumped back, momentarily dazed, and saw a swarthy-skinned girl with dark hair flying with static and eyes that glittered with lightning bolts. She grinned at him, reached to strike again. He grabbed a mortal tough coming at him from the side and threw him at her, tangling them both up and giving the man the shock of his life.

He turned to engage what could only be described as a centaur when he noticed he was beginning to tire. This concerned him, angered him a great deal. He charged the horse-man, slamming his shoulder into his equine chest and bulling him into a small group of other fighters from both sides. The centaur was out cold, along with about half the people pinned under him, and Skye shook his head, feeling marginally better.

He turned to take on what looked like a living scarecrow and felt another wave of weakness wash over him.

He pulled back, slipping into a cluster of his own side to regather his wits. He was still injured from the battle with the hounds, but they did not seem to be the source of this leadening feeling in his limbs. He looked around, trying to assess the battle. His side was slowly falling. Out of the corner of his eye he saw something large wading through the fight, barrelling towards the guard around the queen. He did not think, he acted. Shoving down the increasing lack of strength, he charged the being which could only be described as a bridge troll. The creature saw him at the last second, managed to dodge just enough that he only took a glancing blow before swatting aside one of the last two defenders guarding the queen.

Skye picked himself up, came around for another attack, and saw the troll had been joined by another treant. Another man, leonine and full of piss and vinegar, came up beside him out of the corner of his eye. Their eyes met, and the exchange was brief. The lion took the broad tree-man on the left and Skye squared off against the troll. He drew himself up to his full height, and prepped for a punch.

Before he could throw his own, the troll's fist rammed him, thudding into his shoulder as he twisted just in time to avoid the full impact. The blow rattled his teeth, staggering him back a step. Behind the troll, the queen shrieked for some reason he could not see. Enraged, he lowered his head and speared him, barrelling head first into his breadbasket, winding but not toppling him.

A musical, feminine voice full of high annoyance snapped from just out of sight, "Damn it, Reggie! Watch it!"

Unable to move the troll forward, and feeling the ham fists descending upon him, Skye wrapped his arms around the thick middle and locked his wrists. Exerting more strength than he knew he possessed, he lifted the surprised troll off his feet and tossed him over his head, rugby-style. The creature landed, stunned, and just lay there.

Skye came face to face for a brief second with the deep emerald eyes of the queen. A shock of a different type ran through him. She smiled, and he felt a flow of renewed strength. She reached out and touched his arm, a place that was still marked by a bloody bite from the hounds and something sparked, felt like vines growing through his body just under his skin. He felt stronger than he had in years, refreshed.

He became aware of his surroundings in a rush as the treant staggered back from one of the lion's blows and tripped, began to fall into the queen. Skye's hands shot out, snatched him by the trunk mid-fall and spun, shot-putting the hapless being into the main of the fracas, taking out a few other combatants unable to dodge the falling tree.

Skye turned his back to the queen, after making certain of her safety and that nothing could approach from behind her. The lion nodded to him, turned with him to face the fray and roared, deep and loud, his voice carrying for a great distance. Together they faced all of the Holly King's men trying to capture the queen and found themselves grossly outnumbered.

The wall of defenders in front of them began to fall, even as he felt his limbs turning to lead once more, fatigue ripping through muscles he had already abused greatly today. This was his third fight in as many hours, but it still could not explain this weakening.

Then he saw one of the defenders go down, crushed to unconsciousness by a large man he seemed to remember had been on the Oak King's side in the beginning. The slender, reedy woman fell limp to the ground as her attacker reached for another target, then she slowly sat up. As she rose, she took renewed strength from the breath she drew in, then turned and lunged at the nearest of the Oak King's forces, a broad, goblin-looking man. She grabbed his arm.

He yelled as ice flowed from her hand, encasing his arm to the shoulder. She then backhanded him with her other, an ice-encrusted club. He dropped like a stone and Skye felt another surge of weakness, creeping up his back like a cold hand.

The lion-man beside him grinned at his reaction, seemed to be holding himself up by sheer will alone. "Didn't think we were supposed to win this one, did ye?"

Skye shook his head, trying to batter the concept into his mind. "Doesna mean ah'm no' gonna try," he called.

The lion roared his laughter.

Skye could not see the main battle for the crowd, but he could hear it over the slowly quieting field. It sounded fierce. Then there was silence. The crowd parted before Henry as he strode forth to claim his prize, the crowd folding in behind him. Skye watched the holly spread into a crown between his antlers, leaves a verdant green with small clusters of white flowers. Then he was before them and Skye had no choice, stepping aside and dropping to one knee in exhaustion.

"I am de Holly King, and de darkenin' year is mine," Henry said, pitching his voice for all to hear.

The queen curtsied before him with her head only slightly bowed, straightening and meeting his gaze. "As am I, my king."

He shifted to full stag form, lowered himself onto both knees before her and bowed his head. "A kiss, fair Queen. Yer blessin' on yer people."

She stepped forward and pressed a kiss to his forehead. With that touch, a collective sigh rippled through the gathering in waves of relief. Skye felt the aches and pains earned from his battering in the 'war' melt away like snow before the spring sun, felt the magic extending from her to the king, and from him to his people. Even the wounds he had taken in earlier battles were healed.

Henry rose, stepped in close to her as if contemplating snatching her up and riding away with her. She glowered at him. "Don't even think it, *cousin*. Ye wanted that bit o' the rite, ye shouldna worked so hard to get me t' replace Gabby."

The crowd erupted in laughter and shouts of joy and elation, and the air became filled with the sounds of drinking and music and the squeals of women as they were chased off into the aforementioned woods for a proper hunt. Henry shifted up to a man form, still half naked, still antlered and hooved, and snatched up a swarthy, Romany-looking woman for a deep kiss and a quick feel.

Skye stood about, uncertain what he was supposed to do next. He watched the queen greet a few people, accepting a drink with her father. Ian seemed a little smaller than before, though no less imposing. The oak crown was gone now, and he was vigorously scratching at his head where it had rested. The queen laughed, holding his tankard for him, passing it back when he finally stretched, sighing with relief.

While she was occupied, the lightning woman slipped up behind her, grinning like a Cheshire and pounced, placing a sudden and passionate kiss to the queen's neck. She melted for a half-second, caught the look of amusement on her father's face and then pulled away, embarrassed. "Roulet!" she squealed. "I've... duties to attend."

Gabby, the old queen, stepped up at that from behind Ian, began pushing Liberty towards Roulet. "Aye, ye do. And they're to get fucked and fucked. Now git!" she berated, pressing a flask into her hand and then giving her butt a swat.

She looked indignant, glanced at her father who was very pointedly studying his tankard, then at Roulet who was watching her like a cat watches a mouse, daring her to run. Skye watched the woman with Henry untangle herself from him, sneaking up on the queen. She was identical to the other woman, sans lightning. She reached out slowly, fingers outstretched for the queen's unprotected waist, and tickled.

Liberty jumped with a piercing shrill, whirled and took off running. Roulet watched her run, waiting long enough to take the unopened bottle of whiskey Ian held out, before chasing off after her in the dark, impossibly fast. Shortly afterwards, from beyond the hill, there came high-pitched sounds that said Liberty had been well and truly caught.

Suddenly Ian was looming in front of him, and Skye startled, looking up. He had found himself trapped watching the women for a moment. He felt a shiver develop and remain undelivered at the thought that the Oak King had just caught him ogling his daughter. He was relieved when the man pressed a pint into his hand. "Drink up, boi. Yer a free man now, and tonight of all nights is a good one t' gain it. This is a celebration. Treat it thus." His tone dropped with the volume as he added, as if he understood, "no matter how yeh truly feel it. Don't worry for tomorrow. We'll get that squared away after breakfast. ...Which is at noon, by the by," he called over his shoulder as he walked away.

The man laughed heartily and disappeared into the crowd which was impressive seeing as he was at the least a head taller than everyone else. Skye, unwilling to be rude to his unintended host, drank deep from the wooden mug in his hand, and found it full of rich, bitter Guinness. He drank it dry, went looking for another, the rucksack still on his back forgotten.

4

The morning found Skye sleeping against the hill he'd come out of the night before, feeling stiff and thick-headed. It was late rather than early, the sun already halfway up the sky. It was only just reaching him through the thick branches of the trees into which many had gleefully vanished the night before.

He rose, stretching and taking an assessment of himself. He was a bit damp, but the dew had already begun to dry, his belongings were intact and his clothes where they should be, if a little bloody still. He checked his arm, where he had taken the worst of the hounds' teeth, and found the skin unmarked. He remembered healing of this type over There, but had not expected it here. His sword was still where it should be, and the rucksack on his back seemed unriffled.

There was something about that pack he was supposed to remember, something he had to do. He sat down again, trying to pull from his belaboured brain everything that he needed to remember.

There had been a woman. A rugby match and a woman after. She'd said she needed him. Like a blind idiot he'd followed and he could not explain to himself, then or now, why. He'd had no reason to do so. Still, it begged the question, what was he supposed to do now? He had been taken for a reason. He had served his purpose, what he couldn't clearly recall, but it had to do with the sword on his back. An heirloom, he knew that. There was a fight, and a different woman, and then he was sent away. There was a keen sense of loss at that.

There was another woman, that last one, not the one who had taken him, and a mission, a final task. This woman was the reason he was sent away. He had been charged with her protection. His mind suddenly flashed to a blind girl in green on the arm of a beautiful man with white hair, a man with the distinct air of the Sidhe about him.

He was on his feet immediately, trying to remember where he had seen her last, when. Not that she would be there now; too much had happened since the crowning. That was it, when he had last seen her, being led away by the man in white and blue.

There was a house somewhere. He could start there.

He stalked around the mound and saw a faint pathway and followed it. It had all the markings of a faery trod and was well used. It would lead somewhere useful... unless the man had taken her back into the mound and off to... *Her* lands. He curbed that thought. If he had been one of *Them*, people here would have reacted badly. They had ways of preventing the Wild Hunt from riding through the faery fort in their very backyard. They would not have allowed that to happen in their midst, not that early, before the real drinking had started. But after.... He clenched his teeth and stomped toward the house whose edges he could see gleaming golden through the trees.

When he rounded the wooded corner on the side of the house, he came into full view of the back of the manor. It was glorious: a true antebellum mansion in a tawny gold that caught the light just right. The view of it he had gotten by bonfire had not done it justice. The porch stretched a good two-thirds of the back of the house and was two stories tall. The roof of the porch itself was a broad, sweeping balcony with two sets of French doors and some flowering vine potted in each corner, which spilt over the rails and cascaded a waterfall of pale blue and purple for several yards at either end. He could smell them from here.

It was the occupants of the porch that caught his eye. The woman he was looking for sat, pretty as you please, in a white rocking chair with a cup of tea and a young girl beside her chattering away. As he approached, he felt any resentment toward her melt away, as he realised it was none of her fault. In fact, his brain insisted, she was just an excuse, a rescue. Something about a fight to take him kept picking at him; she had rescued him from the Northern Bitch. That felt odd.

She turned her head towards him as his foot touched the first step. The light Irish lilt of her voice rose and fell musically, soft as a lullaby as she greeted him in Gaelic. *"Top o' th' mornin',"* she began, her small nose quivered a second, *"sir?"*

The girl beside her clapped with glee. *"How you know it man?"*

At that she seemed embarrassed. *"On'y men smell like that. That ...strongly,"* she was quick to turn back to him. *"'Tis no offence I'm meanin', sir, a'tall but... i'tis what i'tis."* She shrugged, then thoughtfully added. *"Not unexpected if ye slept on the lawn?"* She said it as a question, asking if she was right.

His mind began to fit the pieces. She was newly blind. He remembered the face of the thing that did it in a flash, managed not to flinch. She was testing new skills, trying to compensate. What was on his back was hers. He took the rucksack down and started to hand it to her, but suddenly it did not feel right. She should open it in private. If she wanted other eyes, she'd ask for them.

He faltered, suddenly realising as the girl stared at him and the woman sat with her head tilted that they were waiting for an answer. *"Aye,"* he replied, though his voice croaked a bit, having gone suddenly dry. *"Not unus'al a'ter a festival. And noo hardship to meself."*

Ian was suddenly in the open doorway, stretching for the ceiling with loud pops of bone and cartilage. He settled down with a pleased sigh. *"Aye, I'll not be doubtin' the moment the smells o' breakfast start wafting through yon woods, there'll be many and yon young folk traipsin' in from them. Some sheepish, others revelin' in it."* He seemed to make up his mind about something. "Kellain, take yerself in the house and tell Mart'a they're startin' to drift in."

She moved to obey.

Ian shook his head with a grin, "Once the first souls start showin'

47

up, the rest of the army's not far b'hind."

There was an audible growl from Skye's stomach. He had not eaten since... the other side of the gate, of that he was certain.

Ian looked him over critically, from the rucksack in his hand, to his damp clothes and tousled hair. *"I'm bettin' yeh've not had a morsel since yeh left the King."*

At the word 'king' and the way he said it, Skye felt something certain and reassuring run up his back like a flag up a pole. The blind woman also reacted, pausing in her act of pouring a cup of tea by pure feel. Skye nodded. *"Aye, Yer Majesty."*

Ian growled, waved the title off with a hand that was now mostly human. *"A'right, first off, ferget th' bloody title. 'Tisn't a court or formal situation. Rarely use it outside rituals. Name's Ian. Yeh have t' use a title out o' some twist o' propriety, just call me Chief or Chieftain. Are we clear, boi?"*

"Aye, sair."

Ian nodded, satisfied. *"Now, catch up with Kelly and she'll get ye a room an' a shower an' a change. Ye can't come t' breakfast wi' blood on yer shirt. If yer more comfortable 'at way, ask her t' find ye a kilt. I've got one or two running about the house. Yers ain't the first highland arse I've had t' clothe."*

Skye glanced once more at the woman he was responsible for, then nodded and headed into the house.

An had sat quietly, listening to the conversation and trying not to be in the way. She had managed to pour a cup of the good, strong tea without spillage, though it had taken a great deal of effort. The shiver she had suppressed at the mention of the King had not helped, but she managed. She held up the bone china cup on its saucer, loving the expensive feel of it, though noting it was stronger than the delicate service she was used to over... with the King.... She shook the wool-gathering from her head and offered the Chief a cup of his own tea.

"Would ye like a cup, sir?"

She felt his gaze on her, assessing and blushed slightly. Then he was taking the cup from her and there was a smile in his voice. *"Thank ye, miss. I'm of usual a coffee drinker but it smells like Mart'a got in some real Irish Breakfast, not that English crap they pass fer it."* She heard him take Kellain's abandoned seat. *"So, how are yeh settling in?"*

She started to fidget, uncomfortable with the situation and covered by taking another sip of tea. *"Uncertain. I... I don't want to be anyone's burden. I'm only here because the rath is in yer back yard and last night ...well, it would have been rude. Your hospitality was pleasant, but I really must be considering my situation. I can't impose."*

There was something in his voice as he considered her. *"And what exactly is yer situation?"*

"Well... I'm..." she sighed, set her cup down. *"There's just no sugar-coatin' it, 'tis there? I'm out of my time, I know that now, in a strange world, a strange land. I have no papers. I am freshly without sight or vocation and I'll be damned if I go back to the convent."*

"Yeh were a nun?"

She shook her head. She stopped thinking about her answers and just let them come. Some of the cobwebs had been jarred while she slept. *"Orphan. Our Sisters of the Immaculate. I don't think I was with them long, but I believe I'd been educated by them prior. I can... could read and write both the English and the Gaelic though I've forgotten most of my English. I know that now. Bethany helped me a lot last night, though, translating the storyteller. I was able to puzzle a rough match up. A bit more practice, an' might be I'll speak the tongue again. 'Tis been a long time."*

"So, yeh escaped the convent into Faery? Bit o' a pagan trade. How'd they take yeh?"

Of this she was certain, *"Oh, they didn't take me. They hired me."*

"Hired yeh?" He seemed genuinely interested.

"I had few options, ye see. In my day, a village girl like myself could only become four things: a wife, a nun, a servant or a governess, or a ...whore. I'd no dower and were fairly plain, so wife was no option. I'd not the calling fer the convent nor was I yet low enough for the last. I tried t' find myself a situation. I thought I'd try governessing first, as I had some education and the work and pay would be better."

"Thoughtful of yeh," he said. She could smell him smoking something that did not smell like a pipe. She said nothing and continued, wanting it out while she remembered it. She took a sip of her cooling tea.

"There were nothing at first. Then I found an advert in the street, just blowin' down the footpath as trash. Fair put me over the moon, I read it. 'Governess wanted, three children, Irish preferred,' (and how often did that happen this day and age? Even in the Irish country) 'Gaelic a must'. I thought it must be a trap, Gaelic bein' illegal an' all. I only speak it cause m' granfer made sure I did. But I'd found nothing

better and couldn't bear another week with the sisters, so I went.

"Now I'll grant you, I wasn't told quite a few things in the beginnin'. Like where I was t' be stationed, or how long my charges would be children. Faery children are rare enough, but they don't grow fast. Though I've a theory on that, I hope one day to remember."

She heard him chuckle at that. *"I'd like t' hear it."*

"The rest... is clouded for the nonce. I don't know why. I have no reason to not want t' remember." She paused for a sip to collect the emotions threatening to overwhelm her.

"Tell me more about before, if yeh can. Siblings? A Name? A location?"

"County Clare is all I remember. There was a local lord, but he was English. I... I have reason to hate him, I think," she tilted her head. *"My father... worked for him? I had siblings, but they all died. Of that I am certain."*

"So... Before 1893, Irish were illegal up t' then. But likely not before 1830, 'cause that's when they started really crackin' down," he mused.

She took a deep breath. *"So I'm anywhere from 179 to 116 years old."*

"A hefty piece," he agreed. *"Yer still a wee youngin' t' me though,"* he added playfully, trying to cheer her. *"I'm over 300 that I remember. Like as not older. Certainly not younger,"* he laughed as he stretched again and more joints creaked and popped in protest.

An smiled, sipped her tea.

"But it brings us back to yer situation."

She nodded. *"Aye. I'm alone in a strange country, with a strange language, blind, with no skills t' offer fer m'bread. I can't even remember enough o' m' life to teach Irish history, and I'd be hopeless teaching sums or spellin'. I refuse t' be a burden on anyone."*

She heard him sit up, drain his cup, set it gently down.

"I'll tell yeh this, lass. These are the rules and have been the two hundred plus years I've set here and run the Rest. Yer fresh out and disoriented. Yeh need re-educatin' and assimilatin' and even more so in yer case, and I'll begrudge yeh none o' it. Not a morsel nor a protest," he growled as she opened her mouth to speak. *"My hospitality, my rules. Yeh kin help out where yer able, if yeh wish t' stay. Yeh wish to go out on yer own, I kin make it happen. Otherwise, I've an entire village out there wi' empty houses fer the likes o' yeh and my people. I kin set yeh up there. Most who live in the Rest are family and mortal, but they understand most o' the weirdness. Hell, a good chunk o' 'em 'll be showin' up any minute wi' covered dishes and grumblin'*

bellies. I run t'ings on the old Celtic model, like the chieftains of old, and if yeh kin live with that, yer welcome t' stay. What say yeh?"

"I'm overwhelmed. But... why? I'm neither kith nor kin."

He leaned forward, *"Yer hot', lass. Yer Irish and yeh've no family and yer on my land. Fer that alone, I'd take yeh in. Yeh served my King, long and well it seems by what I see hangin' at yer neck."*

Her hand went to her throat, found a strange pendant dangling on a delicate thread of silver. It felt like two figures intertwined, embracing or dancing, she wasn't sure which. It felt... luminous.

"Didn't know about it, I ken?"

She shook her head.

"Never take that off, yeh hear? That there's a faery token, and like as not, will bring them to yer aid an' yeh need it. That's the other reason. Many here think I fled like them and stand again' the gentry t' protect them. I don't. I stand again' all who would take the unwillin', again' the Red Queen and all her bloody names. I take in those who managed to reach my rath and protect them again' those who would take them back, but I send them on when they're ready unless they swear t' me an' mine. Those that come from the Gryphon King, they I'll take as long as they'll stay, cause while I'll not say 'thank ye' to the Tuatha, I'll pay it my own damned way."

She heard him stand, started out of habit to follow suit, but something in his presence made her stay put. She tipped her head up to him, trying to find his face in the darkness.

"Now, I've some business needin' attendance, holiday or no. And I'll leave yeh to the care o' my house. Yeh'll stay here, in the room yeh were given until yeh decide what yeh'll be doin', and I'll have no word more on burdens." He started to walk away and stopped. *"Oh, and yeh'll be pleased to know, we finally did win our independence. 'Tis the Republic of Ireland now. Though Ulster's still bein' the bull-headed fools they al'us were. They're still part o' Queen an' Country."*

Something shivered into place at that phrase. *"Still a queen?"*

She heard him turn. *"Victoria?"* he asked.

She hesitated. *"...Aye. I'm almost sure. Great imposing lady in black."*

"Do yeh remember her jubilee?" he asked hopefully.

She shook her head. *"I don't think I'd have heard of any o' her parties in the village."*

He chuckled. *"Oh, this one yeh'd have heard about. So before '97, tha's n' help. D'ye remember her husband, a'tall?"*

Again, she shook her head. "*Albert was dead before I was born.*" She gave a little start as that titbit poured from her mouth. She had not known it before she had said it.

Again Ian laughed. "*Get used to it. Mem'ries'll slip out o' yeh like a touch o' the bard's tongue or else they'll pounce yeh when yeh least need the distraction. But believe it or no, that helps.*"

And then he was gone.

5

Upstairs, Skye stepped out of the shower and dried himself off. He peeked out of the bathroom into the hallway as he wrapped the towel around his hips, satisfied that there was no one to see him and made a dash for the room he had been given. Two doors down from his, the door was partially ajar and he could hear voices inside, women arranging furnishings.

"No, you have to hang outfits together. The poor thing is blind. It's not like she can make sure her skirt and top matches. Everything has to be put in the same place every time. I'll not have her inadvertently pairing that lovely plaid skirt I found her with a striped blouse."

He slipped past, taking note of which room they were in. He decided he was not ready to confront her yet. When he was dressed, he would wait until they left and slip the pack into her room. He darted into his own as one of the women's voices got closer to the hallway, closing his door just in time. He laid his bloody bundle onto the seat of a wooden chair and looked over the new clothes lain out on the bed for him.

There was a plain linen kilt shirt of a lighter fabric than his own, perfect for the unaccustomed, Southern heat. It was not new, but still serviceable, and of a size that should fit, which surprised him. It was freshly laundered, though smelling it, he thought he caught the hint of gryphon embedded in the fibres. The kilt was a standard Black Watch tartan with a well-worn but cared for broad leather belt. There was an absence of 'other things' on the bed, for which he was kind of pleased. He would have felt awkward. There were socks and a pair of brogues on the floor at the edge of the bed. He threw the towel over the back of the chair and proceeded to dress.

The clothes fit comfortably. The shirt turned out to be a little loose, but it would do until his own could be cleaned and mended. Feeling very much refreshed, he ran his fingers through his hair, pulling back his long, dark locks. He was a little annoyed by the curls at the end, but he was unwilling to chop them off. At least just yet. Satisfied with his toilet, he grabbed the rucksack and left his room.

The door was closed when he got to it, and he paused to listen. He heard nothing from within and took hold of the knob. He took a moment to gather his courage before turning it. Somehow he could face down raging monsters and vicious makar without flinching, yet he quailed at the thought of entering a lady's room. Satisfied there was no one within, he turned the small brass knob and stepped in.

The room was very similar to his own, just dressed differently. It was small and simple, all the furniture against the walls, though it was clear from impressions in the ancient rug that this had not always been the case. There was a simple desk with two very large and awkward looking books with thick pages that did not lay flush with one another. The two chairs in the room, one at the desk and one at the small dressing table, were the same, plain wooden style as his own, save for the fluffy chintz cushions tied to the seats. The bed was a modest affair, with a white, eyelet-edged coverlet. The windows were open, and a breeze flowed into the room through light, airy curtains. Heavier drapes were tied back on the sides of the same chintz pattern as the cushions, for modesty in the evenings. It was a very feminine room.

He started to set the bag on the desk, but then thought it possible she might not find it for days. It was better to put it on the bed. He started to set it up by the pillows and then noticed how shabby and filthy the ruck itself had got. There was no way he could set it on the white spread. But he couldn't set it elsewhere without risking her not finding it, nor did he dare move the furniture which she might, by now, have memorised.

Again, he gathered faltering courage, set the bag on the desk and forced himself to do something he would otherwise have never dared. He opened the bag and breathed a sigh of relief to find the contents individually wrapped. He pulled out the first package. As he drew it forth, it seemed too large to have fit in the bag. But then, these were fey things and sense didn't come into them, or so he told himself. He set what felt like a cloak wrapped around a bundle of clothing just down from her pillow and went back to the desk for the last thing in the ruck.

This felt heavier, was wrapped in a coarse leather scrap that fell away as he pulled the object out of the bag. It was an ornately carved, rectangular wooden box about eight inches on a side. The wood was dark and glossy, lovingly oiled and polished, and the carvings were deep and intricate. There was knot-work all around the edges and a tangle of bramble and roses throughout. Hidden in corners were animals, a fox on one side, a unicorn in a corner, a gryphon in another. The centre was a triquetra. It felt weird in his hands. He could tell the wood was heavy, but had the feeling it was hollow, empty. It felt light inside and heavy outside, and he could not wrap his brain around the idea. He quickly set it on the bed next to the cloaked bundle, took the bag and quickly abandoned the room.

He felt like a thief slipping out into the hall, found he was beginning to sweat a little. He took the ruck back to his room and laid it with his laundry and headed downstairs where he could smell an abundance of food.

Gabrielle, the old queen, was helping An at the buffet table when the stragglers began coming in. An found her pleasant and amiable, and insisted she name everything in both Irish and English. She was trying very hard to remember the language, but it was being stubborn like everything else. And, like everything else, it came easier when she wasn't thinking about it. Some of the incoming people were ones Gabby knew well, as she asked some rather impertinent questions of a pair of young women over the tray of what she had called biscuits, but felt and tasted more like bland scones. But then she could be remembering wrong. It had been a very long time since she had had a proper biscuit.

"Well, yer Maj," Gabby growled good-naturedly at Liberty, "did ye do yer duty?"

An understood most of that, though the word 'Maj' confused her, and the rest she pieced together. There was a touch of embarrassment in the young woman's response. "Aye ...half."

An felt an elbow graze her and guessed Gabby had put a hand on her hip and was glaring. "Which half?" she demanded.
There was a tone of self-justification in the light voice. "I was only *mostly* drunk." This was followed by a giggle from a third party, also feminine. The voice continued. "So, who's yar friend? She's new."

Gabby shifted to Irish immediately. *"This is An Ceobhrán, she came out last night. So far she's only got a rudimentary grasp of English, but we're working on it. An, this is Roulet..."* she said, turning her away from the first voice.

A hand slipped into hers, gave her a light static shock. *"Sorry."* The Irish was fair, but the accent odd, the hint of multiple languages leaking through.

"It's all right. Pleased," An answered demurely.

"And this is Ian's daughter, Liberty O'Keefe. She's the new Queen of the Greenwood."

An flushed, curtsied.

Roulet giggled and was popped from the sound of things. Hands were immediately on An's arms, pulling her up. *"Oi! Enough wi' that nonsense! Did no one explain matters to ya? 'Tis a ritual thing, no more. Yer in America, lass. We take less stock in that like here."*

"Yer more than just a ritual queen," Gabby warned.

Liberty growled, *"Aye, but don't let's confuse the girl."* She turned back to An, *"Outside of the rites, we do not observe the proprieties, ye ken?"*

It was hard to reconcile her upbringing to it, but An nodded. *"Aye, I ken."*

"Good. I'm just plain old Liberty, especially today."

Gabby led her towards a table where they all sat down.

Apparently Kellain had joined them but had remained surprisingly quiet until now. "*I don't think ever want queen to be. Especially on Midsummer or Yule. To suffer attentions of whatever king... Lucky you, Henry is yer cousin. Ye didn't have to... you know.*"

Gabby laughed. "*It's not a requirement, really. Just highly recommended.*"

Kellain persisted. "*Yeah, but Henry? Eww,*" she audibly shuddered, shovelling food in her mouth.

An flushed as she realised what they were discussing. She was entirely unsure if they were in mixed company, but it was clearly not a subject for a dining table.

"*Henry's not bad, when he's got his mind on it,*" Gabby replied.

Roulet laughed, "*And when he's not?*"

An felt the shrug and heard a hint of a grin. "*At least he's quick.*"

The girls laughed and An, embarrassed, concentrated on finding the food on her plate and trying to eat without making a mess of things.

From down and across the table, *came the deep voice from last night.* "*Oi! My antlers'r burnin!*" Henry bellowed, which only served to dissolve the girls into further peals of laughter. An could not help joining them then.

"*Then dunk yer head!*" Gabby shouted back.

There was a huff and a stomp and then no more of it. She heard his voice going further down the table.

An listened to the girls talking, chimed in where appropriate, not used to joining in. People were still coming in and going out, some bringing more food, others drinks. Someone passed near them, hesitated a brief second before apparently deciding on the better part of valour. An smiled. Most men she had known would avoid a gaggle of hens at a table when there were other options.

Before she could wonder how she'd known it was a man, Kellain had leaned in and asked her, "*Have you ever see man on kilt?*"

An swallowed her tea, now blissfully cool. "*Aye, though it seems a silly practice t' me. Impractical, but I'll not judge. The Scots are fond of them, an' even some Englishmen if I remember. We'd tartans and kilts in Ireland, but they were more a formal thing.*"

"*I like it,*" she confided, obviously lusting after whoever had passed wearing one.

An's voice became more stern. "*Yer a mite young t' be admiring'....*" She stopped herself, sighed, "...*No, no yer not. But mind ye, lass, there's more to a man than the shape of his legs. Though how he tends his body will tell ye a lot about him. Same goes fer young women too, so bear that in mind each mornin'.*"

"*Good advice,*" Gabby added to the girl. "*Yer a bit young to be chasin' that skirt though.*"

"*Who was that?*" Liberty asked. "*I've na seen him b'far yesterd'y.*"

Roulet answered. "*I think he came out last night. I gave him a right crack in the grand melee, but while I rang his bell, he kept comin'. He's got quite an arm on him. Threw Charlie MacAver halfway across the field.*"

There was a low whistle. "*He's no light-weight,*" Gabby murmured.

"*He was covered in blood by the time he got to me,*" Liberty said, her voice soft and musing. "*Some not his own. Did he break the rules or enter the fray like that?*"

"*Started that,*" Kellain said. "*Got peek of him before fight and was bloody then. Sleeve cut.*"

"*Hmmm.*"

An wiped her napkin across her brow and dabbed at her throat above the high collar of her blouse. With the sun almost directly overhead, the heat was beating down on her. The air was thick with moisture. She was beginning to feel a little faint.

"*Oh good lord, lass!*" exclaimed Liberty, noticing her start to sway. "*Yer fadin' in the heat.*"

"*I'm... fine,*" she insisted, straightening her back. "*I'm just not use t' the temperature. Thankfully, it's Midsummer and shouldn't get any warmer.*"

There was a moment of silence.

"*This is just the beginning. It's going to get hotter,*" Roulet said.

"*And more humid,*" Gabby added.

"*Why don't ye put on somethin' cooler? No one offer ye a change o' clothes yet?*" Liberty asked.

"*I've not asked. I don't wish t' be a burden.*"

"*Ye won't unless ye faint o' heat stroke. Roulet, you get t'other side,*" Liberty ordered.

An found herself lifted from the bench and aided to walk across the lawn back to the house. She tried to protest. "*I'll get used to it, really. I just need time.*"

"*Aye. Where'd ye come from? The Bitch, the King or some other?*" she asked, every inch the queen without meaning to be.

"*Ireland,*" was her instinctual response. "*But I served at the gates of Tír na nÓg.*"

"*The King,*" Liberty sighed.

"*At least it wasn't the Bitch,*" Roulet commented. "*After ice and snow, it'd have taken forever to acclimate her.*"

"*Did ye also serve the King?*" An asked.

Liberty shook her head. "*No, luv. We weren't that lucky.*"

The women ushered her into the house and up the stairs, sat her in a chair in an unfamiliar room. It smelled different, like spice roses and feathers, a touch of lily and wisteria. There was more of a breeze than in her own room and she could hear Roulet opening up glass doors which must lead out onto a veranda or balcony. Liberty opened a wardrobe and began pushing aside hangers.

"*Ooo, I like that one,*" Roulet exclaimed at something Liberty had pulled out. "*You never wear it anymore and that makes me sad.*"

"*It's a little snug in certain places,*" Liberty complained pointedly. "*But I think it'll fit her. She's more modest in the bust. And the colour will compliment that honey-brown hair of hers.*"

The dress was pressed into her hands and An tried to feel the contours of it. There wasn't much to it. There were no buttons or laces, but a strange metal thing that ran up the back. What she could feel of the bodice was low cut and vest-like. She couldn't be sure of the length of the skirt. "*Where... where is the rest of it? Or is this the chemise?*"

The two stopped.

"*Umm...*" Roulet began, trying to understand. "*That's the whole dress?*"

"*No sleeves? A bare throat?*" she flushed. "*It's a formal gown then? I couldna wear it for a day dress.*"

Roulet started to laugh and cut herself off.

Liberty came to the rescue. "*It's too hot fer what yer wearin'. We wear shorts and sleeveless tops all the time.*"

"*Oh, I couldn't!*"

"*Ye'll die o' heat stroke an' ye don't.*"

"*I'd die o' embarrassment first. It's not modest.*"

"*Times have moved on, sweetie,*" Roulet began. "*It's perfectly acceptable to show a little skin... or a lot. Women go to the beach wearing bathing suits that barely*" *cover their naughty bits and no one thinks anything of it."*

An crossed her arms, *"I would."*

"We don't have t' push ye that far that fast," Liberty said. Her tone gave An the impression she was glaring at her friend. *"But ye can't go round this summer wearin' wool skirts to the floor an' high collars an' long sleeves, fairy cloth or no'. Ye'll no' survive."*

"I'd feel more uncomfortable exposed," An explained.

"Thinner fabrics?" Roulet offered.

"Might work," Liberty conceded. *"Do the sleeves hav't'be solid? If we get ye sommat gauzy?"*

An thought about it. *"So long as the bodice is solid, the throat an' sleeves can be sheer, aye. I'll agree t' that."*

Liberty hit the wardrobe again, handed something off to Roulet who laid it on the bed.

"Here, let's get you out of this heavy linen," Roulet began, offering to help An out of the laced vest.

An stood. *"Oh, I can manage, thank ye kind."* Her fingers flew through the laces, slipping off the vest and passing it to Roulet. *"I'll want t'keep that, though. I'm... fond o' it."*

"Of course!" Roulet exclaimed, folding it up. *"You'll need it come winter."* An passed her blouse over and the woman sighed with envy. *"This embroidery is beautiful. The fabric's so fine, but clearly for more temperate weather."*

"Oh, good Lord," cried Liberty.

Roulet turned, "What? Oh. Um... hmm."

Suddenly self-conscious and uncertain, An's arms went up to cover her now naked torso. *"What is wrong? I'm... am I being indecent? There are only the three of us, aye?"*

Liberty crossed the room. *"It's not that, luv, it's... there's no bra or corset on ya. And with yer level o' modesty I expected one or t'other."*

"From the look of her, she's never worn a corset in her life," Roulet mused, admiring. *"Leastwise not one for its original purpose. Just natural curves."*

An blushed. *"I... we couldn't afford one and the nuns frowned on 'em. 'Tis what the bodice is for. What is a 'brah'?"*

"Don't worry, we'll... get ye some."

A silky feeling blouse was placed in her hands and Roulet helped her to find her way into it. It slid down over her skin like the coarser silks she had worn... where? When? It was finer than anything she'd had as a young woman, with the exception of what she had just taken off... She sat down, trying to wrap her mind around the contradiction. She felt hands on her, but did not seem to notice them or what they were doing.

She remembered two lives, and they contradicted each other in every way. Hardship and hard edges and coarse textures and sorrow. And on the other hand, softness and green things and cool hours and contentment. She'd worked hard, but had loved every minute of it. Her hands remembered the feel of three heads beneath them, the silk of the gilded hair and the lilt of their golden voices. She felt love and loss, regret and grief that threatened to overwhelm her until she remembered she was in the presence of strangers.

"Liberty, she's wearing wool stockings!"

Most of those English words filtered through understood. She pulled herself together sharply, wiped at her dry eyes and reassessed what was going on. One of them had fastened a bodice around her torso and the breeze from the window, though warm, slipped through the fabric of her sleeves as if it wasn't there.

"*Oh, this won't do a'tall,*" Liberty clucked. "*Why are ye wearing granny boots and wool stockin's?*"

"*So no one can see m' legs, why else?*"

Something hit the bed behind her.

Liberty sighed. "*All right. I'll make some concessions here, but ye'll have to make some, too. I'll find ye thin blouses, light-weight vests. Get ye some bras that fit proper. I'll leave ye the ankle skirts...*"

"*They are back in style now,*" Roulet nodded.

"*...but ye have t' give up the stockin's. At least fer the summer.*"

An slowly nodded. "*Fine. But won't the boots be uncomfortable without them?*"

"*Can I get ya in less confinin' shoes?*"

"*In a peasant length skirt?*" An countered.

Liberty sighed. "*They make short socks now. I'll get ye them, too. Roulet, be a luv an' call fer my car. We're goin' shoppin'.*"

6

When An and the girls returned to the house, it was late evening. She had survived her first car ride, which had been disorienting, been fitted for 'intimate apparel' which had been nigh mortifying, been given a crash course on modern markets and introduced to foods for which she had no name and had to learn how to eat to boot. This is not to say she did not enjoy the outing. It was just beyond her experience.

She was thoroughly exhausted by the time she climbed the stairs, and was ready to fall into bed. But first she had things to put away. Roulet offered to help her, and she accepted gratefully.

Before she could follow them, Liberty's phone went off. She stepped out onto the front porch to answer it.

There was one thing the outing had convinced An of, though: the need to remain here under the O'Keefe hospitality for a while yet. It had proved to her that she was not yet capable of functioning on her own.

"Hey, looks like Shannon's been in here," Roulet smiled when they

entered the room. "*There's something on the bed for you. I'll just put these in the wardrobe.*"

"*Thank ye,*" An answered, concentrating to remember the direction and path to the bed, determined to do it without help.

Over the course of the day, Roulet and Liberty both had learned when to help her and when to let her fend, for which she was grateful.

When her hands found the edge of the bed, she felt across its broad linen surface. Up near the pillow she found a soft bundle of cloth, which she unfolded. The air was filled with the scent of... something comforting and familiar. It smelled of Irish summer. The Summerlands. Of Faery. She sat on the edge of the bed, held the object to her face and breathed deep.

As she did so, it unfolded in her hands, spilling the fabric and its contents across her lap and onto the floor. "*Oh, I'll get that,*" Roulet said, moving to pick up whatever it was that had fallen. "*These are beautiful,*" she breathed. "*I haven't seen embroidery like this in my life. Not even from Japan. And that cloak is amazing.*"

"*What...,*" An's voice broke, and she tried again. "*What are these things, please?*"

"*Well,*" Roulet began, laying out each piece for An to run her hands over them. "*This one is a heavy linen blouse, full sleeves and high lace collar the way you like. There's embroidery on the sleeves of ...eagles, oh I think that one's a squirrel. It's really clever. White thread on white fabric. This one is like it but lighter, with very pastel threads. I think it's a forest done in knot-work on the sleeve and collar bands. I ...I don't know what this is made out of.*"

An reached over and fingered the fabric, smiling softly. "*Cobweb.*"

Roulet was quiet for a moment, then busied herself with the rest. "*This one is a tartan vest in blues and greens, a bodice really. Should fit you nicely. And there is a matching skirt in what feels like wool but is just too soft. You'll need to save these for winter. A scrap of buttery leather and a shawl,*" she said, picking up the last object in question and gasped.

An's hand went out and slid through the beaded tassels at the end of the shimmering black lace. "*That one's not so fine,*" she smiled. "*I'm not as good with the faery materials as with mortal, and nowhere near the princess's skill level.*" The image of a beautiful, innocent face looking up at her beneath a crown of golden braids came to her then, warmed her heart.

"*Nonsense. It's beautiful. And the cloak, that'll be warm come winter. It's as*" *soft as suede, but I know it's material. The colour of midnight. So, what's in the box?"*

An let Roulet take the cloak, looked up where her face should be. *"Box?"*

"Mmhmm, just behind you, in the middle at the base of the pillows. Beautiful wooden thing."

An turned, felt across the spread until her fingers came into contact. She pulled it towards her, set it on her lap, let her fingers run across the deeply carved surfaces. The other things, the clothing, she knew those were hers. This was new, something she had never seen. She imagined that the fine, silk grained wood was impossibly beautiful to the eye, but her fingers found it even more so. There were details within the details that only her fingertips saw.

It was not a large box, and only a hand span deep: the kind of box one would keep jewels in. She had never owned jewels, only the silver crucifix she had been given for her confirmation, and that had disappeared a century or more ago, and she'd never given it another thought. The box had sounded empty when she moved it, but it didn't *feel* empty.

Her thumbs slid along the upper edge of the front of the box, looking for the latch. There wasn't one, but the tiny triquetra just under the rim felt different. She pressed it, felt it shift a little and twisted. There was a soft click, and the lid raised slowly on its own. There was a waft of rain on meadows and mild sun on flowering fields, a tingling breath of wind through oak leaves and rowan, and the feel of rising mist at twilight that rose up from within. It caressed her face like a lover or a tender parent, enveloped and settled into her.

She took a long, deep breath, closed her eyes. A voice she knew but could not place sounded in the depths of her mind, setting off small implosions like mental fireworks. The voice was large and warm and musical: a man's voice, a lion's voice, a King's voice and suddenly she knew Him, remembered the fair face beneath golden brows and the eyes the colour of a summer sky.

"For all that has been done to you, I grieve for its necessity. For all you have given, I honour your sacrifice. I give you now what I could not give you then, else you would not have left and things would not go well in the coming seasons. Each of the

children has given you a gift."

She felt them, tiny sparks of light and energy, like miniature stars rise from the box and steal into her body. She could taste each of them, knew which came from which as easily as she could distinguish their voices in the dark.

"The last gift is mine."

This one exploded within her, hot and golden, cooling quickly to something bearable. It settled into her limbs and raced back to her head, piercing and filling the empty holes, doing something to the fog left place-holder. The breath she had not known she'd been holding slipped from her lungs. All the energy seemed to drain from her body and she slid to the floor in a breathless heap.

She became conscious to the sound of voices. She was on the bed, in a cloud of softness, lain carefully on the covers. She remained still, eyes closed, assessing the damage. Aside from a slightly aching head where she had no doubt hit the floor and a faint burning sensation behind her lids, there was none. But she was fully aware that something had changed.

"I don't know," Roulet was saying. "She had that box in hand when I turned to hang up her cloak. I heard something and turned and she was on the floor and that box was laying open like a suspicious spindle next to her."

The sound of claws on wood.

"Is she all right?" Liberty.

"She's breathing now," Roulet sighed. "More than she was a minute ago."

Ian's voice, hard like an eagle's, clipped. "Faery gifts are hard on a body."

"Faery?" the girls chimed.

"But which?" Liberty asked. "Were it a poisoned apple from a jealous queen or a reward fer faithful service? An' don' they usually give those *afore* they send ye on?"

Ian did not answer. "Where'd the box come from?"

Roulet sounded like she'd shook her head. "It was on the bed when we got back. She seemed surprised by it, though she knew some of the clothes; that's what was in the other bundle. Looked like the clothes were sparking memories. But the box... she didn't know it."

"How did it get here is th' question," the gryphon growled.

"That would be my fault, Laird," came the voice from that morning, the growling stomach.

She heard Ian turn, his voice taking on a dangerous edge, every inch an ancient chieftain. "Explain."

"Ah was charged t'bring her oot. Gi'en a pack that were hern. We were chased by the Hunt. Ah think it a fluke they caught ar scent. Ah don' think we were th' object of th' Hunt, jest convenient prey. Ah lost track o' her after ah took on th' hoonds." His voice told her he blamed himself for that.

"Ye fought with that pack on Midsummer's Eve," Liberty commented. "Why'd ye not get it to her afore? Or at least afore now?"

"Truth be told, miss, ah fergot t'were there. Ah put it on her billet this morn, thinkin' it might be a private matter fer openin'."

"So this be from th' King?" Ian asked, his voice beginning to lose its sharp edges.

"Aye, Laird. Sent fer in ma presence an' prepared by prior order."

All this rang true to An as she tried to move her body. It took effort, but she turned her head. It was less effort to open her eyes. What she saw drew a shocked gasp from her lips and all eyes turned to her.

Before her and by the bed, she saw a humanoid gryphon in dark green trousers that left room for his twitching tail, and a green shirt that hung open over an invisible undershirt. In his talons was a glowing box, now closed, which he set aside even as she turned to the next person in the room. On the edge of the bed, by her knee, was a gypsy girl glowing fiercely at the edges, with sparks of lightning in her hair. Beyond Ian stood a marionette with a crown of growing things intertwined in her copper hair. An could tell she wore a dress of some sort, but could only see where it covered, all other details lost to the fog.

What stood past her drew her eye even more than the gryphon man in the Green Man's crown, or the flower queen with her shocked but wooden face. The man was tall, broad-shouldered, but somehow not hulking. His dark brown hair fell about his shoulders with locks obscuring one steel-blue eye as he sheepishly looked up at her from beneath them. There was a sword on his back that seemed to burn to be free.

It occurred to her then that she had seen those eyes once, some twenty years past, peering out of a visor as he and a small group of newly polished recruits were presented before the King by his favourite general.

As with Liberty, she could not see his clothes beyond knowing he wore a shirt with the sleeves rolled past his elbows and a kilt.

Ian's voice of concern drew her attention back. "Lass?"

"I... I can see ye!" she breathed, struggled to sit up.

Taloned hands moved to help her, sitting her up against the headboard. Roulet moved like lightning to arrange the pillows behind her.

"I'm fine but..." she frowned, glancing down at herself. "Now that's disconcertin'. I'm floatin'."

"Floatin'?" Liberty puzzled.

"I can't see the bed, then. I am on the bed, aye?"

"Aye."

A soft 'hmm' came from Ian. "Tell me what yeh *can* see."

She leaned back, looked around to obey. "You, not fully gryphon, but enough. The ladies: a doll an' lightnin'. An' th' Highlander hoverin' over yon. Odd, though. I can see yer clothes an' Roulet's, but not Liberty's nor the gent's." She glanced down again, blushing. "Or m' own fer that matter."

The Scot suddenly vanished, presumably behind the doorway.

"I can see that ye've sommat on," she almost growled. "Just no detail." The Scot reappeared, though by the arms crossed over his chest, he was still uncertain. She cast her gaze to the rest of the room.

"I can see somethin' hoverin' on that wall, but only partly, like sommat's in th' way. They're likely clothes. And the box in the air there," she pointed to where a nightstand should go.

Ian nodded knowingly. "Fey sight." He glanced at the box. "He must have treasured yeh fine t've gone t' such lengths."

"She saved his children."

Ian's head whipped back to the doorway, then turned to her. "Yeh didnae tell me that bit."

Skye nodded his head. "Aye, Laird. Th' governess," he said, nodding his head in An's direction, "gave her eyes t' protect 'em and damn near her life."

An felt embarrassed. He was making more of it than there was. "I merely ran. I fought nothing. I drew the creature off from the wee ones. I weren't fast enough."

"Is anyone else noticing she's been speakin' English this whole time?" Liberty demanded, her fists on her hips. Something in her wooden face told An she knew how uncomfortable with the subject she was getting and had changed it deliberately.

It only worked marginally, as attention was still on An. "Something else from the box?" Roulet asked.

An shook her head. She didn't think so. Not completely. "I knew the tongue afore I went beyond. I merely forgot," she shrugged.

"And now yeh remember?" Ian asked pointedly.

"I was beginnin' to remember bits. The ladies ha' been helpin by translatin'. I was piecin' it t'gether. But many things only half remembered are clearer now."

There was something hopeful in his eagle's eye. "Yer name, perhaps?"

She shook her head sadly. "Alas, I lost that a century ago. Surrendered it fer 'Nan' an' '*múinteoir*' and of course, '*bean an ceobhrán*'."

Ian began to draw the others with him, away from the bed. "All right, the lass has had a tryin' day and..."

"We only took her shoppin'," Liberty protested.

"Aye, I've been shoppin' wit' yeh, lass. She's like fair shot. Now out."

"Wait," An said, barely able to raise her voice to be heard. "Commander, I'd... speak with ye a moment. Then, if Roulet or Liberty would ...help me dress fer bed?"

"Aye," Liberty began, then seemed to remember something vital. "Bloody.... Roulet, can ye manage? I came up t' tell ye Tori called. There's some trouble at th' bar. I'll have t' go down. Da', we'll need a wee talk beforehand." There was a meaningful look exchanged between the two of them as he nodded.

"I got this," Roulet said, dismissing the matter. She stepped aside to allow An a private moment with Skye, moving to the wardrobe to fetch her the old-fashioned eyelet nightgown they'd found for her.

Skye crossed the room to her bedside, helped her to sit up as she held out her hand to him. She did not get off the bed, but held onto his hand a moment, squeezed. "Commander, I am terribly sorry for what I've cost ye. I realise now I'm the reason ye had to leave. For what it's worth, I'm sorry."

He gave her what she took for an indulgent smile. "Lass," he said. "I've not left. I've just been reassigned is all. Yer safety is my charge."

She groaned at that thought. "But here is not There," she insisted.

"Battlefield venues change. An' I don' begrudge ye th' duty. Now ye should rest." With that, he turned and left the room, closing the door quietly behind him.

For the next few weeks, An drifted about the house, trying to learn the patterns, to avoid the furniture she still couldn't see, and establish some sense of autonomy. If she couldn't manage to navigate the house without a constant assistant, she could never expect to make her own way, and she feared she was on the cusp of taking advantage of Ian's hospitality. Primarily, she needed something to do. Something of worth. She felt lost without a purpose.

She awoke in the middle of the night, uncertain of the time. She slipped on her dressing gown and tried to puzzle through the braille primers that had been thoughtfully procured for her, but nothing was clicking. She was just restless. Going back to sleep was not an option.

Finally, she dressed in one of the light-weight, ankle-length skirts Liberty and Roulet had bought her, and one of the silky, nearly sheer blouses, her modesty protected by the bodice-like vest that matched the skirt. She could feel some kind of embroidery on it, but could not fathom the design. She left her hair in the side braid she always put it in for bed. It did not matter that the house was likely dark at this hour. She lived in the dark.

She navigated the stairs easily enough with the rail, stepped into the back hall of the house. She was starting to be able to tell where she was by the sound of the floors. It was all polished hardwood, and some of the rooms creaked differently than others. She walked down the hall, trailing her fingers along the wall, counting doorways. She was coming to know the hallways by the various scents, too. Shannon, the head-housekeeper, had taken to putting certain flowers in certain places. Always roses in the west back halls, carnations in the east wing, and roses and lilies together in the front.

Tonight, as expected, the house was mostly quiet, but she could hear faint noises from the back halls and followed first her ears, then her nose to the scent of bread preparation. She had never been back here before, but knew immediately that she had found the kitchen. "Hello?" she called, seeing only the empty grey that filled her vision until something magical crossed it.

"Oi, lass, what are ye doin' out o' bed?" came the frumpy, motherly voice of Martha. She heard her setting something on a board near her, the rustle of an apron cleaning hands and smiled.

"Couldn't sleep any more. I'm not intruding?"

"Tsk, no, just caught me at startin' th' dough. There'll be soda bread fer breakfast an' cherry almond scones fer tea."

"Sounds positively homesick."

"Homesick?"

An shook her head, "I'm sorry, I don' know why I put it that way. But th' smell..."

There was a knowing tone in the woman's voice. "Smells'll do that to ye, take ye home. Like nothin' else fer the memory. Have a seat an' ye like. Can ye find th' table? 'Tis but straight across."

"I'll manage, thank ye."

"I've some coffee on, fer mysel', but if ye like I can spare ye a cup?" she offered.

An shook her head as she reached out with her hands, taking cautious steps forward. "I've no love of coffee. ...Thank ye," she added, as if forcing herself to say it and slightly embarrassed by it. "Fergive me. I'm... out of the habit of thanking."

"I'm of the understanding ye don't thank the fair folk. I've had a few o' the Touched such as yersel' under my wing a time or two. Mind the cat," she added, her voice beginning to turn around just as a suction sealed door opened and a waft of chill filled the room.

An tried to mind her step, making sure not to pick up her feet so not to step on the animal.

"He's a right annoyance, but he keeps the mice and *púcaí* out o' m' pantry. Thankfully, he leaves th' brownies alone." Her voice had a strange echo to it, as if she had her head in something.

An's foot slid against something furry, which reacted by leaping, not away as she expected, but the exact perfect direction to trip her. Her hands went out in front of her to catch herself and she found the cold stove. She managed not to do any damage to herself or the cat until her hand brushed against something on the stove-top that burned as if it had been red hot. She jerked her hand away with a hiss, took a half step back and fell against a pulled out chair, tumbled awkwardly into the seat.

"Lass, ye all right?" Martha bustled over, fretting like a mother hen. "Oh, thank heavens I left that chair out from gettin' down m' stash o' dried cherries. Shoo, ye wee monster!" she cried, flapping her apron at the cat who obediently fled. "Nothin' too bad I ho..." she paused as she saw An nursing the back and side of her hand. "Nothin's on, how'd ye...? Och, ye great fool," she snapped at herself, taking An's hand in hers and examining it. "None o' ye usually come in here, so I didna put th' iron away."

"Ye iron while ye bake?" she asked, gasped as the woman slathered something cold and slimy on the burn.

"No, child. The skillet. It's cast iron. It's yer holy water."

An was confused. "My holy water?"

"Tsk, havna they taught ye nothin' yet. Vampires, they burn when they touch holy water or crosses. The fair folk, and those they've touched, react poorly to iron. Cold iron is worse, lucky you that was cast. Lord knows the master keeps a bit o' cold iron around the house somewhere fer emergencies, but... only cast iron down here. I like that skillet. T'were m' gran's, so I ain't likely to be rid o' it. Not usually a hazard on the back burner... but then, I wasna takin' a blind girl an' an infernal tom inta account."

An had no choice but to let the woman fuss over her. Half an hour later, after tea and biscuits, her hand had stopped hurting, and she was able to escape the kitchen while Martha attended to her soda bread.

She headed towards the front of the house. There was a sitting room where she had left a braille copy of a book she knew by heart. It might help her to learn the feel of the letters better. She counted doorways and turns and smelled for the roses and lilies. She heard voices before she smelled the flowers and slowed down. They were masculine voices, some angry, some distressed, all kept at a low tone she could not understand from this distance.

She tread softly, trying not to disturb them, hoping they were in one of the other three rooms off the atrium and not in the little solar she was headed for. Her luck held. They were in the larger of the three, something Roulet had called a 'living room' where they had one of those television boxes, a large array of couches and a fireplace. From the sound of it, there were two Irishmen, an American and an Englishman, and the Englishman was the one under duress. She glided past like a ghost, reaching for the doorway just beyond it when she felt a twinge in her chest.

She stopped, pressed her good hand against her breast-bone, frowning. It didn't feel like indigestion. Ian's voice cut clearly through her distress.

"Yeh didn't approach th' Cossack?"

"No, sor. 'E came t' me! 'ad me snatched off th' street-like, shoved inta tha' fancy car o' 'is." That pain again. Maybe it was a reaction to the speaker?

"Why'd ye go an' tell him who ye worked for, Chatham?" someone growled. An recognised the voice as belonging to Reggie, Ian's right hand and heir.

"I didn' bloody 'af ta'. 'ad me dead t' roights, 'e did."

No twinge. Truth.

She stopped. How had she known? One of the gifts?

Yes. It tasted like eagle feathers and lily water.

She started to continue on to the solar, to ignore the interrogation she was certain was neither legal nor her business. The next exchange nearly robbed her of her breath.

"Did yeh tell him anything important? Like regardin' m' daughter's business?" Ian snapped, at the end of his tether but on the verge of leniency.

"No, I didn', sor. On me mum's grave, I swear. What I did tell 'im was months out a'date. Tole him ye don't confide me much."

LIE, her senses screamed. She stopped, made up her mind and turned back to the door, stepped just into the frame. Within she could see Ian and Reggie, both mostly human. Ian was leaning on the back of something she could not see. "Beggin' yer pardon, Mister O'Keefe," she said, bobbing a curtsey and trying her best to look like the help. Someone came towards her but was called off, perhaps with a gesture.

"I'm a little busy, Miss An. Can it wait?" he said, trying to be kind and polite, but something in his voice reinforced her impression she was in the wrong place at the wrong time.

"I'm afraid not, sir." She shifted to Irish. "*Does the Sassenach speak?*" she asked pointedly.

Something crossed Ian's face at that, alerted to something in her manner or her features. "*Nay. Be brief.*"

She took a deep breath, praying she was right. "*He's lyin' to ye.*"

Ian went from halfway across the room to looming in front of her in what seemed to have been a single stride. His hands on her arms were gentle but firm. "*How do yeh know?*"

She shook her head. "*I'm not entirely sure. The gifts, I think. When he said he was taken off the street, I felt it here,*" she said, touching his breast. "*When he said he told them lies, it near sucked th' breath out o' me. Truly hurt. Forgive me, chief, I'd no intention o' eavesdroppin'. I was just goin' to the solar for a book I left there and then it hurt, and I had to listen. It didn't hurt when he said he didn't have to tell them who he worked for. Just th' rest of it. I know in my soul he's lyin' something awful. I don't know what's goin' on and I don't have to know. I was just dead certain if I didn't tell ye what I knew, somethin' terrible would happen.*"

His hand moved up to her shoulder, fully taloned now. His anger was coming off of him in waves, but he maintained his outward calm. It wasn't aimed at her. "*I intend this man no harm,*" he said, not taking his raptor brown eyes off of hers.

She felt that pressure again, returned his fierce stare. "*Aye, but ye do. If I'm tellin' ye true, I'm guessin' ye'll kill him. ...And rightly so fer threatenin' yer family. Just bear in mind ye not get caught. These people need ye with yer neck unstretched.*"

At that Ian laughed, his talons becoming more hand-like. "*They don' hang people anymore, lass. But thank yeh. Get yeh on to yer book, but take it t' yer room, mind. I'll be up later to have a word with yeh.*"

She curtseyed again, switching back to English. "Thank ye, sir. I'll take care of it right away."

As she felt her way to the solar, she heard his knuckles crack as he re-entered the room and closed the door behind him. She found the book fairly quickly, feeling her way from chair to table to chair to the table she'd lain it on. Her fingers drifted over the spine, swiftly told her she had the right book and she left again, a little more sure of her position in the room. As she reached the staircase, Reggie came out of the living room, looked up at her with confusion on his face, then headed out the front door.

An drifted back upstairs to her room, curled up in the over-stuffed chair in a corner by the window and ran her fingers across the bumps on the page, reading aloud to herself as if to confirm she was reading aright. *"Whether I shall turn out to be the hero of my own life, or whether that station will be held by anybody else, these pages must show."*

7

The conversation with Ian had been enlightening.

More than a few centuries back, Ian had noticed that members of the O'Keefe line were apparently very popular targets for the Sidhe. To save his people, he made a bargain with one of the Seelie: the Gryphon King. In exchange for a century of service, all O'Keefe's everywhere, born or adopted, were protected from being taken against their will. They could still bargain, agree or be tricked into crossing over, but never by physical force. When he returned, he found his people still in need, just from more mundane sources. He came to the New World, unable or unwilling to compete with the current mortal chieftain, and began unifying the family there, helping other poor Irish as he was able.

He quickly foresaw New York as a bad place to stop. It would soon be overcrowded with immigrants coming in with no money to keep moving on. So, he moved the bulk of his people South, to the Florida territory, carved himself out a nice little stretch of land when he found what amounted to a faery fort, a rath. There was a clear trod there, and one of the reasons the natives avoided the area.

He built his house, put up homes for the people he brought, found ways to manage the rath and built himself a fortress on the old model. This meant the main house was the centre of the land, with everything else radiating out from it, and a wall surrounding the property. It was not at all what an Englishman or American thinks of when they hear the word 'fortress'. It wasn't extremely defensible, but didn't really need to be. When the Civil War broke out and stretched far enough, they were more than capable of defending the land. When the Wild Hunt came through, they found ways of confining it and protecting the people from its predations.

A rath on the property meant the occasional Taken found their way out. It also provided an avenue of approach for those who would offer their services to the Dé Danann. This meant an unusual concentration of the Touched living in the region and from time to time the Taken from other places found their way here. He found places for them all as if they were Irish or family if they desired it, and all he asked was allegiance so that everyone's needs could be met.

While the nearby city began growing, he insinuated himself into the general doings of it. He got involved in the politics for a while, but never more than he really had to in order to see that his people got what they needed. He frequently paid to bring scores of Irish immigrants south to the Rest, got them citizenship, jobs, and homes and settled in a place where they could breathe and be Irish. He even set up a primary school that taught Irish in addition to the regular classes, and made certain that every child, and some of the adults, who lived there could read and do their sums. He paid heavily into the nearby government to make certain that the laws never became hostile to anyone because of their original nationality, and that his community was left alone. Heavy enchantments on the wall helped with that.

When Prohibition came along, he naturally ended up on the wrong side of things. Thus began his career as a crime boss, especially when other 'families' tried to take over. Ian was Irish Mafia. Not the kind seen in films or read about in stories, though An was unfamiliar with what he'd meant by that. He provided for the family however necessary, not always legally. He ran some drugs, but nothing hard-core or dangerous and, in fact, deliberately kept out the hard stuff. He ran gambling halls and other 'vice clubs', or rather, ran the people who did. He used toughs to enforce his will and his people's needs. In short, he was still a chieftain of old, he just occasionally broke a few laws to do it. In order to keep out real gangs and mobs, he had to become one himself.

The Russian mob was a nasty bit of business. No heart, no compassion, no higher purpose, just unbridled capitalism backed by violence and underhanded tactics. They had moved in over the last twenty years and Ian was hard pressed to keep them under control. This was what Ian had been doing when An had her revelation, for which he thanked her. He said he might call upon that talent at a later date, but that he would try to keep her out of the business as much as possible.

It was mid-July, and the weather was suffocating for An. The new clothing was helping as much as anything could, but she could tell that the people around her were sweating, even in their short pants and revealing tops. She was learning quickly, figuring out modern life as well as learning to deal with her handicap. Having finally got the hang of braille, she began reading history books by the dozen in an attempt to catch up. In a joint effort to learn and help Bethany and Kellain with their homework, she had them read to her from whatever textbooks they were studying at the time.

Liberty and Roulet had taken her under wing and were fond of dragging her out on excursions. Ian had managed her a legal ID and the requisite papers, so she was able to get a library card. The library quickly became her favourite place to go, much to the frustration of the ladies. The mall just made her feel lost, but she would never say anything. The two women were getting almost possessive of her, highly protective. Once, on an outing, someone had commented on An's attire, and before she could fashion a reply, Roulet had countered with "It's a religious thing."

She was eternally grateful for the two women, but she was getting restless, feeling useless and without purpose, and depression was setting in.

An's favourite room in the house was the front sitting room, what she thought of as the Magnolia room for the heavenly citrus fragrance from the large, waxy blossoms Martha filled it with. The room had four large windows on two sides, and an open doorway to catch both errant breezes from other parts of the house and the people who wandered in and out at all hours. She had long ago learned the house was an open one. No one ever knocked unless they did not belong, and often as not, the door was propped open.

She had asked Ian the safety of that, with the situation with the Russians, but his response was simple. Anyone coming to the house had to pass through the majority of the rather active Rest. If they were new or did not belong, the house knew long before they arrived.

This particular July morning, An was in the sitting room, in her favourite wing-back chair in the corner, trying her best to crochet while she listened to the conversation going on around her. Some of the men, Reggie and Henry and a few others, were in the Living Room very loudly watching a basketball game. An thought she heard a feminine voice in there as well, but she couldn't be sure. She and Bethany were helping Kellain with her Irish, while Gabby sat nearby, knitting needles clicking madly away. Others came, stayed for a bit and went, but the four of them remained constant.

"*They're getting loud,*" Bethany grumbled in Irish from the floor where the girls had sprawled and spread out their books and papers. "*I don't really get that sport at all. Chasing a ball around a court and not allowed to touch other players.*"

Gabby chuckled over her needles. "*You must really hate golf.*"

She shook her head. "*Oddly enough, I understand that. There's skill to it, but no real competition. It's the head to head, no-contact sports that bug me.*"

Kelly shrugged. "*Takes more skill no to touch?*"

"*Not,*" An corrected. "*Not to touch. And I suppose. I am still surprised that men can make a living playing such sports. And get paid the insane amounts they do.*"

Bethany laughed at that. "*Aye, that they do. I've a cousin just got in with the Dolphins. That's an American football team. He's making a million-five a year and keeping only two hundred fifty for himself and his mother. The rest he sends up here. Course, any time he needs extra, Uncle Ian's more than happy to make sure he has it.*"

An was surprised to hear Ian's voice before she sensed his presence or heard his footsteps. But then, she was concentrating very hard on working her lace by feel, and the boys were being awfully loud. "*A fair chunk o' that sits in a college fund fer those what want it. Investments and all.*"

"*Wise*," An smiled. "*I am somewhat surprised you're not in there with them,*" she added, nodding her head in the direction of the game.

"*Nope. Prefer my sports full contact.*"

"*This does not surprise me.*"

She listened as Ian crossed the room to the window between her and Gabby, chuckling. "*When the football season rolls around, boi, I'll be right in there with them. Now, Friday... heaven help any idiot who causes trouble. That's the Guerrero/Hinojosa fight and I don't aim to miss it.*"

"*Preference for pugilism?*" An cocked an eyebrow. "*Again, I am not surprised.*"

Bethany piped up, "*What is it about Guerrero that you like so much?*"

"*The man's got pluck, that's what. ...Well, I'll be damned,*" Ian muttered.

"*What's the matter?*" Gabby asked.

"*The Scot, um... Skye. He's out on the lawn with some of the Younger boys showing them swords.*"

"*If it be something ye don't want, ye need t' speak to him on the matter,*" An advised. "*To my memory, that's what he did over there: trained.*"

Ian looked over at her. "*Really? That's interesting and useful to know. Let's go have a chat with th' lad.*"

The girls were off the floor quick as jack-rabbits and headed for the door to watch. An and Gabby rose at more sedate paces and as An moved to cross the floor, she tripped over a book Kellain had left behind. She would have gone sprawling had Ian not snaked out his arm and caught her. "KELLAIN!" he bellowed.

The girl popped immediately back in the room, quailed at the dark expression on the chief's face. She understood instantly and ran to sweep up her things. "*I'm sorry, examine. I wasn't thinking.*"

An's eyebrow went up and Gabby stifled a giggle.

"Are yeh tryin' t' say 'Miss'?" Ian growled in English, though An could tell he was amused.

Kelly looked up, startled. "Aye?"

"Try *iníon not iniúch*," An offered with a tender smile.

Kelly looked mortified. "What'd I say?"

"Ye called me an auditor, I think. No mind," she insisted curtailing any further embarrassment on the girl's part. "Now, I know it seems I can see everythin' now, with the faery gift, but I can't. I can see th' Touched, but I can't see you or yer things."

"What you need is a guide dog," Bethany offered from the doorway.

That thought did not please her for some reason. "I don't know..."

Gabby shook her head. "Might be a problem with us. Some of us anyway. We'd have to have a dog raised among us fer that, and that'd take too long. Maybe a tap stick?"

"That might be better, easier to get used to at least," An sighed. "How do I...?"

Before she could finish her sentence, Ian was gone from her side and out the door with a flash of feather and wing.

"What was that all about?" Kelly muttered, from the sound of things still gathering her homework from the floor.

"No telling with him," Gabby sighed and stepped up to An, taking her arm and guiding her around the mess. "Come on."

They were in the hallway when he returned from the east wing where he kept his private study, with a shillelagh in his hand. An stopped, registering the stick immediately. Its edges were sharper than other things around that she could see, except for the tip which shimmered as if something invisible were there. He crossed to her and held it out. She reached up for it, felt a tingle run through her hand up her arm as she touched it. For a full second, both their hands remained on the weapon. The tingling subsided and Ian let go.

"Thank ye," was all she could manage. "But... 'tis magical."

"I know," he said mildly.

"It can't be," Gabby frowned at it.

"I can see it."

"Beware th' tip," he warned.

"It's shod in iron, Ian. How can it be magical?" Gabby insisted.

He shrugged. "That's cold iron, by th' by."

An lifted and turned the stick, sliding her hand down within inches of the cold iron she could feel throbbing at its base.

"What's wrong with getting her a normal tap stick?"

"I don't have one."

"Or a mundane shillelagh 'til we can?"

He chuckled. "Girl's got to defend herself. Plus... it won't let her get lost." With that, he moved out the front door onto the porch.

An let the others go, though Gabby stood by her a moment more. She stood there, running her hands over the old, knobbed wood. It had been polished smooth by years and hands, not by any tool or varnish. It felt right to her. She let it slide through her loose hand to the gently curving end. It fit in her palm perfectly. She turned towards the door. She knew where it was by the breeze on her face. Sweeping the tip across the floor experimentally, she found nothing in her path, but noticed the edge of the carpet runner without having touched it. She stepped forward with more confidence than she had in weeks and followed Gabby's footsteps onto the front porch.

Bethany was sitting on the porch rail next to where Ian stood watching Skye showing a young man the sword he always had at his back. She gathered the impression that there was more than one young man when bits of the one she could see kept shifting out of view for no reason. Gabby stepped back beside her, out of her way so she could see.

The young man's features were dark, like polished wood, and seemed to have a very fine grain to them. His fingers were long and delicate and when he spoke, there was a faint twing to it, like harp strings. Gabby noticed her studying the boy and commented. "Can you see what he was?"

An shook her head. "I'm not sure. I see... something... he were no beast like most I've seen, nor altered as the Commander was, for a soldier."

"But you know he is one of the Taken."

"Oh, aye. That I can see him at all tells me that."

Gabby nodded. "That's Billy Younger. He was taken and made into a harp."

"That explains that."

"His brothers are here because they came to us to get him out." She laughed. "It was all very Jack and the Beanstalk, sans Jack of course," she added with a sigh. "Him we couldn't rescue."

"There's a cloud castle with a giant?"

Gabby shrugged. "There are lots of little realms, most are under siege by one o' th' big ones most times unless they're well hidden or really small. We've got people from all over. Liberty came from th' Sky King, too. We found her when we rescued Billy, and a small handful of others. Couldn't get Jack though."

"Jack. THE Jack? Jack of th' tales?"

"Yup. He's chained t' th' throne. Next time Jonny's around, ask him t' sing ye Jack's song."

Their attention was diverted by Ian leaping over the rail to the ground and crossing the lawn to the group. An could hear other voices than the three she could see and heard one of them pelting away towards the carriage house when Ian told him to go get something.

"Yeh want t' learn swords, boys?" Ian asked. There was a resounding ascent. "Yeh want t' learn it from him?"

"We think so, sir," one of them chirped.

Ian turned to Skye, "Well, afore I let yeh teach m'folk, I need t' assess yer skill." Ian held his hand out behind him as the footsteps came running back. From what An could tell, a sword was placed in his hand. "Now, I'll not want yeh goin' easy on me, my bein' an old man and all..."

Gabby and the girls snickered at that.

"But we'll go a few rounds of serious fightin'," Ian began.

Skye cleared his throat. "Begging yer pardon, Laird, but... I've never lost on th' field. And if either of us gets hurt serious..."

Ian's thumb jerked over his shoulder to the porch. "That's what Gabby's over there for. She knows th' faery healin', same as m' daughter."

Skye shrugged and settled into his stance. "Very well then, sair. On yer own heid be it."

Ian laughed, muttered something about young pups or rips, and set to with a will.

An watched for a few minutes before getting bored with it. She could see the combatants, but only one of the weapons, and it made the whole thing look rather silly to her. She could not appreciate the finer points of the matter. Besides, there was something in her hands that wanted her attention more. She found her way to one of the numerous rocking chairs and sat, running her hands lovingly across the satiny wood. The clanging of metal and grunting of men faded into the background.

There was only her and the shillelagh.

She knew things about it, more the longer she stroked it, felt out every nick and gouge and imperfection in the wood. For one, she would never get lost with it. All she had to do was tap the ground with it in front of her home, (and it had to be earth, not stone or wood,) and it would always guide her back to that spot if she but asked, or to any location so set. It was also more than happy to be used as a weapon and would make her an excellent one, it promised; would come to her when called, resist the hands of others. All she had to do was name it.

And the iron tip? she thought to it.

Name me and touch it.

She thought only briefly, and smiled, loving the irony. "*Cipín.*"

Without thinking on the matter, her hand reached for the iron tip and she gasped as the stick slid down to prevent her touching it. She tried again. The same thing happened: the stick moved of its own accord to prevent her from hurting herself. She knew instinctively that the iron tip would never land on anything she did not intend it to that would take special damage from iron.

She stood, drifted to the steps and, with the shillelagh guiding her feet, descended to the front walk and turned aside to the lawn. She raised it a hand or two above the ground, then rapped it sharply on the grassy earth thrice. She felt the power surge through her fingers, sent a shiver down her spine. She smiled, knew without a doubt, no matter where she was, that if she had Cipín with her, she would always return here.

She suddenly became aware that the fighting had stopped and the combatants at least were looking at her. "Fergive me, am I in th' way?"

"Nay, lass," Ian chuckled. "So... what'd yeh name 'er?"

"Cipín."

Skye scowled even as Ian grinned. He wiped sweat from his forehead. "Ye named it fer a drumstick?"

She gave a soft laugh. "Aye, fer drummin' sense inta thick heads."

The Younger boys, and apparently a few others who had drifted up, laughed at that.

Skye ignored them. "Ye need sommat t' find yer way. One o' those white wands with the red ends."

"This'll find me m' way fine, thank ye kind," she countered delicately.

"But that's a shillelagh. Folks see that and take it fer a weapon, they're liable t' test ye. What'll ye do an' some punk loon decide t' mug ye?"

Her smile crept shyly up one side of her mouth. "Drum some sense inta his thick head."

There was a moment's silence, then the lot of them fell out laughing; some of them at the very notion, others at the way she said it. She did not mind either. She pitched her voice so she could be heard. "I'll admit, I've some drawbacks to work around. An' I'd never stand up t' swordsmen such as yourself or th' chief, but... I'm no shy hand. I supervised children. I am very good at takin' things away."

The laughter died down.

"I'd be obliged to ye, ye showed me a thing or two to compensate," she added.

Skye sighed as Ian threw up his hands and stepped back. "Fine. Ah'll see what ye ken first, though." He took up his stance with a weapon she could not see. Apparently during the fighting they had switched to practise swords made of wood. "Ah'll go easy on ye."

She turned a little sideways, watching the way he held himself, trying to judge the length and placement of the weapon. "Don't do me no favours," she taunted. "I'll not thank ye t' baby me."

"Fine, lass. Have it yer oon," he growled and lunged.

The blow would have landed on her shoulder, but she swung the stick up and in the way. Cipín had obviously helped a little, giving her just the hair of an edge. The force of the blow was not his full strength, she could tell, though she could not gauge what those limits were. She didn't really want to find out yet. She needed to get that weapon out of play. She look a step back and waited again, watching every twitch of his enormous body. She saw the incoming swing and ducked under and into it, cracking him at the base of the wrist at the thumb, forcing him to drop the sword. She took advantage of his surprise and rapped him smartly on the ribs, though not hard enough to do any real damage.

Without warning, one of the Younger boys came up behind her and grabbed her. As he pressed against her, the head of the shillelagh came up and rapped him in the forehead and as his hands belatedly flew to protect himself, the iron shod end was dropped sharply onto the top of his foot. He hopped away from her, yelping over to where Gabby waited to patch him up.

This time she saw Ian's signal to another bystander to try and attack her. Skye laughed when Billy shook his head vigorously, throwing up his hands. An's stick flew out with lightning speed to crack Skye sharply across the calf. He jumped as if he'd been switched, yelped as he danced back.

"Watch that end, ye vicious quine. Thar's iron there."

"Aye," she snapped. "An' it'll nary touch ye, an' ye behave yerself. Now, get serious. I need t'know these things."

He sighed, straightened up. Leaving his weapon on the ground, he went at her. She struck out with the shillelagh, made only glancing contact that was brushed aside as he tackled her, lifting her bodily from the ground and throwing her back to it. She landed hard; the wind knocked out of her and the shillelagh from her grasp. She rolled to her hands and knees, held out one hand, and Cipín flew directly into it. She used her to stand.

She bowed to Skye. "Thank ye. Now, ...show me how not to let that happen again."

He stood straighter, looming taller somehow, reassessing her. Finally, he nodded. "First though, ah want ye t' hit me again with tha' stick. No' th' back end!" he yelped, dodging prematurely as she held it just below the knob. She deftly flipped it, letting it slide just past the halfway mark. "As hard as ye can. Ah want t' ken yer strength."

She obliged, watched his eyes bulge for a second, though he did not move or yield to the blow she landed on his thigh.

There was amusement in Ian's voice. "So, how hard can she hit?"

Skye's voice was strained, trying to control the pain. "If ah weren't... what ah am... it'd be broken, sair." He hobbled back, held up a hand. "Gimme a mo'."

There was another round of laughter at that, himself included.

It was getting towards dark when Martha stood on the porch steps and called out over the sound of laughing and good-hearted melee. "Oi, you lot!" They paused exactly as they were, Skye bent over in a headlock with Reggie. They all looked in her direction, even Ian, who was supervising a round robin at An with some of the mortal lads. "I'm putting dinner on the table in exactly thirty minutes. Any o' you lot not bathed and dressed proper and at the table at that time will be fed out in the kennels with the other dogs. Bethany, pet, go set m' table fer however many louts as happen to be out there what ye think might make it." With that she turned and went back into the house, wiping her hands on her apron, more out of habit than any real need.

Everyone remained frozen for a half second, then made a mad scramble for the house. Skye tucked himself deeper into the headlock, closer to Reggie's belly, then lifted, neatly tossing Reggie off him and onto his back with a loud thump. He turned to help him up, both men laughing. Reggie grimaced, closing his eyes and turning his head away, making a face. "Regimental? Really?"

Skye laughed. "Yer just figgerin' that oot?"

An allowed Ian to take her arm to escort her back into the house. He pointed at a cluster of boys who were apparently dirtier than the rest. "Oi, you lot can shower in the carriage house. Shannon'd have my hide I let yeh track that in th' house." He warned her about the steps, went up them at a pace she could match. "I really need to build more bathrooms," he chuckled.

Dinner was like any large family affair: noisy. Without remembering details, An found herself in familiar territory, even down to competing for the last rolls. At a glare from Ian, whoever's hand was in the basket next to hers rolled the last bun into her grasp and withdrew. An thanked them and was rewarded with a mumble. Conversations were mixed and many. An was engaged in a light conversation with Gabby and Bethany about gardening. The boys were going on about the basketball game. At the far end, Ian and Skye were discussing serious matters of skill with Reggie.

"I think the boys could use the training, and they certainly want it. It'll keep them out of trouble this summer," Reggie was saying. "Besides, think of the look on the Russians' faces when our boys start wielding lead pipes like claymores," he laughed.

"I agree there are advantages," Ian conceded. "And if they have to fight off one o' *them*, they'll have an edge. The discipline will be good for them. But they'll need to know other things, brawlin', dirty-fightin', that rugby spear-chuck yeh do. Think yeh kin handle it?"

Skye shrugged. "Aye. Ah taught sech things over there. S'ards, drills, close combat. Ah loik th' work. Will need a place though: a field, a hall. Ah prefer a field fer somm'it, a gym fer others. Not always goin' t' fight outdoors. Need to learn to work aroond."

Ian nodded.

"Also, though ah doubt there'll be a whole lot o' call, might want t' teach them battle calls: signals fer things like fall back, left flank, charge ...retreat," the last Skye said with distaste.

"Might surprise yeh how much call there'll be," Ian said softly. "If we ever get in an open fight with those bloody Russians... I'd like t' be able t' call a fade out when th' police are incomin'. Leave th' bastards t' face th' music alone."

Reggie frowned, weighing the pros and cons, though there was a gleam of hope for it in his eye. "You really think it'll come to that?"

"Might like," Ian said shortly. "So, yeh acceptin' the job, Skye?" he asked, turning back to the man. "Knowin' yer teachin' mob-boys t' better do their dirty work?"

Skye didn't really hesitate. "Aye, Laird. Ye've given me a roof and a bellyful." He lowered his voice, "ye've taken in what ah'm charged with. Ah can't bloody well wander off elsewhere, and I might as well make myself useful. The illegalities don't bother me much, though ah'm not gonna do any 'hits' fer ye unless they're gunnin' fer me oon, but other than... what's a little rum-runnin' atween friends?" he grinned. "Asides, where else this day an' age am ah goin' ta find a job teachin' lads t' break heids? Or t' use a s'ard. Who else has a wooden *claymore* 'just lyin' aroond'?"

They laughed.

Gabby had patched them up, but Skye could still feel the bruising he had taken from his battle with Ian. As Reggie and the chief discussed details and he refilled his plate, Skye mulled over the fight. They had begun lightly enough, assessing one another. Eventually, they had realised the other was holding back and had laid it on thicker. This escalation had continued until they realised they were close to really trying to kill each other and were very closely matched sword to sword. Ian had told him that if it had not been for what Ian was, Skye might have been able to take him. He knew without being told, though, had the fight gone to brawling or wrestling that he was hopelessly out-matched.

He had a mouthful of potatoes when he realised he had been addressed directly. "Sor?" he mumbled, trying to be polite and not open his full mouth more than he had to.

"I said, welcome t' the family. Yer role'll be minor, but significant."

Skye swallowed quickly, shook the extended hand. "Thank ye."

"I'll introduce yeh t' Danny later. He's our builder. Let yeh work the specs on yer needs. I've a cul-de-sac I'm finishin' up just on the other side o' the wood from the rath, not a bad place to put it. Yeh'll have a house right near an' yeh like. M'daughter's is in that cul-de-sac and just finished. Which reminds me," he raised his voice to be heard across the table. "Any o' yeh lot be wantin' another free supper and maybe a round or two at the pub, best be showin' up on Liberty's doorstep Tuesday mornin' at nine an' help her move."

There were several ascents and a few groans from those that would be unavailable.

Skye basked in the warmth of it all. A place, not just as a soldier. Something essential to do without resorting to menial tasks. The idea of bussing tables had not appealed to him, though he had not been able to see himself getting any other kind of work. Maybe construction if he was lucky, but he hadn't the references or really the skills beyond the muscle. Now he would be able to do what he loved. *And* he was getting a home out of it, something completely unexpected. His eyes went around the table, paused at the governess. An. His responsibility. He turned back to Ian.

"After dinner, if ah could beg a private word?"

Ian nodded readily. "We'll go t' m' study after pie."

"Pie?" he echoed, perking up. "What kind of pie?"

Ian took a deep breath. "Maple apple-pear crumble, I'm thinking."

Skye caught the same scent Ian had and quickly cleaned his plate.

Ian's study was a comfortable affair. Thick, dark wood panelling, shelves of books, an antique mahogany desk that looked like it had been here since the house was built. There was a fireplace on one wall, above which was a painting of a fey-looking woman in a medieval gown smiling mischievously with several Irish wolfhounds lounging around her. The hardwood floors were covered by a thick, elaborately patterned rug from India and from somewhere cold air was piped in. It was an interior room with no windows, so ventilation of some sort was needed. So far, this was the only room he'd encountered that had air conditioning.

Ian sank into a large, padded office chair behind the desk, propping his stockinged feet up on its edge. Skye took the couch, sitting with his elbows on his thighs and his clasped hands dangling between his knees. Ian patiently lit a cigarette, offered him one, which he accepted. It gave him something to do with his hands while he thought. Ian waited him out.

"Ye've not asked me a terrible lot o' questions," he began. "But then ah've not got th' mem'ry loss th' governess has. Ah didnae get th' kiss of forgetfulness she did."

"Kiss of forgetfulness?"

Skye nodded. "Aye. Ah've seen it, been told. Sometimes it's easier when they leave, to no' remember that place. Ah couldna afford it. Ah had t' remember. 'Protect her fra th' wolves', he seid. That's m'duty an' ah'll do it til me last but... ah cannae do it fra a distance, ye ken?"

Ian watched him a long moment, taking a deep drag on his cigarette. "So yer concerned with her living up here at the house and you living all the way out yon and not trustin' m' security?"

Skye was quick to refute that. "Noo, no'a'tall! Ah'm..." he wracked his brain, sighed. "'Tis no' a *security* issue. Yer no' always aroond. She's blind. There's a million little dangers aboot. Th' iron in the kitchen fer ex. An' naw that twig ye gave 'er," he groaned.

"Yeh know yeh can't shadow her every moment of her life, right?"

Skye leaned back on the couch. "Aye. She'd hate me fer it too an' ah did."

"Rightly."

"But what's a man t'dew?"

"Let her live her life. Aye, keep an eye out fer the big stuff. But out here, there's not a lot o' the big stuff. There's plenty in this house t' keep that kinda eye on. Yer problem'll be when she decides she wants t' go out

91

there, beyond the wall. And she will. Likely soon," he observed. "I've noticed she's been a mite restless o' late. Yeh may keep her occupied a while with the self-defence..."

"But that'll backfire in th' end, won' it? She'll believe she's right an' fine and th' wolves'll have governess fer tea."

Ian studied him carefully. "Any particular wolves yeh've an eye out fer?"

Skye took a draw on his forgotten cigarette, shook his head. "Na. He just seid there were wolves out here and he'd have her safe. Ah assumed he meant those would prey on th' blind an' helpless."

Ian gave an amused snort. "Like as yeh noticed this afternoon, she's not as helpless as yeh thought, boi."

Skye chuckled at that. "Well, ah do feel fer any unnatural what tries his hand. 'Tis th' ones she cannae see what worry me."

They smoked in silence for a bit. "Does she know yer th' one saved her life?"

Skye's head snapped up at that. "How d'ye ken that?" As far as he knew, no one on this side knew but him.

An eyebrow went up. "I'll take tha' fer a no. I have m' ways, lad. The hedge is only up when we expect unwanted visitors, like Bealtaine or Samhain. Keeps th' Bitch from ridin' through and takin' what pleases her. Other than that, we know how t' open it. We can come an' go as it please us. Those that desire t' risk it."

"Ye sent a letter," he said flatly. He remembered the occasional missive coming up that road from the watchmen, having to choose a man he thought ready to deliver it to the castle. He should have known. Not all the letters were of Fey origin.

"Do yeh care for her? Beyond yer duty?"

Skye looked down at that, thought long and hard.

"Yeh don't have t' tell me," Ian said, crushing out his cigarette. "Just so's yeh know yerself, why yer doin' what yeh are."

"She were good with th' bairns," he finally answered. "Ah've seen her, onct or twict, fram a distance. An' in th' pavilion, saying her good-byes. Ah saw how deeply it hurt her t' leave them ahind, but she niver let it be shown on her face. Ah think ah'm th' on'y one saw tha' tear."

Ian let him ruminate a few. His fingertips found something stuck to the edge of his desk by the blotter and he concentrated on scraping it up with a fingernail. "Are yeh still loyal t' th' King?" he asked casually.

Skye stared at him; watched him meticulously peel up whatever was stuck to the wood, trying to assess why he was asking and how he might react to the truth. He found he didn't really care. "As far as ah'm concerned, ah hav'na left his service," he said flatly. "If that changes whether ye still wish me t' teach yer lads, ah'm sorry fer all tha'. Ah'll take th' girl an' go."

Still not looking directly at him, "What makes yeh think it would?"

Skye was beginning to get irritated. His hand itched, and the sword seemed more obvious on his back. The fact that he should be leaning on it and wasn't never occurred to him. It was never really all here unless it was in his hand, anyway. He got himself under control. "Ah've talked wi' th' locals, some o' th' Taken. Fox fer instance. Some o' th' lads are downright hostile aboot th' gentry what kept 'em. Seem t' think they be all same cloth, ye ken. Ah know better. But ah'll respect yer right t' yer 'pinion."

Ian laughed. "Yer fine, laddy-buck. Stand down. I feel th' same. I've done my time an' made my trade, but I begrudge them nothing. Some on th' other hand,... they're right wankers, yeh ken? I just needed to know yer stance. If yer still loyal t' Him, we'll be havin' no conflict. Though I'll need yeh t' understand, yeh answer t' me now. The old way. Yeh've called me Laird 'til now an' I've let it slip. But it means it now. We do this, I'm yer liege, e'en as he's yer King."

Skye did not waste time thinking about it. "Aye, ah'll dooit. So long as ye ken she goes anither way ah'm honour-bound t' folla." He rose, moved to bend to his knee, but Ian held up his hand.

"No need. Yer word be enough. Time was I'd ha' gone through th' full formalities, but those days are long gone. Yeh swear in th' King's name t' accord me all th' rights an' duties as yer liege lord?"

"Ah so swear, in th' nam' o' the Gryphon King, t' obey ye, Laird Ian O'Keefe, the Oak King, as my liege laird until sech time as ye release me fra m'service."

Ian smiled at the added titles. "When ye swear, boi, ye put some weight into it!" He laughed and poured the two of them a whiskey.

8

An found traversing the house easier with Cipín. She no longer stumbled at carpets, or cracked her knees against chair seats before her hands found the backs. She still had a few minor issues. It wasn't a guide dog. She had to use it properly and she could still be waylaid by small things, and things she failed to touch it with. But still, life was a little easier. She remained restless though, felt useless. The depression still threatened.

She came downstairs one afternoon, planning on a walk to test her limits, and saw a man standing where she knew the vase of flowers to be. He had white hair that fell like snow down his back that was badly braided. He was bent as if taking in the scent, one hand held up, cupping the rose that was slowly fading into view. Her eyes widened, drinking in the simple beauty of that single, perfect blossom. It was red, singed a bit on the edges now with what appeared to be frost. It only made it more beautiful.

"Tell me how ye did that," she asked softly. "Please?"

He looked up sharply, saw her standing halfway up the stairs. His eyes were an earthy brown set in the most beautiful face she had ever seen on a man. His features were half Irish, half Native American perhaps, but there was an elven delicacy to them. His skin was on the fair side with a faint brown undercast which promised to tan nicely if he ever went out in the sun for any length of time. "Ceobhránach," he breathed, and the soft, lyrical voice told her he was the bard from Midsummer.

"Mister Sorrow, it was?"

He gave a soft embarrassed laugh at that. "No one calls me Mister Sorrow. Jonny, please. Ye've... adapted," he said.

She could not be sure if he was pleased or disappointed as she continued down the stairs to the floor, using him and the rose as a guide.

"Ye... kin see now?" he frowned.

She stopped abruptly when she took the table in the hip, winced. It was wider than she had calculated; the legs tucked far enough under to be missed. "Not everythin'," she said wryly.

"How?"

"The gift of fey sight."

His manner changed slightly, a discomfort whose cause she could not identify. "From yer fey King?"

She nodded.

"Needs ye beware faery gifts, lass. They're never what they seem."

She smiled softly, turning her head away a little, made shy by his nearness. "I know. I'm on good terms with this one. And I trust him. I raised his children."

"So I've heard." He was close, very close, and seemed almost embarrassed in her presence, something she had not felt from him when they had met. "So... you can see... everything fey?"

An nodded, reaching out to touch the rose, felt the frost as a real thing on its petals. "Aye. Well, things magic touched, or themselves magic. I see them as they are, or can be. Ian, fer instance, always has something of th' gryphon about him, even when he's human. I met Billy Younger th' other day. I knew he was Touched, not just 'cause I could see him, but his skin reminded me of wood-grain and his voice sounded like th' harp he'd been."

Jonny gave a soft laugh at that. "Aye... unusual fer the Sky King to take a man fer the harp, though. Normally he chooses pretty young girls with high, pure voices."

"Oh, he's a pretty voice, a'right. He yelps like a girl," she chuckled. "Now, tell me how ye did this, please."

"Did what?" He followed her hand to the flower. "The rose? I... have a small problem *not* leavin' frost everywhere."

"No, not th' frost. I'd just see th' frost were that it. Ye did something t' th' rose. I see th' *rose*."

"Oh, that." He turned, stood next to her and covered her hand with his under the base of the flower. "It's simple really, though not all the Touched can do it. I doubt Billy could. You might. Yer steeped in their magic, ye might be able. Just... here," he directed her hand to a different bloom, careful not to touch it himself. "Just stroke th' outer petals, try to extend yerself to it. Touch it with all yer bein', want it t' be part of you."

An closed her eyes, took a deep breath, trying to control her reaction to the delicious coolness of his body beside hers. She cupped the rose from below and delicately ran her thumb across the velvety softness of the petal's lip. She tried to breathe herself into it. She found herself humming very softly. She opened her eyes and could see the beginning edges of the flower taking shape mistily. She smiled. "I'm doin' it."

"Good. 'Twasn't too hard, was it?" he asked.

She was suddenly aware of how close he was. It left her breathless. She chided herself for reacting like an untried girl. He was a bard; completely out of reach. That he was handsome only assured she would never have a chance.

"Thank ye. Ye've solved my crochet problem." She was blushing, she knew, as she drew her hand back from the rose. "And...," her face completely lit up, "I kin write again!"

He shifted back a little, pleasantly surprised. "Ye write?"

Her blush deepened, and she looked down, suddenly embarrassed. "A wee. Used to. From time t' time. Nothin' noteworthy."

His long, delicate finger reached out and brushed aside the protective veil of her hair, tucking it back behind her ear. "I'd like t' see some of it, some time. If yer willin'."

She shivered at his touch.

He drew back, closed his hand. "I am sorry. I'm cold."

"It's not that. I like cold," she said quickly. She realised what she'd said and blushed more furiously. She set her hand against her cheek and shook her head, sending her hair to once more hide her face. "Oh, I'm blushing like a witless fool."

He chuckled. "I find it very becomin'. It speaks of innocence. A rare commodity these days."

"It speaks of modesty," she corrected. "Something even rarer," she added. She collected herself, gave her vest a tug to settle it in place and assure herself she was not in disarray. "Fergive me, I... I've never shown anyone m' poetry. And I'm certain a Bard would find my little rhymes quite silly and banal."

"I doubt it. But let me judge, when yer ready fer them t' be seen. 'Tis been my experience that those the author keeps hidden away, certain they are unworthy, are the best of all, the most passionate and telling about them."

"Sometimes I just can't help m'self. Something occurs to me and I have to write. I don't control th' words. I remember... from before, I remember hiding them, some of them anyway. The ones I *had* to write. Them I had t' hide cause they made my mother uncomfortable when they...."

There was an interested spark in his eye as he tipped his head to regard her, the ghostly beginnings of a smile. "When they what?"

She fidgeted. "They don't come true in th' sense that they tell of someone falling off a cliff and then someone falls off a cliff. But..." she was clearly uncomfortable. She rubbed her hand unconsciously on the head of the shillelagh.

"Ye write of blood and there's blood, ye write of high drifts of snow and ye get record winters?"

"I write of gunpowder and tears and a brother comes home in a box."

He allowed the silence to stretch out, let her soak in suddenly remembered grief and assimilate it. "Ye've th' bard's tongue."

She shook her head, dared to look up at him. "Nay, only when I write. And only ...once in a while. But," she continued, taking a deep breath, "ye came fer a purpose, I'm thinkin'?"

He smiled boyishly, dipped his head slightly, "What brings ye t' that deduction?"

"Well, yer hanging about th' foyer like a guest awaitin' audience, fer one. Ye were startled by me, fer another."

"I'm not used t' people bein' able t' sneak up on me," he grinned ruefully.

She shook her head. "Ye were absorbed."

"Ye were quiet," he insisted. "And t' answer yer question, I came t' discuss Lughnasadh with th' chief. But it seems he'll be a mite busy fer th' next hour."

It was her turn to be confused, "How do ye figure?"

He tipped his head towards the open door. "Some of th' boys just pulled up, and it looks like they've some trouble brewin'. Reggie doesn't get that look often; when he does, it means bad things for bad people."

An stepped sideways until the flower arrangement was out of her way. Sure enough, she could see Reggie, looking positively ferocious, coming through the door and hear two or three others behind him.

"Said he's in his office and to come straight back," one of the others was saying, closing something small in his hand with a click.

Reggie nodded politely to An and Jonny as they strode by, disappearing down the east wing. Jonny sighed, drawing her attention back to him. "Looks like I shall have to come by again tomorrow. Matters of festival can wait in th' wake of whatever that is. And what were ye up to this fine afternoon? Ye came down with a sense of arrested purpose."

She felt the blush threatening her again, "I was going to try to go fer a walk, in spite of the fact that no one has th' time t'day. I thought I'd test my new friend out," she said, holding up Cipín.

He gave a little whistle. "That's a nice knob-knocker ye have there, miss."

"Ian loaned her t'me."

"Aye," he nodded solemnly. "I'm familiar. I know where he got her."

"Oh?" she brightened. "I would love to hear it."

He spread his hands in apology. "Sorry, Ceobhránach, but that is not my tale to tell. Would you be kind enough to allow me to escort ye on yer walk, though?"

She felt herself turning faintly pink again. "I would be honoured if it will not inconvenience ye."

He held out his arm to her. "Well, it seems that a certain block of time I had set aside has suddenly become unoccupied. A walk sounds nice."

She smiled, reached out to accept his arm, felt her heart skipping erratically. "Then lead on, good sir, wither we shall away."

Skye stood at the very top of the stairs, watching An walk out the front door with the man in the patchwork denim vest. He had seen the white-haired man before in her company, and though he seemed to be behaving like a perfect gentleman, he still did not trust the man. He was tempted to follow them, to make sure he did not try anything, but remembered what Ian had said about having to let her go her own way sometimes. He knew what would happen if she found out. Any attempt to stay close enough to her to protect her would be hopeless after that. Still, he was tempted.

He heard someone on the hall behind him and turned to see Liberty walking up with a box of things. "Lemme get tha'," he said, taking the box from her.

"Oh, thank ya," she chirruped, happy to unload the box into his arms. "Ah'm just takin' a few thin's t' m'car. Gettin' th' new house up an' ready. Skye, was it?" she asked, following him down.

"Aye, ma'am," he said, carefully avoiding using the royal title his instincts and upbringing insisted on. When they reached the main floor, he stepped aside for her. "Lead th' way."

She gave him a traffic stopping smile and moved a little in front of him. "So, what had yer attention so intent?" she asked.

"Huh? Oh," he said, realising she had caught him out. As they stepped onto the veranda, he saw Jonny and An going around the side of the house, on the path that led to the fort. He stopped on the top step. "Wha'doya ken of tha' white-haired gent?" He made an effort not to call him something ruder.

Liberty looked where he was watching, caught a last glimpse of white braid and denim quilt. "Jonny Sorrow? He's the local bard, why? Have ya no' met him yet?"

"I havnae, noo. He trustworthy?"

She stopped on the last step, looked up at him. "Why's yer concern?"

He read no hostility in her face or voice, just genuine curiosity. He continued down the steps toward her. "He's ta'en th' governess fer a walk. Ah'm concerned. She's m' responsibility."

Liberty laughed softly, led him to her car, which was parked in the round drive just ahead of the panel van Reggie had pulled up in. "M' Da set ye t' that? Or she of personal import?"

He sighed, waited for her to open her trunk. "Th' King charged me with getting her t' safety. Ah need to know she's safe with him."

She lifted the trunk lid and leaned against the bumper, one fist on her shapely hip. "Ye know that kinda ended when ye walked out the gate, right?"

He set the box in the trunk with the others, shaking his head. "No' for me."

"You know, th' best way t' do that would be to woo her and win her. Then ye can watch over her an' ye like," she suggested, studying him carefully.

He looked at her, threatened to lose himself in her flashing eyes. "Ah don' see her tha' way. Admire, aye. She's a rare woman, and vulnerable. But m' heart's nae involved. Just m' duty."

She hummed softly, nodding her head. "If she is 'that type' of woman, then he is 'that type' of man."

"What type?" he asked, confused.

She closed the trunk. "Whatever type she is. If she's the type what wants t' be taken advantage of, he'll likely take advantage. If she's a prudish lady, he'll remain th' perfect gent. She's Victorian, could go either way; but ah'd guess she's safe with him. If yer talkin' other dangers, she'll come t' no harm in his care. He has his own sense of honour, and he is a Bard with a capital B. The old kind."

He nodded, only partially reassured but accepting her assessment. There was nothing else he could do. He had to take some time and think about why it still bothered him, how he really felt about her. Without thinking about what he was saying or doing, he did the polite thing. "Is there aught else upstairs ye need manhandled?"

Liberty giggled at that, causing him to blush furiously. "Um, if ye mean heavy thin's lifted, aye." She led him back into the house, unaware that he was suddenly nervous as hell.

They had just reached the table in the foyer when Ian came charging out of the east wing with a phone to his ear. "What th' bloody fuk!" he was growling. "Hold on, don't engage yet. Yer not enough. I'll round up some help an' come through th' warehouse. Wait until we get there."

Reggie and the other boys were right behind him, checking their guns. Ian pulled up as he saw Skye. "Yeh want a little action?" he asked.

Skye felt the old familiar itch in his hands and shoulders. "What kinda fight? Ah'm not much a gunman," he warned, nodding in the direction of the weapons.

"Champion."

Liberty paled.

Skye cracked his neck. "Oot here?" he growled. It was not like the Northerner to send her champion into the real world. There had to be a reason, and it wouldn't be a good one.

"Aye, they're at a skate park just off downtown, stealin' kids."

The sword was in his hand before he had completed the thought. Ian nodded, taking that for assent.

"Liberty, luv, I need yeh t' get Gabby and th' sisters, whatever others yeh can and meet us in th' warehouse. We may need some patchin' when we're done."

She pulled out her phone and ran off down the hall towards the kitchen, yelling for Martha. Ian walked over to the wall along the side of the grand staircase, pulled out a ring of skeleton keys and fit one into the lock of a door Skye had never noticed before. When it opened, he caught the cold, musty smell of concrete floor and storage, wood crates and packing material. Skye went through the door without hesitation.

The other side was just what it smelled like, a warehouse. It was mostly empty, but there were crates here and there, a forklift, catwalks, and an office which they had apparently just walked out of. He moved a little ways in, turned, and could see through the windows to the dark office; the dim LED light of the monitor's power switch glowing off to the left. The door opened back into a bright hallway through which others were pouring, followed by Ian. He watched Ian step out of the frame, heard the keys click onto a side table before Ian entered the doorway without them.

Reggie was already heading to a delivery van parked just inside the tall doors. As he climbed in, one of the other boys opened the bay door. Everyone, Ian included, piled into the van with Reggie in the driver's seat. They pulled through as soon as the door was up enough, and the man who opened it jumped into the back. Before the door had been completely closed, Reggie peeled out.

The skate park was less than a mile away, and there was not a lot of traffic. This was an industrial/residential area and not well driven at this time of day. Skye was not entirely sure what city this was in, having not yet left the Rest, but it didn't matter. There were kids in trouble.

The skate park was in an area that did not seem to get much use. There were a few mobile homes buried in wooded lots, quietly falling apart across the dead-end street, and a lot of straggly bushes and overgrown weeds leading up to the first half-pipe. They pulled into the cracked parking lot next to Mikey, a broad boulder of a man, and his handful of toughs. They piled out of the van, moving cautiously into the concrete jungle of ramps, half-pipes and bowls, following the sound of teen boys cussing and yelping in fear or pain or both.

The boys were corralled in the bottom of a skate bowl, huddled in a small group with five goblins stalking them with nets and ropes. Three more goblins stood off to the side, blocking off any chance of running past to the other half of the elongated feature, through the half-pipe tunnel. They held their boards up, wheels out, to defend themselves, but they were hopelessly out-matched. On the rim above them were eight more, watching the fun, holding various arms and cheering them on. Standing aloof and grinning a little past them on the bridge over the half-pipe tunnel, arms folded over his chest, was Champion.

There was a flap of wings as Ian shifted to full gryphon and leapt into the air after Champion, and the rest of them began running along the upper rim of the bowl to the goblins. Mikey took half the men with him down into the bowl to rescue the kids and Reggie ran right while Skye went left. The two of them had just mowed down the first of the goblins, when Ian's screeching flight was arrested mid-air as a makar jumped out of the pipe and attacked. They rose up over the park and closer to the nearby woods in a snarling ball of feathers and fur.

Reggie and Skye charged forward, intent on pinning Champion between them, slicing through the goblins that failed to get out of the way like cord-wood. In the bowl, Mikey had got himself between the kids and the goblins, the ones guarding the tunnel now striding forward, grinning. Suddenly, Mikey bellowed. One of his men beside him gurgled and went down. Mikey turned, a knife in his back, saw that the kids were goblins themselves just before they swarmed him.

Reggie took all this in and issued orders. "Skye, get Champion. I'll be there shortly." With that, he shifted completely, becoming a large lion-man, and pounced on the nearest goblin in the bowl. He was followed by the rest of his men who fired at the goblins when it was clear, used them as clubs when it was not. The bowl swiftly devolved into a mosh pit of violence.

It did not take Skye long to reach the bridge and Champion. Most of the remaining goblins either dived into the pit out of his way or were just cut down by the now faintly glowing claymore. As he stepped onto the first foot of the concrete stretch, Champion raised a blunderbuss and fired. It caught Skye mostly in the shoulder, but he was already swelling with battle fury and shrugged it off. As he closed, Champion managed to get a rapier up and in between them, and the two began to dance in earnest.

Champion was a tall man, very dapper and something of a dandy. He was Errol Flynn and Tyrone Powers, all rolled into one heart-throb of a package. He had sparkling blue eyes, a dashing smile, and amber curls that fell to his shoulder. The smile was mocking at the moment, and faced with a rage-swollen Scotsman in a kilt, he appeared positively petite.

They traded blows in an effortless dance. The claymore would come crashing down, only to be deflected into a glancing blow. The rapier would flash in, only to be skidded aside to land no more than a nick, and then the larger sword would lunge again, hungry for his throat. It was an endless back and forth, tit for tat that soon left the bridge and began to meander around the park.

Champion was seeking higher ground, found it on a stepped platform for rail-slides and stair-jumps. Skye was impressed with Champion's skill. But then, he told himself, the Northerner would hardly have named him Champion if he wasn't capable of living up to it. He had heard the man's reputation and long desired to test it for himself. Hell, this might have been the very man he would have had to battle in the

Northerner's challenge, and he was very interested in how this would have fallen out. It was turning out to be a serious fight.

An and Jonny were somewhere just past the rath, enjoying a pleasant walk in the growing dusk. The gloaming had always been one of her favourite times of day, when the mists would begin to rise and the birds came in to roost and the world seemed in between everything. Here by the rath she could see a few things, mostly the grass on the slope and some of the flowers blooming on the edges. The trod itself was only marginally visible, but she imagined that would become clearer when it was active.

She was trying to use her ears to get a feel for what was around her. Jonny had stepped away from her for a moment, watching her, she was certain. It got warmer out of his immediate presence, but she was determined to tolerate it. She concentrated, could sense the edges of the trees and the light wind blowing through them just off to her left and in front of her. She could feel the edges of rain several hours away. There were birds near, twittering happily, and somewhere a squirrel running up a tree. Not far from that was something bigger, also climbing, but she was unable to tell what that was. As she started to turn that way, she heard a clanging from the direction of the house: three even strikes of a mid-tone bell, a pause, then repeated.

Before she could ask, Jonny's hand was at her elbow again, taking her arm and drawing her back the way they had come.

She did not resist, but asked, "What does that mean? 'Tis obviously a signal."

"'Tis a call for healers and other support personnel," he answered, setting a brisk pace but one she could keep up with easily. "Either a number of people are hurt or are going t' be. Either way, we head t' th'house. We'll find out what we need t' know there."

"Are ye a healer?" she asked. It would not have surprised her.

"Not of significance. I've other uses."

They did not take long to reach the house. Apparently he had taken a fairly circuitous route outward, but the beeline coming in. Others were trotting up the steps to the house, some of whom An could see and more than a few she could not. Liberty was in the main foyer with a ring of old keys in hand and issuing instructions.

"Bethany, take that crate o' bandages an' antiseptics to th' warehouse and start settin' up a triage station. Martha, ...oh, good, hot water! Jeremy, take that from her an' carry it through, set it up where Bethany tells ya." She turned to a woman coming in from the back of the house that An could not see, "Peggy, hand sanitisers, excellent idea. Makes sterilizin' easier. Put that in Bethany's crate then grab a handful o' th' boys t' drag out the pallets an' cots from th' crates in th' warehouse."

She paused as Jonny came in with An in tow. "Sight fer sore eyes, Jonny. We'll need a mite o' scoutin' t' tell us what t' expect, if ye'd be s'kind."

Jonny nodded, gave An's hand a light squeeze before letting go and going behind Liberty to an open door under the stairs.

An approached her friend who looked every inch the Queen of the Greenwood.

"Anythin' I kin do? I'm versed in first aid. I kin triage if needs, do th' quick things."

Liberty hesitated, then relented. "Ye kin tend t' th' ones ye kin see, there'll be a few. Lord hopes all th' prep is for aught, but one shouldn't plan fer th' least." She turned, yelled over her shoulder. "Kellain!"

The girl trotted up in short order, her hands full of something which Liberty took from her and passed to someone else going through the door. "Take Miss An through and give her th' run down o' where everythin' is. She'll be tendin' th' Touched if there's wounded among 'em. An, ye hollar fer me or Gabby should anyone need more immediate attentions. We tend t' heal th' mortals afore anyone else unless they're in danger o'dyin'."

"Understandable," An nodded, allowed Kelly to take her arm and guide her through the door she could clearly see standing in the middle of nothing.

Skye and Champion had managed to land very few blows on each other, none of them of any significance. The rake's expression had gone from cocky to serious concentration in the matter of minutes. Behind and below them, Skye could hear the goblin battle. There was the clanging of metal weapons, the thudding of hard objects against flesh, the harsh scraping of skateboards and the occasional sharp retort of gunfire. From sound alone, he could not tell how it was going.

Both he and Champion realised they were at a stalemate. Skye did not like the fact that he was biding time for someone else to come help, but facts were facts unless he just got lucky, ...and he did not expect to get lucky. In fact, he was extraordinarily unlucky.

He got in a serious strike, but Champion was a sore loser. Realising he was not going to win the fight on skill alone, and how much danger he was actually in should another blow like that fully land, Champion pulled out a flintlock pistol and shot Skye point-blank in the chest.

Skye felt like he'd been kicked by a hippogriff. He went down, his sword falling from his grasp and vanishing. Champion stood over him, drawing back his sword to finish him off. Skye blinked, trying to get breath and sense together enough to dodge. When he opened his eyes again, a split second later, Champion was no longer standing over him. There had been a blur of golden fur, but nothing clear. Skye rolled enough to look down the staircase to the lower level. Champion lay on his back with Reggie on top of him, something bright glinting out of the lion-man's back even as his claws tore into the man's face and side.

Champion pushed him off of him, stood and drew his sword from Reggie's chest. He whistled and something black flew up out of the nearby woods and snatched him up, flying off with him. Skye raised his hand, too weak to do anything but trying anyway. The hand fell, stretched down towards Reggie and went limp.

An stood off to the side, staring out the open doorway into the gathering night. A large, white raven dropped out of the sky and landed just inside the warehouse, shifting smoothly into the form of a man before his feet touched the concrete. It was Jonny. He went to Liberty immediately. "Ian's on his way with th' most egregious. Ye've a minute, maybe two. Mikey's bringing th' walking wounded in th' other van."

Liberty nodded and turned to issue orders as he shifted back to raven and flew out once more. The whole operation moved like a well-oiled machine. It was clear to An, from what she could see, that this was not the first time they had done this. She waited near the door, prepared for triage. She did not have to wait long. Ian landed with something heavy carried in his talons.

The moment he came to a stop eight feet from the ground, metal doors slid open and people were being pulled from the space below him. Ian slumped on the roof, his beak coming down with enough force to crack the windscreen. A few seconds later, he slid off on the far side with a wet thunk and the weak struggling of wings on pavement and Liberty ran over with a screech. Gabby was right behind her.

An stepped far enough to the left of the van to see around it, and Ian was in bad condition. She was amazed he had been able to carry the vehicle as he had. He was ripped to pieces. Then others were coming into view that required her attention. She did a quick assessment of each man she could see, told the stretcher bearers where to put them and what needed to be done immediately. For one or two of them she had to call Roulet and her sister to attend, as they were the only healers free at that moment. The last out of this van was the highlander, the man who had brought her safely out of faery.

She had him brought to a pallet and checked him over. He was bad off, shot in two places and cut in many more. He was not in immediate danger of dying, but needed faery healing. She did what she could, tearing open his shirt and pressing a bandage to the peppered hole in his chest.

He opened his steel-blue eyes and grinned ruefully at her. "Ah should just give up on tha' shirt. Not meant ah should keep it, ah guess." He grunted as she applied more pressure to stop the slow leak beneath her fingers.

"Liberty!! Someone... soon!" she called, beginning to think her initial assessment was less than accurate.

"Be no trouble to ya," he chuckled, ended up coughing. "Bairns 're safe as fuckin' houses."

An staggered at that, thrown further off balance by Liberty's hands taking the place of her own, peering under the bandage. "Peggy, forceps! I've got a ball t' remove! I got this one, An. Ye kin help some o' th' others."

She rose, took a half step and backed into someone. Cold hands grabbed her arms, gingerly guided her around something on the floor she could not see. She turned, saw Sorrow behind her, looking at her with concern. She nodded, telling him she was all right. He let her go, and she headed to the nearest man she could see, Mister. Younger, who needed his leg bandaged.

Sorrow knelt beside Liberty, lending a hand even as he gave his report. "Th' remainin' have fled. Champion and th' last surviving makar opened a doorway the moment the sun was down and gone back. Fox and a couple o' th' boys are dealin' with goblin and makar bodies."

"What are ye tellin' me fer?" she asked, concentrating on pulling the ball out of Skye's chest without doing more damage.

"Yer father's still out cold."

"Tell Reggie," she snapped. "He's th' heir an' I'm busy."

Jonny paused. An looked over, reading volumes into that silence. His voice was soft, full of sympathy, and understood grief. "I'm sorry, Liberty. Until yer father says otherwise, yer th' heir."

Liberty looked up at him, her face stricken. "But I'll tell Mikey as well," he added. He rose and moved off, looking for Mikey.

Liberty took another second to process, steeled herself, and went back to work. A second later and the flintlock ball hit the concrete with a wet *tink*.

An moved away, giving Liberty time to work. She made sure this time to step nowhere Cipín had not cleared. The words Skye had spoken had sent her mind reeling in a fit of memory. She had been sitting, her back to a tree, her face blazing with new pain, gelatinous tissue melting away. And there was that voice saying those words 'bairns're safe as houses'. Not just those words, but that voice. She would have to ask him, later, when he was more aware. First she had to get herself under control. She could feel the pain again, smell that thing that had attacked her, smell makar. She shuddered, took a deep breath.

She heard someone moan at her feet. She turned, slid the end of Cipín out until she came in contact with a pallet. Running it to the edge of it, she quickly figured out where she was in relationship to it. She knelt, slid her hand over from the corner of the thin mattress until she came in contact with blood matted hair. She trailed her fingers down the side of his young face and then to his shoulder where she found a bandage. The chest fluttered in pain, and she withdrew. A hand came up out of the darkness, seized her wrist and squeezed.

"Don't go… it just hurts. They'll get back to me. Just… don't… go," he wheezed.

"Shhh," she whispered, "I won't." He released her and she settled herself against the pallet, her legs curled up under her and softly stroked the side of his face with the back of her fingers and began to sing a low lullaby in Irish. It was the first song that came to mind, what she'd always sang to the young prince when he refused to sleep. "*Come over the hill, my bonny Irish lad…*"

She never noticed when the area around her grew quieter, the moaning and small grunts of pain stilled. When the hand from the next pallet over touched her knee, her other hand automatically slipped into it. She sang the song through, fished for another in her memory. She'd never had to sing more than one and she knew her voice was less than perfect. There was one song she remembered, though not where she'd learned it. It was suited to her voice, sweet and soft.

"I wish I was on yonder hill
'Tis there I'd sit and cry my fill
And every tear would turn a mill
Is go dté tú mo mhuirnín slán

*Siúil, siúil, siúil a rún
Siúil go socair agus siúil go ciúin
Siúil go doras agus éalaigh liom
Is go dté tú mo mhuirnín slán…*"

She sang the song through, and when she was done, there was silence. At first she thought she had been so horrible no one could say anything. Then she felt the tears on the first boy's face, felt the grip of the other hand ease. There was a coolness behind her and a hand on her shoulder. "'*Siúil A Rún*'. Interesting choice."

She looked up, saw Jonny bent behind her. "It… was all I could think of."

"T'was good. Ye've many talents, Ceobhránach. And a haunting voice."

She blushed, started to turn away, but he stopped her, brushing back her hair with his frost cold fingers and taking her hands. "Th' healers are here," he said softly, drawing her to her feet. "Best we get out of their way."

She allowed him to lead her away from all the activity near the stacks of crates. Before she could react or protest, his hands were on her waist, had lifted and perched her on a short stack and fluttered away again as swift as they had seized her. It took her breath away for reasons she could not allow. It placed her knees at about his waist, as he rest his elbow beside her and leaned against the crate. "There's not much better ye could have done fer them, ye know."

She fought the blush trying to bloom. "I know my skill is small. I don't know th' faery healin' a'tall…."

He set his hand on her arm, made her look at him. "That's not what I meant. Ye did them a world o' good. Their bodies are one thing. Gabby an' th' others can manage that. Ye did fer their souls. Where'd ye learn t' sing like that?"

She felt her cheeks flaring. "I was never taught. Th' songs… I learned those from m' mother, I think. There are others I think I know, what I learned from other o' th' King's servants. Songs I never heard before I hired on. Sad songs, o'course. Some of them I love, but then I'm Irish, aren't I?" she laughed.

"Like what?" he asked, settled back against the crate.

"Oh, nothin' like yer repertoire. Yer knowledge far exceeds m' own."

He frowned slightly. "I didna ask about m' own. I asked what ye'd heard. I'm curious."

She inwardly drew back in the face of his displeasure, tried to think. "Well, there's one about a boy named Danny. I like that one fair. And one about a graveyard in France. That one talks of a great war, and then more and more. I love th' sentiment an' th' melody. 'Do all those who lie here know why they died? Did you really believe them when they told you the cause? Did you really believe that this war would end wars?'," she quoted.

Jonny began to sing, his voice sweet and cool like a fresh breeze in the hot July night.

There was a tear welling in her eye, drawn forth by the pain and purity of his voice. "Aye, that one."

"'No Man's Land'. Also known as 'Th' Green Fields of France'. Always a good choice."

She smiled shyly, turning her face a little, letting her hair fall in the way. "A good war song. Like 'th' Foggy Dew'. I'll have t' read their history if I can find braille references."

"I'll look." He brushed her hair out of the way again. "Why d'ye hide yer face so, Ceobhránach?"

She cut him off, looking over at him, "And why is th' Bard wasting his time over here with me talkin' music? Surely yer needed elsewhere? I know I'm just in th' way right now. I've done what I could. But you…"

He let her divert him, glanced out over the room, seeing much that she couldn't, though his eyes paused long in the area where Ian still lay unconscious. "Stallin', really. Though any bard likes talking shop."

"What are you stalling from?" she frowned, watching the furtive flicker of his eyes.

"Tellin' th' chief his heir…," he took a deep breath. "That his heir is dead."

An's eyes swept the room, found Liberty still bent over Skye, though he was starting to sit up now. She breathed an unexpected sigh of relief. "But I thought Liberty…"

"…Is his daughter, aye. But he's only known of her fer th' last year or so. Didn't even know she existed until they stole her an' Billy Younger an' a few others from th' Giant. There was no doubt when they met, though. She remembered her mother right enough, as did he. He'd already chosen an' groomed an heir before that, ye see. Reggie was a cousin or grandnephew or sommat. Hard to delineate without a family tree in front of ye when one is hundreds of years old and on th' tree several times. He adopted him as son an' has been groomin' him t' take his place as head o' th' family fer th' last five years or so."

"Ye mean the family or the 'Family'?" she asked, making the air quotes she had seen Roulet use.

"In all senses. Though mostly th' criminal sense," he added, seeing as she already knew. "There is a great deal he's tried to protect her from that may not be possible any more."

There was a sudden wail from across the warehouse. An looked up, saw Roulet covering the lower half of her face as she stepped back from something on the floor. Someone moved towards her, but backed off immediately as lightning began to ripple off of her.

Jonny's eyes narrowed as he watched. "That's interestin'. An' I thought I knew all th' gossip."

"What? Who is it?"

He turned to look up at her. "Ye can't see? He's uncovered now."

An stretched upward a little, trying to see over things she couldn't see, but saw nothing over there except Roulet, and now Solitaire, crossing to comfort her. She shook her head. "Nay. There's nothing there fer me."

"Hmmm, also interesting. It's Reggie. She's just seen his body."

An looked confused. "I thought Roulet and Liberty... they had a Sapphic relationship."

"They're lovers, aye. Apparently that wasn't all." She felt him tense up next to her, followed his gaze, and saw Ian staggering to his human feet, shrugging off Gabby's attempt to hold him back. "Excuse me, Ceobhránach. I have m' duty t' attend. I hav' t' tell th' gryphon how he died."

"You know?" she asked softly.

He paused, drawing himself up, clearly stalling and not ashamed of it. He nodded. "It's one part of what I do. I watch. I report." He started to slowly walk across the floor. "*And then I get t' sing their dirges,*" he added in Irish, softly, as if to himself.

An remained where she was, watching as Solitaire pulled her sister away from the bodies, ignoring the lightning and the minor shocks that were starting to make her hair stand up. She watched Ian fall to the floor on his knees, tears freely flowing with no attempt to wipe them away. No one approached him for several minutes, not even Sorrow. They waited until he rose, looked over the dead and the wounded. Most of the latter were slowly getting up now. He saw the Bard standing purposefully near one of the vans, waiting, and crossed to him.

An did not hear the conversation. She didn't have to in order to know he was getting the overview of the whole battle. She watched their body language. Jonny remained in a loose stance, a good position to dodge from, though she could see the tension in him, like a coiled spring.

Ian was easier to read. There was pride, and anger, frustration, acceptance. She assumed Jonny had gotten back to the details of Reggie's death from the change in Ian's posture. He was facing half away from the bard, but his hands were curled into taloned fists and his shoulders were tight. He rolled them to try and loosen them up, glanced over to where Skye sat watching Liberty a half yard away, watching her father.

When Ian reacted, it was swift and explosive. He spun and ploughed his fist into the side of the van, caving it in and shifting it a good eight feet. Gabby put her hand to her forehead, a pose of long suffering. Liberty flinched and took a half-step forward, then changed her mind and went to Roulet instead. Skye started to his feet in an instant, sword in his hand, and ended up on his knees instead, still reeling from the pain of recent healing. He looked to be debating an approach of the chief, then decided discretion was the better part of valour at the moment and remained where he was.

An started to continue her survey, but her gaze lingered on the Scot. She was almost certain it had been he who had rescued her from the fomoire. Did this change anything? She wasn't sure, but it certainly begged questioning.

Liberty drew her attention as she led Roulet and Solitaire to the office door and opened it with the ring of skeleton keys that An could see clear as day in her hand. She guided the two of them through and turned to others, clearly telling people An could not see to gather up and go through. She could see isolated people picking things up from the floor and rolling them up, packing them into more things she could not see. From the flickering in and out of sight they were doing, she deduced that everyone ambulatory at this point were doing the same: either packing up or heading back to the house.

Jonny distracted her from her observations by taking her hand. She was a little startled that she had not noticed his return. "We'll have t' move ye in a moment," he said. "They'll need th' crates yer perched on. We'll wait until they've carried th' dead through, though."

An accepted his assistance in getting down, held Cipín close. "Ye don't have t' babysit me. Surely yer time's better spent."

"My part in all this is done. I'm as in th' way as you. Were it no' fer you, I'd likely be winging my way home."

"An' ye don't resent not doin' so?"

He shrugged. "All I'd be doin' is dwellin' on matters."

She had taken a breath to ask a question, stopped at that and let it out. His eyes studied her. "What?" he asked. She shook her head. His finger tilted her chin up to face him. "What?" he softly insisted.

She met his gaze, but blushed. "I... was going t' ask fer... details. But I can stifle m' curiosity."

He smiled. "Never stifle yer curiosity. I don' mind. Tellin' isna dwellin' and kinda what I do."

She sighed, nodding. Jonny led her out of the way as someone came past them and opened the crate that had recently been her perch. "If yer comfortable tellin' I'd like t' know. It'll distract me from... other thoughts."

He nodded, led her at an ambling pace through the warehouse, avoiding activity as they worked their way to the office door. An was certain when they were done, no one would be able to tell the warehouse had been in use.

"Well," Jonny began, using the storyteller's cadence that he had used the night she had met him, "the whole thing was a trap. A set up."

"To catch whom?"

"Ian is my guess. They had makar."

An gasped, shuddered visibly. "Explains why I smell them. I thought... I thought t'were memory."

His hand stroked her hair. "No, t'weren't imagined. They had a pack of hobs masked as teens and 'attacked' them. When our people arrived, they lured Mikey's group in to protect th' 'children' and when they had their backs, stabbed them. It was a mess. Champion was watching th' whole. Ian went for him but was attacked by a makar."

An thought a moment at the extent of Ian's wounds. She shook her head. Makar were gryphon killers, but they were flock animals. "Just one did all that? I was of th' impression it took at least three makar to kill one gryphon. I imagine it'd take five fer Ian."

"Seven," he said ruefully. "Thankfully, they only had six. They lured him into th' woods where th' other five were waiting. Meanwhile, th' Scot kept Champion busy whilst Reggie rescued Mikey an' his boys. They'd have gone back an' forth forever I think, but th' Scot got lucky. He got a good hit in. So Champion pulled a pistol an' shot him. He was about t' finish him off when Reggie jumped him. He had th' sword back, so I don' think Reggie saw it. He got Champion good, but Champion got th' last strike. Right through th' heart. One of th' makar came and grabbed him.

"Ian came out of the wood beat t' hell, but still managed t' carry th' van o' th' worst wounded. Granted, this is as far as he got. Had there been a seventh..." he left it deliberately unsaid as they stepped through the threshold into the manor.

Even though An could not see but a tenth of it, she could tell the house was bustling, and about to get worse. Jonny guided her around people into the sitting room and into her favourite chair. She sank into it gratefully, glad to be out of the way but near enough to observe. Jonny sat beside her. She was going to tell him he didn't have to sit with her, but guessed it might make him angry again. He was a Bard and entitled to sit where he liked. And she was grateful for his company.

"Tell me, what all is it ye do fer th' Rest?" she asked, seeking to make conversation to ease the uncomfortable silence. Outside the window beside her, she could hear the rain she had sensed earlier. It felt appropriate.

"Many things. I scout fer one. Th' raven form allows me to be largely inconspicuous... until folk notice I'm white. 'Tis a matter of learning where to fly and rest," he added with a chuckle. "Other than that, I heal a very little. Enough to keep someone from dyin' maybe. I tell th' stories, th' old ones and th' new. I do what I can t' teach those fresh out."

That explained his interest in her, she thought. She settled her disappointment deep inside her and paid attention to his words.

"I do what Bards do. And then... when folk die... I sing them to their rest."

"That must be the hardest part."

He nodded. "Especially fer me."

There was something more to that statement. She could feel it, feel his grief coming off of him like a wave. She reached out and set her hand on his, gave him a soft smile of comfort.

His eyes met hers for what seemed forever, reading whatever he found in their foggy depths. "Fer me it is a painful duty, beyond th' obvious. The Northerner..." he paused, glanced out the door, then back at her, leaned back in his chair, but did not relinquish her hand.

"I was due to be married, ye see. Or so I think. I'll explain that later. Lovely girl from the village. Then one eve I met this woman... beautiful beyond angelic beauty. Red lips, pale skin, blood-red hair. Should have been m' first clue, but I was fey-struck. She led me through th' wood to a meadow and a pavilion, made love t' me fer hours. I played for her, sang for her. She danced, we loved.

"In th' mornin' she took me back outside and showed me the beautiful meadow we'd walked through th' night before. It were a battlefield, a carnal field really, full o' th' dead and dyin' and more fightin' still for her favours. She told me she wanted me t' be her dirge singer. Men seized me and bore me to th' ground, held me while she kissed me, long and deep.... and with every second a lifetime of someone else's memories was pressed into me, merged with my own. Lifetimes of sorrow and loss and regret. So many I don't know which is my own anymore.

"She stole from me m' life and th' face of my true love and then had th' audacity to hand me m' harp and ask me t' sing fer her." There was a quiet venom in his silken voice, all the more frightening for its softness.

He took a moment, took a deep breath to control his anger. "I did. I played one song: 'Minstrel Boy'. That was th' last song I ever played for her. For, like that bard o' th' song, I broke my harp across my knee and never played fer her again.

"She turned me into a raven, made me serve her spy. An' when she fancied, she made me a man again to torment me." He pulled back his sleeve, showed her the back of his arm. It was covered in an artful tracery of fine white scars. The effect was as beautiful as it was horrifying. "After every cut, she would ask me t' sing again. And every time I'd tell her no, she'd cut me a little deeper."

An was silent after that. It was a tragic tale, and there was nothing she could think of to say. Her own story was a fairytale compared to it and it made her even more self-conscious in his presence. She glanced away, though he did not relinquish her hand.

"I didna mean to make ye sad, Ceobhránach."

"Oh, it's not that," she demurred, barely daring to look back at him. She rest her head on the high back of the chair, half peeking at him around the upper wing. "It's... what ye must think o' me... and my life o' privilege." She gave a laugh at that. "Though a century or so ago I'd have mocked you sore fer callin' me privileged."

"I didn't call you privileged."

"No, but... compared?"

His eyes captured hers and would not let them go. "I never compared my life t' yours, never would. Ye got lucky. Like as not ye earned that luck. Ye were Irish in Victoria's time. Ye were a governess, which tells me ye weren't one of th' few Irish with any money, property or luck. Yer life was likely alternatin' 'tween hell and heaven. Yer family made life worth livin', but that livin' was hard."

"I... there were many of us to begin. I were th' only one left... when I hired on," she said softly, her voice catching. She didn't know why she was telling him this, or how she was remembering it.

He leaned forward, his smile disarming her completely. "And teaching faery children can't have been a picnic."

She couldn't help but smile back. "Sometimes it were. Sometimes.... There was one time when th' Lion Prince changed his sister into an acorn and hid her so well even he couldna find her. O' course, then he got distracted and stopped looking. We hunted fer near two weeks fer that girl," she laughed. "An' then one mornin' there's this oak beside th' moat that'd never been there afore. We go out there t' check it out and one o' th' branches hit him. He changed her back o' course, but not without gettin' a runnin' start first."

Jonny chuckled with her.

She relaxed a little, still smiling, but sadly now. "See, this is what I mean. Even m' hardships were nae hardships compared. Ye were tortured, I..."

He squeezed the hand he still held captive. "An' ye buried everyone ever meant anythin' to ya. Ye had joy, aye. An' ye paid fer it, too. Don' sell yerself short."

He looked up at the doorway, nodded sombrely. He gave her hand a last squeeze and stood. "I have business to attend, Ceobhránach. Mayhap I'll see ye again afore I leave?"

"I'm not going anywhere," she smiled ruefully.

He bowed over her hand, kissed the back of it and walked away with someone. An unconsciously rubbed the place his lips had touched. It burned cold and sent tendrils of heat through her body at the same time.

She sat thinking, her elbow on the arm of the chair and her chin resting thoughtfully on her thumb, her forefinger curled at her lip. There was a lot on her mind, words primarily. She needed a pen, paper, and had no idea where to find them. She was not about to pull someone away from what needed to be done right now to ask for some. It was a trivial want, or so she told herself. There were people all around her grieving.

A woman was brought in, crying, held by some male relative. They hesitated when they saw her. "Are we... there's ...no where else at th' moment really," the man apologised.

She waved her hand towards the other side of the room where she knew there was other seating. "Please, don't mind me. If ye need privacy I can leave, but ye'll not disturb me."

"Thank ye. Ye don't have t' leave on our account. There, there, Mother. Set here. It's terrible, but... Mikey said he died bravely. Made an accountin' of himself."

The woman devolved into quiet sobs, unable to speak for a moment. An tried not to listen, grief at this stage was private, but it was difficult. From his sudden gasp of pain, she assumed the woman had grabbed his arm. "I've lost one son t' th' family business. I'll not lose another. I don' care what th' chief bloody says. Ye'll not follow his footsteps," she hissed.

"Mother, loosen yer grip. Criminy! I won't. Uncle has other plans fer me, anyway. They include college, law school."

She sniffed, and from his sigh of relief she'd let go. "Well, that's all right then. He owes me, after all, what I've given this family."

An was thankfully distracted by the appearance of Skye in the doorway. He hesitated, but crossed to her when she waved him over. He sat in the chair Jonny had vacated. An could feel his heat beginning to erase the comfortable chill that had been there.

"How are ye holdin'?" he asked, almost shyly.

She gave him a tender smile. "Better than ye, likely. That shirt is ruined. I don' think th' seamstress can repair it this time."

He shrugged. "The curse of a warrior. Better m' clothes than m' body."

"Though it nearly was that too," she offered.

"Aye. Tha't'were."

"I've... a question for ye," she began, though reluctantly.

"Ask."

"Were ye th' one killed th' beast who took m' eyes?"

He remained silent, watching her. She read the confession in his body easily. "Thank ye. I mean that sincerely," she said. "Why didn't ye tell me?"

He shrugged. "Why? Ah didna want it t' change anythin'."

"Change what? I've been trying t' figure ye out fer th' last month 'r more. There was sommat I were fergettin' an' it felt important. I was beginnin' t' fear there were a relationship I'd lost. Yer always there, at the edges o' things, ...watchin' me. I couldn't understand it. I still don't. Ye... is there somethin' more I don' know?"

He shrugged again. "There's nothin' more. Ah were charged wi'yer safety. Ah mean t' see to it."

She gave a quiet laugh. "Ye know I'm safe here, right? Yer job's done? Ye kin go on with yer own life. Go back an' ye like."

He shook his head at that, an action he instantly regretted as it made his head swim. He could still feel the healing creeping through his system, not done yet. The brink of death was not crawled back from lightly. "Ah can't go back. ...Ah don' think. There were..." He wasn't sure he wanted to tell her everything, still trying to avoid even the appearance of debt. But then, he thought, it might help make them even in her eyes, as it should in his own but... he sighed. He was confusing himself. "I was chosen because th' Northerner challenged th' Gryphon King to a duel of champions."

"I heard."

He stopped. "Wait, what?"

She blushed. "Th' children led me to back o' th' pavilion. They wanted t' eavesdrop. We heard it all. I know why they chose ye. For what it's worth, I'm sorry."

He growled, standing. "Confound it, woman, ye owe me nothing," he hissed, keeping his voice lower for the sake of the grieving humans in the room.

Her brow creased slightly, "Likewise."

His hand curled into a fist, was uncurled again with obvious effort. "Ah... ah'll do my duty where ah see it," he insisted.

She chuckled, causing him to turn. "Are all Scots bull-headed mules?"

"Aye." The voice from the doorway kept Skye from making the response that nearly exploded from him. He and An looked to see Ian standing there, with Jonny just behind him. "To my experience, they are. Skye, if yeh would, I need t' borrow Miss An."

She rose, confused, looking to Jonny for an explanation that did not come.

"Excuse me, Commander," she said, bobbing a brief curtsey and moving past him, Cipín firmly in her hand.

He stopped her with a hand on her arm. "Please, dinnae call me Commander n'mar. Ah don' hold th' title here."

She looked sweetly up at him. "But if ye've no' left his service, why wouldn'ya?" so saying, she untangled herself from his grasp and crossed to Ian. "At yer service, Chief." She turned her head to the Bard. "Mister...," she caught herself. "Jonny, the lady in there could use some comfort. She's just lost a son," she said softly.

He peeked in, frowned, looked back at Ian in question.

"Duncan's mother," he explained. "One o' th' mortal boys lost their lives to goblin knives." Jonny nodded and entered the room. Ian offered his arm, which An accepted, and guided her across the atrium to the hallway that led to the East Wing. They passed the formal dinning room, within which she could hear people talking and getting things together, plans being made. She could smell the carnations that marked this as the East wing for her. He took her a long way down this hall, past other doors and down a side hall to a cold room with a strange smell.

It smelled like an interior room. It was a little stuffy, cold but artificially so. Like the shops Liberty had taken her to, but smaller, more confined. She smelled leather and books and the bitter ashes of whatever it was Ian smoked. A lot of wood, which helped to mitigate the lingering smell of blood and makar. He guided her to a comfortable, padded chair and bade her sit, crossed behind what she took to be a desk and lowered himself into a larger chair. For a moment, it looked as if whatever weight rest on his shoulders had doubled, but then he took a deep breath and leaned back, looking every inch an Irish king of old.

"Are ye fair recovered, sir?" she asked. "Makar are nothin' to be trifled with."

He looked her over. "Ever seen one?"

She nodded solemnly. "Overhead and close enough t' know th' stench," she said softly.

He sniffed his shirt, wrinkled his beak-like nose. "Sorry about tha'. Ever seen a pack in a fight?"

She shook her head.

"Pray yeh never do." He sighed, set a hand on the desktop. "I called yeh back here cause I'm in a small spot. Lughnasadh is upon us in th' matter of a bare week and I've funerals t' plan, wakes t' do and my heir t' bury. Ironic. As th' holiday was originally a funeral game t' celebrate th' life of Lugh's foster-mother. Hate that I have ta..." he growled, deliberately not finishing his sentence.

"What can I do, sir?"

He sighed. "Jonny said yer sommat of a poet. Pretty good from th' one yeh recited him. I want ta ask yeh t' write an elegy fer Reggie."

Her breath caught. "But... wouldn't that be Sorrow's bailiwick? His job even? I wouldn't want t' tread on toes... I...."

Ian shook his head. "He's th' one said I should ask yeh. An' normally ye'd be right. But I need help. Liberty's managing th' one end, getting everyone dancin' t' th' same tune. Rowdy's doin' th' paperwork with Doc Calloway, he's a mortal doctor serves th' Rest and some outlyin' areas. Always good fer a hasty death certificate with suspect circumstances. Makes them all 'legitimate' an' less suspicious. Jonny's doin' Reggie's job o' arrangin' th' wakes an' th' funerals with Echo, our... grave tender. He's got his plate full. I'd do it but..." he sighed, rubbed at a mostly dry eye. "I've got th' mortal families t' deal with an' my own grief asides. I've also got t' go t' Chicago t' Reggie's mother, tell her tha' th' son who was supposed t' be safe wi' me died savin' another, and bring her back fer th' funeral.

"It's a small thing, but no small thing just th' same, yeh ken?"

She nodded. "I... I am glad t' be of service, an' just hope I do it justice."

He breathed a sigh of relief, a weight visibly off his shoulders. "Thank yeh, lass. Whatever yeh do should be fine. I trust Jonny's judgement in matters o' th' arts. He is a Bard, after all. Oh, an' he said he might ask yeh t' sing at th' wake if yer game. Get Kellain or Bet'any... no, not Bet'. Mart'a'll have her runnin' ragged helpin' her with th' food an' like. Kelly, get her t' acquire yeh some o' the traditionals yeh've no' heard, let yeh learn what yeh don' already know. 'Danny Boy' an' th' 'Green Fields o' France' were his favourites. Maybe 'th' Foggy Dew' if yeh kin manage it. Jonny can if yeh think it too high."

She blushed at the thought of officially singing at a wake. "It's a good thing I can't see most o' the audience, then, aye?" she asked, laughing nervously.

He chuckled. "Yeh'll be fine. Normally we'd ha' someone sing 'Danny Boy' at th' graveside, but this time I think '*Siúil A Rún*' terribly fitting."

The way his eyes watched her, she got the impression he had heard her in the warehouse. She blushed even more furiously. "I... I've served as keener afore, sir. I'll... no' let ye down," she said softly, unable to look up.

There was interest in his voice. "Do yeh remember whose?"

She shook her head. "Family," she choked. "We were too poor t' hire."

He nodded, left it at that. "I'll leave yeh to it then. I'll have Shannon or Liberty see about gettin' yeh a mournin' gown. An' assign Kellain t' play secretary."

An smoothed her skirts over her knees, collecting herself again. "That won't be entirely necessary, sir. I'll just need a pen, paper and ink, I think." His eyebrow disappeared into his hairline at that. She smiled, shy again. "Mister Sorrow showed me how t' glamour things, that I might be able t' use m' sight t' see them. I've not tried it with writin' but we'll see. As good a time as any t' test th' theory."

"Here," he said, pulling a sheet from a drawer and handing her a pen.

She was taken aback by the suddenness, but accepted them. She was a little self-conscious about trying this observed. It was different with Jonny: he had been teaching her. She ran her hands over the pen, trying to acquaint herself to its nature while she glamoured it. She had never held one like it before. "Ink?" she asked, feeling across the desk for the well.

"In th' pen," he said. "Just put it to th' paper as if yeh'd dipped it, an' write."

She mentally shrugged and pulled the paper to her, set the pen to the page and wrote her name. Like invisible ink put to heat, the lines flared into existence for her, the neat, slanted letters and even loops. She smiled broadly, having been half-afraid it wouldn't work. She set the pen down and rose. "Aye, it'll do fine. I just need th' paper and a pen, enough I can make mistakes and adjustments. Ask Kellain t' find me th' music and I'll listen an' learn. How much time have I?"

He leaned back in his chair with a loud creak, calculating even as he spoke. "Th' wakes will be held at th' Hedge Gate on Friday. That's th' Rest's pub, if Liberty an' th' girls havna taken yeh yet. Th' funerals will be Saturday mornin' at graveside. We'll have them all side by side at Reggie's site. After service we'll shift th' other three boys down where they're families want 'em. One o' them is t' be shipped t' Upstate New York. We'll have th' Lughnasadh games after, an' th' banquet'll double fer th' funeral feast. Ye have about four days. That enough?"

She nodded, reached out and Cipín jumped to her hand. "Will be plenty. I'll be in m' room if anyone needs me."

He nodded. "I'll send Shannon up t' take yer measure and bring yeh a bit o' supper. Dinin' table's occupied at current," he said with a rueful raise of brow.

She smiled, understanding. She was painfully familiar with the practice.

9

The Hedge Gate was huge as pubs go. Certainly larger than its counterparts in the home country, easily on par with modern nightclubs. The main tap room was capable of seating a hundred patrons comfortably. It was darkly panelled in plank wood for a rustic look, with a stage on one end and enough room for a small band and a reasonable dance floor in front of it. The lights were filtered through empty glass bottles which cast interestingly coloured patches of light on the patrons below them. The tables and chairs were sturdy oak, handmade, oiled by decades of handling and well-sanded and scrubbed over years with tender attention. The bar itself was a rich, dark wood that had been imported from Ireland. The mirror behind the bar was etched with Celtic knot-work borders.

There was a substantial kitchen behind the bar, accessible through a side door, serving both American and Irish traditional pub food. Just to the right of the bar was a room dedicated to pub games. There were three green-felted pool tables with all the equipment, and a slightly raised back section designated for dart tournaments. At the moment, the pool tables were draped with black cloth with the four bodies laid out in state for the benefit of the mourners. Reggie was on a separate table that had been set up in the dart area.

At the other end of the game room was a roomy snug, set up as a private meeting room or for the benefit of the immediate family who 'needed a moment' on occasions such as this. Everything about this pub screamed that it was exclusively for the use of members of the Rest. There were also subtle clues that it was the official wake site, used for all celebratory purposes that were not the major rites of the year. It was the hangout of choice for those who did not wish to attend the rather pagan rituals.

A true public house, kids were welcome and there were benefits to the bartender knowing everyone. He knew the ages of all the kids and when they were allowed to get their own alcohol. Those from the old country felt instantly at home. The American-born family found it a taste of the old country. There was something here for everyone.

Jonny was already there setting up when Liberty brought An by.

The pub was blissfully cool, colder than normal due to the presence of 'those in state', for which An was grateful. Shannon had access to a closet that contained clothing worn by the men and women of the house going back a hundred years and more, in varying conditions, but most were well preserved. She had found An a Victorian era mourning gown complete with black crepe veil. It was made of silk and deceptively light, though if she had to spend too much time out of doors, the heat might become overwhelming. It had needed to be taken in a little in places, and re-hemmed, but was still a good fit. An was very pleased. At the moment, she wore the veil hanging down her back.

While Liberty headed into the kitchen to check on wake preparations, An took the time to acquaint herself with the layout of the room, as she was able to see none of it. It was fairly straight-forward, though the tables were annoyingly staggered. There was a clear path along the bar side and there was still some dance floor available, though someone had set out extra chairs, taking up about half of the floor. Jonny was on the stage setting up something she could not see but assumed were images of the deceased.

126

His clothes were sombre: high-waisted black trousers, tall polished boots, a fine linen poet's shirt without the ruffle, and a black patchwork vest. It did not surprise An that she could see them. His hair, however, was pulled back in a poorly done braid.

She stepped to the edge of the stage, hesitant to call attention to it. "Um,..." she began, trying to find the polite words.

He looked up, flashed her a sad smile. "Evenin', Ceobhránach. Yer looking fine. Wouldn' think widow's weeds so easy t' find these days." He gestured for her to turn around and, blushing, she obliged. "Bustled even," he commented.

Her hands unconsciously went to her back, smoothed her gloved fingers down over the modest bustling. "I... I've always liked the silhouette," she said shyly. "I... just could never afford one. Granted, it's not for every day. I don' see how a woman could wear this for years but... it'll suit for the occasion."

"And appropriate for keener. Are ye ready? Did I presume too much askin' ye?" he frowned slightly, seeing the expression on her face.

She smiled, embarrassed. "It's not that, it's..." She half raised her hand to point. "Yer hair..." His hand went to the snow-white braid, lifted it to look at it. "It... it won't do. Unless ...yer after dishevelled?"

He gave a soft laugh, a little embarrassed himself. "I do m' best. But... 'tis hard to braid back on one's own."

She put her hand down, flushing into her collar. "I apologise. I'm out of place," she sighed, started to turn.

"Are ye volunteerin'?"

She stopped, looked at him over her shoulder. He was crouched on the edge of the stage. His face said he was sincere. "If... if ye want," she said softly. "I wouldn't mind. Ye should present a uniform front, at least. All disarray or none."

He hopped off the stage and pulled over a chair, straddling it, pulling out the elastic at the end and shaking out the badly done plait, resting his arms on the back of the chair.

"I... I'll need a brush," she said, trying very hard to maintain her composure. She could not understand what it was about this man that made her self-control just fly out the window. She turned and felt her way to the bar, calling for Liberty. A young woman she could barely see came out of the kitchen with arms full of something which rang like glass when she set it down on the bar.

"What can I get you, miss?" she asked.

An was taken a little aback at being able to see the woman at all. It didn't help that she looked like a ghost. "I... I need a brush," she managed. She gestured back behind her to where Jonny sat watching her with an amused expression.

"Oh. Sure!" she exclaimed and rummaged around behind the counter, popping back up and handing her both a brush and a comb. "Just leave them on the bar when you're done," she smiled broadly. "By the way, *love* that dress. It really flatters you."

An blushed, thanked her and returned to where Sorrow waited. She tucked the comb in her pocket and pulled off her gloves. She finished undoing the braid, began running her hands through the cold silk. "How would ye like it? Braided as ye had it? Or something more intricate?"

He shrugged. "I need it back from m' face. Do what ye like otherwise."

"Very well," she said, forcing herself to have confidence. "If ye want me to do th' straight braid after all is done, I will. Then ye don't have t' worry about it fer a bit at least."

"That'd be fine." She couldn't see his face, so she couldn't read anything into the statement, but she was sure she had missed something.

She took her time brushing it out. It flowed like water over her hands. Not even the princess's hair had been this fine. Finally, she switched to the comb and pulled back the front and sides, plaiting them into three fine, elven braids that bound the front of his hair back. She braided both sides all the way down to the end, then wrapped them around the flowing remains of his hair, weaving them into a basket pattern where they crossed. Only then did she secure the ends of the braids together, hidden away under the rest of his hair.

She set her hand on his shoulder to tell him she was done and stepped away. She pulled the strands of his hair out of the brush as she crossed to the bar and was startled to have them melt away in her hand like so much snow.

As she tucked the comb into the brush and found the bar to set it on, Jonny passed her to take a gander in the mirror at what she had done.

He seemed pleased. He turned, pressed a kiss to the back of her hand as he set her dropped gloves into it and returned to the stage, setting up his instruments. An was left feeling more than a little flush. She paused to glance at her own reflection, was further embarrassed to see her cheeks in high colour and turned away. She was thankfully distracted from everything as the front door opened and mourners began to drift in.

The wake began as all wakes do, quiet and mournful. People came in, went to the room where the dead lay in state, and paid their respects: to the dead, to the mothers and the widow and family. Ian spent most of this time brooding in a large chair in the corner by the dartboard. He accepted what came his way with a quiet dignity. He paid his own respects to the family, assuring the survivors they would be taken care of.

Eventually, folks migrated to the bar, began with drinks, devolved into knots of quiet conversation. Soon enough they would come to the portraits at the stage and drink a shot with the dead, leaving one or pouring it out on the wreaths that Liberty assured An was there. Some left small trinkets with the bodies in the other room, tokens of remembrance; some were just not as comfortable with that.

Echo hovered in the 'state' room, never leaving the company of the dead, watching over them like they were sleeping infants. Jonny had begun to play simple music on his harp after An had finished his hair. He sat on a stool with a beautifully carved Irish harp on his lap and made the strings weep.

After about an hour, Ian left the back and entered the bar proper, and all the quiet talking ceased. He strode to the stage with several shots in his hand, passed one to Jonny and placed one in An's hand. She started to protest that she did not drink, then stopped. This was Rite, and she realised it, settled back into her seat near the stage and kept her mouth shut.

Ian cleared his throat and waited as other shots were handed out and passed around. When he thought everyone was ready, he spoke up. "Michael Murphy, Duncan Padraig O'Keefe, Patrick Mc'Kellum, Reginald Collin O'Keefe. Yeh lived fer yer families. Yeh died fer strangers. T'was a foul ambush an' an act o' war we'll not be ignorin'. Rest yeh well, gentlemen. Yer sorrows an' pain are done and the clan will attend what yeh left behind. *Until we meet again in the Summerlands, eat, drink and love with*

God. Sláinte!" with that he tossed back his shot, and everyone in the house followed suit.

An hesitated but a second, then tossed it back, and nearly choked on the burn. Ian turned to her, and someone put a hand on her back for support.

"Not used t' whiskey?" Ian asked, mildly surprised.

She shook her head until she could breathe enough to speak. "No, sir. I were too young an' whiskey too dear. I wisely avoided fey brews."

He chuckled. "Yeh'll get used to it. Sip th' next one 'til yeh do."

An silently decided she'd pass, but nodded. She found her way to the bar for water, sipped it. It was not long before someone touched her shoulder and said in a low voice. "Jonny needs ye at the stage. Said it's time."

She thanked the man and downed the rest of her water quickly, much the way folk near her were downing their pints. She followed the precise path she had scouted earlier from the bar to the stage, only having to dodge people who soon started to get out of her way on their own. She mounted the few shallow steps and carefully crossed to where she could see Jonny waiting, Cipín assuring her the way was clear.

Jonny stepped to her, stopping her where she was needed, turned her gently to face the audience and adjusted something in front of her. She could feel a strange thing before her face, a few inches away, but she ignored it until she cleared her throat nervously and the echo of her voice reverberated all the way to the back room. She jumped, stepping back, finding a chair or another stool with her heel. Jonny was suddenly right there, a comforting hand on her arm and a cool whisper in her ear.

"Calm, Ceobhránach. 'Tis a microphone: a bit o' technology t' make ye heard. Just ignore it."

She swallowed, nodding, trying to ignore the quiet laughter that trickled through the room at her reaction. She felt heat on her cheeks and took a deep breath, determined. She stepped back to the microphone, feeling its presence just below her chin, and began. Her voice was clear, carried well even without the mike in the now silent pub. She kept her eyes on one man, standing in the back of the room, one she could see. Why she chose Skye she could not have said, but he calmed her in her recitation. He was someone she knew, who would understand.

Lady of the Mist

"The warrior's blade lies idle
Upon his plate, no meat
His horn hangs limp upon his chair
The hunt no more he'll greet

The hedge grows cold and empty stands
He'll hunt not Gentry's prey
No more lost souls he'll rescue
From life as Northern slave

No more, my friend, no more
In hall your voice shall ring
Your presence upon our hearts now tread
No more, lost soul, no more

Good soldier lost in glory
To the enemy hell was paid
Raise we our glass to the soul who's last
And final tattoo has played

No more lass's charms to drink to
No more pints deep in foam
No more the lads to brawl so brash
Our lion has been called home

So march ye on to fiddler's green
Where the weather's fine and the ladies fair
The pipers play only jigs and reels
No more the martial air

Bear no mind to us left behind
We'll find somehow our way
Your battle is done, your burden gone
No more, our lion, no more"

The room remained silent, but An could hear something. It wasn't until she noticed the raised arms of everyone she could see that she realised every soul in the bar had raised their glass to her. She had spent the last four days asking about Reggie, trying to understand him; worried if what she had written would do him justice. She had worried in vain. She flushed, bobbed a curtsey and started to move away, but Jonny's soft voice called her back. "Ye can't leave," he whispered, began plucking the strings of his harp. "Yer th' keener, remember?" There was a ghost of a smile on his face. "There's a chair behind ye, an' ye need. Do ye ken this one?" he asked, playing a soft air.

She nodded.

"Which version did Kelly get ye?"

"Sinéad."

"Good. Can ye manage?"

Again, she nodded, suddenly more nervous than she had been reciting her own work. She stepped back to the mike. This time she closed her eyes to block everyone out, concentrated on the soft sounds of Jonny's fingers on the strings. She took a breath and began to sing: high, sweet, and mournful. She let the song pour through her, feeling the words. She did not have the technical perfection of the Bard, but she had a purity of soul and the ability to express it. Her voice was suited to soft and mournful, to lullabies. By the time she was done, she was not the only one singing, and that was good. It gave her confidence when he launched immediately into the next song, a duet. Thankfully, it was one she knew well.

She opened her eyes, sang the back and forth with him, letting her sweet softness temper his own clear tenor. This song allowed her to drop down into a more comfortable mid-range that she preferred, complimenting him. His voice made her heart stop, bleed with the pain in it, and the cool purity of the notes. They paired well.

She let him sing on his own for a few more, let him make the choices. He knew his audience better. The ghostly girl came up during the third song and set up a small table between them, placed a bottle and a cup of tea on it and flitted away again.

An's hand slowly reached out, came in contact with the bottle first, which she picked up and sniffed. It was a nut brown ale which she turned her nose away from, setting it down. Jonny chuckled, guided her hand to the cup of tea by tapping the saucer lightly with the tip of his bow. She smiled and gave him a tiny nod, picked up the cup and sipped gratefully. The hot fluid felt good on her throat, helped her to loosen up.

Then Jonny was tuning up his fiddle and began playing a far more rousing tune to which An remembered words and sang along. So did about half the audience who by this point were fairly loud and well on the way to drunk. Ian stood near the front with Liberty, with a bottle of something in his hand which he spent a good deal of time drinking from.

There were tears and toasts and drinking. There was food and good cheer and stories that even the bereaved mothers laughed at. Skye felt almost out of place in the midst of all of it. He had worn a solid black kilt, with a black kilt shirt and green garters. He looked smart enough, but even with a half-drunk pint in hand he felt like an intruder.

When most had left the stateroom, he found his way in there, partly to escape the bar, partly because he hadn't been in yet. He paused at the second table, recognising one of the boys who had joined the makeshift practice not that long ago, the one that had earned him a place here and the right to train them. It was the young man who'd been stabbed in the back by the 'children' he had thought he was protecting. Skye set his hand on the cold wrist and squeezed, even knowing it was for his own comfort.

There were small things left around the bodies, notes tucked into the breast pockets. Someone had even slipped a five-dollar bill into Michael's pocket. There were shot glasses lined up next to them, being carefully re-arranged by Echo. Skye stepped back, startled by the man.

Echo was a tall, gaunt individual, bat-like in feature, and seemed to only be half there. He looked up and saw Skye and stepped back to the wall, crossing his long, spindly arms over his chest at the wrist, becoming, not invisible, but unnoticeable.

Skye waved a hand in his direction to tell him it was all right and headed to the dart area, where Reggie lay. He approached the body, lost in his pain and guilt. He had not been able to face Ian since Monday. Facing Reggie... was only marginally easier.

He stared for a long moment in silence, looking at the leonine face in quiet repose. Echo had cleverly hidden everything, even the one slice which had gone up the side of his neck to his ear. There was a rosary carefully tucked in his folded hands, artfully draped. Skye remembered seeing that rosary in his hand just before they had got to the park. It had been in his pocket when he died.

"Damn it, man," he swore softly. "Ah was just gettin' t' know ya. Ye were th' first man here aside yer uncle t' gi'me th' time o' day. Though we spoke so little, we communicated more in a glance than most wi' a mouthful. We worked well in tandem an' got th' job doon." He sighed. "Mebbe we shoulda stayed t'gether. Ah wasna good enough on ma oon. Ah was too ba'heidit thinkin' ah could take th' bawbag masel'. Ye had t'rescue ma arse. They were right t' send me awa' fra Faery. Ah'da lost tha' fight too, and then where'd th' King be? Ah owe that wee bit mor'n ah wanted t'admit," he added, thinking of An. "Ah owe ye ma life though t'were my fa'lt ye lost it. If only ah'd..."

His rant was interrupted by the sudden presence of a woman beside him. She barely came up to his chest, with flashing grey eyes that were red with weeping. He stopped, stared at her for a second, trying to register her. He opened his mouth to say something when her hand snaked out and slapped the tar out of him. His cheek was suddenly on fire. He looked down at her in shock.

Her voice was deep and hoarse from hours of crying as she snarled at him. "Don't ye dare cheapen my Reggie's death with yer damned self doubt! How dare you make my son's sacrifice about yer failure!" she accused.

Skye took a step back as she squared off against him.

"I don't give a shite about yer feckin' survivor's guilt," she shouted, poked him in the diaphragm. "Did ye fight to yer last?"

This question threw him off, "Aye," he gasped. Her fingers were hard and accurate.

"Did ye hav' 'im?"

He was more taken aback by this question than the assault itself. "Aye?" He took another step back, off the dart platform.

There was venom in her voice as she snapped, "Did the bastard cheat?"

Skye found an inch of backbone. "Aye," he responded, more stiffly than before.

"Then where is th' failing in that?" With that challenge, her face softened. "Could anyone else have done it? Taken him?" her eyes begged him for the right answer, without knowing herself what that answer was.

"Aye, Nae,.. ah don' know, ma'am. Honest. Mikey mebbe... Reggie...."

She shook her head, stepped up to him and took his face in her hands. "My Reggie, he had a hate on for that man. Him and th' Rook both." Skye stiffened just a little. He knew the Northerner's Chosen well. "But he admitted t'me onct that he couldna take him alone. It says t'me what he thought o' yer skill that he let ye face him alone. Even fer a moment."

They stood there a long minute before she let him go. He stared at his shoes a bit before meeting her stormy eyes with his steely blues. The words suddenly came easier. "Thank ye, Ma'am. Fer yer son's life. Ah loiked him fine. Though ah wisht he'd nae had t' trade his life fer mine."

She nodded solemnly, taking a step back. "Make sure ye make it worth it."

Skye understood himself dismissed and walked quickly from the room, aware of Echo's large, bat-like eyes watching him go. He stepped out the door to find himself chest to chest with Ian.

The chieftain took in the handprint on his face, his rattled look, and glanced beyond him to the woman calmly adjusting something on her son.

Skye, unable to avoid the confrontation now, unable to bear the scrutiny, felt the overwhelming need to say something to the man whose heir had given his life for him. He opened his mouth, but nothing came out. He was at a loss. "Chief, ah..." was all he managed.

Ian's large, slightly taloned hand came to rest heavily on his shoulder. "It's all right, son. I understand." Those golden brown, eagle's eyes held his intently. "Yeh do know that had someone not occupied that man, he'd a' picked yeh all off one by one?"

Skye actually hadn't known that. The thought had not crossed his mind. He breathed a sigh of relief.

Ian glanced once more at the calm way Reggie's mother was going about her business, gave Skye a look of shared suffering. "It's all right. Mrs McNeil can do that to yeh," he chuckled. He put a companionable arm around Skye's shoulders and drew him back into the bar. "She

135

slapped the devil out o' me when I told her. Then cried her heart out in m' arms. Hell, I didn' even hav' t' tell 'er. She opened th' door, saw th' look on m'face and slapped me on principal."

Skye chuckled, rubbing his jaw. "She packs a punch."

"Aye, that she do." He lifted his arm to wave at the girl behind the bar. "Tori! Get this lad a pint!"

10

Early the next morning, the priest came knocking on the pub door. Solemnly they filed out, stepped into the processional formation. All but the immediate families and the pallbearers had gone home hours before, leaving the parking lot, such as it were, empty. It looked eerie in the cool, foggy dawn. It was peaceful; fitting.

Skye shouldered his burden gladly, stood behind Henry at the back of Reggie's casket. Ian had asked him not an hour ago, when he had gathered the men together for a ritual shot of whiskey and a final toast to their dead. Reggie's mother had asked for him. Insisted, he'd said. He was honoured.

Two altar boys in black cossacks and white surplice walked in front of the priest, swinging the censers on their chains. The priest carried his staff solemnly forward, leading the flock onward. As head of the family, Ian walked immediately behind the priest. Jonny and An flanked him, walking three paces back. Jonny in his black patchwork with a black ribbon now woven into the criss-crossing braids and a bodhrán drum in his hand. An marched solemnly beside him without her shillelagh, her veil falling to her breast, covering her carefully dishevelled hair, giving forth a high, keening wail that carried eerily through the fog. She kept her eyes on Ian's back, trusting her sight to lead her. Then came the boys, carried high on black-clad shoulders, Reggie, Michael, Duncan and Patrick, followed by the immediate family. Echo trailed along at the rear, reluctant to let the dead out of his sight.

They wended their way down the lane, the long way, through the main street of the Rest toward the Parish Church. It was a haunting procession. The drum was heard beating out the time, and the keener's voice carried like a siren through the mist, all heard before the priest could be seen. The curtains and doors of every house were closed, but as the procession passed, people dressed in black filed out of the houses and joined the line. The people who came out of the houses were more than those who lived there, as folk who lived off the parade route had come to wait in the homes of those who did. In this manner they came to the small parish church nestled amid ivy and myrtle trees.

At the church steps, An fell to her knees beside the door, out of the way, her face buried in her hands, weeping. Jonny took up station on the far side, standing like a statue, still slowly striking the drum in his hand. It was not difficult for An to actually come to tears beneath her veil. One funeral or another, it was all the same one. She had walked this road before, before brothers, a sister or two, both her parents. For some reason she felt those losses keenly this morning, perhaps because everything was as surreal yet painfully solid as it had been on those mornings. Perhaps it was because she could not remember a single face or name.

When the last of the procession had entered the church, Jonny silenced the drum and bent to help her to her feet. She looked up at him, a little lost at first, allowed him to pull her up. Drawing a black-edged kerchief from her pocket, she dabbed at her eyes, discretely blowing her nose before throwing back the veil and tucking the kerchief away. She walked into the atrium of the church with him.

An listened, found the door to the sanctuary by the sound of people settling themselves in. Her hand found the small font at the jamb by instinct, dipped her fingers and crossed herself. She slid her hand around the edge of the door-frame, feeling her way along the back wall for the chairs that were always set there for deacons or ushers. She perched on the edge of one, listening to the mass.

As a child, she had found comfort in these places. Had loved the coloured glass and the music, the rites. The Rest's priest had a good voice, comforting and warm, the kind of voice that would be easy to confess to, but his words seemed to have no effect on her. This disturbed her. The little rituals that always gave her a sense of peace and comfort left her strangely cold.

She distracted herself by trying to analyse why this might be. It wasn't that she was now one of the Touched. She could see many of them in the congregation as engaged in the service as she had once been. She thought perhaps it was the act of having lived in close proximity to older gods and by their laws and dictates for so very long that had her just 'going through the motions' and left favourite parts of the mass feeling hollow to her. Unable to take it, she rose and felt her way out of the sanctuary with only the soft hiss of crepe against the floor heralding her exit.

The atrium was empty, but the front door was open. She could see the edge of Jonny's arm just outside and reached for the doorway. Stepping out, she saw him sitting against the wall with his drum at his feet, smoking something that he did not hold like a pipe, nor did it smell like one. She felt for the step and gingerly sat on the top one, arranging her skirts around her. She turned her face to the morning, could still feel the mist in the air, even though the sun should have burned it off by now. "Is the fog still as thick as it feels?" she asked softly.

"Aye. Prob'ly burned off in th' rest o' th' village already. But there's a river near, 'tween here and the cemetery. Fog always lingers here. ...It seems to like ye," he said. She looked over her shoulder at him. He was observing her casually. "It clings to ye, seeks ye out. On the march here, it was almost like ye were th' source."

She blushed, looked back out into the darkness. "My favourite time of day, when the fog rises. I used t' go down t' the stream to watch in th' gloaming. It always seemed to trail after me on the way in. One o' th' reasons they called me *bean an ceobhrán*."

They sat in companionable silence for a little while before Jonny spoke again. "Why'd ye leave the mass?"

Her shoulders twitched. "It... didn't feel right. It ...hurt."

She heard him move, glanced back to see him leaning forward over his knees. "Physically?" he frowned.

She shook her head, and he seemed relieved. "It... just... I don't know. I've lost the... taste, I guess. The old ways..."

"Are more appealin', aye."

"It's not that... I... I just don't feel it anymore. Mayhap livin' with the nuns fer nigh two years had sommat t' do with it. I don' remember my faith bein' a chore afore then. What? Ye thought I might feel physical pain goin' in?"

He leaned back against the wall, taking another drag of smoke. "It has happened."

An watched the smoke curl in the air above him, making interesting patterns. "What are ye smokin'?" she finally asked. "It's not a pipe. Yer holdin' it wrong and it smells different."

"It's a cigarette. It's tobacco wrapped in paper. They're cheaper, more convenient than pipes."

"Why doesn't it smell bitter, like the ones Ian smokes?"

"I roll my own. Add things from time to time. Ian buys his, uses filters. I don't. It's a preference thing. So, one more little hint as t' yer age," he said with a twinkle in his brown eyes.

"Not necessarily. It might have been a city vice at th' time. Th' village was rather poor. We were all beholdin' t' Lord..." she frowned, sighed. "Still can' remember names."

"It's all right." He cocked his head over his shoulder, listening to something inside the church. He took a last, long drag from his cigarette and rolled the remains between his fingers, tucked something in his pocket and gracefully rocked to his feet. "'Tis time." He held his hand out to her and as she set her hand in his. This time it was he who commented on how cold it was. "No time fer nerves, lass. Yer fine. Now, this time you lead th' way."

"Wait, what?" she cried. "But the priest..."

"Leads ye *to* church, not from it. At least here. I'll be right b'hind ye."

"Surely th' chief should lead...?"

"He's takin' his turn as pallbearer. As chief, it is his right and

140

expected of him. It shows he bears a share o' the burden and th' grief. It's his promise t' th' family. A'carse, this time he *is* family, but that's neither here nor there." He turned as someone came out of the church door, bent to accept something from someone small.

"But how will I see the way? I've never been..."

He gave a soft laugh. "Don't fret. Timothy here and I have that covered." He breathed on something in the boy's hands and she watched as frost grew across the surface of a glass lantern. He struck a match and lifted the glass, lit the candle stub within and closed it. The effect to her was a soft glow. "Mister Smalls here will lead the way with his lamp. 'Cause o' the fog an' all," the look he gave her said this was just an excuse. "Just follow th' light."

He crossed to her, began lowering her veil into place. "Is it always this way?" she asked.

"No," he said, adjusting the lace edge of the crepe. "We haven't had a beansidhe fer nearly as long as I've been here. My first funeral we had one. The effect is... memorable." He held her eyes with his through the veil, seemed to be trying to read things in their foggy depths.

"What happened to her?" she asked in a hoarse whisper, unable to look away.

"She got bronchitis and lost her voice. We haven't had anyone with the pipes in a long time."

He let her go, turning to take the drum Timothy handed up to him. She grabbed his arm gently. "How did you know I'd make a good keener?"

He smiled sadly at her. "Yer voice."

The graveside service was touching. Skye stood at military attention behind the immediate family with the rest of the pallbearers. It was all he could do to maintain his comportment when An began to sing '*Siúil A Rún*' in her soft, haunting voice.

The service done, most people wandered away from the gravesite. Some remained to help as the pallbearers picked up the three who did not belong at this grave and carried them to their final resting places. This had Echo in a small fit, unable to see to all of them at once. Skye stayed to help lower Reggie into his grave, rolling up his sleeves to help fill it in.

Once the dirty work was done, everyone left migrated towards the big house. Once they left the cemetery and the full weight of the morning sun began to bear down on her, An began to flag in the heat. Jonny took her arm and did not let go of her until they were in the main house and on her hall. She assured him she would be all right and went to change into the darkest, coolest clothes she had.

She carefully hung her widow's weeds up in the back of the wardrobe, folding the veil and putting it away in its drawer. Shannon had been very clear that she was to keep it so long as she wanted it, and at least as long as she served keener here.

When she finally brushed out her hair, pulled it back and came downstairs, she found Jonny hovering in the atrium by the flowers again. She could see all the lilies and roses on the side of the table he was standing on. He looked up at her approach.

"Ye look a mite cooler. Ye goin' t' survive th' heat? August in Florida can be mighty unforgivin'," he warned.

She gave him a shy smile. "I'm as cool as modesty will allow. I'll survive. Cooling drinks, et cetera. Stay in th' shade." She accepted his hand as she left the last step. "Will ye be participatin' in any o' th' games?"

He set her hand on his arm and led her out the back to where all of the festivities had been set up. "I might. I hear they're doin' an insult contest this year. An' I'm t' judge a bardic event."

"I may have t' watch that."

"I'd hope ye'd participate."

An blushed. "I was meanin' th' physicals."

He shook his head. "I know my skills. I've no need t' show off or know that I'm better than any o' them. They're skills I don' like t' use."

She nodded. They stepped off the veranda and he hailed a small young woman over that An had not yet met.

There was the hint of raven feathers about her hair, and something bird-like in the bright roundness of her black eyes. She was almost painfully thin, with long fingers and a narrow face. There was a ring on her finger that immediately drew An's eye, though she couldn't say why.

Even her voice was bright and ravenish without a trace of Irish. "Whatcha need, Jonny?"

"An, this is Raven. Raven, An Ceobhrán."

The girl, who couldn't have been sixteen though her eyes said she was so much older, smiled and held out her hand. "The Keener," she said brightly. "Pleased t' meetcha." She giggled. "Yer voice had me in tears, darlin'."

"Thank you?" An replied politely, unsure if it was truly something to be thankful for.

"Raven, I be needing a favour."

She turned back to Jonny. "Sure, what is it?"

"I have to go and set up for th' bardic contests, but An needs to be taken around and shown where everythin' is. She can see anythin' touched by magic but naught else, so she's liable to overlook th' mundane. Would you please help her map th' area out? That way she can wander on her own later..."

"And still have a clue where she is and what to avoid? Got it."

"It shouldn't take long," An injected. "I just need th' general idea."

Raven waved the protest off. "Not like I got anything better to do. ...Well, I do. But I don't like dealing with food other people are goin' t' eat, so I'm tryin' not t' get pressed inta table duty. I'll help clean it all up later. I just hate settin' up. Asides, Martha gets so particular about what goes where."

An smiled at her. "If yer sure."

Jonny took her hand, his other rest lightly on her upper arm as his eyes pleaded his pardon. "Fergive me for abandoning ye?"

She bobbed him a curtsey. "I have taken up more than my share of your time as i'tis. Thank ye. I hope I did well?"

"Better than hoped." He pressed a cold kiss to the back of her hand. "'Til later."

It wasn't until he had walked away that An realised he had done something to her sleeve. She had braced herself for the heat, only to find it bearable. She looked down where his hand had been to see that he had frosted her sleeve. She smiled shyly, turned back to Raven. "When yer ready then?"

"Absolutely."

The games were vigorous, to say the least. An drifted through the different areas and activities with various escorts, sometimes alone. There were hammer tosses, wrestling, sword fighting, boxing, archery and even marksmanship. In the afternoon there was to be a footrace that circled the manor and the surrounding woods, as well as a few shorter races and a horse race to follow. There were prizes for the Touched and the mortals separately in most of the events, especially where the Touched had an advantage. An could only see about a quarter of the events, though she did enjoy seeing one particular Touched getting badly beaten in wrestling by a mortal. She laughed as she hadn't in years, watching what amounted to her to seeing him rolling around in the dirt, twisting himself into strange and painful positions.

Roulet was taking part in what seemed like everything, pushing herself past all sense. An stopped to watch her in a bout with Mikey. She was using a metal staff and Mikey his great sword. Standing on the sidelines with her sister and Liberty, An noticed there was a conspiracy going against Roulet. Liberty was doing something subtle to Solitaire, who was looking a little weak and annoyed, but carefully watching her twin.

An watched the fight.

Roulet was relentless, using the metal of her staff to deliver frequent jolts to Mikey in spite of his parrying attempts. There was something in Roulet's eyes she did not like. She stepped up to Liberty and, without taking her eyes from Roulet, asked in a whisper, "What, pray tell, is goin' on?"

"My sister is going to get herself hurt or killed trying to beat her grief," Solitaire growled.

"She won't stop," Liberty added. "She ran th' marathon, th' sprints, has been in three fights, two wrestling matches and one round with th' hammers. All without stopping. She's goin' t' run herself inta an early grave she keeps that up. We're goin' t' stop her. ...Just as soon as Mikey gets a hold on her," she added, keeping her eyes on the fight.

Seconds later, Mikey deliberately took a shocking hit on the back, slid in under the staff to disarm her. Dropping his own sword, he wrapped her in a bear hug and just held on, letting her expend herself in electrical surges. At that point, Liberty placed her hand on Solitaire's shoulder where it met her neck and poured something into her. Solitaire slumped, caught neatly by someone standing behind her, and Roulet went limp in Mikey's arms.

Liberty stepped up, began issuing orders. "Mikey, carry her inta th' house. Put her in m' old room. Malcolm, would ya be so kind as ta folla him wi' Solitaire?"

Henry came strutting up at this point, his crown of Holly still gracing his antlers, but the flowers were now well on to becoming small, hard, green berries. "What's all dis? Interfering with de sacredness of de games, woman? Ye know better."

She waved him off. "Back off, bucko. This be a matter o' savin' her from herself. It were th' on'y way we were gettin' her t' stop. It weren't an official match, though she didn' know that. Mikey agreed to it."

He was a little taken aback by being so addressed, but as she squared off against him and the floral crown began to become more apparent, he put up his hands and took a step back. "All right. So long as it weren't official." She turned to follow Mikey and Malcolm. He called after her. "Just be back before five. Ye have t' hand out prizes, my queen," he said the last with a mocking bow.

She rewarded his cheek by snatching an apple out of a bystander's hand and pegged him right between the antlers.

An did not laugh out loud like everyone else, but hid her smile in her hand and turned politely away. She followed Liberty's retreating figure back to the house, using her to stay clear of obstacles and the worst of the crowd. Once at the house, she proceeded on to the solar and reached into a canvas bag tucked behind her favourite chair, containing her ball of thread, hook and the band of lace she had started. She headed back to the veranda and cast her gaze across the broad lawn and the myriad of activities. She located the bardic affairs and headed off into the quieter part of the lawn, privately hoping she'd find an unoccupied seat.

She didn't, but someone gave theirs up for her. She couldn't see the gentleman, but thanked him, even as she told him it wasn't necessary. She fingered the length of her thread for a bit as she listened to the end of the insult contest and looked around at the people she could see. Skye was there, across the way, nodded to her when they met eyes. There were several of the Touched among them, all having a good time. The last contestants were a centaur and a middle-aged, mortal woman with a scathing tongue.

Her last volley was biting, sending the audience into a mix of shocked silence and embarrassed laughter. The centaur coloured visibly, tried to bite back and couldn't. Finally, he tucked one front hoof and gave her an equine bow. "Well fought, Molly Suggins."

An set her glamoured thread and hook down in her lap to applaud the sharp-tongued woman, then picked up her thread and began to crochet, happy she could work again without fearing she had miscounted or made other glaring errors. She settled back with her lace to watch the bardic half of the competition.

She could hear people setting up, and tuning instruments, warming up voices. She was counting stitches when she felt the temperature around her drop. She looked up to see Jonny looking down at her with a wry smile. The way his hair framed his face and the sunlight behind him haloed him for a brief moment, he looked positively elven accept for the earth-brown eyes.

"Aye?" she asked shyly.

"And what will ye be doin' fer th' contest, Ceobhránach?"

She shook her head, running out a yard or so of extra thread from the ball. "Oh, I think they've had quite enough o' m' banshee's wailin' for a while."

"Yer voice...," he stopped himself, changed tactic. "Will ye recite then? Tell a tale, a joke, somethin'?"

She blushed. "I couldn't."

"Ye should. Ye should enter at least one thing, fer th' ritual's sake. Bad luck an' ye don't."

"Ye shouldn't have had t' tell me that," she sighed. "I've been... there too long it seems."

"So, unless ye've a mind t' try yer hand wi' th' fightin'..." he glanced pointedly over his shoulder at the makeshift stage, which was little more than a glorified pallet tossed onto the ground. "There's also a dance competition later," he offered.

She took a breath. "I'll recite. But... I only have th' one. I... don't remember my others."

He flashed her a cocked smile. "That one will most certainly do. I'll call ye when it's yer turn."

An couldn't crochet anymore, she just slipped it back into her bag. She was profoundly nervous. She could hardly pay attention to the singers and the musicians, the tale teller or the comedian, even the few other poets were only half followed. Her fingers fidgeted in her lap.

Finally Jonny called her. She rose, clutching Cipín tightly, feeling more like she was striding to her execution than a performance. She could not understand why she felt more nervous now than when she had stood and presented the elegy at the wake, or sung as keener this morning, or even joined her untrained voice to Jonny's perfection. There were only about a dozen people she could see, scattered in front of her, but she could feel more. Jonny sat just off to the side with Gabrielle, watching her, encouragement on his face.

She gathered herself, took a breath, and lifted her voice.

> "When ships have left the harbour
> Seventy sailors on a random sea
> Floating helpless to distant horizons
> Hoping for shelter in the lea.
>
> When hearts have parted undesired
> Forced away by other's will
> They slowly fall to chaotic pieces
> Washed away by th' blood they spill
>
> When angels leave you loving
> The darkness moving in
> Filling spaces once held sacred
> By a heart that's caving in
>
> Such are times when hearts break open
> Shattered, abandoned and dying
> When life it seems just can't continue
> Ruined where hearts left it lying

When ships have abandoned seaport
Seventy sailors strong
Following sun-path west-ward
List'ning t' the sea's wind-breasted song

When hearts drift long and empty
Half-dead to face the heat
Love too long in absence
From kisses angel sweet

When angels fly to heaven
Leaving man in need
Hearts break in their attempt to follow
Where holy feathers lead

Such the time when hearts so broken
Take up the pieces and then
Time to say farewell to angels
And take the human side again"

An stepped off the platform with a graceful swiftness, grateful the ordeal was over. She aimed herself for her lace, waiting on her seat. Picking her work up, she felt for the arms of the plastic chair and sank into it. She felt fully flushed in wake of the applause she could barely hear, so relieved was she to be off the stage. Hands patted her shoulder and back, murmurs of 'well done' and other encouragements. They surprised her almost as much as the discreet sniffles and not so quiet blowing of noses. Apparently she had moved some people to tears. She sat back and was actually able to enjoy the rest of the performances.

It was an hour or more later when Martha rang the dinner bell on the back porch, telling everyone the feast was ready. The comedian who was the last on stage laughed at that. "Well, I guess that's my cue to get offstage. Those tables are groaning with food and it ain't gonna be my fault if they break cause I held up the feast. Martha'd skelp me within an inch of my life."

People laughed good-naturedly as he took a bow and they began to move off en masse. Someone touched her elbow as she stood, about to offer to walk her back when they suddenly backed away. An frowned, confused until Jonny took the unseen person's place and offered his arm. "May I?"

She blushed, nodded, shifting her bag up her arm and Cipín to her other hand.

"Now that weren't so bad, was it?" he asked.

She gave a short laugh. "It was terrifyin'. I've never recited my own work in public before."

"Ye wrote the elegy."

"That were different,... somehow," she insisted. "I don't pretend to understand it. I were nervous then, too, but not like this."

He shrugged. "Ye could recite someone else's. Charlie did. That piece he did was a Pablo Neruda."

"Surprisingly, that would have been easier for me."

"Well," he said, giving her hand a pat, "'tis good to stretch yer limits."

The feast tables were indeed groaning with food. Skye heaped his plate with things he was familiar with and dishes he did not recognise at all. It was a feast of ancient proportions. Across the table he could see An beside the Bard, watched him help her to select foods by describing them. Stouts, beers and whiskeys were available, though aside from the ritual drink near the end when Ian stood to exemplify the dead and the reason for the ritual, he noted that An did not touch the alcohol. When Ian finished his speech, the table in perfect unison chanted "Sláinte!" and drank. Others continued drinking. An satisfied herself with her cup of tea.

After dinner came the music and dancing. There was a full band, so Jonny was not required to perform the whole evening and took a turn on the dance floor with An, who was flush by the end from both the exertion and his nearness. Thankfully, by then he was asked to go up on the stage to sing, giving her time to get herself together. Inwardly, she chided herself for even thinking of reaching above her station, because a Bard was *well* above her station. She was soon lost in the sound of his voice, singing one of the many sad but spirited Irish songs.

When he was done, the band began a rousing reel, and An found herself swept up in it, indulging herself in one of the Irish country dances she remembered from her youth and throwing herself into it. When everyone fell out, laughing and clapping and the music moved to something slower and more a couples thing, she found herself off to the side with Roulet and her sister. She looked the former over critically. "Ye look better," she commented. "Got it out o' yer system?"

Roulet gave her a sheepish look. "Got it shocked out, yes."

An put her hand on her shoulder. "The guilt will resolve itself in time." Roulet looked at her, surprised. An smiled. "I know the look. Think ye yer th' on'y one what's felt guilty aboot their past?"

Roulet seemed to relax after that, gave An a hug.

"Uh oh." Something in Solitaire's voice made both of the other women look up.

Roulet followed her sister's gaze and groaned. "*A fute,*" she cursed in French. An tried to follow where they were looking. "What is *she* doing here?"

"You know she can't stay away from him for very long," Solitaire drawled.

"It was over a year this time, damn it all."

An tried to see, caught only glimpses between milling mortals. Finally, she saw Jonny standing off to the side with an unknown woman. He gave her the impression of a stag facing down a wolf, torn between flight and embrace. His eyes were full of pain, like a man who wants a drink and knows he shouldn't.

The woman drew An's eye the moment she came into view. She was breath-taking. She almost shone, giving off a cold perfection, an absolute, artful grace. Her clothes were unseeable, but the sleeves were three-quarter, the skirt just above the knee and the neckline more daring than most here and highly inappropriate for a funeral no matter what the era. Her hair hung in perfect waves off her shoulder, coy little ringlets hanging at her jewelled ear, the colour an odd dichotomy between the Autumn red it was supposed to be and the blonde she had glamoured it to be.

As her hand reached out to trace one of the tiny braids An had woven Jonny's hair into, An felt a surge of anger at what she was convinced was a derogatory remark at her handiwork, followed by jealousy of the hand on him. The pain in her heart came as he half-closed his eyes and leaned into her palm. The tightness of his jaw was lost on her. She did not realise she had been holding her breath until Bethany came trotting up, out of breath herself. An's hand slipped to her chest, her fingers wrapping unconsciously about the two dancing figures around her neck, seeking comfort. She listened, but could not tear her eyes off the pair.

"So what does she want?" Solitaire asked Bethany. "I know you were eavesdropping."

"Of course I was," Bethany snorted, "and of course you're the first I'm going to share with. I hate the bitch as much as you do."

"So what does she want?" Roulet pressed, echoing her sister perfectly. If the voice had not come from a different location, An would have said Solitaire had repeated herself.

"Apparently she's asking Jonny to perform at her husband's funeral."

"It looks more like seducin' than askin'," An replied with a bitterness that surprised her.

Solitaire groaned. "Which means he'll say yes."

"He never could resist her," Roulet sighed.

"Few men can, not when she tries," Bethany snarled. "Some even when she doesn't. She doesn't belong here."

Something occurred to Roulet. "When did her husband die? She's not exactly dressed like a widow," she added sourly.

"That's the worst of it. He hasn't."

At this, An finally managed to tear her eyes from the pair. "What?"

Bethany explained. "She's in a May-December marriage."

"She's a fucking Gold Digger, is what she is," Solitaire growled.

Her sister laughed. "And you're not?"

Solitaire had the foresight to sound indignant. "No. Well-off is just *one* criteria. I have to actually like the guy to put up with him. And I'd never marry a guy old enough to be my grandfather and deliberately move to cut his kids out of the inheritance."

Roulet explained to An. "She married some old guy with a heart condition or terminal something. Not really sure in what order or what he's dying of, I never really pay her much attention when she's not eyeing our men. He must have taken a turn for the worst."

"Or she's planning on working him up to a heart attack," Solitaire snapped.

"She could do it," said Beth.

An glanced back at Jonny, watched the pain on his face as the woman pulled away from him and he fought the urge to follow her. An turned away, angry with herself for her reactions. Here was concrete proof why she kept her heart to herself. He was tantamount to falling for the Lord of the Manor's son, and this woman was everything she would never be. "So who is she?"

"Serephina …Morelle now? We lose track of her last name," Solitaire answered. "She's been married three times that I know of since I've been out, and I know she's been around longer than that. Her and Sorrow go back."

"Weren't they an item once?" Bethany asked.

"From the look of it, they still are," An snapped and turned back for the house.

Skye stood off to the side, watching the dancing and the musicians. He had noticed the governess in deep conversation with the twins, saw her distress but not what had caused it. He was starting to go towards them when Liberty appeared in his way, smiling coyly up at him. "Aye, Miss O'Keefe?" he asked. "Or is it Yer Highness t'night?"

Her eyes flashed. "Liberty will do fer now. Yer Majesty later."

He swallowed. "What …can ah do fer ye, Miss Liberty?"

"Spare a dance fer yer queen?"

He blushed. "Ah've seen ye dance, Miss. Ah'll just embarrass ye."

She grabbed his arm and began pulling him out onto the floor. "I'll tone it down," she grinned.

Skye found himself torn between wanting to run and hide and staying as physically close to her as he could manage. By the time he was able to make up his mind, which was the stronger impulse, he was in the middle of the crowded dance floor and the choice was moot.

An found herself in front of one of the bonfires. She could not see it, but she stood there, soaking in the heat that was very different from the ambient swelter of the August night. She ignored everything around her for the most part, staring into the flames as if she could see them, wondered if she would be able to see it if they used a magical source to light one.

Someone offered her a drink, but smelling the alcohol, she politely declined. Another individual came up behind her and accepted it in her stead. This second person did not go away, but came up to stand at her elbow to watch the fire with her. She caught a glimpse of him from the corner of her eye and realised he was one of the changed. He was a short, stocky man; very much a long-fingered, walking badger. Even his face was that of a badger. He stood quietly, drinking from the bottle for a long moment before he ventured to speak.

"Ya would be Miss Ceobhrán, would ya not?" he asked in a quiet, infinitely polite voice. His accent was lightly Bostonian.

"I would. And ye?" she asked with equal formality.

"Danny O'Keefe. Family buildah." He did not offer to shake hands. In fact, he continued to mimic her position as long as she chose to not look directly at him. "I unda'stand ya pose a very pahticulah challenge foah me."

"And what might that be?"

He grinned. "Buildin' a house ya kin see."

This gave her pause. "And can ye do such a thing? Build a house with magic in its very stones?"

"It's only gotta be lightly magic, right?"

She turned to look at him, taking note of his waistcoat and the watch chain that ran from one side to the other of it. "Aye. I can tell that yer vest is but lightly touched, magically coloured perhaps, but yer watch is heavily of th' other side."

He ran his furred hand down his front, smiled. "'Twas only put togethah by magic, notta magic thread. So yeah, I kin build ya a house ya kin see, Miss Ceobhrán. And I shall take a great deal of delight in doin' so. As foah my watch," he pulled it out of his pocket and held it out to her, "I found it on the way out. I'm quite fond'a it."

The moment it touched her hands she knew things about it, things that were not quite a whisper in the back of her mind, but almost. "And it is quite fond of you, Mister O'Keefe. It helps ye t' work more quickly than others, faster, cleaner. And that hand ye have no idea what it does… it marks th' time ye've left."

He paled, accepting back the watch from her as she held it out. "Time I've left?"

"Aye. On this earth. Unless somethin' or someone interferes, an' takes ye early unless I misunderstand it. Yer natural lifespan. I suggest ye make th' most of it."

"H-h-how, howdoyaknow…" he stammered.

She looked him over carefully. "It told me."

"How?"

She shook her head. "I don't know."

"Can ya read othah things this way? Mundane things?"

She thought about that, turned to face him. "May I?" she asked, holding out her hand. He readily nodded, and she reached out and touched the shoulder of his vest, stroking the fabric. "'Silky, pretty, aren't I fine.' That is all yer vest says t' me." She fingered the cloth of his sleeve, which she could not see, could tell that it was ordinary linen. "This… this does not speak."

He nodded, as if it all made perfect sense to him. "Excellent. Well, if I find anything magical I don' unda'stand I now know who to ask, don't I?"

"I would be pleased t' be of some service. Now, you wished something of me?"

"Yeah. Yoah house. What kind would ya like?"

She pulled back. "Oh, I hardly qualify for my own home. I have no way yet to earn my keep."

He grinned, showing a mouthful of badger teeth. "Oh, somethin'll come along. Always does. Could take months. I seen folk come t'rough took nearly a yeah to find theyah place. But boy, did they make up foah it," he blushed. From the way he fidgeted when he said it, she guessed he was talking about himself. "Besides, Ian said I wasta build ya one, so what would ya like?"

She did not have to think long on the matter. "If I could have anything I wanted, I would like a small Irish cottage, a stone wall around, maybe a yard high, with roses and ivy and those lovely blooms that hang from the veranda of the main house. I love their smell. I'd build a small garden in th' back, preferably with a small stream running through th' bottom of th' garden, maybe trees. But I will settle for something small and modest. I understand there are apartments here."

He shook his head. "Yeah, we have an apahtment complex for those what like that sort of livin'. But yoah not gettin' a place at the Unicohn Ahms. I was told ta build ya a house. Ya shoah ya don' want anythin' biggah? I just finished Libehty's, and it's a two-starry, foah-bedroom, wit' a cellah and an attic big enough ta convaht ta livin' space."

"I am fine with something small. I have small needs. A sitting room with windows overlooking the garden, a modest kitchen and a bedroom is all I need."

He began sketching something down on a pad he pulled out of his pocket. "Hmm, ya know, I think I got just the spot, too. What kinda trees?"

"Old ones? I like fruit trees. If I have th' space, I'll likely put down raspberries or blackberry canes, herbs and some flowers. A bit of a vegetable garden fer m'self an' I can get th' seed. Nothing extravagant. I'm no farmer. Just a country lass what misses home."

He tucked his pad away again, reached out to shake her hand. "Ohp, mind the claws," he warned, taking her hand more gingerly than normal folk. "I promise ya'll be absolutely delighted oah yoah money back, guahanteed. Now if you will...."

She paled. "I... haven't any money. I've told ye, I've no means."

He laughed. "Don' fret, pet. It's a sayin', a waya speaking. It's Ian's money regahdless and not mucha that. I have plans foah this house. This will be my mastehpiece, a wohka aht," he beamed. He was so worked up at the prospect of the project that she hadn't the heart to call him off.

He wandered off looking for someone else and An finally turned and used Cipín to return to the house.

Danny took several minutes winding through the crowds before he found who he was looking for: the man in the kilt. He was with Liberty on the dance floor. He waited only long enough for the last strain of the song to start before he cut in. "Cousin!" he exclaimed, kissing both Liberty's cheeks and ignoring the looks she was giving him. He turned to Skye. "And the man I've been looking for."

"Ye have?" he asked, eyebrow raised.

"Oh, yes, indeedy. Danny O'Keefe, family buildah," he said, thrusting out his hand. "Mind the claws," he warned as Skye hesitantly reached out.

As they were shaking, it suddenly pinged in Skye's mind who the man was and why he would be looking for him. "AH!"

Danny grinned. "Good, ya know what's up. Shall we go discuss the pahticulahs?"

Liberty looked down at her watch and growled. She grabbed Skye's arm. "Ye'll have t' wait til after th' awards. I've t' go present an' this lad's been in so many contests t'd'y he's bound t' end up wit' one or two."

She left neither man room to argue and dragged them back to the dance area and the short stage that had been set up for the band. Henry was already there, waiting, getting the results from the various judges. Liberty dropped Skye and her cousin off by her father and headed to the stage. Ian glanced over at the two of them, nodded, turned back to the stage and frowned.

"Ye know, Danny. I think I ought t' invest in a permanent stage or bandstand," Ian began. "We used t' have a gazebo thing over yon, last century, I think it was. Hurricane took it out. Or was that a tornado? I ferget."

Beside him, Gabby snorted. "You, forget?"

"Old man brain," he growled in response.

Skye did his best not to chuckle. Ian gave him a sidelong glare, which helped his self-control immensely, and then Henry had taken the mike and begun his announcements.

An quietly dressed herself for bed. She set her clothes in the hamper Shannon had thoughtfully provided and was about to slip in between the sheets when there was a knock on her door. She paused, felt for the chair over which she had hung her dressing gown and, slipping into it, cracked the door open. It was Liberty. An let her in.

"What can I do fer ye, Liberty?" she asked softly.

"Ye kin sit down an' tell me why ye left early," Liberty answered, not unkindly.

An sighed, made a precise turn and crossed to the wicker wing-back chair in the corner. It was yet another addition by the Head Housekeeper when it was noticed how much she enjoyed the one in the solar. She indicated for Liberty to take the other chair by the desk.

Liberty closed the bedroom door and pulled the indicated seat over to face An's and sat down, waiting.

An nestled herself back in the comfort of the chintz cushioned back, her hand unconsciously drifting over to stroke the intricate details of the carved box on the stand next to it. "I... became overwhelmed."

Liberty sighed. "Solitaire and Roulet told me what happened with Serephina."

An's reaction was sharp and quick. "They should have kept their comments regarding my reactions to Master Sorrow to themselves." Her cheeks had flared a dark red.

Liberty started to soften and bend, sorry she had offended, but quickly stiffened up, looking more the Queen than she had in a while. "No. I understand about privacy and yer Victorian sensibilities, but they've not gossiped it across th' Rest nor t' anyone else. They care about ye and what happens to ye, as do I. When ye missed th' award ceremony, they brought th' matter up t' me. Roulet's th' one said she thought she knew th' cause and there are things ye need t' know."

An simmered down, took a deep breath, her thumb stroking a small carved hummingbird in a corner of the box. She calmed. "Very well. What?"

"Unfortunately, some of them aren't my place t'tell. But Serephina... she's a right black widda, that one. I don't understand what's a'tween them, but somethin' is. An' ye can't blame a man fer strayin' when that woman is involved any more'n ye could blame..." she struggled for an analogy and had trouble coming up with one with names. "Well, th' tales are full o' sorceresses what stole another's man through magic. That's her."

An shook her head. "It's no matter. I've n'right t' set my heart for him in any case. I haven't, an' I won't."

Liberty laughed. "Ye think yer heart'll give ye that option? Yer more naïve than I thought, then. And what d'ye mean ye've no right? Ye've every right."

An was adamant. "Nay. 'Tis only heartbreak there. A governess might look t' th' servants fer her heart's ease, or a farmer or small landsman or craftsman, but never t' the lord or his like."

Liberty softened, slid her chair closer, set her hand on An's. "Ah, luv, yer not 'th' governess' any longer. We're not a class-based society any more and ye've every right to set yer heart for any ye like. E'en m' father should ye choose. Though I don't recommend it."

She gave a small smile in spite of her shock. "'Tis a hard thing to reconcile."

"Aye, there's a lot o' adjustin' t' do. Ye've more to do than most."

"I... had accepted th' fact that love for me was unwise and not t' be. I don't even know if this is th' case here, just that...."

"Seeing him with her hurt?" she raised a knowing eyebrow.

An nodded. "I don't understand it."

Liberty leaned back. "I do. Ye've just met him, he's swept ye off yer feet an' left ye breathless..."

"He's done nothin' improper," An was quick to add.

She smiled. "Nor will he. He'll be as proper as ye like him t' be. Or as improper. But he's knocked th' wind out o' yer sails none-the-less. There's a chance. Then ye see evidence he's either courtin' another, or plain spoken for. It's a shock, that things weren't what ye expected. It's goin' t' hurt."

"But what do I do?"

An shrugged. "Ye just go on as before. Then, when it seems right or ye decide ye really need th' answers, ye ask him. He'll answer or he won't and that's th' way of it."

She frowned. "And how will I know he's not lyin' t' me? All men lie and all men cheat. It's just what they do. I can accept that, was raised t' th' expectation, but I won't be th' one he cheats with."

Liberty didn't know which statement to address first. "Wow. I... all right. One, not all men lie or cheat, and I feel sorry for whoever taught ye that. Though I suppose in your day..." she shook it off. "As fer Jonny lyin'... to put it baldly: he can't. Not *won't, can't.* He's under a geas or sommat."

An seemed to shrink into herself at that. "I thank ye fer comin' t' see t' my wellbein'. I appreciate th' concern. I'll manage, thank ye."

"If yer sure?"

"I have better self-control than folk give me credit for," she smiled.

"I've been taking care of m'self fer a long time now. Though 'tis wearin' on me at th' moment that I can't."

"I can understand that. I'll keep an eye out fer somethin'. Oh, I nearly forgot why I realised ye'd left early." She pulled something out of her pocket and placed it into An's hands. "Yer award fer th' Bardic contest."

An looked up in shock from the small book in her hand. "I won?"

"Placed second, but th' twins are hard t' beat when they work t'gether. I'll have ta get th' dancin' as a separate contest next time around. It's not fair."

She blushed, sat back and ran her hands over the soft leather cover, felt the tooled indentation of a spiralling triskelion on its face, but nothing else. "What is the title?" she asked, sadly realising it couldn't be in braille from the thinness of the book.

Liberty laughed. "No title but what ye give it, luv. It's a 'blank book'. Glamour it so ye kin see it, then ye put yer thoughts into it, or more poetry, that'd be nice. Write me somethin' happy. Or at th' least hopeful."

An flushed further. "I... can't begin t' thank ye enough."

"Psh," she clucked. "Don't thank me. Ye won it, fair an' square. Jonny picked th' prizes. We had somethin' fer each type o' art, dependin' on what won. Which tells us we should have individual contests..."

An was so overwhelmed, by the idea, the crisp blankness of the book, by the smell of the leather and clean pages and the faint crack and creak of its spine as she opened it for the first time, that she did not hear Liberty take her leave. She rose, crossed to the desk and sat down. Never once did it click that the chair should have still been in the corner, not at the desk. She took up the pen that she had glamoured to write Reggie's elegy and opened to the first page, letting the words flow from her to the paper.

It was a sweet little piece, something akin to a lullaby. She felt slightly drained when she was done, but then she often did after writing. It was a release. She blew on the page to dry the ink out of habit and closed the book. She put the pen in its place and set the book on top of the braille books on the back corner of the desk, then thought better of it.

She rose and crossed back to the small table beside her wing-back chair by the window and opened the box that had contained the children's gifts. The book nestled quite nicely inside it. She closed the lid and crossed the room, slipping out of her dressing gown and into the bed, ready to sleep in spite of the sounds of revelry still flowing through the open window. The smells of the fires lulled her, providing comfort without the extra heat she could not have withstood at the moment. She was asleep immediately.

An rose the next morning and went about her day as if the events of the night before had not occurred. She breakfasted with the family and the other Taken who currently resided in the house, of which there were only four. There was Skye, of course. A handsome young selkie, who filled the air with the aroma of salt seas, making An feel inexplicably homesick. The other two were a gnomish engineer who was moving out that day to work in the wide world beyond for Danny's construction company, and a frog boy who kept using his tongue to grab whatever he could not reach at the table. The latter had not yet acquired a fully human form and was struggling with the concept of needing to have his 'curse broken'.

At the end of breakfast, as she was taking out the plates, Shannon remarked to Ian, "I'll take that one under wing if ye need, sir. I'll do fer him what I did with that 'lost boy' ye brought through in '86."

"An' ye did right well by him, if memory serves, Shannon. What was that he's doin' now? Yer in touch still, aye?"

She gave him a reproving look as she stacked his plate on top of the others in her grasp. "Of course I am. Phillip is teaching literature at NYU at the moment. Got his tenure last year."

"Good. Have at this one," he said with a baleful glare in the frog boy's direction.

The young man visibly wilted. It made following Shannon the preferred course and the two of them headed out, with the boy carrying a tray with the cups and silver.

From breakfast, An went into the solar to work on her crochet whilst the rest of the family went to mass. She was asked if she'd like to attend, to which she politely declined and surprisingly, no one pressed or asked her to explain. She sat in her chair for hours, working on her lace, listening to the various people who came and went throughout the day after church. A great many paused to congratulate her on her success the night before, which both pleased and embarrassed her to no end. No one mentioned either Jonny or Seraphina, for which she was grateful.

Liberty came round for supper with the family and An was pleased to show her what she had written. She fetched the book and handed it to her as they sat in the solar after the meal with coffee whilst others watched whatever game was on the television in the next room. Liberty opened the book and began flipping pages. "Wow! Did ye sleep at all? Ye wrote all this in one night? Some of these are amazing. 'The well-turned phrase, like th' turnin' moon--waxes and wanes in its light--Brighter and brighter like a candle whose flame--burns from both ends of the wick...','" she read. "Breathtaking."

An frowned, "What? I dinnae write that last night, I wrote that..." she leaned over to look at the book, "...years ago... over There...." She fell silent as she noticed the hand in which the pages and pages of poetry were written. Liberty handed her the book and watched her face as she turned page after page. An sat down.

The first was written in her own hand, with the modern ink pen she had used last night. The rest... the rest were in the hand of the young prince, though far neater than she remembered, in the flowing strokes of his swan-feather quill and fey-flower ink, which was faintly purple in the right light. "I don't understand."

"Don't understand what? Did ye sleep-write?"

She shook her head. "No. I wrote these... whilst I was in service. I left them behind. Not intentional, mind, but none-the-less...."

Liberty thought out loud. "Where'd ye set th' book? Mayhap some brownie did ye a favour?"

"Brownies are a Scottish sprite," An frowned. "And 'tis th' young prince's hand."

"What, ye think just cause they're Scot we don't have one or two lurkin'? We call 'em by other names but they be brownies all th' same."

"Well enough, but it were in th' box th' King...." An stopped. She only thought a moment more before she darted upstairs, letting Cipín keep her out of trouble. She was aware Liberty was following her, so she left the door open. She picked up the box and thought about it, felt the box respond, insinuating the understanding of what she wanted to know without 'speaking'. She sank into her chair by the window with it on her lap.

"Well?" Liberty asked.

There was a smile of wonder and love on An's face. "It... it's a ...well, I put things into it and they go There, to th' children. And vice versa."

"Clever. And the poems?"

"I guess th' prince found it and thought...." The book in her hand corrected this impression. "No. It was taken from th' box. Th' prince loved th' poem. Th' princess remembered my old collection and fetched it. She read them out and th' young prince copied them with great care."

"Explains why they're in Irish."

An decided she would pen a letter before bed. It would take careful crafting to thank them without thanking them. She rose, set the book beside the box to remind herself, and followed Liberty back downstairs to the solar. She had crochet to put away, and she was not yet ready to retire. She thought about taking a walk in the lovely twilight. The gloaming still came late and lingered long, and the mists would be rising from the river.

Before she could ask Liberty if she would like to join her, a man ran in the front door, saw Liberty and skidded to a halt. "Where's yer Da?"

The two women paused on the stairs in confusion. "His study, I think," she stammered.

"No," Ian said, stepping out of the living room. "I'm in here watchin' th' bloody telly. What's th' rush, Sean? Aren't ye supposed t' be watchin' th' Tallow girl?"

Sean took a moment to catch his breath. "Jacob's on it now. I had t' leave. Was seen. Jacob can watch without being seen at all."

"Activity?" Ian asked calmly, leaning against the doorframe.

Sean nodded. "Night hag this time. Had two hobs with her. We got them, but we're goin' t' have to do something. We can't keep watch like this forever."

"I know, but... what else can we do? We have t' protect her. She's not one of us but she will be if we don't take steps."

"I agree," Sean said. "'Tis rare for magic to show up this strongly and this young without a legacy being involved."

"Legacy?" Liberty asked.

Sean looked up at her, took his hat in his hand. "Aye, Miss O'Keefe. A family line where this happens more often than not. In which case, they're trained from an early age and we don't get this sort o' problem. This child is what I supposed ye'd call a 'muggle-born'," he said with a wry smile, "if it helps to use those terms."

Liberty nodded. "Actually, that does clear it up fer me."

"It still leaves me in th' dark," An ventured. "Providin' th' conversation isn't a private one."

Ian looked up to the staircase, and a strange look crossed his eyes. He stood and moved forward. "Actually, let's call it private and take this to m' office."

Sean nodded and turned down the appropriate hallway immediately. An bobbed a brief curtsy and continued down the stairs, preparing to cross to the solar to put away her lace. Ian stopped her with a hand in her way. "Um, if yeh'll be so kind, Miss Ceobhrán, as t' follow Sean?"

An looked up, confused, but nodded.

"Liberty, will yeh be joinin' us or headin' home?"

Something out on the darkening lawn caught her eye, and she smiled, spoke without turning to her father. "Oh, I think I'll walk home. An, I'll read th' new poem later if ye'll let me. Ye have a good night."

"Good night," she murmured in confused response. She allowed Ian to take her arm and escort her down the hallway to his office while Liberty stalked out the front door with a determined look on her face.

In the office, Sean pulled out the chair for An, seating himself on the couch. Ian dropped into his chair and lit up a cigarette, tossing one to Sean. "I wanted a cigarette anyhow. Now," he said, lighting up. "Please t' explain t' Miss An who ye are and what th' situation is."

Sean took in the expression on Ian's face then turned to An, studying her a long moment before he lifted the cigarette to his lips and snapped his fingers in a manner that reminded An of the lighters modern men used to light their tobacco. Though there was no lighter in his hand, a small flame burst into existence between his thumb and forefinger. He drew in, and when the cigarette was properly glowing, opened his palm outward to show her there was no fire and no source.

An watched the process, less impressed than she felt she should be.

She looked back at Ian, feet propped up on the edge of his invisible desk, watching her with care and amusement, then back at Sean. She studied him more closely. She was certain there was more here than Taken tricks. She had seen Fox light his habit with his finger before, so that wasn't it. She could see him clearly, if a bit shimmery, as she could any of the Touched, and then she realised he wasn't Touched at all!

There was a particular resonance to the Touched, a duality to them, being both real and of Faery. There was none of that in this man. Her sight of him was straight-forward and clear, wholly of this world. The magic which she saw him through was all of this world and almost more real than her own. It was also a great deal less confined or defined.

"You're a *draoi*."

He laughed at her surprise. "Aye, Miss. I am a wizard, so to speak. I work my will on the universe." He held out his hand. "Sean O'Keefe."

An accepted it, introduced herself. There was only a flicker of amusement at her name, but unless you were looking for it would never be noticed.

He got right to business. "As I was telling Miss O'Keefe, Elizabeth Tallow is a *draoi*, as you said, as well. But she is only nine. She's come into her power this young in a household of people who have no idea what their daughter is. Were she a legacy, she would be taught how to use and shield her powers so that others would not realise what she is and come hunting her before she's able, if she ever will be, to defend herself. As it is, we have to watch th' house every night and fight off th' various monsters of all supernatural bents who are drawn to her power like a moth to a flame. I had t' kill a vampire last week. Th' problem lies in keepin' her safe whilst her parents remain clueless. She's seein' things they can't but some of us can."

An mused quietly, her hands sitting primly in her lap. Her voice was soft when she spoke, "A child with such an 'active imagination' would benefit from special attentions. How's her schoolwork?"

Ian grinned. Sean's face went momentarily blank, then it was his turn to light up in surprised realisation. "Yer...," he looked at Ian. "She's... Is she?"

Ian shrugged, waved his cigarette hand dismissively. "She's no' got th' certifications she needs to teach school these days but she's th' skills."

Sean looked back at her. "I was under th' impression ye were from th' late 1800s. How well versed are ye in modern teaching?"

"Have mathematics changed that much? Readin'? What I don't know I can learn, quicker than th' child, likely. My problem will be knowing if she's gettin' things right. I can't exactly see her writing and I am blind as far as normals understand," she added as she thought things through. She looked over at Ian. "I see what yer doin', an' it won't work. I'm blind. No one'll hire a blind governess, fey-touched or no."

Ian's grin was smug. "Oh, I kin weave a reason so sound they'd be fools t'refuse it. There are reasons fer yeh t' be there other than teachin'. Sean, yeh've a friend at th' school board, aye?" Sean nodded. "See an' yeh can get her transcripts, see where she's lackin'. Gimme a backdoor."

"I'll get right to work. Find a guidance counsellor's reason for the 'intervention'."

"And then I'll sweep in t' th' rescue with Miss Ceobhrán here. That is, if she'll take the job," he added, turning to her.

"What exactly will be expected of me?"

"First and foremost, keep th' child safe," Ian responded. "We need someone what can see th' dangers who can notify us should there be sommat needin' discouragement. Second, guide her along, help her get her powers under control. Yeh've taught magical children afore, do what yeh did fer them."

"But I couldn't teach them how to use their powers," she protested.

"That's what I'm for," Sean interrupted.

Ian put his feet down and leaned forward on the desk. "Yeh taught them *when* t' use their powers an' fer why. Thanks t' yeh we have three less Tuatha likely t' snatch people and alter them fer their own amusement. Three less lookin' at us as toys t' be played with, broken an' cast aside, an' three more allies against those what do."

An took a deep breath. A purpose at last, she thought. She sat up straighter, one hand settled on Cipín's knob confidently. "One: where will I be stayin' and what will be done on my days off, as I'll need at least one a month. Two: I'll be needin' t' learn t' battle these beasties, in case one slips inta th' house afore help can come."

"Ye'll likely be stayin' with th' Tallows," Sean answered. "We need ye on premises at night. Maybe after a few months they'll get th' hint that she's guarded and ye can relax yer watch a hair."

"I'll have Juan teach yeh t' use that twig yer so fond of," Ian grinned. "He knows a few special tricks fer sticks."

Sean frowned. "He doesn't teach weapon styles. Says they're for th' weak."

Ian chuckled. "He'll teach *her*. One could argue she *is* weak." He turned back to her. "As fer days off, I'm sure we can manage two nights o' th' old watches a week."

An was startled. "Two nights off a week? Sir, that's outrageous. They'd never go fer it."

Sean laughed. "They'd ask too many questions if you asked for less."

An flushed, made once again aware of just how out of time she was. "Well, I should still remain there six nights a week for a month or two. Until things settle a little."

Ian shrugged when Sean looked over at him. "Might work. Be a good idea, regardless. We'll get her ID's claiming her an Irish au pair. Rowdy should be able to handle th' paperwork. He has a knack for making papers no one takes too close a look at."

"Very well, then. I suppose someone should tell Danny that I shan't be needin' the house after all."

Ian chuckled. "Oh, I'll not be th' one t' break his heart. Yeh'll be needin' it in any case. Yeh'll have time off an'll need a place to spend it." He narrowed his eyes as she started to protest and she closed her mouth. "I'll let yeh know as soon as we're ready t' present yeh. Yeh'll have t' fill th' child in on everythin'. She's met us before. She'll be delighted with yeh."

Sean frowned. "Might want to get her a better name, though," he mused. "An Ceobhrán isn't... exactly normal. That and no middle name..."

The right corner of Ian's mouth twitched smileward. "Well, I suppose I could adopt her, an' she be willin'. Afford her th' protections."

"It's what I was thinkin'," Sean agreed. "If she deals with hobs or other fey things, they won't be able to snatch her and leave th' child helpless."

An watched the two men talking about her as if she wasn't even in the room. If they were hoping to use this to get a rise out of her, they were disappointed. It was something she was used to.

Ian finally turned to her. "Well, lass? Yeh interested?"

"Th' job or th' surname?"

"Both, either?"

"Well, since yer askin' direct...," she said with an infuriating, prim calm, "Aye, and aye."

Ian grinned, leaning back in his chair, took a long, slow drag from his cigarette. Sean sank back against the couch as if a great weight had suddenly been lifted. Even An underwent a small change, though there was no outward indication. Purpose settled into her every pore, suffusing her with a sense of calm and rightness.

11

The child was striking in ways beyond just An's ability to see her. She was pretty, of course: a head full of blondish curls that hung halfway down her ribcage, large eyes that particular shade of blue that could be any colour from sky to grey to lavender at a whim and a precocious little mouth. From the moment of introduction, those eyes latched onto An, watching her warily, trying to figure her out. What enabled An to see her was very different from any of the Taken she had so far encountered. She was more like Sean, but different even from him. If she could set eyes on another like them, she might be able to compare and separate out what marked them what they were and what was just their individuality, but in absence she had to make do. There was something untamed about the girl, shimmering and wild. She was vivid. It was beautiful to watch.

They sat in the Tallows' living room: Sean's School Board friend, John-Michael Wells, sat in one chair with a cup of tea; Miss Tisiphone Jones, an O'Keefe lawyer, sat in the other, with the family on the couch across from them. An was perched primly in another chair off to the side. Elizabeth was leaning forward, her arms folded and resting on her knees as she studied An. The adults were talking around her, paying neither the child nor the governess any mind. An's eyes rest on the girl, and, though she knew no one could tell what she was actually looking at, (with the cloudy cataracts that she had been told was all mortals saw), she also knew the child was aware of just where she was looking.

"I understand the necessity. Miss Jones explained it all very well but... my concern right now, Mister Wells, is that fact that she's blind," the mother, Sharon, protested.

"I assured you, in the matters where your daughter needs help, she is more than qualified to assist," Miss Jones injected, no trace of the light Irish accent she had displayed when An had been introduced to her an hour ago. "She was chosen with a great deal of forethought. She's cared for children in your daughter's situation before."

"While blind?" George Tallow asked.

An spoke up, though her gaze never changed. There was only a trace of her Irish lilt, leaving behind a light and very proper sounding British accent. "I assure you, Mister Tallow. I am not completely blind. Every once in a while something comes through. And while I shan't be able to help her with her writing or her arithmetic, I shall in all other ways be able to tutor her. Teach her ways of helping herself."

"But..." Sharon began.

John-Michael spoke up with a long-suffering sigh. "Look. I understand this is not what you were expecting, but she is what the agency sent. She *is* uniquely qualified for this position, and with the Americans with Disabilities Act in place, I can't deny her a post. Her previous employer, I am told, has left her in possession of certain skills..."

At this point Elizabeth had suddenly made up her mind about something and leaned back on the couch between her parents, a smug grin on her face. An gave her a soft smile in return.

"Who was her previous employer? I might be more comfortable with this if I knew that much at least," the mother protested.

"I'm afraid that part of her file is sealed. There is a glowing letter of recommendation in it, but all indications of who it was have been blacked out. I am assured it is a matter of a national security," Mister

Wells responded, flustered.

There was a sound of further protest from George, but An interrupted it. "Forgive me, Mister Tallow, but all I can say about my previous employ is that the children in my care were highly imaginative, precocious, often puckish youngsters in very real danger of acquiring the spoiled and entitled attitudes to which indulged and privileged children are prey. And that when I left them, they were well on their way to becoming what I hope will be well-behaved, fair and just rulers of their father's country when the time comes, interested only in the wellbeing of the people who rely on them."

"Royalty?" Sharon's voice was soft and awed. "Why... why after caring for royal children... would you want to care for mine? We're ...just middle class. Hell, we can't even afford you." She turned back to Miss Jones. "I still don't understand why anyone would be taking such an interest in us or our daughter."

An smiled, her head slightly cocked. "Your daughter's case intrigued me. And your benefactor is a philanthropist. One should consider gift horses."

George cleared his throat. "Yes, but one should also check to make sure it doesn't have a belly-full of Trojans."

An's eyebrow arched. "That would be Greeks, Mister Tallow. The Trojans were the ones who were slaughtered by the horse's contents."

She heard Elizabeth giggle, noted her feet up on the couch and her slouched position. "And put your feet on the floor, Miss Tallow. While that may be appropriate behaviour when you are alone, we are still guests in this house and you should comport yourself as a proper young lady."

Elizabeth gave her a startled look, but sat up immediately. The swiftness of this action prompted a surprised response from her mother.

Afraid she had overstepped, An turned her head in the direction she had heard Sharon's voice and attempted to soften the blow. "I also taught comportment, manners and etiquette. I understand America is a relaxed country where working man's clothes are everyday wear, but I also understand that impressions matter. I would enforce whatever behaviours you desire for relaxed, at-home situations, but I will also teach her appropriate behaviours for the company of strangers and occasions where impressions are to be made. In short, at home she can be the absolute heathen if you so desire, but in public she will know how to act the perfect lady. I have taught princesses, I understand these matters."

An could not see the expression on Sharon's face, but read much into the quiet way she whispered, "George..."

George, however, still had some issues. "I am still concerned with this mystery billionaire's motivations. I do not wish to accept a gift, however generous, if there are strings attached."

The lawyer leaned forward at this. "Mister Tallow, I understand your concern. And while I am legally forbidden to reveal his identity, I can assure you that he has only the utmost concern for your daughter's welfare, and through that, your family. I will not pretend to know his mind as to why he wishes to do this. You know these eccentric billionaires," she chuckled. "But I can say that he clings to the concepts of hospitality and honour and the onus of those better off to those less fortunate. Perhaps he sees some potential in her. I cannot begin to know. But I can assure you, sir, that what this is is a gift. And gifts, by the codes he follows, come without strings. You have not asked for this. He owes you nothing and you owe him nothing. There is no expectation beyond your daughter's welfare. And yes, you still have a say in that welfare and raising," she added, cutting off any protests in that vein.

"I am given to understand that there is a college fund set up in Elizabeth's name?" George said.

"Yes, sir. All you have to do is sign the contracts I have with me accepting Miss O'Keefe into your home and employ, and the stipend and college fund will be set up and handed over. The college fund cannot be touched accept by Elizabeth at twenty-four if she chooses not to go to college, or before that by the school of her choice. The stipend is set up to offset Miss O'Keefe's upkeep, and her personal salary will be drawn through my office."

Sharon piped up, her mind now on business matters. "One of my bosses once had an Au Pair, and I am aware there are certain things we are required to do for her, or allow her to accomplish?"

"Yes. Not all of that is applicable in this case. Miss O'Keefe is slightly older than most who apply, and she will not be attending school while here. Her visas and documents are all in order and she is in the processes of applying for dual citizenship. Everything will be handled by my office, as will any problems if you feel you have any. All she requires is a private room and instructions as to how you wish your house to be run and your daughter to be taught. She will feel out the rest on her own. Give her a tour of the house and try not to rearrange things too often or without showing her after and," she added, turning to Elizabeth, "don't leave things lying around that she cannot see and could trip over. Once she knows where everything is, she should be pretty self-sufficient.

"If we are agreed, then?"

There was a sigh and a whispered conversation of half sentences and then a silent acquiescence. Miss Jones then opened her briefcase and began pulling out papers to be signed.

Sharon stood, began collecting the tea things. "When will she be moving in?"

"As soon as is convenient to all parties," the lawyer assured her.

"We'll perhaps have to switch the rooms around, George," she began. "So Miss O'Keefe can have a downstairs room?"

"Where does Elizabeth sleep?" An asked politely.

"Upstairs," Sharon replied.

"Then an upstairs room will be fine, Mrs Tallow. I am not physically incapable, I can manage stairs right fine. My current residence has an abundance of them. I only need room for the basics, and I would like to be as close to the young miss as possible as I will be helping her with homework and other matters." An stood. "I hope you will not think that I am trying to take your place, Mrs Tallow. You are and always will be her mother, and I will encourage her to confide in you as always or more than she has been. I hope you will consider me a member of the family, albeit a lesser one, of course."

Sharon blustered at that, "Oh nonsense. I'm sure everything will come out for the best. George, that small room in the attic we were going to make into an office..."

"You mean the one that has just ended up as a storage locker?" he scoffed. "We can reconvert the study next to Elizabeth's room. It'll take longer but an attic room..."

"A garret room?" An interrupted. "I am certain it will be more than sufficient. I am not used to large rooms and have only modest needs. No need to turn the house upside down on my behalf."

George didn't seem to know what to make of this, but relented. "I'll get it cleaned out this weekend and we can have it ready for you by Monday. ...If you're sure."

"Positive. Is it so cluttered at the moment that I could not get a feel of it? I will need to know what furnishings to bring with me, what will fit."

Elizabeth jumped up. "I'll show her, Mom." She stepped up and stopped in front of An. "Ummm, how do I do this?"

An smiled, taking a more tap appropriate grip on Cipín, "Ye take my hand and set it on yer shoulder. I will walk beside or behind ye depending on which shoulder ye place me on."

Elizabeth eyed her suspiciously. "Your accent changed."

"Aye. It did. And it will. And if ye pay attention, ye'll learn what it means when it does."

They stared at each other for almost a minute before Elizabeth nodded and said, "Ok," in a tone that said 'challenge accepted', and then proceeded to lead her through the living room and up the stairs.

On the second floor, Elizabeth led her around the small balcony railing off to the left. "My room is right here across from the stairs," she said, letting An trail her fingers across the door and the wall. "Next to it is my 'study', as Mom likes to call it. It was too small to be much of a bedroom, though it used to be my nursery, so Mom just turned it into a craft/study/library room. That's where my computer and books and stuff are. Bathroom's next. It's pretty big. And this door is yours."

She let An feel the narrow frame and turn the crystal knob herself. It felt like a closet door. She swung Cipín out in front of her gently until she tapped the bottom step, discovering a narrow flight of stairs going up. She allowed Elizabeth to lead the way to the small door at the top and followed her in.

"There's a lot of stuff in the way, so be careful, but I think you can walk the parameter. Dad's got filing cabinets on the left wall and some boxes on the back by the closet."

"That's perimeter, and well ye know it, lass," An said, less sharply that she might have.

Elizabeth fixed her with an intent stare, waited until the woman edged away from the door and began to feel the walls and the slanted ceiling that she could sense was near on the right side. Then she closed the door behind her and locked it, leaning against it. An turned to face her, unconcerned.

"Spill it, Mary Poppins."

"Excuse me?" she asked, the stiff British pronunciation creeping back into her voice.

The girl sighed, rolled her head and her eyes. "Look, forget the manners and the blind act, lady. I know you can see. Why you're playing at this, I haven't figured out yet. Why you're here at all, I haven't grokked yet either but..."

An set Cipín in front of her and set both hands on her knobbed handle and fixed Elizabeth with an intimidating stare. "If we are going to make this work, you are going to need to know the rules, young lady. The first one is: you cannot lie to me, so don't try. The second is: be polite. All rude will get you is a cold eye and no answers. And trust me, Elizabeth, I am your key to *many* answers."

When the girl stood up straighter and looked intrigued rather than sullen, An took a less imperious stance and softened. "First, I assure you, as far as your parents are concerned, and this house is concerned, I *am* blind. Oh, I can see your pert little self all well and fine, but of your parents and this room I see nothing. The reason for that is why I am here.

"You are magic. I can see magic. I can teach you when to use your magic, grant you access to someone who can teach you to wield your magic, and protect you from those things you keep seeing outside yer window every night tryin' to eat yer magic or to just steal ye away so they can use ye. That answer any o' yer questions?"

Elizabeth didn't answer at first, just studied the governess for a long minute. "So... if it's magic you can see it?"

"Aye."

"And you're magic too," she said, her eyes narrowed slightly, daring her to deny it.

An tipped her head minutely in reply. "Aye, after my fashion."

"And you can really do all those things that lawyer lady told my parents you can?"

"That and more."

"Did you really teach princesses?"

An smiled. "One. And two princes. ...'Twas my occupation for th' last century and a half or so."

Finally, something that caught her off guard. "Century..."

"Aye."

It was the firmness of the way she said it that made the girl believe her more than anything. "What kind of kids stay kids for a century?" she gaped.

"Elven ones." She allowed the fact to register before she continued. "Now, I'm going to need some idea what this room will hold, so I will know what furnishings to acquire before we are missed. Which your mother will no doubt begin to do shortly."

She started to turn to approach the wall when she caught a glint in the girl's eye. As she turned to examine that look more closely, her eyes went wide as the whole of the room, stacks of boxes and open filing cabinets and all, shimmered into view. Elizabeth's voice was soft, "Can you see it now?"

"Aye." An got her astonishment under quick control, ran small mental calculations in the back of her mind. "How big is that closet?"

Elizabeth shrugged. "Not too big. It has a shelf and a bar to hang clothes from, if I remember right. Not much wider than the door though."

"I don't need much," she replied, turning back to the girl. "Does doing this tax you?"

"Doing this much does, a little," she shrugged again. "I can do bits and pieces all day though."

"Don't do that," An corrected. "It's bad posture and speaks ill of you. It says that you are lazy and indolent."

"What does?" she frowned.

"Shrugging." She gave the room one last glance. "You can let it go now. Thank you. And we shall keep our natures secret from your parents, shan't we? They will not understand, or all this would not be necessary. Now," she said, turning back and stepping up to the girl, "do you agree to my terms? You will not attempt to lie to me. You will keep no secrets from me. You will tell me when you fear and what, what you feel or sense. Ask me whatever question you desire so long as you use discretion in what you ask where, and accept my answers even if they do not satisfy you?"

She eyed her warily. "What if I don't understand the answer?"

"That would require other questions. But if I tell you I cannot tell you a thing, you must accept it."

"Can I ask why you can't tell me?" she asked cannily.

An smiled, pleased. "Yes. You may not always like the answer."

Elizabeth held out her hand. "Then I'll trust. So long as you trust me."

An accepted the hand in a firm grip. "I promise you, I will always have your best interests at heart in everything that I do concerning you."

Elizabeth felt a ripple through the room at those words, felt the need to say something else. "I... I promise to... trust you ...even if I don't always obey you."

A single eyebrow lifted. "Fair enough."

With that, their contact was broken and whatever had filtered through them and the room faded. Elizabeth turned and opened the door, led the way down the stairs. Halfway to the second floor she stopped, though she didn't look back at the governess. "You go English when you're teaching."

Behind her, An smiled again, thinking to herself, *'Oh, yes. This one will do very well.'*

12

Elizabeth sat on the bed watching An take her clothing out of a small trunk, and feel her way to putting certain items in the short dresser and hanging others. She watched her place each item meticulously, organising everything by feel. Finally she spoke up. "How do you know what's what, what matches? You have some stuff that won't go together. Or are they all magicked?"

An smiled, brought her a blouse and held it out to her. "Feel it, just there, under th' cuff."

Elizabeth obeyed, frowned. "There's bumps. Doesn't that irritate you?"

"'Tis braille. Shannon was thoughtful enough to translate short descriptions of the clothes and embroider them in discreet places, so all I have t' do is check the cuff and read. Though some things I can identify without that, it helps. And no, it doesn't. None of my cuffs are tight enough for that to be an issue. Now, if ye want t' be of service, ye kin unpack that trunk of books onto m'shelf."

The girl got up and opened the trunk in question, groaned when she saw what was in there. "Encyclopaedias!" She hefted the first one out and frowned at the thickness and strangeness of the pages. She opened the book and laughed at the blank pages and the small bumps that covered them. "These are for you!"

"Aye. I don't know everything. I shall need to learn as you do in some cases. I'm here to help with your schoolwork, not teach ye. I'm t' help with th' other things."

"Like the night-thieves."

She looked over her shoulder at the golden waves bent over her chest, pulling out books. "Night-thieves?"

"Aye," she said, falling into An's speech pattern easily. "The ones who come at night trying to get in to take me or something from me. One got in once." She did not look up, but her voice was small and sombre as she shelved the heavy set of books. "Really long, gaunt woman, like she was made from sticks. I woke up and saw her drawing something off me. It hung in the air like... pixie dust. She was collecting it, just waving it out of the air into a bag. Then suddenly there was this dragon-like shadow man in her face and they were fighting. There was another woman there, kinda crackly, who pulled something that felt like a blanket off me, and suddenly I could move again. They shoved the thief into her own bag. It was creepy. They told me not to worry too much, they were trying to keep an eye on me and not to tell Mom and Dad.

"I've seen the woman since, at odd times. And other people that look different like they do, like you do. But I can't always tell which are the goblins and which are the ones fighting them. They haven't spoken to me since."

An stepped up behind her, set a hand on her shoulder. "You don't have to worry about that ever again. I've got wards I can put up to alert me if they try to get in and I can be in your room in but a moment."

She turned, looked up at An hopefully. "But how are you going to run them off? The dragon-man had a sword."

"And I have Cipín," she said, waving her hand to the shillelagh leaning in a corner. The shillelagh bounced against the wall in answer. "Trust me, I know how to use her."

"But you won't be here every night. You said so."

An frowned lightly at the girl's stubbornness to keep from smiling. She rose, went to her night-stand and opened the drawer, pulled out an ordinary torch. She handed it to Elizabeth and then held out her hand. "Come on. Take me to your room."

Confused, Elizabeth got off the floor and led her to the door, jumping back with a squeak when Cipín leapt from the corner into An's other hand. She led her downstairs to her room and closed the door behind them. "Now what?"

"A window? One that faces th' street?"

Elizabeth led her around the few obstacles in the room to the window, kicking the odd toy out of the way. An felt in front of her, found a small night-stand and the bed to the immediate right. "Perfect. Can you see out this window?"

"Yes."

"Can you see a tall oak tree across th' street? There should be a picket fence."

"You mean next to my bus stop?" she frowned, looking.

"Perhaps I do. Now, there is a comfortable fork in that tree, I am told. On nights I am not here, if you hear anything, or are afraid, there is going to be someone hidin' in that tree, watchin' th' house, like there has been every night before now."

"I've never seen..."

"Exactly, but they've been there none-the-less. Now, if ye see sommat, or hear sommat, or I tell ye to, I want ye t' aim yer light at that fork and flash it. Yer watcher will see it and come to th' rescue. I'll only be gone one night a week for a few months until it becomes clear t' these beasties that yer well guarded. This would be so much th' easier if ye lived in th' Rest, and so much less needful, but we'll make do. In a month or so we'll arrange some special lessons of a sort and I'll introduce ye to one o' those watchers who'll start t' teach ye how t' do th' things ye can."

Elizabeth laughed. "So I get a wizard tutor until I'm old enough for Hogwarts, huh? And a faery governess on top of that. Cool."

"What is a ...Hogwart?"

Elizabeth didn't answer. She got up and went into the next room, bringing a hardback book and pressing it into An's hand. "This will explain."

An turned it over, felt the raised letters on the dust jacket and slowly deciphered them. "And what, pray tell, is this?"

"You wanted to read what I'm reading? That's the first book in the series."

"Harry Potter and th' Sorcerer's Stone?"

"Yup. I've read them all. We can probly get you a braille copy from the library. I mean, I can fix that one for you, but Mom might ask questions and it wouldn't last. So," she said, plopping down on the bed. "Where do we start?"

"Well, your manners could use some work. But other than that, I do not know. It is a little early for 'princess lessons'," she added pointedly, reading the look on the girl's face. "Besides, I still need to get a feel for this house and th' way th' family works and figure out what you actually need. That and your mother is coming upstairs, likely to call us to dinner," she added.

"How do know that?"

"Elizabeth! Miss O'Keefe?" her mother called from the top of the stairs. The creak of a floorboard told them she was headed for the garret door.

"You heard her?" Then Elizabeth grinned. "Right, the over-compensating senses! What else can you do?"

"Nothing appropriate for th' moment," she said, setting the book on the nightstand and turning toward the door.

Elizabeth frowned. "Aren't going to read it?"

"Perhaps you can read it to me later. School hasn't started for you, so there isn't much to teach. Literature is a good place to start. And of course stories, questions. I'm sure you're full of them." She opened the door and stepped into the hallway. "We're in here, Mrs Tallow." Behind her, An heard a small drawer open and the thunk of the torch going into it and the drawer sliding closed again.

The woman jumped a little, caught in the act of opening the door to the stairs. "Oh, you startled me. I thought you were still upstairs settling in and couldn't hear me. Supper's ready, Miss O'Keefe."

An gave her a nod. "I thank you, Mrs Tallow. And please, call me An. Calling me Miss O'Keefe makes me look around for a friend of mine."

There was a moment of quiet that caused An some concern. It was frustrating to not be able to read the woman's expressions. "Well, if I'm going to call you Ann, you can't call me Mrs Tallow."

"It's 'Ahn', Mom," Elizabeth piped up, slipping past the governess to the bathroom to wash her hands.

An gave her a shallow bow of acquiescence. "Sharon then."

Sharon began to move past her, back to the stairs. "I hope you like spaghetti."

"Can't say as I've ever had it."

Elizabeth poked her head out of the bathroom door. "You've never had... Oh, are you in for a treat," she grinned.

"Actually," Sharon said, a frown in her voice, "It's going to take some... tricky forking to figure out how to eat it if you've never had it." She waved it off. "Oh, we'll muddle through. You're going to help our girl with her... issues, least we can do is help you acclimate to your condition."

At this An hesitated. "Acclimate?"

"Yes. Miss Jones explained that your cataracts aren't... well... you haven't had the degree of sight loss you have for long. I hope that wasn't too intrusive?"

An softened her expression, even though she was still a little irritated. "It is water under the bridge, madam. ...Sharon," she corrected. "We will 'muddle through' as you put it."

"See you downstairs. Elizabeth, you stay up here and escort her to the table once she's washed."

"Yes, ma'am," she sighed when An gave her a glare. She followed An into the bathroom. "Water's right in front of you on the left, soap's on the right," she directed as An felt her way to the spigot. "So... why'd you get so upset? Was that lawyer lady not supposed to tell?"

An washed her hands, frowned at her reflection hovering ghostlike in front of her. "I will happily answer questions about myself or discuss what of my past I can. But I dislike being the subject of conversation."

"Oh," she said sheepishly. "Towel's to your right on the wall."

"Thank you."

Over the last few weeks, An had put up small charms and runes in discreet places around the house, some with the help of Sean whilst the family was out. In the yard, she hid several tiny garden gnome figurines and drove iron nails into the four corners of the property. Elizabeth saw her placing the last nail when she arrived home from school and asked what they were for.

"Th' gnomes were given to me by my employer. They alert me if anyone enters th' yard."

"So garden gnomes are real?" she asked, making a face.

"Oh heavens, no, child. There are garden spirits, aye, but they don't look like these silly things. These are just wooden talismans with magic on them. It alerts me to th' intent of th' people crossing their perimeter."

"Oh. And the nails?"

This she answered more forcefully, her displeasure at the need obvious. "To keep out th' Fey."

Elizabeth hitched her backpack up on her shoulder, "I thought the faeries were helpful."

An sighed, stood. "Let's go inside to have this conversation and put that heavy weight down." She led her into the empty house, going upstairs to the study. "Some are. Not all," she explained. "And they are easily offended and dangerous even when they are. At the moment, we fear that some of what are attacking you are Fey or agents of the Unseelie. You would be a... dangerous addition to their ranks."

"Unseelie?"

"The Fey are largely divided into two courts: Seelie and Unseelie. The Seelie are the light court, those who respect that human beings are people and individuals. They are often inclined to be helpful. The Unseelie are more... darkly inclined, prone to viciousness at times and more easily insulted. This does not mean an Unseelie cannot be kind or beautiful, nor the Seelie always so."

"Ah. How can you tell the difference? Between Seelie and Unseelie?"

An did not answer immediately, but found her way to the rocking chair in the corner, and settled herself with her crochet first. "Before I start regaling ye with cautionary tales o' th' Gentry, ye need t' set yer things down and change yer clothes. Yer mother also asked me to have ye turn on th' oven for her. She said 350° and t' set a timer fer forty-five minutes. We're t' turn it off when th' bell rings."

Elizabeth obediently went into her room and changed into shorts and a t-shirt, then rushed downstairs to turn on the oven and back again. An glanced up at her attire from her crochet and frowned. "I never shall get used to th' clothes these days. Scandalous."

Elizabeth grinned. "I half expect to see you in skirts to the floor."

An twitched the edge of her shin-length skirts dis-approvingly. "Yes, well, it has been pointed out t' me that it would call attention to my age. It has taken some gettin' used to. In my day I'd have been branded a harlot fer showing off my ankles like this."

"And the sheer blouse wouldn't?" she asked with her head cocked.

"While unorthodox, it is acceptable, due to th' heat and th' fact that my vest covers everything I need covered. But now is not the time fer history lessons, though one day I might tell ye what I remember."

Elizabeth settled in as An began to tell her the tale of Tam Lin, a Fey knight rescued by a mortal woman who loved him. She followed it with several others, some short, some long, about mortal dalliances and run-ins with various types of Fey, illustrating the dangers and the benefits. "The true Fey do not like to be called 'faeries'," she said. "They are the Good Folk, or the Gentry, if they are noble. They accept that they are fey, but grow angry to be called Fey. Pixies, what you think of as faeries, don't mind it so much, but one should be careful in any case."

She paused long enough for Elizabeth to go turn off the oven when the timer went off and did not finish telling tales until the lace glove she was crocheting was complete and Elizabeth's mother had arrived home from work.

Elizabeth did not say anything about the gnomes, and her mother apparently didn't notice them.

After supper, Elizabeth started on her homework while An sat in the rocking chair with a braille copy of her school book, trying to decipher what exactly it was they were trying to teach the girl. Finally, she gave up and decided to find out the subjects of each chapter and go to the library to try and look up other books on the subjects that were more straight-forward.

When she tucked Elizabeth in for the night, she paused at the window, taking note of a man walking his dog down the opposite pavement. She started to move away and then stopped, frowning.

"It's the man with the Rottweiler, isn't it?" came Elizabeth's voice from the pillow, muffled by the covers.

"I don't know what a Rottweiler is, but there is a man with a dog, aye." She did not take her eyes from the pair as they walked by, both of them glancing up at the house at the same time as they walked out of sight. "How do you know about them?"

"Well... I didn't, ...until you could see them. I wasn't sure. I saw them when I went to school this morning, and across from the field at P.E. I couldn't study them without being noticed, so..." she shrugged. "Are they goblins?"

An shook her head, closed the curtains carefully and took the torch from the nightstand, tucking it into the bed with the child. "No, likely though they are agents. People like me, not all of whom are good, like any person. And ye've no more worries about goblins, *a'chuisle*. I've told ye, they can't cross now."

"But... won't that keep you from crossing? Doing what it is you do?"

An brushed a strand of hair from the frightened girl's face. "I'm not magic in that way. It won't stop me any more than 'twill stop that man who may be fey magic, but is very much not Fey. But they can't find th' nails to remove them and they can't find all th' gnomes, so even if they try, something will go off. One of th' reasons fer so many. Besides, th' nails only keep th' Fey from crossin' th' boundary. It doesn't squelch th' magic or I'd be no good to ye, considerin' fey magic is how I see them. Now sleep."

To silence any further resistance, she sat on the edge of the bed and softly sang a song called 'Red is the Rose'. Elizabeth thought it sad but lovely and fell asleep before she was done.

An slipped quietly out of the room and closed the door, locking it the way that Sean had shown her. A week back, An had slipped a slim golden thread woven with a strand of hair from Elizabeth, her mother and father and herself around the doorknob. Now, once she activated it as she had been shown, only the four of them could open that door from either side. If her mother checked on her, she would never even notice the door had been locked.

An drifted downstairs long enough to pop her head into the living room, to inform the girl's parents she was asleep and bid them a good night and then felt her way back to her own room. She locked her door and went to her nightstand, from which she drew a cell phone. She had been taught how to operate the thing by feel, but she had quickly discovered it was not necessary. Things just liked her, in general. Once she had got used to the idea of the gadget and had it for a little while, she found it eager to please her in any way it could. She opened it, cradled it in her hand and asked it to dial the manor. Eventually, someone picked up. She recognised the voice and smiled.

"Evenin', Shannon. 'Tis An. I need a word wit' th' chief if he's available."

"He's at th' pub t'night. Gimme a mo' an' I'll ring down there, have him call ye."

"Thank ye, Shannon. Oh, and Shannon..."

"Aye?"

"I miss Martha's corned beef."

The woman laughed. "She trying t' make ye 'feel at home'?"

An smiled painfully. "'Tis the thought."

"Come by after mass on Sunday next. I'll have her make it special."

"Now don't be goin' out o' yer way fer me."

"Pish posh, child. I'll have someone fetch ye Sunday. 'Night." Without leaving her time to protest, Shannon hung up.

An sat on the edge of her bed, running her thumb across a groove on the head of Cipín, waiting. After a few minutes, the phone in her hand rang. She answered it quickly, hating the sound it made. It immediately offered to change the ringtone to something more pleasing.

"Miss Ceobhrán," she answered automatically, thinking 'later' to the phone. In the background, she could hear the noise of the pub getting a little dimmer, the sound of billiard balls cracking against one another and then everything but Ian's voice getting muffled.

He chuckled at her response. "Yer a Miss O'Keefe now, lass."

"That is yer daughter, Uncail."

She could hear him sobering at the word uncle. "Fair enough. There are a lot o' yeh. Now, yeh never call, 'Niece',," he said pointedly, responding in kind, "so there is sommat afoot. Am I wrong?"

She leaned back against the wall that served her for a headboard, shifting to Irish. "*Ye would be correct, sir. I'm not sure, but there's been a man with a cú hound following her, today at the least. She saw him at th' bus stop and outside th' school and I saw him t'night across th' street. 'Tis possible him or one o' his saw me bury th' nails.*"

"*They'll compensate then. Yer mighty casual about this, so there's a little time, aye?*"

She laid Cipín on the bed beside her, wanting her close. "*They may not even try t'night, but I want t' be prepared. I may need th' back up.*"

"*Remind me t' put Roulet's number in yer phone and show yeh how th' speed dial works. If it's ever a 'they're here now' situation, I want her called first. Dial it an' drop th' phone. She's learned this nifty little trick of telegraphin' herself through th' line. She'll get there afore anyone. How long yeh think yeh have?*"

"*Maybe an hour or two. The Tallows are still up and watchin' the television. They'll be in bed by quarter after, maybe asleep by eleven. Don't think they'll try anything 'til they're sure the house is asleep.*"

"*Unless they don't care and plan on killin' or takin' th' parents too. If they're trollers, they'll sell th' parents at th' markets and call it a bonus. Yeh think they're Touched?*"

She sighed. "*I didn't study th' man long enough, but that dog o' his is. Not sure if he can cross th' line, though. May have too much in him.*"

There was a pause on his end as someone came in and he issued an order. An figured he was in the snug. "*All right, I'll have a roundup, call Sean and send a few over. Yeh won't see them, hopefully, until something happens. When yeh think they're abed, yeh remember that mark Sean made on their bedroom doorframe?*"

"*Aye.*"

"*Well, do to it what yeh do with yer yarn. Should activate it and keep 'em asleep. We could have a full donnybrook next to th' bed and they'll not wake 'til cock's crow.*"

"*Hopefully it won't come t' that, sir. And it might not be bad idea t' sneak a cock inta th' neighbourhood, speakin' of such things.*"

"*Might not at that.*"

188

Skye was at the bar with Danny, looking at new drawings for the long hall being built for him when Seamus, one of the numerous O'Keefe cousins, slipped up behind him and tapped him on the shoulder. He tilted his head to the wiry man, listened as he said only, "Chief. Sidebar."

He nodded, confused, but turned to Danny, "Sorry, lad. Duty callin'. Looks good so far, though ah'd like somethin' over here t' keep real weapons handy, an armoury as it were, in addition t' th' trainin' pieces."

"I'll sees what I kin do. Go. Uncle don' call sidebahs unless somethin's up."

"What exactly is a sidebar?" he paused to ask, then drained the last of his pint.

Danny laughed. "It's a lawr tehm. But when he uses it, he means the side of the bah, that room ahff the game room?"

He set his glass down a little harder than he intended and nodded his thanks to the bartender. "The snug?" he asked.

When Danny nodded, rolling up the plans, all Skye replied was "Ah," and followed Seamus, Mikey and a couple of the mortal bully boys he didn't know by name into the room where Ian sat waiting.

He was hanging up the phone as they entered. "All right.... Close th' door, Peter. Yeh know better." The young man sheepishly closed it behind him.

"An called. There's a man she can see and a fey hound watching th' house and th' girl. They haven't tried anything yet, but she expects tonight or th' next few days for something to happen. She's asked for backup. I'm sendin' you lot to meet with Sean near th' house. Mikey, set up corner watches with Sean's help so yer not seen until yer needed. Nccd I remind yeh, this is a clandestine job. Watch, take it out if it tries sommat stupid and get out. Meet up at Courtz when 'tis over. I'll meet ye there."

"Why Courtz?" Peter asked. "Why not back here?"

"Cause Courtz is closer, ye shite," Seamus growled, smacking him on the back of the head.

"And there's healers there, if any o' yeh blockheads need it," Ian growled. "If nothin' happens by four, call me and I'll send a relief team and we'll set up watches fer th' next few."

"Yes, sir!" Mikey said, and began to usher them out.

As Mikey led the way, Skye asked, "What is Courtz?"

"A nightclub in the city. Liberty and Roulet own it."

An sat in the rocking chair in the study with the door open and the lights out. Her crochet was in her hands as she listened intently to the activity in the room below her. She was already working on the thumb of the glove she was making, when she felt the last buzz of electricity go out downstairs, felt more than heard the Tallows settling into bed. She waited another five minutes before setting the piece aside and rising. She flowed down the stairs like mist in the dark, barely aware of the tendrils trailing behind her on the steps, as she found her way to the parents' bedroom. She ran her fingers along the outer edges of the door-frame, stopping about head height when she felt the minute ridge of the carved rune.

She had been nervous and felt over cautious when she had let Sean into the house the week before to carve these runes, and to place the other precautions around the house. She felt a surge of pride that her charge had already found everything that was active. She rubbed the rune, infusing it with a touch of her own magic, much as she glamoured her threads and writing supplies that she might see them. The door flared to life in a flash of light, something Sean had not warned her about, and faded to a silent, but felt pulse. The faint snoring from within deepened immediately, and An was satisfied they would not awaken until she released it.

She drifted across the room to the back door and let herself out, locking the door behind her with an antique skeleton key which she then slipped into her pocket. Had she been able to see the lock itself, she would never have thought the key would fit it. She held Cipín firmly and confidently in hand as she crossed to a shadowed corner of the manicured yard, where an ancient wisteria tree hung over the privacy fence from the neighbours, and simply waited.

She did not have to wait long. She saw the man and his hound appear on the pavement from beyond the tall hedges that framed the neighbours' yards. They seemed to be out for a stroll, except for the way they turned as one to look up at the now darkened house. She wondered how many times they had passed this way. The 'dog' turned off from his straight arrow path and began to wander into the edges of the yard, sniffing purposefully. The moment it tried to cross the boundary An had set four inches in from the edges of the walk, it yelped and jumped back. Its handler abandoned whatever pretence it had of innocence, glanced around and then let go of the hound's lead, stepping over the iron-bound threshold without a wince.

She let him come halfway up the walk, gazing at the parents' windows, then up at Elizabeth's while the hound stood watch. The man stopped and snapped his fingers, and in an instant four other beings puffed into existence in various locations outside of the yard. Two were across the street and one on the neighbour's roof. The fourth An heard in the yard behind her, the soft 'pff' barely audible on the other side of the high fence.

In that instant, one of the goblinoid creatures crossing the street suddenly turned to fight off something An could not see. Then everything happened at once. She saw a flash of bright movement from the tree across the street, the one she had told Elizabeth to signal in case of trouble, and then the dark, spindle-limbed woman on the roof began to slide out of control towards the rosebushes. She shrieked as she clawed for purchase on the tarred shingles, pulling a few down with her. Mikey was there to meet her, tearing into her with his sword.

The scuffle in the street continued unabated, even though the hound ran to help, attacking a second unseen individual.

Skye charged out from the side yard and attacked the man with the leash. It was all he could do not to come at him screaming like the highlander he was and allowed the claymore in his hand to do it for him. The leader managed to avoid the first strike, to close with him to make the enormous sword less effective. Skye merely let the sword go and wrapped his arms around him, pounding him with his fists.

The other one from across the street was a swampy thing, with seaweed hair and the fetid, damp smell of the bog about it, vaguely man-shaped. It surged across the lawn, barrelling into Skye and his opponent, throwing the Scot off balance and giving his friend a chance to put a little wary distance between them. It continued past them, lurching for the side of the house as Mikey blocked the front door, dragging the spidery woman by her hair.

While the man with the leash was staggering back, pulling something from his coat, Skye did not think. He caught his balance by turning, carrying the motion around into a massive swing in the midst of which the sword re-materialised into his hand, slicing the man from armpit to ear. He did not stop to make sure he was finished, but turned to run after the swamp-creature. As he rounded the house, he saw An step forward from the shadows, say something in challenge to the thing trying to get in the back door. Skye rushed forward, swinging his sword where the thing had been, and saw it rush the governess. She never flinched. She merely said something he could not hear clearly and, gripping the shillelagh midway down the shaft, swung and stove the creature's head in.

An watched as its deflected momentum sent it into a heap next to her. She looked up, saw Skye standing there twenty feet away, staring, shocked. She felt and heard the whirl of colder air above and behind her on the fence. She did not turn. "As you can see, the child is well guarded," she said, her voice intimidating with its calm, low tones that showed no trace of fear and suggested a great deal of hidden power. "Whatever you bring, I will bring more. I live here now. Your chance is gone. Leave now and live. Stay..." to finish her sentence, she merely held Cipín's bloody head up and out to the side of her, showing the thing on the fence what it would face.

Skye swallowed as the being which had been little more than a swirl of air and smoke vanished with a muffled hiss. He felt the surging of power that told him where and how the smokeling had gone. He looked down at the dead swampling at An's feet. He let his sword go.

"Remind me niver ta get on yer bad side," he said flatly, brows raised.

Mikey strode around back, saw the body and Skye and chuckled, "Not bad, Skye. Hey, Ian's been called and sending clean up. Sean's going to wait here for them. We've got to get Peter and Harry down to the club, get them patched up. That hound did a number on Pete's leg."

An stepped around the body with distaste. "Thank th' lads for me, Mikey. They did a fair swift job." She gave him a nod of thanks and started to go towards the house.

"Why don't ye come down to the club with us?" Mikey offered.

Skye immediately thought that was a bad idea and tried to communicate this to Mikey without An being aware of it.

She gave him a tight smile. "Thank ye, but no," she demurred. "I've m' duties here to attend to. Out o' th' woods we may be, but there still be trees about."

Mikey held out his hand as she moved towards the back steps. "Ian is there and will want to speak with you."

She paused, looked over at him. "That is a different matter. Ye should have told me th' chief wanted a word. Lead th' way."

Skye, full of apprehension in the matter, fell into step behind her as she followed Mikey around the front of the house. His sword was already at his back again, but he was in no way relaxed yet.

She paused at Sean. "Ye'll see to it she's guarded tonight?"

Sean set a reassuring hand on her shoulder and smiled. "A cricket would be hard pressed to enter that house. I'll stay here until you get back, never fear."

She nodded in acceptance and followed Mikey to the side of the vehicle, which she heard pull up to the curb. She could not see either of the men she could hear in the back, but she could smell the coppery taint of blood in the air. Skye helped her into the front passenger seat, pausing to fasten the seatbelt for her before he climbed into the back with the boys and closed the door.

Mikey drove around to the back of the nightclub, pulling into the service alley up to the delivery bay where three bouncer-type gentlemen stood waiting to help bring in the wounded. Skye let two of them form a chair from their arms and carry Peter inside, while he turned to help An out of the van and guided her up steps he was not sure she could see.

He himself had not been to Courtz yet, wasn't sure at all if it was the right kind of environment for the governess, but kept his mouth shut and his hand firmly on her arm, making sure she didn't trip over anything.

They entered through the storeroom, adjacent to the kitchen where an energetic and loud little man in a tall chef's toque and jacket shouted orders and insults in an obnoxiously bad French accent. The man, as An caught a glimpse of him in passing, was the very caricature of the 'French Chef', but, angry as he seemed, she saw a hint of joy in his work as he managed several pans at once. Then they were turning up a back staircase to a set of upstairs rooms.

There was an entire suite of apartments up here, including a private lounge complete with comfortable chairs, a pair of couches, and the requisite coffee table. There was a door on the far side of the lounge through which, when it opened, came the sound of dance music and a lot of people having a good time. Liberty closed the door immediately behind her, muffling the noise, and crossed to the couch that had been thoughtfully covered with a plastic sheet before they laid Peter down on it. She immediately went to work.

Skye set An down in one of the chairs, out of the way, and watched the queen work in silence. She was in a spangled green top that fell off one shoulder and black capris, but she looked every inch a queen in spite of it all. Even the strappy heels did not detract from her grace and nobility. The crown did not manifest itself fully as she exerted her magic, but the room filled with the fragrance of flowers and spring. He watched in fascination as tiny, transparent vines came from her hands and began to 'sew up' the huge gashes in Peter's leg.

The door opened again and Roulet entered, Ian right behind her with a bottle of Jameson in his hand. Ian went to a cupboard and opened it, taking down a pair of high-ball glasses and filled them halfway with the potent liquor. He handed the first immediately to Peter, who drank gratefully, and the second to Harry, who took a sip then pressed the cool glass to his left eye.

"Pack a punch?" Ian asked him.

Harry gave a rueful laugh, taking the ice pack Roulet handed him and pressing it to his eye so he could drink the whiskey. "A wee. That hound was a bit of a corker, though. Trouble was when he took pore Petey here for a chewtoy." He grimaced down at his cousin and gave a little laugh. "At least ye don't squeak like one."

Peter threw him a glare that said if his glass weren't full, he'd like to throw it at his cousin's head. Instead, he drank more and sighed as the pain began to subside under Liberty's careful ministrations. He grinned besottedly up at Liberty as she leaned over him, checking for other wounds, and found nothing more egregious than a bruised cheek and a torn rotator cuff. "Yer a right angel, ye know that, love?"

She growled with a smile. "Peter McCullum O'Keefe, don't make me slap ye."

The lad grinned, a wild glint in his brown eye. "Promise?"

Beside her, An felt Skye stiffen, then force himself to calm. Her hand went up, gently touching his arm. He looked down at her in surprise, saw the soft understanding smile and was more able to control himself because of the interruption. He thought to himself, and not for the first time, that there were layers to this woman. Though he was still not sure how he felt about her.

He stopped to think about that. When he had seen the swampling headed for her, he felt panic and rage all at once, certain she was going to be cut down. It was not just the feeling he got when he was set to guard someone. He had felt that particular brand of panic before, and this was different. He had to admit that he actually cared for her, though in what way he had not yet sussed out.

Ian interrupted his contemplation as Mikey arrived and the two called him over to give the report.

"There were five of them," Mikey began.

"Six," Skye corrected.

Mikey turned. "We only killed five," he exclaimed. "We need t' warn Sean!" He started to reach for his phone when Skye's hand went out, shaking his head. But it was An's voice which stopped him.

"The last will not be back. 'Tis better this way, that one escaped to report. They're not so likely to try again." She did not get up until she saw Ian's hand gesture her over. She rose, stumbling over the coffee table before she could get Cipín around to clear the path. She came to stand with the men.

"What was it?" Ian asked.

"A smokeling," An answered. "It never entered th' fray, but stayed back t' watch. I think it might have tried to slip into th' house if it had not seen what it had. I gave it a warning. I think we will see less of this now."

"What th' hell happened?" Ian growled. "From th' top."

Mikey began. "We waited in hiding as you told us to. The man with the hound came up to the house, letting his beast approach the yard as if to do his business, only it jumped back from the iron border. The man then walked up towards the house and summoned back-up. That was when we attacked. There was a spider woman on the next roof over who jumped to the Tallow's roof. Sean made her fall, I believe, and I took care of her. Harry pounced a hob in the street and Peter dealt with the hound when it turned to help the hob. Don't know why the hob thought it was going to cross where the hound had failed, but..." he chuckled.

"It was an actual hob?" Ian asked, eyes narrowed slightly.

Mikey nodded, "Full bore hobgoblin." He paused to recount the events, thinking out loud. "Let's see, there was the witch on the roof, the hob and hound in the street. Skye handled the handler. That'll be a bit messier a cleanup, but Sean's got it. There was the thing An mentioned which only these two saw... oh, there was the swampling. It came from across the street, knocked over Skye and the handler, and charged around the house. Skye finished off the handler and went after it. He got it before it got to the door. Man, did that thing stink!"

Skye shook his head. "Ah dinna get th' swamplin'," he grinned, feeling pride swelling in his breast.

Mikey frowned. "But you were the only one back there." Something clicked and his eyes flicked to An standing demurely between Skye and Ian. "You?" he said in delighted surprise, pointing at her. He laughed. "Well, damn it all, lass! That's right craic!" He turned to Ian as the chief cocked an eyebrow. "The colleen's got an arm on her! Had to have. She cut the thing's head in half like a melon."

Ian smiled wryly as he glanced down at the now blushing governess.

Skye chuckled. "Ah thought it was gonna git inta th' hoose at farst. Then, as ah came 'round th' hedge it turned fer her an' ah thought she was gonna be swamped. She dinna flinch as it charged 'er, took one swing an' it jist crumpled. Made its heid an innie insteid o' an outie!" The men laughed at his description. An blushed more furiously and looked elsewhere. "Then th' smoke-thing was up top o' th' fence and she warned it doon. Made m' glad she weren' threatenin' me. She's right deadly wi' yon twig."

An had had enough. "It wasna expectin' resistance. If it had, I'd a ha' more a fight on me hands, and may not o' landed so strong a blow."

"Ye taunted it, lass," Skye growled, feeling so much pride in her he refused to let her make light of it. "Ah heard ye say sommat to it afore it turned. It woulda passed ye by."

"An' let it get inta th' house?" she snapped sharply. "Not bloody likely." She coloured darkly at that, embarrassed by her slip of language. Ian's chuckle did not help.

"But ye still called it on yerself when it coulda ended bad," Skye insisted.

"Aye. To protect a child. I got lucky. Th' last time I drew off an enemy, I lost my eyes. This time I was armed an' wit' some skill and not alone. I knew someone would be along. 'Twere nothin'. The next time it might be m' life. But I'll do it again in a heartbeat fer that child," she growled and went back to her seat, this time avoiding the table.

The men watched her go. Mikey frowned. "I'm confused. What was she arguin' about?"

"It was a hell of a hit," Skye agreed.

Ian watched An for a moment before answering in a low voice. "She's embarrassed, gents. Not used t' praise, that one. Yeh've made her uncomfortable with it. And I dare say she's confused, hersel'. Like as not her Victorian modesty won't let her brag. She's a conflict o' th' old ways an' what th' bloody English Queen did t' civilization," he almost growled the last. He looked over at his daughter. "That lot ambulatory?"

"Aye, Da. An' a more incorrigible cuss I haven't dealt with 'ceptin' Henry," she called.

"Fine, then we're all goin' downstairs fer a tot. Yeh too, An, lass. Yeh kin have tea an' yeh prefer."

Put that way, An could not very well refuse and allowed Roulet to take her arm and guide her down the stairs beyond the door and into the noise of the club.

The sound was maddening. The front stairs came down between the door to the kitchens and the hallway to the bathrooms and faced the end of the bar. The ghostly girl that An remembered from the wake was behind the long mahogany counter, mixing drinks with flair and expertise and a fair amount of speed. The rest of the bar was wide and open and filled with a seething mass of humanity from the sound and smell. There were glimpses she could catch of people she could see, but she could tell they were surrounded by mortals.

As she set her feet off the last step and moved out of the protection of the stairwell walls, she was assaulted by the sounds from the speakers off to the right past the bathroom hall. She flinched, and Roulet took a firmer hold of her arm.

"It's all right, dear," she soothed. "There's a stage there, and we're right by the speakers at the moment. They're pretty big. We've got a dance floor in front of it. We do karaoke Friday nights." She read her expression of confusion easily and explained. "That's where the audience gets to go on stage and sing to their favourite songs. It's a Japanese thing that's really taken off. Brings in good business. You want to sit at a table or at the bar?"

An raised her voice to be heard over the cheers of people on the dance floor applauding the mortal who had been singing something loud and rough and bouncy. "I'd best stay with th' others. 'Tis why I'm here after all."

Roulet nodded and brought her to them, helping her to the barstool. She leaned over the bar and grinned at the ghost girl. "Tori, my angel, would you get us a pot of tea?"

Tori set down the whiskeys and the pint of Guinness in front of the others and began wiping down the bar in front of them. She looked An over. "You want 'tea' or just a 'cuppa'?"

An was surprised at the response and thought about it a second. "Well, I could use a bit of a pick me up. It was an... exerting night. I'd not mind a biscuit with m' tea."

"Sugar? Milk? And are scones ok?"

An smiled, relieved. "One lump, no milk, and a scone would be perfection."

Tori grinned and disappeared for a moment, leaving the bar in the hands of someone else from the sound of things. She turned to Roulet and, quietly as she could, asked, "Why is it I kin see her?"

Roulet laughed. "Oh, she's... touched. Just not like you or I. She wasn't taken or anything. She's not like Elizabeth or Sean at all, but she has the Sight at the very least."

An relaxed a little, setting Cipín in front of her, leaning against her knees. "That explains why I can only see her a little. I seem to remember knowin' women like her."

The music had paused to change and suddenly a familiar voice began to fill the room with a softer, more lyrical melody, singing about pain without love. An felt her heart skip, a knot in her chest and her breath caught in her throat as she slowly turned to face the stage. Jonny stood there, in white pants and shirtless save for the patchwork denim vest he almost always wore. He poured his pain and tortured soul into the microphone cupped in his hands, eyes closed until he stepped back for the opening bridge. He returned to the mike, to all but moan the first verse, eyes still closed until the refrain which got harsher to An's ears. His voice, growling the chorus, remained beautiful, perhaps for all the pain in it. At the vocal bridge his eyes opened, casting over the audience, singing to the foot of the stage and the people that seethed there. When the chorus softened, his eyes caught hers and suddenly they were the only people in the room and he was singing to her soul.

Then the song was done, and the microphone stood alone on the empty stage.

She forced herself to turn away, thanking Tori for the tea she had just placed in front of her. An slid her hands cautiously over the bar, letting the heat of the cup guide her to it, discovering its placement and orientation. There was a triangular confection on the side of the saucer covered in a coarse grain sugar. Whatever it was, it was not the scone she was expecting, but she picked it up, taking a small bite of the corner as she tried to get herself back under control. The flavour of oranges and cranberries melted into her mouth with the thick, buttery shortbread. She sighed happily, her heartache momentarily shocked into silence. They reminded her more of rock cakes, though they were decidedly sweeter. Thankfully, the orange and cranberries provided a nice counter to the sugar.

Beside her, Roulet laughed. "Heaven, aren't they?" An nodded. "You're lucky. Lafayette doesn't make them often."

Tori set a second plate down in front of Roulet. "And that's the last of them," she grinned. "Don't say I don't love you, boss."

Roulet laughed, chattering some French endearments to the girl before she moved away.

Beside her, An could hear Skye going on to Peter and the others, regaling them with the tale of her staving in a swampling's head with one blow. To her chagrin, he made just as big a deal of her cool, unflappable demeanour throughout. She hesitated to tell him that that unemotional exterior he was so proud of was a façade designed to help her cope, that she had been absolutely terrified.

Again the music distracted her, as someone began singing a song about a lion man whose melody deeply appealed to her even though it was the 'lion man' that caught her attention. It called her to mind of the prince, though the rest of the lyrics did not apply at all. Then it was suddenly much cooler around her and she stiffened. She did not turn, but sat sipping her tea. The cold spot stopped instead of passing by and Tori placed a bottle of something brown and bitter in the space between An and Harry.

"Ev'nin', Mister Sorrow," she said with cool politeness even before his hand reached over to take the bottle.

"Ye stab me through th' heart, Ceobhránach. Sudden so cold?"

His voice sent a chill of a different sort up her spine, placed a quiver in her belly. She turned, fighting to keep herself under control. "I've no reason t' be warm, sir." She met his eyes more to prove to herself that she could than anything else.

He reached out, brushing aside a lock of hair that had slipped her knot. "Tell me it's th' harrowing night I'm hearin' ye had. Though from all accounts ye showed herself not to be trifled with."

"If that is what ye wish to hear," she evaded. "T'night was no fomoire. No makar. T'night was easy."

He gave an almost imperceptible, acquiescent tip of his head at that. "Still, first true combat. Not everyone takes it so well."

She nodded. "True. I ran from th' last one, for all th' good it did me." She stopped, took a deep breath. "That's not right. I mean... it did *me* no good, but th' sacrifice was worth it. Their lives for my eyes."

His voice and expression were softer as his fingers stroked her cheek, tender as a snowflake. "Aye. Their lives are better for not spending them in Her care. But you.... How are *you* faring?"

An reluctantly turned from his touch back to her tea, making room for him at the bar should he desire. "Well. I have a situation now and purpose, so I am content again. Thank ye so kind fer askin'."

If her sudden formality disturbed him, he did not show it. He merely turned sideways and rest his elbow on the bar and drank his beer, listening to the young man on the stage hamming it up to a rendition of 'Mister Cellophane'.

"Mabon is next week," he offered finally, watching her take the last bite of her 'scone'. "Will ye be takin' time off t' come?"

"'Tis ritual, is it not? Will I be needed in any official capacity?"

Roulet watched the exchange painfully, drinking the multicoloured concoction Tori had made for her. She kept her mouth shut.

"Not that I'm aware. 'Tis mostly a harvest festival. There'll be minor games, like horseshoes and lawn bowlin'. Like as not th' lads'll get up some races, a ball game or two. Nothin' formal like Lughnasadh. There'll be music and dancin', o'course."

"Ye'll be singin' then," she said politely.

He nodded, peering at her from beneath a fall of his snow white hair, "Some. I'd be delighted if I can convince ye t' sing with me fer one or two."

She did not look up at him. "I'll have t' see."

Roulet decided to add her two cents, not liking what she was seeing. "There'll be a bonfire. Always is. And a straw man. Liberty and Henry will have formal things to do, but no one else, I think. Everyone else's job is to enjoy."

"'Ceptin' the cooks," An added pointedly. "I'll have t' see," she repeated. She drank the last of her tea and set her cup down, reaching under the bar for Cipín. "Well, I best be gettin' home. 'Tis late and I can't leave th' Tallows in an enchanted sleep. Mister Tallow has to go in t' work tomorrow, Saturday or no. And I promised Elizabeth we'd go t' th' park." She got off the stool and pressed her cheek to Roulet. "Evenin', luv," she said softly. She nodded formally to Jonny. "Mister Sorrow."

She crossed behind the others at the bar, pausing to place her hand on Ian's back for his attention. "Evenin', Uncle. I'm headin' home. Thank ye fer th' assistance and th' company."

He narrowed his eyes as he studied her. They flicked over Sorrow, then back to her. "Ye've marked th' Tallow's as home?" he asked.

"Aye, sir. Th' Rest is still marked as well. Cipín is bein' very accomodatin' on th' matter, thank ye."

"Yeh'll be out to th' house for Mabon, aye?"

She took a deep breath. She had seriously considered skipping it, but couldn't now. "Most likely, Uncle." It was taking some getting used to, calling him Uncle instead of Chief, but it was wiser in mundane company. "Keep well."

"Very well, then. Yeh should come out t' th' Hedge Gate once in a while. More comfortable surroundin's. This place has got to be a shock."

"I'll consider it," she smiled politely, bent to press her cheek to Liberty.

"Come by anytime, luv," Liberty told her softly. "You're on th' house."

"An' ye wish," An sighed and proceeded to tap her way towards what she hoped was the exit, following the unconscious signals from Cipín.

Liberty flicked a signal to a waiter to escort her to the door, and he went without a word. He offered his arm to the blind woman with a polite but warm, "If you will allow me?" and a "This way, miss."

Ian growled low to Harry. "Follow her. She's a bad street to cross. Don't let her know you're there unless yeh have ta."

"Aye, chief."

Skye was tempted to take Harry's place and follow her himself, but Ian was probably right to send the mortal. Skye would be seen for certain. He sipped his pint and stared into the mirror over the bar, watching the tail end of An's skirt disappear into the other room which led to the outside.

Her attitude tonight puzzled him. She had a triumph and yet was very angry about the praise and celebration. She was a conundrum. And then her sudden coldness and exit. He looked over at Roulet through the looking glass and saw Sorrow watching An's retreat as well, with that confounded, pretty frown of his and his fist tightened on the glass in his hand. He watched Roulet lean over into Jonny's ear, and whisper something, and the look on the man's face changed to understanding, then anger, then self-recrimination. The man tossed a bill on the bar and was gone without a sound. Skye turned to Ian, not sure how much of his irritation was jealousy.

"Chief," he said, keeping his voice down. "Are we allowed to just... disappear like that? In front of *them*?" he asked, indicating the host of mortals around them.

Ian chuckled. "We have no laws other than 'don't be foolish' and 'don't endanger th' rest of us'. Depends on how yeh do it. Vanishing in a crowd is perfectly fine. And in this dim light, who knows what they saw?" he shrugged, popping a pretzel bite into his mouth.

Skye turned to stare at the door and found himself face to face with Liberty, her eyes flashing. "Dance with me?" she asked, then grabbed his hand and pulled him out onto the floor.

An followed the instincts Cipín fed into her, keeping to the pavement and avoiding the scattered people walking along it this evening. It felt busier to her than it should have been for the hour. She came to the corner and felt the drop of the curb, paused to listen for traffic. She had been warned that the motor cars of the day were far more dangerous than the horse-drawn carriages of hers.

The street was silent. She stepped down to the asphalt and had begun to cross when a cold hand seized her and pulled her back. There was a rush of air past her as a car came around the corner at unreasonable speeds, too fast for her to have heard it, or moved if she had. She found herself breathless in Jonny's arms, overwhelmed by the smell of him, clinging to keep from falling in the street. He smelled of a winter morning, crisp, clean, and full of the promise of the coming day.

He loosened his hold on her, looked down to meet her eyes. Reluctantly, she looked up at him through hair that had escaped her knot in the bustle. "*All right?*" he asked softly in Gaelic.

Breathless, she nodded. "*Th...thank ye.*"

"*Ye need a guide dog,*" he smiled.

She shuddered. "*Not... not fond of dogs just at the moment.*"

"*Th' Wild Hunt,*" he nodded, understanding. "Am I permitted t' walk ye home?" he asked, shifting to English.

Angry as she was at him and herself over him, she did not allow it to override her reason. "It would seem t' be th' wisest course."

He set her hand in the crook of his arm, the perfect gentleman. She reached out and took up Cipín where the shillelagh had remained standing beside her. Even when An had let go of her, Cipín had refused to fall over. Using her more as a walking stick than a tap stick, she allowed Jonny to help her across the street and into the wooded neighbourhood sprawl beyond.

"Tis only a couple blocks," she said, by way of idle conversation. "On Tallyrand."

"We'll find it," he assured her.

It was nice, walking with him, even in silence. It was more than that he made the warm night bearable, but she couldn't put her finger on what it was, beyond just feeling... right. There was nothing she wanted more in the world at that moment than to keep walking into the night with him. But that would not have been proper, nor was it very likely to happen. "You needn't take me all th' way if ye'd rather go back to th' club. Cipín will get me there from here."

"Like Cipín got you across th' street back there?" he asked quietly.

His voice was like a caress. She sighed. "There are no other dangerous streets to cross now. No noises to drown out the sounds of engines."

"Still," he said, keeping a firm hold of her arm, "there are other dangers, and there is no point in tempting fate. Unless you object to my presence for some reason?"

She heard the question beneath the question. It took her another forty yards to respond. "It depends on th' purpose of yer presence. I enjoy yer company, but I'll not stand in another woman's way when... she was there first and I've not.... I'm just not."

He stopped walking. She turned to look at him. There was pain in his eyes. "There is no 'other woman' and there are many 'women'. I've told ye my history."

"Aye, what ye remember, if that is even yours," she said pointedly.

He gave a choked laugh. "I'm not even sure from day to day who *I* am." She started to pull away, to continue walking, but he held onto her hand. "Serephina is not... 'my woman' as ye mean it. We are old acquaintances who sometimes..."

"Take comfort from one another?" she offered, not sure why she was helping him.

"And torture each other in th' same breath. I can't... resist her. I don't want to explain. Not now. Not here."

"Another time, then."

He tried to draw her closer, but when she resisted, he let her. "Just don't gi'me th' cold shoulder 'cause of her," he said softly. It did not sound like the plea it was. He let her begin walking again, slower now, still with her hand on his arm.

"From what I've been given to understand 'tis not somethin' any man can help," she said, more sharply than she intended.

They walked in silence until they stopped at the foot of the Tallows' walk. Jonny knew it was the right house by the young wizard sitting in the shadows beside the rosebushes, watching them. He took her hand in his as he lifted it off his arm.

"Come to Mabon. We'll talk there. I'll answer... what I can."

She sighed, knowing she would regret this, "Fine. And great is th' fool I am fer it."

He bent over her fingers, his cool lips barely brushing the knuckles above her neatly trimmed nails. "Until then, Ceobhránach." He released her, remained standing at the end of the walk, watching as she turned and went up to the house with a stately grace, sparing a thankful nod to Sean.

She took the skeleton key from her pocket and turned it in the lock. The door sprang open in her hand. Once it closed on her, Jonny looked up at the dark upper windows, saw the figure of a little blonde girl watching him from behind her curtain. He smiled, shifted into a white raven and flew away.

13

An dreaded the following weekend. Apparently Ian had manipulated things yet again, ensuring she would be able to come. Sharon had somehow 'won' a weekend getaway for a family of three to Orlando. To be polite, George said he would try to find a way to bring An, but she had smiled and thanked him, and declined. "I'll be fine, Mister Tallow, truly. I have friends I've been meanin' t' spend more time with and this is th' perfect opportunity."

"If you're sure. It's no hardship to make arrangements."

She had been firm, but polite, and had locked up the house, magical and mundane, the moment they were gone, going to the curb to meet the car that pulled up for her. Someone held open the door for her and guided her into the back, taking her small overnight case and putting it in the trunk. She sat in silence, dreading the odd vertigo she always felt in these contraptions. She knew she was moving and could feel something like movement, but at the same time she couldn't and she did not like it at all.

She had brought her book with her to distract her from the light-headedness and now pulled it from the small bag at her side and opened it. She had written in it this week, the first time in a while, and what she had written bothered her a more than a little. It was not one of the poems she dreaded, the ones that heralded bad things, but it was disturbing to her none-the-less. She ran her hand over the page, making the words spring to life before her eyes and reread them again, trying to assure herself that it was not the maudlin, angsty, badly written poetry of the lovesick.

> Caught in the breath of winter
> I sit in the rose bower
> Surrounded by thorns
> Waiting for the roses to bloom
>
> I sit and wait
> My heart full of thorns
> My fate hanging on an unkind word
> Fragile, my butterfly heart
> Waits ill-patient for spring and the coming change
> Still wind
> No word spoken, I die unchanged
>
> Unloved, I die forgotten

The second mention of thorns bothered her, but she could not think of something to replace it with. She knew for certain then that this was not one of *those* poems. *Those* poems always hit the page the way they were meant to be.

She felt the vehicle slowing and looked up, saw the wall that surrounded the Rest by the wards and other enchantments that made most folk pay it no mind. In no time at all they were pulling up to the front of the manor and Cipín led her over to the spot she had marked months ago. She stood there, looking up at the house she could sense by its shadow, and sighed. There was something about this place that made her feel stable, something the world outside the wall lacked.

The driver handed her bag to Kellain, who trotted out to meet them. Kellain was overjoyed to see An. "I'll put this in your room," she crowed, running back inside as Shannon came out and glared at her. Shannon took An's hand and led her more slowly into the house.

"Welcome home, dear," she smiled, patting the top of An's hand. "Everything is th' way it were when ye left us."

An took a deep breath as she entered the cool interior of the front room. The fragrance of roses and lilies welcomed her, along with the hint of magnolia from the solar to her right. Even Shannon smelled as she always did, of furniture polish and lemons and sachets. There was comfort here. "Thank ye, Shannon. Yer a dear."

The older woman chuckled. "Oh, 'tis not but my duty. Not often I get them come back."

This reminded An. "How is your 'frog prince' doing?"

"Fairly useful. His manners are much better and he's a great help around the house. He can get to places I can't without a ladder. He's looking more normal, though. I don't know what it is about the change. Some, like poor Danny, never go back to being human enough to walk among men. Some alter by fits and starts. Some, like th' O'Keefe, can change back and forth and in-between at will. Not sure yet which he'll be."

An's laugh came easy, and she began to wonder why she had been so against coming. "You'll sort him out if anyone can."

The woman's thanks was translated through the squeeze of her hand, but she said nothing of it. "Most everyone is out back. And some are right eager to see ye."

Any further questions were forestalled by An stepping out the back door onto the great veranda. There were things she could see out here. She walked forward, unaware of when Shannon had let her go, and slipped quietly back inside. There were banners draped and streamers wrapped around nearly everything in a riot of reds and golds and ambers. Banners and streamers that she could see wrapped around things she could not. She laughed with joy and crossed to the rail, easily avoiding the rows of chairs and rockers which were each marked with a glamoured ribbon.

There had been some changes to the fields since she had been gone.

She could tell the places where the bonfires normally stood by the motions of the few Taken piling the wood. Beyond that, in a place that was nearly the centre of everything without getting in the way of the battlefield, was a permanent bandstand, draped in gold fanned banners.

Raven came up to her while she was standing there taking it all in. "It was Roulet's idea."

She looked over, feeling relaxed and the beginning of herself for the first time in over a century. "What were?"

"The streamers. They had some left over from various parties at Courtz. But they were all different colours and none of them enough to do much anything with, so Liberty decided to glamour them to the colour we wanted. Voila! You can see them. Then Roulet got the idea to wrap them around everything so you could see what's where. Sweet, huh?"

An wasn't sure quite what that was supposed to mean, but she smiled. "It is very effective and quite lovely, thank you."

"Listen," she began. Something in her child-like voice told An the subject was not one she was comfortable with. "I've heard... a rumour you can talk to things." She said it all in a rush, like one long word in an attempt to get it out before her courage failed her.

"Been talkin' ta Danny, I see," she answered, her smile softening. "Aye, I do."

"I have this ring... it was a gift and... I'm worried what it can do. That it could be... telling on me?" she said, unsure, once more child-like.

"The one on your right hand?" she asked. It was the one she had noticed the day she met the girl. A shy nod was her answer. "And how did ye come by it?"

She examined it without touching it, eyeing it warily.

Raven's voice was soft, almost not heard. "The Red Queen. Put it on my hand herself. Said it was our promise and... I worry..."

An set her hand on the girl's shoulder. "I'll talk to it."

"There she is!" Roulet exclaimed and ran over from around the side of the house. Solitaire was on her heels. "An! Welcome back. You're needed in the queen's private chambers," she crowed, taking the steps two at a time.

"Excuse us, Raven," Solitaire said. "Though I think you can come, too. She wants all the women."

"Well," Roulet corrected. "Most of the reliable ones. You specifically," she said, pointing at An. She and her sister each took an arm and began to pull her back into the house.

Raven laughed and followed, having some idea what was going on.

"Can I at least ask why? I was told I'd have no official duties t'day," An protested, though she was laughing.

"Can't say," said Roulet.

"Not here," chirped her twin.

"Too much testosterone."

"Too much what?" An asked, beginning to feel like a badminton bird looking from one sister to the other.

"Men," Raven supplied.

"Oh."

In short order, An found herself in a room full of women, most of whom were mortal. Liberty was presiding over them with Gabby at her side. Liberty lit up when she saw the quartet enter. "At last. Now we can start. All right, Gilly, give An yer chair an' ye please. It's easier for her t' get to. Don't want her tripping over the lot of ye tryin' to find one."

With only a little grumbling, Gilly stood, taking An's hand and guiding her into the chair in her place.

"Now, with that settled," Liberty began with glee. "Roulet, the door?"

Roulet grinned evilly, going to the door and laying her hands on it. Suddenly, the entire room, wall to wall, surged with electricity. There was a yelp from the next room and several of the women giggled. Roulet smiled, leaning back against the door and maintaining a lower level of the current to discourage further eavesdropping.

"All right. Yule is not that far off. Most o' ye know th' tradition. We hold a Winter Masque every year and it's going to take us this long t' manage th' costumes. This year we're goin' in with a plan." Liberty stepped back and let Gabby take over.

"Every year for the last twelve, our Holly King has gone rutting among the ladies tryin' t' root out his queen. He's got to find her afore the Oak King does, or he'll be at the disadvantage come the battle. That's tradition. If he succeeds, we get a longer winter. If he fails, spring comes early, or so they say. And let me tell ye from experience, that's the way it's always gone. Well, this year the horny bastard has been braggin' and layin' bets as t' how long it'll take him. An' he's bettin' short. Claims he has a way o' findin' the real queen and I suspect he thinks the crown will give her away."

"How are we to circumvent that?" someone asked. "Not to mention that it's not that hard to tell which of us are Touched and which not."

Liberty grinned like a Cheshire. "I've paid a visit to th' witch. She was more than happy to help." She glared at someone on the floor, "And no, she didn't charge me m' firstborn," she snapped. "Superstitious shite," she added in a mumble. A glint appeared in her eye. "She just wanted a few... special thin's. Now, she's goin' t' give me a box o' charms, which we need to work into our masks or costumes. It doesn't have t' be seen, but it does have t' be there. They'll go active at noon on Yule and will last until midnight. What they'll do is give all of us th' same glimmer o' glamour." This brought a spate of laughter. "It will make us all equally magical in seeming. Even An wouldn't be able t' tell us apart. Mine will suppress th' crown."

"But if they see our costumes before then, they'll know who's who," one woman complained.

"That's why we're going to work on them in secret," Roulet grinned. "We have a place set up where only we can go and we can work on the masks and costumes and not even your husbands will know who you are."

The conversation devolved at that point into plans of who was going to be what, when they were going to get the materials, and when each of them could come over to work on costumes. An began to tune them out. She was thinking, her mind turning over in veins she was hard-pressed to stop. She was finally rescued when Raven touched her arm. "Aye, dear?" she asked.

"The ring?"

An glanced around the room, then at the ring. "This is hardly the place for that. Perhaps we should go to my chamber?"

She rose and followed the excited raven girl from the room, stepping carefully in her wake to avoid people. Because some had stood and were moving around, it was less successful than usual. They were finally clear of the room and headed down the hall when she realised she did not know what room she had been put in.

Bethany's voice came from the stairs.

"There you are! Danny! I found her!"

Raven sighed, realising it wasn't happening now either.

"Bethany?" An asked. "What...?"

She didn't have time to finish her question before the girl was on her and drawing her towards the stairs. Her excitement was infectious even though it made An suspicious. She turned to Raven as she reached the stairs. "I'll take care of it, I promise." She turned to Bethany, "Can't this wait?"

"Nah, it cahn'," Danny injected, coming up to the other side of her and gingerly taking her arm.

Between the two of them, she had no choice. They carried on a conversation over her head. "Should we drive or wahk?" Danny asked.

"It's not far, and like as not, she'll be walking back and forth, so... let's take her the route she'll take to get there," Bethany answered.

In spite of her protests, neither one of them would explain as they took her out the back door and across the lawn towards the rath. It wasn't until they were on the path through the woods and past the faery fort that An stopped, forcing them to tell her, or she wouldn't take another step.

Danny sighed. "Skye's long house is done. He wants ya to see it."

There was a prickling within that told her, while the words were not a lie, they were not the answer to her question. She gave him 'The Look', the one that had quailed elven princes. He swallowed and opened his mouth.

Bethany warned him before he said anything. "Don't even try to lie to her." He shut his mouth. "Please, Miss An. It's a surprise for you and if we tell you, it will spoil it. It's not much farther, I promise."

An felt nothing. She could tell they were both very pleased with whatever surprise they had for her and keen to show her. She relented. "Very well. But I do not wish to miss the festivities."

"Oh, you won't," Beth assured her. She took An's arm and the three of them proceeded down the wide path through the wood.

They had only gone another hundred or so yards when the wood opened up. Not far from where they walked, An could see a door standing in the middle of nothing. She frowned, tilting her head. "Why is there a magical door in the middle of ..." She stopped realising that the building it was attached to was of course mundane.

"That's the doah ta Skye's long house," Danny said, veering her off from it slightly. "I'll explain why ya can see it in a bit. You'll be able to see somma the inside 'cause I had to do some special things in theah. The buildin' itself was easy and went up quick. Had an old-fashioned bahn-raisin' foah it," he chuckled. "The inside was the tricky paht that only I could do," he said as they walked. An could feel the presence of the tall long house on the one side and another house on the other. "It did not, howeveh, take any time outta my pet project," he grinned. "I'm almost sad to see it done," he added with a sigh.

Then Bethany let go of her arm and set it on her back instead, giving her a light push forward, while she and Danny stood back and watched her.

An started to turn to ask what was going on when she saw the edge of a stone wall around the corner of whatever building they were beside. She closed her mouth and kept walking, her curiosity peaked. The short wall continued to a small gate which she stopped before, drawn to it like she had been drawn to few things in her life. Cipín, resting lightly in her hand, told her, *Here*, with no question of what she meant. An's hand rose and came down with a sharp 'tak' on the ground by the gate, marking the location. Tears of wonder and joy filled her eyes.

Rising beyond the small gate, at the end of a little garden path, was a small stone cottage built in the style of Irish houses that was old when she was young. The whole building screamed 'Home' to her. There were vines climbing up the side of the wall that did not look like ivy, and the front yard, though small, had empty beds set by waiting for whatever she would choose to plant come spring.

"Go ahn in. It'll never be locked to ya," Danny encouraged from behind her.

She set her hand on the gate and felt it want to open to her. She heard her boot heels click softly on the paving stones that glittered in the sunlight. It crossed her mind that they would glow under the moon. The door was thick oak, oiled and polished to bring out the character of the wood while protecting it from the elements. It was bound in scrolled brass. She reached up to touch the shining metal, felt the warmth of the sun on it.

"Sorry about the brass," Danny said. "T'ahn woulda been a bad idear all thin's consideahed. Ya'll have ta be careful of the shillelagh. In any case, ya won't need it inside. I set up a stand foah it to keep the tap off the floah."

Almost without thinking about it, she slid the shillelagh further up in her grip, holding it at the halfway point. She reached for the latch and the door opened under her hand. The smell inside was inviting, new, and magical. She stepped inside and Cipín pulled her hand out towards a corner where a small stand waited. The moment the tip touched the bottom, the stand vanished from An's sight, but nothing else happened. The knob rested against the corner and became still.

An turned her attention to the rest of the house. Next to the stand was a bench-styled coat rack, the likes of which she had only seen in the lord's house when she had gone with her father to pay the rent. There was a bench with a chest under the seat for one's boots and shoes. There was a mirror set between two rows of pegs for coats, cloaks, and hats and a shelf for gloves and other small things.

The room itself was not large by modern standards, but enormous to her for the needs of one person. It was only a little smaller than her bedroom at the manor had been. There was a fireplace, and a stuffed chair in the style she found so comfortable. There was a small table at the right height to the chair for tea or books, with a place underneath for her crochet and lace-work. There was a single window overlooking the front garden with a nice view of the gate with dainty eyelet linen curtains.

The small kitchen was not completely separate from the main room, with its own window over the small porcelain sink. There was a stove of a kind she was unfamiliar with, which Danny took a moment to explain. As well as a refrigerator, which he didn't have to.

There was a small table in the kitchen, just large enough for two people with a single chair, and there was a door next to the cupboards by the sink. She made the mistake of glancing out the window over the basin and was surprised to be able to see more outside. She went to open the door and was startled again to note that the door was in two halves. Before she could actually open it, Danny called her away.

"Come see this fahst. The gahden last," he suggested.

She looked at him, saw that glimmer in his eye that she knew was why Ian had refused to tell him the house wasn't needed. She nodded and came to him, was pleased to note that although there was only the one window in the front room and the kitchen window, the chamber was fairly bright and airy. She suddenly knew that if she wanted it darker, it would be. She smiled. She should not have been surprised. The house was a magical thing. Of course it would talk to her like everything else. She also knew without being told that subtle changes would occur according to her needs, more easily if she was in direct contact with things in the house. She took the hint that bare feet were preferred.

Danny was holding open a second door near the fireplace. An drifted past him into the small bedroom. This room was filled with light. The walls were painted a pale, silvery white with just the hint of blue to it. There was a tall brass bed under the window which was set high enough that she would have to sit up to see out properly, but would afford her a nice view of the night sky if she wanted when she lay down. The bed was dressed in white eyelet and crisp, soft linens over a deep, feather mattress. The night table had a single lamp and a book on it, with a small drawer for necessaries.

There was a modest dressing table in a nearly white wood that proclaimed itself made of Holly. It had an oval mirror, a matching chair, and a wardrobe beside it. There was a fireplace, smaller than the one it backed, but more than adequate to keep her warm if it ever turned cold, something she was seriously beginning to doubt would ever happen. There was a single door in the room other than the bedroom door which opened into a small water closet with a dainty sink and appropriate facilities.

Danny grimaced as she looked in, apologised profusely. "I tried ta put in a bath or a showah, but ...the house wouldn' lemme," he pouted.

She smiled, her hand on the door-frame as she closed the door again. "It will provide when I want one."

He brightened. "Really? I was hopin' that wer the case, but.... I wish I could talk to things like ya do."

She shrugged. "There might be a way. What one Gentry grants as a gift, I am sure could be acquired by another somehow."

"I'll ask the witch," he said, nodding. "She'll know. Maybe I'll find it at the Goblin Mahket. It'd be easier ta get ta nearer Samhain."

An frowned. "Beware the Goblin Markets."

He waved off her concern. "Oh, I know. I goes theah often enough. I'm getting bettah. The witch might get a bettah deal though," he mused. Suddenly he looked up. "Oh, theah's one thin' I fa'got!" He took her hand and pulled her back through to the front room.

Bethany was poking through the pantry, taking note of what would be needed, and was surprised to find nearly everything one could want. She looked up as Danny dragged An to the fourth door in the room, the one opposite the fireplace, next to the coat rack.

Danny presented the door as if it were his grandest achievement. An looked at it, found it rather nondescript. She looked back at him, watched him deflate. He waved his hand at it. "Touch it, ask it what it does."

An raised her hand, caressing the polished wood. Immediately she saw what she had to do to whatever door she desired. Once done, from then on, but only when she willed it, that door would open to this door, much like the door between the warehouse and the one under Ian's stair. She smiled. "Thank you," she said, both to Danny and to the house. Now she had a reason to keep the house, and it would not sit abandoned for too long. She had the feeling it wouldn't like being left alone. "I will just have to figure out how to get the alarms to alert me here."

"I'm shoah theah's a way," Danny said dismissively. "Wouldya like ta see the gahden now?"

She turned to the now open door, felt almost drawn to it. The back was decidedly bigger than the front. The wall ran all the way to the bottom of the garden, which was fairly deep and sloped gently down to a stream that ran under the walls with a pretty little footbridge. There was a small orchard of about eight trees, a pair of apples, pears, peaches, a walnut and a pecan. There were some late blooming roses along one part of the wall, a profusion of reds and pinks. One smaller, more straggly bush caught her eye, a little further down the wall from the others. Its blooms were a deep yellow, though they looked wilted and drooped.

Danny followed her eye. "I took the libehty of havin' some o' this cultivated for ya, to get ya stahted. Litehally Libehty. She's the reason ya can seer it all. That one oveah theah," he said, seeing where her attention was. "It ...kinda tuhned up. Libehty hasn' been able ta do anythin' wit' it. Thought ya might like ta try ya hand. Ya got places fer a vegetable patch if ya like and ready spots along th' walls foah those berries ya mentioned. Jus' lemme know whateveah ya want ta get. I kin manage just about anythin'."

Bethany interrupted him. "Liberty might be the better choice for getting seeds and seedlings. She is the one with the green thumb after all."

Danny nodded. "Right, right." He pulled out his watch, flipped it open and consulted it. He snapped it closed and back into his pocket in one smooth motion. "Well, we're just right out ta time. Gotta get back. Cah's waitin'."

Danny led them around the house along the side yard and An was pleased to note that the wall was only a little higher than a yard and made with good stone, only trimmed as necessary. It did not take long to walk through the lush grass to the front walk, where An paused to look back at the house.

She smiled, feeling the welcome in her bones. The house closed itself up, and the gate opened for her. Cipín stood waiting for her against the outside of the wall. She took her up and followed Danny to what she could tell was a waiting car. Before she got inside, she bent and gave Danny a kiss on the cheek. "Thank you," she said. "Deeply, I thank you."

He blushed into the collar of his shirt, pleased as punch.

When An returned to the manor, the festivities were just getting under way. There were only a few others coming in still, carrying their potlucks. Kegs were being broached, and the tables were laden with food. The band was tuning up and people were beginning to laugh and mingle. Liberty and the twins met her at the porch, grinning. "Like it?" Liberty asked.

An beamed. "I love it."

"Danny tell ye yer right next door t' me?"

An glanced over at Danny, who had the decency to look sheepish. "No, he didn't. I have figured out that the buildin' on the other side is

Skye's Long House."

Liberty laughed. "He's callin' it his 'Mead Hall'. Swears it still suits, even though 'tis mostly for trainin'."

Skye came up from the tables with a plate of food. "Though ah still espect ya ta make an appearance there now and again fer trainin'. Yer gonna get involved like last week, ah want ta be comfortable that wasn't a lucky crack."

She nodded, taking her usual stance with Cipín on the ground before her and both hands resting lightly on the knob. "Very well. I'm off Sundays. If nothin' else happens by Samhain, I'll have two days."

"Ah'll take 'em both."

Liberty popped his arm hard enough to make him have to scramble to keep from losing his plate. He cried out more in surprise than pain, though it hurt. He rubbed his arm with his free hand.

"Ye'll take what she gives ye, lummox. Chances are she's got things she'd rather do with her days off than take a beatin' fra you."

"Like what?"

Liberty fixed him with a withering stare. "Noneya!" she snapped. She turned sweetly to An. "Will ya mind comin' over t' my house Sunday fer lunch? We'll work out 'things' before supper."

An smiled mischievously, remembering what 'things' must be. "Aye. I see no problem with it."

Roulet and Solitaire came over and took An's arm, leading her off into the crowd, leaving Liberty to deal with Skye. Then Solitaire saw someone she wanted to talk to and wandered off in another direction without a word.

"Ingenious, with the ribbons," An said.

"Glad you like it. It looks good to normal eyes, too, so no one's complaining."

The whole event had the feel of a town fair. Children ran in and out among adults, laughing and playing their boisterous games. There were places where folk were cooking over an open fire or in covered smokers, handing out chunks and slices of various meats as they were done and ears of roasted corn hot on the cob. Corn was something An had got used to eating at the Tallow's. She wasn't used to people eating it. It was animal feed. She was pleased to discover what she had been missing out on, for the corn here was sweet and flavourful.

The ritual was short and to the point. Just before the sun began to set Henry carried a whole, freshly killed deer to the altar that had been set up and Liberty carried a basket of grain, fruits, vegetables and flowers. The holly in Henry's antlers was full of ripening berries, and Liberty's crown was full of asters and roses and other late blooming flowers. Her leaves were beginning to change colours and there were sprays of barley and wheat among them.

As night fell, the pair led a procession followed by a group carrying a straw man. Everyone else followed in their wake. Once the man was bound to the stake in the midst of the bonfire, Fox stepped forward and made a great show of breathing fire on the torch Liberty held out. Henry then took the torch and set the wood ablaze. An watched the torch come to light, gazed with fascination as the fire began to spread. She could not see what was burning, but every tongue of flame, every glowing coal was bright and alive to her eyes. She saw the straw man come to life even as he died in a blaze of red and orange.

Some people danced around the bonfire, Liberty and Henry included, at least until the straw man was gone. Even Roulet and her sister joined in, from opposite sides of the fire, but they spun and cavorted in opposite directions, linking arms and reversing when they met. It was not long before a great wheel had begun around the fire, with people joining in that had previously abstained. They danced in two rows in opposite directions, as the twins did, but linking arms with the next person coming at them, passing themselves along from one person to another. Even An let herself be pulled into it, trusting those she could not see to take her arm and pull her along when she held it out. When the straw man collapsed into the body of the fire, there was a shout and the dancers came to a halt, some of them falling in a heap, laughing and trying to overcome their dizziness.

Roulet found An again after she untangled herself from the heap she had ended up in, and took her back by the buffet tables, making sure she ate and drank something.

When An asked where her sister was, she grinned, "Trying to keep Henry from getting his antlers untangled."

"Should we... wait, *keep* him tangled?"

Roulet laughed. "Yeah, she's the one who tangled him up... in her skirts. Come on, they're starting over at the bandstand and I want to dance some more. But we need to eat a bit first."

She was a little disappointed when An got her drink from the children's selection, but she said nothing, respecting An's choice to remain dry. She guessed the blind could ill-afford the loss of equilibrium.

The band was in full swing when they came to the well-trampled green. An let herself be pulled into one of the great reels that she remembered from her youth, where the whole dance floor moved in wheels and patterns, changing partners frequently. She enjoyed herself, pleased that there was something familiar here for her.

They began the Wild Horse Stomp, and she threw herself into it. The men and women lined up in opposite lines, each taking their turns at the dance: the women prancing prettily as they turned and the men pawing the earth with their feet before they cut the steps. Then the pairs linked hands, trotting several strides, first one way and then the other, then lifting their arms high for the couple at the end of the line to run through to the head and rejoin. The dancers separated and spun in place, each line taking steps to the right, switching partners, with the luckless guy on the end, now partnerless, having to run all the way down to even out the lines and pick up a new partner. The entire dance went on in this riotous fashion until the dancers were worn out or were back to their original partners. An ended up paired with a great many mortals and more than a few Touched, including Ian and Skye at one point.

An had just run through the gauntlet with Peter, the mortal who had tangled with the cú in front of the Tallows', when the partner change left her in front of Jonny Sorrow. Her heart stopped, and it was all she could do to remember the steps expected of her. When he took her hands and they began the trot left, instead of reversing and returning to the right, he kept them going left until they were off the dancing green. He pulled her with him as he turned away from the dancing and the crowd completely, leading her away from everyone.

She didn't know why, but she let him, too startled and flustered to protest. He slowed when the noise level died down. From what she could tell, they were in a garden she had not encountered before. She could see there were decorative hedges from the strings of fey lights someone had draped them with. He brought her to a halt at a small bower with a trellis arching overhead, wrapped in Roulet's red streamers.

An looked around nervously. She could still hear people not far away, on two sides, near enough to distinguish parts of loud conversations, and she could see glimpses of some of the Touched over the hedge so she deemed herself uncompromised. He set her down on the bench and sat beside her, her hand still resting lightly on his as he leaned back against the wood of the bench.

"I'm sorry about that," he said. "We can go back if ye like... when ye've caught yer breath. But ye said we might talk."

His eyes said she hadn't resisted, though he was hoping she would not, now that she had the chance. She shifted in her seat a bit, turning a little to face him. She blushed when her knee touched his, but did not move for fear of calling attention to it. She did, however, slip her hand from his and into her lap. "Aye, I did."

He took it as encouragement and gave her a sad smile.

She just sat there and breathed for a moment. She was acutely aware of his nearness and his elven masculinity. He smelled of snow and winter air and sleeping earth. There were notes of mellow smoke and a touch of whiskey, all of it putting her at ease and on edge at the same breath for very different reasons. Eventually he rescued her.

"And how have ye found th' evenin' so far?" he asked softly, his voice like the landing of snow flakes.

"Fair. It has been... exhilarating. Oddly freeing."

One white eyebrow arched over his earth-brown eye and there was a hint of amusement about his perfect lips. It only served to make her feel more plain compared to him. "Oh? A chance to let yer hair down?" He reached out and caught a lock around his finger at her temple, delicately coiling it behind her ear and draping it down the front of her vest. "I like it down, ...but out o' yer face."

She blushed, tipping her head so that the other side fell across her cheek, obscuring one mist filled eye. "My eyes... disturb some folk."

"I find them beautiful." As if he realised it was a tender subject, he changed it, fingering the white on white embroidery at her wrist, running his finger over her pulse point as if unaware of what it would do to her. "This is beautiful. Elven work that. Cobweb silk is rare this side."

Glad of something safe to discuss, she focused on the delicate lace at the cuff. "The princess made it for me, for my hundredth year."

They were interrupted by a mortal couple running past them, giggling and excusing themselves when they found the bower occupied.

"Glad they found one another," he said softly.

"Who?" she asked, confused.

He smiled, nodded in their direction. "They've started cosying up to each other since th' wake. Mayhap they'll post their banns in Spring, parents willing."

She gave a soft chuckle. "Not much has changed from th' old country."

"Not here. Out there," he said, waving his hand towards the distant outside world, "life has certainly moved on. They do things differently and I don't completely understand it. One of th' reasons I stay here, venture out only on specific days."

"What do you do with yerself?" she asked, suddenly curious.

He shrugged. "I have my work for th' chief, for th' Rest. I am one of th' dreamwalkers. I've learned th' faery dreamin'. I also teach and entertain as I should as Bard. And when th' chief calls, I act th' scout when 'tis fitting." He paused as they could hear Solitaire and Henry chasing each other the next hedge over. He took her hand up again. "Perhaps this wasn't th' best place for this conversation?"

"More like not the best night. These events do seem to bring out the... ah..." she blushed.

He nodded. "I know what you mean." He turned to look over the hedge behind them, to determine how close they were to the rutting activity he was sure was about to commence. "Perhaps we should..."

They were interrupted again, this time by Raven, who landed in bird-form on the edge of the bower, bent to look in and then jumped to the ground, shifting back into a girl before she landed. "Hi, sorry, been looking, you said..." she gushed, pausing finally when she saw who else was there.

An sighed, knowing she would be hounded until she read the ring, held out her hand. "Give it."

Raven brightened, pulled the ring from her finger and placed it in An's bare palm.

As her fingers curled around the warm metal it grew warmer, and her mind was flooded with images so real she could feel the flames that licked up from the coals beneath her and began to melt her human body down to base metal. The pain was intense, pulsing, real enough to make her scream in a rising pitch that seemed to have no end. Her actual body writhed on the bench as the hammer came down, pounding her into the desired form. The ringing pain seemed to go on forever, blow upon blow until she was right, then she was cast into the ocean deep to cool for an eternity.

Skye was by the drink table hefting a new barrel onto the pouring stand when the scream rang out in the night. It ran through his blood like ice. It was the same voice as the fey wood, but the sound was different. The sound was agony, not terror. He dropped the keg and tore off towards the lover's maze, kilt flying. Others were running, but he passed most of them, bulling through those he could not go around quickly enough. As he ran down the hedgerow, his sword fell into his hand. He came around the corner and saw the bower: An's rigid body arching off the bench, her lungs sucking unsuccessfully for air, her fist clenched in front of her, and Jonny on his knees before her trying to pry her fist open. Raven fluttered, terrified, just back from them.

He hesitated, not sure what to do or make of the situation. Then Sorrow had the fist open and pulled a ring from it, casting it away from her, and Raven dived to pick it up. Skye let his sword go and came closer, aware that others were joining them. An was still not breathing and fighting to do so. Sorrow laid his hands on her, frost creeping up her arms and over her chest from his touch. Skye started to surge forward, but a burst of ozone near him and a hand on his arm stopped him. Jonny had a helpless look on his face as whatever he was doing did not seem to be working.

A long, hard gasp came from her as she reached out, flailing like the drowning for something to pull her out. She found Jonny's hand and seized on it, clinging desperately. For a brief moment, she smiled, and Skye noticed that she wrapped her whole hand around the ring finger of Jonny's right hand. Then just as suddenly she was sobbing in his arms, pressed to his chest, her hands clutching the ragged denim of his patchwork vest, moaning "No more, please. Not another one. Not another..."

Another minute passed, and she began to tremble, her sobs growing more quiet and eventually ending. Skye was aware of Liberty behind him, beginning to shoo people away.

An took a deep breath, opening her eyes to find herself on the grass in Jonny's arms. Skye was looming near, looking ready to draw his sword against something. He just didn't seem sure what. Liberty was just behind him, and Raven had shifted to bird and was sitting on a branch with a worried look in her black eye.

Self-conscious, An loosened her grip on Jonny's vest, smoothing it out where she had creased it, blushing at the wet spot she found. Her hands went to his muscled arms as he stood, drawing her up with him and guiding her back to the bench.

He knelt again in front of her, not letting go of her. "Are ye all right, now?" he asked softly.

She took another trembling breath before nodding.

"What did ye see? If ye can stand to tell," he added.

"I... I saw," her voice sounded hollow to her ears, as if she had been crying for hours and she felt wrung out. "I was a person. Man or woman I dinna ken but... I was melted down in a furnace, a forge I think, hammered into a ring. I was thrown into the ocean to temper, left... forever." A tiny, lost sound escaped her throat. "Then She reached in and pulled me out again. Put me on the hand of a little girl. I was her promise, she said, the bond between them. So long as the child always loved her mother, they were bound.

"Oh, god," she gasped, "Her love is so deep, so *fierce*, I... it's obsession, all-consuming. You're fine as long as there is no room in yer heart for another, though she herself loves many. Her love burns," she whispered, closing her eyes and shuddering.

"Then something happened. The... the child... she stopped loving Her. And another little girl came along and killed her, and the ring... I was put on the new little girl, and then another, and then another. I thought there would be no end."

She looked over Jonny's shoulder at Raven, her eyes burning. "Ye were the last. And so long as ye love yer mother she'll leave ye be, though she wants ye home." She shook her head, answering the question in Raven's face. "I don't know what else it does. I'll not touch it again."

Skye was afraid to ask, so whispered to Liberty, "Who's 'She'?"

"The Northerner," she said flatly.

He stiffened, clenched his fist until his joints cracked. Liberty flinched, and he stopped.

Jonny stood. "All right, I think it time t' get ye home." He helped her to her feet, then swept her up into his arms, an act which startled a squeak out of her.

From over her shoulder at the top of the trellis, they heard Raven's voice croak a quiet, "I'm sorry," before flying off.

Jonny turned to face Liberty. "Where am I takin' her, Miss O'Keefe?"

She took charge immediately. "Home. The cottage next t' my house."

He nodded. "By the training hall or th' other side?"

"In between them."

With that, Jonny turned and began walking deeper into the lover's maze. "Cipín," An protested. "I left her by the bandstand."

"Got it," came a voice she did not see, and then there came the burn of ozone.

Feeling weaker than she had after the fight with the fomoire in the gryphon King's wood, An surrendered to being carried, putting her arms around his neck to make it easier for him. She felt fevered and relished the cool touch of his neck against her forehead.

Skye watched them go, started to follow, but Liberty's arm stopped him. "Do ye want her for yerself?"

He thought about that, jaw tensing. He stared into her eyes, felt lost and unsettled. He looked after the white hair disappearing into the dark and thought about An's eyes, what he'd felt looking into them. It wasn't like this. He felt something, but not this. One of the men in the camp had commented just before the parley, that it was a shame the governess had lost her eyes, as they were the only beautiful thing about her, but he didn't see that. He saw a different beauty, something more lasting, ...and that something was not for him. He looked back down at Liberty's glittering greens, and sighed, crossing his arms. "Nae."

Her hand grew gentle on his arm. "Then let her have her chance. Who knows?"

"I'm still responsible," he insisted.

She smiled at him. "And ye live next door. We can check up on her when you take me home, just after I tell Da what happened." She gestured off after the Raven girl, "He's goin' t' need t' know about her in any case."

She slipped her hand under his arm into the crook of his elbow and made him turn back towards the manor and escort her to the main house.

Jonny carried her slight weight with ease through the wood and An allowed herself to take comfort in his strength even as she fretted over the embarrassment of the need. The wood was mostly dark, but there were dapplings of moonlight through the thinning leaves. The light breeze that sprang up as they left the shelter of the trees was deliciously cool, far more in keeping with her preference in weather. The day had been too warm for her tastes, and if the night had been as hot as the last, she wasn't sure if she could have withstood it in her current condition.

Jonny found his way down the path to the cul-de-sac. There were several plots there, some standing empty. Directly across from him was a lot with a fence around it and a large Romany wagon sitting prettily in the middle. Beside that was a modern two-story house, and the Mead Hall stood to his immediate left. He turned towards Liberty's large, two-story affair and did not need to see Roulet glittering at the gate in the little stone wall beside it to know which was the right house.

She opened the gate for them, stood there holding Cipín patiently.

"How is she?" she asked Jonny.

"Well enough t' answer fer m'self, thank ye," An snapped, though her voice sounded weak even to her.

"Sorry, love," she said, reaching out to touch her cheek tenderly. "You looked so pale in this light, I thought you were asleep."

Jonny turned in the gate and strode down the path to the door. An took note that the paving stones did indeed fair glow by moonlight. The door swung open as they approached, and An sat up a little straighter in his arms. "I'll thank ye t' let me cross my threshold on my own," she said curtly.

With a wry look in his moon-darkened eye, he nodded and set her to her feet, though he did not let her go until he was certain she was stable. She seemed to be, mounted the first step on her own, then staggered against the door frame. He grabbed her again, though this time he just let her lean on him, helped her into the house. Roulet followed them in, setting Cipín in her stand, and turned to assist.

There was a fire crackling merrily in the grate and the green damask wing-back chair placed perfectly in front of it. Jonny took her over to the chair and eased her into it. She winced as she sat, surprised at how tender she felt at the moment, as if she had truly been burnt and not just experienced the memory of it, however vivid.

Jonny hovered by the arm of the chair, reluctant to leave her.

"Can I get ye anything? Take care of anythin' for ye?" he asked in his soft voice.

"I'll... be fine. I just need a cup of tea and I'll… I'll go t' bed," she breathed.

Roulet started for the kitchen to get the tea when there was a tiny rattle of porcelain at An's elbow. All three of them looked to find a delicate cup of Irish porcelain steaming fragrantly on the tiny table. An smiled gratefully and picked it up, sipping it. It had just the right amount of honey in it. The perfect blend of bite and sweet.

"'Tis a marvellous house ye have here, Ceobhránach," he said appreciatively.

She smiled. "I've Daniel O'Keefe to thank for that. Though I'm sure I'll find there are house spirits to tend to matters in my absence. I think it'll handle any need but takin' m' boots off."

Jonny started to move to offer and stopped himself. He took her hand instead, placing a light, cool kiss across her slim fingers. "Until later, then. Our conversation can wait. Roulet, will ye stay and help her to bed?" he asked, looking up at the gypsy woman.

"I'll take care of it. No worries," she smiled.

He looked back down at An. "I'll leave ye then. Until…, Ceobhránach." He held her eyes almost longer than necessary, then turned and left the house.

Roulet approached her chair. "Can *I* get you anything?" she asked. The look in her eye and the tone of her voice told An she thought her a fool for turning the man away.

"I would appreciate help with my boots," she said first, then, as Roulet bent and began to unlace the old-fashioned, sueded leather boots, she answered her disapproval. "I am not a modern woman, Roulet. I don't fall into bed with any man who catches my interest."

Roulet slipped the first shoe off and An sighed with relief. She had not realised how uncomfortable they had got until they were off.

"From what I hear, a Celtic woman could sleep with any man she fancied, even once she married. And a man is afforded the same."

An gave a wrung out laugh. "I am a contradiction, luv. I was raised Irish Catholic in Victorian Ireland. Modesty and chastity alongside th' Celtic virtues of Loyalty, Generosity and Vengeance. Aye, I watched th' Tuatha live by th' old ways. Even their people who were not all my people, some of them embraced it. But I've never... I find it hard... ahh," she sighed as the other boot came off and Roulet began to rub her stockinged foot, "to change that. A blind eye is turned when a man strays, but women must remain chaste and true or be considered loose and of less worth."

"I can't imagine being a hundred and fifty-year-old virgin," she grimaced. "No offence."

"None taken, dear. One can't miss what one hasn't had. My job requires propriety. I'll hold to my virtue. I'm just glad th' weather's turning finally and I can wear proper shoes. I was feeling a bit th' harlot with my ankles bare to th' world."

Roulet chuckled, held up An's foot, turning it slightly one way then another. "I suppose there is something to be said for a glimpse of the forbidden. Like the song says: 'A glimpse of stocking was something shocking, now heaven knows, anything goes'."

"That's a song?" she asked over the last sip of her tea.

"Would you like me to sing it for you?"

"I think I would, but I would also like to go to bed."

"Here, I'll help with that," Roulet said, getting up. She helped An out of the chair, was not happy to find how difficult it was, how stiff An had gotten. "Are you sure you're all right? I can do some of the healing like

Liberty, just not as much."

An smiled, accepting her help towards the open bedroom door. "While I'm sure that is apt to be a shocking experience, I don't think my pains are real. I felt everything that poor soul went through before it became that ring. And b'fore you ask, no, I don't think it can be made human again. There's nothin' human left."

Roulet got An into her room and helped her into the nightgown that lay waiting on the bed. She sang the song "Anything Goes" by Cole Porter for her as she brushed out An's hair. The thick waves of amber were soft and Roulet found it a delight to play with, was almost sad to have to stop and braid it up. She pulled down the covers and helped An into the tall bed, tucking her in.

An stopped her with a hand on hers before she moved away. "I want to thank you fer everything today. Liberty, too. I owe the family so much. I... I love my house. Yer too good to me, and I'm such... such a trial."

Roulet pressed a kiss to her forehead. "Nonsense. Now go to sleep. You've earned it."

As she moved away from the bed, she paused to check the fireplace, to bank the fire and found it set for the night. She slipped out of the bedroom and softly closed the door behind her. She went to collect the teacup and the boots to put them away and found them gone. "Hmm," she said softly. "Either you've got yourself a brownie, An, love, or your house really likes you." Behind her, the fire began to slowly die down, faster than it should, and she took that as a hint to be on her way. She paused on the threshold and said to the house at large. "Remind me not to get on your bad side."

14

An felt a little better in the morning, though not completely rested. She rose and dressed, pleased to find that Shannon, or someone, had put all of the clothes she had brought with her in the wardrobe. Unbraiding and brushing out her hair, she put it up in her usual knot and headed into the kitchen. She set a kettle on the boil for tea and set about making herself porridge for breakfast. She ate in comfortable silence and set her dishes in the sink with a little water in them, intending to wash them when she got back, and headed out into the garden.

She found a small potting shed on the bedroom side of the house, and a new pair of gardening gloves. She went down to investigate the strange yellow rose that had caught her attention the day before. It looked decidedly unhealthy. She went back to the shed and looked through what was available. There was bone meal and several other types of plant feed and flower boosters. She decided to start with the bone meal and water.

She fertilised it and took a pair of pruning sheers to the dead branch tips, cutting with expert care. It was a particularly prickly rose, with a lot of little thorns all along the stems. It had several really long, wicked thorns that were a purplish-red and thicker and longer than any rose she had ever seen. She kept catching her gloves and sleeves on them. Humming softly to herself, she worked, doing what she could for it. When all that was left was to wait and see, she took off a glove and cupped one of the yellow blooms. It filled her hand as she ran her thumb over the petals. She frowned to find it limp and soft instead of the firm velvet of the other roses in the garden.

"'Tis it your location, I wonder?" she mused aloud. "Or something ye need? The other roses are thrivin' down wall. But here ye are, all by yer lone."

She felt a sudden awareness of someone else near and looked towards the house. She moved her hand from the rose and reached out to the wall, cutting herself on a thorn in the process. She gave a tiny gasp but paid it no other mind, set her hand on the stone. Suddenly, she could see Skye standing at the gate trying to figure out whether to knock on the post or to go up to the door and knock. She smiled. *Let him in,* she thought, and laughed as he jumped back when the gate opened on its own for him.

Skye cautiously crossed the threshold into the front garden, turned to watch the gate swing ominously closed behind him as he backed down the path. He turned towards the front door and saw her standing at the corner of the house watching him. It was odd seeing her look at him and standing there without her stick, like a sighted woman but for the cloud-filled eyes. There was a faint darkening under those clouds, but otherwise she looked none the worse.

"Ye... ye seem recovered," he stammered.

"Morning, Commander. What brings ye by?" she asked, drawing on her other glove and bending to a patch of ground to begin marking out new beds.

"Um... jist checkin' up on ye fra las' noight. There are others worried an'... we're neighbours after a'." He watched the concise movements she made with a small clawed tool, grabbing chunks of earth and deftly turning them. "Where'd a foin lady like yersel' learn that?"

She gave a humph as she worked. "One, I'm no Lady and never

were. My father was a laird's grounds keeper on lands our family owned
for seven hundred years b'fore th' Sasanach came," she spat. "I worked
fer my bread from th' day I was old enough t' hold a trowel. Oh, I
learned m' letters an' that's what saved me in th' end. And my Irish,
secretly, at my grandfather's knee." She sank back on her heels, wiped the
little bit of sweat from her brow with the back of her glove, and looked
over the freshly turned black earth.

She looked up at him. "I've not remembered so much at once b'fore.
Thank ye, Commander. Apparently I need t' get my Irish up to remember
where it comes from."

"No worries, lass."

"Was there sommat else I kin help ye with?"

Skye felt uncomfortable under the scrutiny. "I..." He took a breath,
stood straighter. "We need to talk, *bean an ceobhrán.*"

She set her tool down. "I have not heard that title in..." she shook
her head.

"Too long," he breathed in agreement.

She rose, pulling off her gloves. "Well, I suppose I should invite ye
in and put on tea."

He followed her into the house, watched her set her tool and gloves
on the bench by the door and slip off the simple, low brogues she had
worn outside. "Ye'll have t' pardon m' bare feet. The house is particular,
I've learned.

She got a warm, happy feeling from the polished wood beneath her
toes at the statement and smiled. She took note that there were two chairs
by the small fire now, and she gestured for Skye to take one of them. She
crossed to the kitchen to fill the kettle, only to find that her breakfast
dishes were gone. She ran her fingers along the edge of the cupboard
tenderly, thinking even as she turned the stove on, *Should I put out honey
and milk? Or is this all you?*

She got the distinct feeling that she should, though leaving a little tea
in the pot once in a while would also be welcomed. That, and she might
want to set out the honey and milk at the bottom of the garden. "I have
pixies, do I?" she mused out loud, surprised.

Skye looked up. "I'm sorry?"

"Nothing," she smiled, going to the pantry for the tea. "Just musing to myself. It seems I have pixies in the garden."

He frowned. "That a bad thing?"

She shook her head. "No. Not if I keep them happy. And that should be easy. I'll need to learn the path through the wood from the gate down garden, though. Easier than walking around the long house every time."

"Ye mean m' Mead Hall?"

She nodded, "Aye."

He waited until she brought the tea tray to the small coffee table before he attempted to make himself say what he needed to. He watched her frown at the table that she did not remember being there this morning. Then she moved on as if it were no matter at all, began to serve the tea. He smiled to see little shortbread biscuits on the tray and helped himself to one. They were as crumbly and buttery as he remembered them being.

She sat back in her chair, cup and saucer in hand, and sipped quietly, waiting for him to say what he came to. It was important to him, or he would not have used that name, so she waited him out. It was apparently a difficult thing for him to express.

After a few swallows from the delicate cup and the whole of the first biscuit, he made himself start. "Ah have concerns." He held up his hand to ward off any protest, having caught a hint of something around her eyes. "Ah ken ye think 'tis nunna mine. An' ah know ye ken how ah feel about what ah've been charged ta. We'll have ta agree ta disagree on tha' p'int."

She sipped silently, watching him. That had been more diplomatic than she had expected from him.

"But, ...Look. Ah've been gi'en charge o' folk's safety afore, an' discharged ma duties wi'out a hitch, emotionally speakin', e'en when ah had ta guard through combat. Ah had one take it inta his ba'heid to wander off an' got hi'sel' near throttled fer his trouble. An' niver did ah react in ma gut th' way ah reacted las' night t' yer scream."

She sat up a little straighter, confused. Was he declaring himself? She didn't know how she felt about that. She knew she took comfort from his presence, but... that was a different thing, wasn't it?

He thought she was looking at him, and it disturbed him just a little that he couldn't be sure or really read those cloudy orbs. "Ah give a damn what happens to ya, lass. If ah dinna, ah'd be on guard twenty-four/seven and damn yer complaints t' th' contrary. That ah've stepped back and let ye... have a life a yer own... tells me a lot aboot how ah feel. If ye kin accept ma occasional over-protectiveness..."

"Only occasional?" she asked softly.

He gave a self-depreciating laugh, "Aye, likely ah deserve tha'. But if ye kin accept it... ah'll try t' stay mostly out o' yer way."

"So, yer just wantin' t' make sure I stay safe?" He nodded, taking another biscuit. "An' so long as I accept occasional interference, ye'll not be movin' in and reorderin' m' life?"

He winced. "When ye put it like tha'..."

She set her cup aside on the table by her chair and regarded him. He now knew first-hand how she had managed three of the Gentry's children for over a century. "It will all depend on whether ye'll accept that there'll be times when I tell ye t' go boil yer head and mind yer own."

He started, biscuit in his mouth, as what she had said and how she'd said it sank in. He hurriedly swallowed, began to say one thing, then changed his mind. "Jist don' hit me wit' tha' stick. 'Tis an ugly mug ah ha' on't, but ah'm fond o' ma heid," he complained, rubbing it.

She laughed. "Very well. I shan't hit ye in th' head."

That didn't bode well, but as she reached under the table to pull out her lace-work, he decided to let it go. He watched her hook flying through the thread with fascination a moment before he remembered there was a reason he had brought up the subject. "As ah said earlier, ah have some concerns. The house is fine, an' ah'm glad 'tis tween Liberty an' m'sel'. Roulet and her sister are across th' way. But th' Bard worries me. He has a reputation ye see..."

He couldn't tell if her eyes were on her crochet or on him. "That, Commander, is one of those 'times'," she warned.

He bristled. "At least hear me oot, woman!" He set the cup down lest he break it. "Ye'll make yer own mind on't but ah'll be damn an' ye don' know what ye risk." She continued to crochet, saying nothing, and he went on, "Ah know how ye treasure yer virtue an' integrity. He's well-known fer beddin' lasses aroon' here. Breakin' hearts as he clings t' none o'em long. They say he walked away fra' his own betrothed fer that

Northern Bi..." He bit off the word that came to his mouth, conscious of the governess's sensibilities. "Fer Her. Says sommat that he left e'en th' Red Queen. Ah jist don' want t' see ye hurt. Or yer reputation tarnished by yer association."

"S' don't go off alone wi' him or entertain him alone here. I understand. I have some sense, Commander. We weren't alone last night an' I made sure we were near enough t' others for propriety afore... well," she demurred.

"M'name's Skye," he protested. "Ah'm not th' Commander n'more."

"Fine then, Skye," she said, made a gesture with her eyebrows that could very well have been a shrug.

He stood, not trusting his frustration. "That man's gonna ha'e his hands full wi' ye! Thank ye fer th' tea an' yer time," he growled, turning and let himself out. He stormed down the walk and opened the gate, jumped again when it slammed behind him faster than he could get out of the way.

Inside, An set aside her lace and sighed, staring into the fireplace. "What am I gettin' m'self inta?"

Liberty's presence at the gate made her jump. She rose as Liberty was coming down the path and met her at the door. "Hello, dear," she smiled, trying to put a less beleaguered look on her face. "Did I... am I late?"

Liberty laughed. "No, luv. Tha's t'morra. I nthought I'd come by t'day and either visit or invite ye over. Thought we could talk."

She nodded, stepped back from the door. "Come in. I've got a whole pot o' tea and plate o' shortbread."

She led the way into the house, intending to go to the kitchen for a clean cup when she noticed that there was one, turned neatly upside down on the saucer next to the plate. Skye's cup was nowhere to be seen. She smiled and offered Liberty the other chair.

"So," Liberty began as she took her seat and let An pour her a cup, "What'd ye do t' put poor Skye in such a state?"

An chuckled. "Accepted his terms and issued a challenge, I think."

"Did that lummox offer you an ultimatum?" She added a bit of honey to her tea, stirring.

"No. Well, maybe. He said he'd stay mostly out o' m' life so long as I accepted the occasional buttin' in. I told him fine, so long as he accepted

I'd occasionally tell him to stuff it." She huffed. "I swear he sounded like m' brother. ...One o' 'em," she frowned. "I'm pretty sure I had more'n one. And that they were as insufferable as all brothers are."

Liberty smiled as she chose a biscuit. "Unfortunately, I never had that problem."

An daintily crossed her ankles as she picked up her crochet from the table and Liberty took note of their nakedness. She gave a mock gasp, hiding her smile behind her hand. "An! I'm surprised at ye, entertainin' a man in yer bare feet!"

She raised an eyebrow at that. "He doesn't count as company," she said curtly. "He's goin' t' act like a brother, he'll haf ta concede t' bein' treated like one." She looked down at her crochet while Liberty dissolved into laughter, frowned to note that there were at least two rows more on the doily than she had put there.

She sighed and addressed the house at large. "While I am not ungrateful fer th' thought, I'd prefer if ye left m' busy work alone. I need somethin' t' do with m' hands at night afore bed, and as ye won't let me do dishes..." Through her feet she got the impression that the message had been received and not unkindly.

Liberty sat back, watching the odd exclamation. "House-elves?"

"Aye, apparently. How d'ye like th' shortbread?"

Liberty smiled. "I always like Martha's shortbread."

An stopped. "Ye... ye mean my pantry is the Manor's?" Liberty nodded. "An' ye didn't tell me?"

"Danny made th' arrangements. Martha knows. So 'tis likely your brownie is one of the family's, lookin' t' set up their own housekeeping. Lucky, that. So," she grinned, "do ye have an idea what yer wantin' t' be fer th' Winter Masque?"

An put down her discomfort at finding out she was tapping the manor's pantry and concentrated on trying to count her stitches, finding out where the brownie had left her. Once she figured that out, she began working. "I... have an idea, but... I don' know."

Liberty sipped her tea. "Tell me anyway."

"Ye said ye want to keep Henry guessing, so he doesn't know who ye are?"

"That's the idea," she smirked.

An tipped her head, concentrating on her stitches so she wouldn't have to look at her friend. "What if there were a queen present? Or someone who could very well be one?"

Liberty's eyes lit up. "What had ye in mind?"

"Well... all the ladies are goin' t' be vaguely magic... I won't have to worry about bumping inta them, and Roulet's solved the object issue. I might be able ta... but I'd be a bad choice..." she shook her head, cutting herself off.

"Nah. I think yer perfect. Provided yer ok fendin' Henry off. He can be pretty handsy."

An gave a small shake of her head. "What I'm thinking of, he won't make so bold. Either way, it'll distract him, wonderin' if ye dared."

She tilted her head, eyeing An carefully, her doll's eyes trying to read the governess's expression. "What are ye..."

An shook her head. "If I'm gonna do it, I need it all to be a surprise. I'm not sure yet if I can manage it. I'll ...let ye know if it falls through."

"All riiight," she drawled, not sure about this but willing to trust. "Will ye need the charm from the witch?"

"I'll let ye know. But I don't think I will. What are you goin' as?"

Liberty fairly crowed. "That is the best part! Roulet and I are goin' as Jack an' Jill! I'm Jack. Henry'll never find me. 'Course, likely neither will Da...."

An smiled at her deviousness and poured herself a second cup of tea from the still steaming pot, sitting back to enjoy the company.

Later that night, before she lay down to bed, she wrote a letter to the children. It asked after their health and progress, detailed some of her life here so far. She gave details of the creatures they'd fought off at the Tallows', in hopes there might be something familiar about them or their method, or some titbit that might be of use to the King. She asked the Princess if there were any subjects she would like books on. Only then did she ask for a chance to speak with them on a small matter, a personal favour. She set the letter and the lace gloves she had made in the carved box and closed the lid.

When An woke the next morning, she did not feel like she had slept much. There had been dreams, she knew, but she couldn't remember them and felt actually grateful for that. She had the impression they had been horrid. She rose, found she had sweated in the night, and stumbled to the kitchen to set the kettle. She was pleased to find a large claw-footed tub steaming in front of the fireplace. There were towels warming on the hearth and the curtains were drawn and dark.

With a small exclamation of joy and relief, she drifted over, slipping out of her gown and into the hot, fragrant water. There was a small table next to the tub at her elbow, with a sponge and a bar of soap that smelled of roses and a hint of citrus; actual roses, not the sickly sweet perfume they called rose in this modern day. She washed, using the soap on her hair as well, then lay back and soaked, determined not to get out until the water was cold. The moment she thought that she realised it never would unless she wanted it to. She decided she would soak a good fifteen minutes before getting out and sensed an agreement from the house.

She sank beneath the water, holding her breath as she had since she was young, and suddenly the water seemed endlessly deep and eternally cold and she was boiling hot. She flailed in a panic, and just as suddenly she was lying in an empty tub, shivering, with reassuring thoughts washing over her from the house. She crawled out of the tub which was apologising profusely, grabbed the towel and wrapped it around herself. She stood, fled back into the bedroom, assuring the house it wasn't its fault.

In the room, her bed was made, the linens changed, and an appropriate dress was laid out for her. She dressed hurriedly, remembering she was supposed to meet Liberty for lunch after mass.

She heard something in the distance and stopped tucking herself in to listen. The sound grew louder and she could hear the church bells ringing. She finished getting dressed, turning to her dressing table for her brush, and saw the box. Immediately she forgot the brush and opened it. Inside was a letter on pristine white parchment sealed with a roaring lion's head in gold wax.

She sat to read the flowing script of Irish words. His handwriting had matured greatly, the words drawn bold and firm.

Greetings favoured Teacher,

Your letter finds us well and thriving. Our brother says he misses you, but hopes you are happy. Teddy sends his greetings as well. Though our brother has aged as he should, Teddy still stands guard while he ...does what he does.

Eagle requests books on this thing called 'electricity'. She says is it like lightning but harnessed. We have begun dealing with elementals of this type from the Swamplands and she believes understanding this principal will help us fight them.

As for your request, I intend to go on a hunt this evening. Meet me in my pavilion near the gate at dusk. I ride at moonrise.

The Lion Prince

An closed the letter and put it in a drawer, nervous now that she was so close to having to ask for what she wanted. She still wasn't sure what exactly it *was* she wanted.

She brushed out her hair and pinned it up hastily. She found her boots waiting for her on the bench by the door, along with a medium-sized, black leather handbag. She peeked inside and smiled to discover her crochet. She slipped into her boots and laced them up, grabbing the bag and Cipín on her way out the door.

Liberty had decided they were going out for lunch and piled An into her car, driving them out of the Rest. "What's in the bag?" she asked as they drove slowly through the ambling streets towards the wall. "I've never seen ye carry a handbag."

"My brownie seems to think I'll need my crochet t'day. Though it does give me an idea. I know I should have some money set by. Miss Jones said something about an account, but I have no idea how much is there or how to access it. I would like t' pick up some more thread and some books."

"We kin do that. Ya want a bookstore or the libr'y?"

An gave a half laugh. "I don't think these books'll ever be returned, so I'd best buy them. I might need yer help picking them out. What I'll be gettin' can't be in braille."

"All right, I'm game."

The two of them spent a pleasant Sunday afternoon out and about. They had lunch in a quaint little cafe, eating outdoors where the

September wind played endearing melodies through the dying leaves. At the craft store, An bought several skeins of yarn that, while not wool, were certainly soft and warm, and Liberty helped her to pick out colours. She also got a second set of hooks in a neat leather case and a large spool of white crochet thread. At the bookstore, Liberty helped her find several good volumes on electricity and lightning without ever asking what they were for.

It did not seem long before they were headed back to the Rest for Sunday dinner at the Manor. Martha had made corned beef as promised, and it was every bit the savoury concoction she remembered. It was a pleasant dinner, with only one new face and less a few others, but she had come to expect that at the manor. The newly rescued came and went.

As it got closer to evening, she began to feel more nervous, worried she would be too late. Finally, Shannon announced that the game was starting shortly and if folk wanted, they could take dessert in the living room. This was greeted with enthusiasm and caused Ian to pull the woman in for a kiss on the cheek. "Yer too good t' me, Shannon, my love," he crowed.

She gave him a swat and told him to go stuff himself and watch his confounded ballgame.

An lingered back, getting up slower than the others, calling Cipín to her. She politely declined the caramel apple bake that Martha was doling out for the pack in front of the telly. "Too rich fer me t'night. I've t' go home t'morrow. I'd like an early night." It wasn't a lie. She wanted an early night, as she was tired beyond belief. She just wasn't going to get it.

Martha sighed, accepting the excuse. "Well, if ye want any fer breakfast, I'll set some in the back pantry fer ye. Don't be a stranger now yc've a home o' yer own."

An bent to press a kiss to her doughy cheek and headed for the back door. She adjusted her shawl on her shoulders and took her bag tightly in hand, told Cipín to lead her home past the rath.

She hadn't gone more than a few yards past the veranda when Skye caught up with her. She tightened her jaw, forced herself to put on a pleasant smile. "I've Cipín with me, Skye. I can find m' way home fine. Ye needn't miss th' ballgame fer my sake."

He dismissed the notion. "They said they were goin' t' watch a football game. What they're watchin' an't football, more like carry-ball. Ah'm goin' home, anyway."

She got no tinges of untruth from him at that and had to accept his escort. The settling of birds in the trees for the night told her that dusk was well-advanced. She could hear the waking calls of owls and knew time was thin.

They walked in silence on the path through the wood. As they neared the rath, An found she could see bits of things, getting brighter the closer they came. The path wound past the old faery fort at a little distance, and Skye frowned when An turned aside from the main route onto the one that led directly to the mound entrance.

"Ah thought ye said Cipín knew th' way home? That way's th' knoll."

"I know," she said reluctantly.

When she kept going, Skye reached out and took her arm, pulling her to a halt. "What are ye up to, lass?"

She turned on him, embarrassed, but knew from the look in his steely eyes that she wasn't going any farther until she told him. "I've a meetin'. An' yer makin' me late."

He scowled. "Has this t' do with tha' ring ya talked ta Friday last?" He was worried she might be being compelled to go to Northerner's realm or meet one of her people.

"No," she protested, jerking her arm out of his grasp. "It has to do with... sommat yer not allowed t' know."

"Well, yer not takin' a step more until ah do, so make up yer mind," he growled.

She glared up at him. The full impact of her gaze was lost in the swelling dark. "Only if ye swear t' secrecy. Ye can't tell a male soul in th' Rest."

"What ye mean..."

"Swear it!" she snapped.

"Fine! Ah'll not tell a male soul. Now where are we goin'?"

She straightened, startled. "Yer no' comin' with. I'll tell ye where I'm goin', but yer no' comin'."

"Then neither are you," he said, folding his arms across his chest and scowling down at her.

The growing light from the mound made him more visible to her than she was to him. She could tell by the set of his jaw that there was no moving him. "I'm goin' t' meet th' Prince, and I need t' get there afore moonrise!"

His stance loosened a bit. "Why'd ye no' say so? There's n' trouble t' escort ya to th' castle..."

"I'm not goin' t' th' castle," she said curtly as she turned and began walking towards the glowing hill. This time he let her, following along behind. "I'm t' meet him at his pavilion afore he leaves on his hunt."

"Then ye need me. If he's not in his father's lands, there's n' tellin' what might try t' stop ye."

An said nothing, stood before the small hill, waiting for the door to appear. When the last light of the sun faded from sight, it shimmered into view and came open under her hand. She stepped through into the faery world and paused to take a deep breath of the sweet, vivid air. She looked around, saw everything, the grass, the trees, the brightening trod. Tonight it was a Seelie road.

Skye noticed the hedge maze that had been here when he left was gone and the landscape was slightly different. A quarter league up the trod was the tree-lined curve in the road from whence he had sent An on alone and turned to fight the first of the Wild Hounds. Sitting just before this curve was a large tent glowing softly gold in the night. It was towards this tent that An headed and set a brisk pace.

Skye took uncomfortable note that the tent stood alone with only a single guard at the flap. If the prince were going on a hunt, where were his horses, where were his huntsmen?

The guard started to challenge them, then he recognised Skye. He snapped back to attention, "*Commander Skye, sir. I was not told ye were accompanying the Governess. If you'll give me a moment, sir.*" He ducked into the tent, and returned a half moment later, holding it open for both of them.

Stepping inside, they were welcomed by familiar and comforting smells. Skye could smell metal and leather and armour oil, the scents of battle preparation. An smelled books and faery fabrics and lily water. Lion was seated beside a table, sharpening a dagger. Eagle stood behind him in a dark hunting gown, putting a book away. Lion stood when they entered, crossed to An to take her hand as she sank into a deep curtsey. The prince pulled her to her feet, kissing her hand. Eagle smiled and drifted nearer.

His voice was as warm and deep as his father's, with a faint rumble that made her think of lions. *"No. Rise, Teacher. You of all people have earned the right to stand before us."*

She blushed as she rose, looking into his piercing blue eyes. He had grown into a strikingly handsome young elf. He was taller and broader of limb than Jonny, she noted, and far more beautiful if that was even possible. *"Lion,"* she said, being careful not to thank him, and to use the name she knew he would prefer.

Eagle fluttered closer. Her hair was just as long as ever, drawn up in her impossible braids and gleaming like liquid gold. If her brother had grown into a handsome man, she was a breath-taking young woman. Behind her, she noted that even Skye was affected by her, going stiffly formal. Her dark blue eyes were piercing as she took An's hand from her brother. *"Salutations, Teacher. You have been missed."*

"You look well, Princess. I confess I am a little shocked by the changes, but they are good."

"And overdue," Lion said dismissively. He turned to Skye. *"You were unexpected, Commander. I hope everything goes well?"* His eyes communicated more than his words, and Skye felt the weight of the responsibility handed him.

"Aye, your highness. As far as she is letting me," he added sheepishly.

Lion actually laughed at that. *"Never was one to allow security constraints to interfere with life."* He clapped Skye on the shoulder. *"Good luck with that."*

He turned back to his seat at the table, leaving Skye glowing with pride. He gestured An towards the only other chair in the room. *"Please, Teacher. Sit. Tell me what you wish."*

"Well," she began, then remembered what was in the bag as she set it down. *"Oh, I have brought..."* She carefully leaned Cipín against the back of the chair as she began to fish the books out of the bag. She did not notice Eagle eyeing the shillelagh warily, but Skye did, though he said nothing as he took up his place behind An. The Princess looked at her brother briefly before crossing to An to accept the three volumes held out to her.

"These were the best I could find that might suit your purposes. I just hope ye remember your English. I think I taught you that one very early on. The third one is a

current dictionary of the English language, just in case. There are new words even I do not know yet, especially scientific ones. I'm not sure how much of it will work here, but," she gave a gesture of 'oh well' with her hands and sat down.

"I remember a good bit of it. And will remember more as I read," Eagle said as she looked over the volumes. *"These should be acceptable. We will discover with suitable experimentation what will and will not work. Mister Sawgrass,"* she said the name with distaste, as if he were beneath her, *"is fielding a lot of this type of elementals. While they do not work in our realm as they work in his, they still function. This could make a difference."* With that, she drifted to the back of the tent to another table and sat down, began reading immediately. She set the dictionary open beside her for quick reference.

Skye did not like the mention of Sawgrass's encroachment on the King's territories. He remembered dealing with the minions of that particular Gentry: full of muck and mire. He was a minor factor in the daily struggles of the Fey, and not even the Northerner bothered to ally with him.

An turned back to Lion and tried to smile, feeling very nervous now. Lion repeated himself. *"Tell me what it is you wish."*

She clasped her hands in her lap, keenly aware of Skye behind her, and tried to proceed without fidgeting. *"There is a ritual coming up... Yule, and the O'Keefe's celebrate it with a Winter Masque, where the Holly King and the Oak King both have t' find the Queen among the masked women to win an advantage in the coming battle for supremacy of the seasons. My friend, the Queen, wishes to play a prank on the Holly King."* She saw him smile and the light go on behind his eyes and knew she was on the right track. The Prince still loved a good prank. *"She has asked a local witch for charms which will obscure the crown and make all the women appear equally magical,"* she glared over her shoulder at Skye whose eyes were wide with surprise and amusement. *"Which she can easily do, but making another appear to be wearing a hidden crown is beyond her skill."*

Lion leaned forward, elbows on his knees and a grin on his fair lips. *"And you need something to make you appear to be the Queen in disguise."*

An took a breath of relief. *"Aye, my prince. You have the way of it."*

"So what is it you wish to be? For there is more to this request or you would have simply asked in your letter."

Her relief dried up instantly. She looked down at her fingers. He was always more astute that she would have liked, even as a child which he most certainly wasn't any more. "*I... I wish....*" An got hold of herself, inwardly chiding herself for behaving like a shy little girl asking for a kiss. She sat up straighter and spoke less softly. "*I want the faery tale.*" At this Eagle looked up, but said nothing. "*For one night I want to be unforgettable. To be Cinderella and have a chance to win my prince.*"

His eyebrow went up at that and she feared he might think she meant him, but his words soothed that even as they startled her. "*So which have you set your cap for? The gryphon or the Stag?*"

"*What?*" she gasped. "*Neither. I'm not that much the fool. I...*" she blushed.

His voice was gentle as he coaxed it from her, "*Who, my teacher?*"

She all but whispered. "*Just once I want to be beautiful, to be the kind of woman who might catch the eye of a Bard. To be worthy of his attention.*"

Skye caught the look in Eagle's eye as she turned her head to her brother, her finger marking her place in the book. Lion did not look back at her, merely smiled sadly and shook his head slightly. "*Ah, my Lady of the Mist, for one so wise, you are so naïve.*" She looked up at him in panic, fearing he would say no. "*Fear not, Teacher. You shall have your wish.*" Her hand went to her necklace, and he shook his head. "*Nay, this is my gift to you. Let us say it is for the prank.*"

"*Yes, let's,*" Eagle said dryly, still staring at her brother.

He ignored her, "*Meet me here again, just before dawn the day of Yule, the day of the Masque. Come dusk, you will be ready. Now,*" he said, standing and tucking his dagger into his hard riding boots. "*Now, the moon is rising and we must be off.*"

An rose, taking Cipín in hand and curtseying once more to the royal pair as Eagle almost lazily rose from her chair and set her book on the table. "*I wish ye good of your quarry.*"

Eagle smiled as she pulled on a pair of leather gloves that made her delicate hands look more like eagle's claws. The expression was predatory. "*And them the worst of us.*"

"*Aye.*"

The princess stopped before she pulled on the second glove, remembering something. She went to a box and pulled out a small bundle of white cobweb silk thread. It glittered on the skein as if even the dewdrops had been caught up in it. She placed it into An's hands. *"For your new little princess. Make her a pair of gloves as fine as the ones you made me."*

An started to curtsey again, stopped and pressed a kiss to her cheek instead, much as she used to do when the woman had been young. She was taller than Skye now, and more stately. She could have imagined the blush she felt on Eagle's cheek. *"I will strive to make my work worthy of my materials."*

Eagle smiled. *"Just remember a little coltsfoot oil on your fingers. It helps keep it from being sticky and tangling."*

"I'll remember."

With that, the guard was opening the flap and she and Skye stepped out into the night in the midst of an active hunting camp. Two fine and high-spirited horses stood by, held by a grooms-man and dressed in such a way as there was no confusing to whom they belonged. The stallion was a tawny gold with a rippling mane and a lion skin for a saddle blanket. The mare, a high-stepping bay with a white crest that stood up, and was adorned with feathers.

Before the flap fell behind them, An heard Eagle's voice raised to her brother. *"Is it wise to encourage her? Is she strong enough to go where that road leads?"*

"She has to be or..." and the conversation was cut off as the silk fell, leaving An wondering the wisdom of her heart.

They stepped aside and An let Skye guide her back and out of the way, protecting her from the last minute bustle as the huntsmen mounted up and the sleek, white, massive cú sidhe gathered near, eager for the blood of whatever they were hunting. Skye set his hand on her shoulder, to still the expected fear at seeing the hounds; but she was calm. One passed them by and sniffed them, and An surprised Skye by holding out her hand and letting the beast sniff before she ran it through the fur below his ear. The hound gave her a chuff as he was called away, trotting up to the golden horse as his master strode from the tent and mounted up, the princess right behind him, mounting her own restless steed.

The pair of them stayed to watch the faery host ride out. It was an impressive sight, one An had never seen, not this close. The children had never been old enough, and they had watched from the battlements as the King had ridden out without them. It was much more impressive from down among them. The host rode towards the gate, but veered off on a different path not far from it. An held her position until they were out of sight; only then did she allow Skye to take her back down the dimming trod towards the gate, and the Rest beyond it.

They were out of the mound and back on the path to their respective homes before she spoke again. It was almost a mumble. "He's right. More the fool's me."

Skye bristled. "He seid ye were naïve. 'Tis not t' say yer a fool."

"Comes to the same end."

She strode on ahead, walking a little faster, and refused to say another word.

He followed a few paces back, close enough to catch her if she were to stumble, but far enough to give her the illusion of privacy. He stopped between the buildings at the edge of her wall and watched her go to her little gate. She paused just inside it. "What ye heard, t'night. No male ears. Understood?"

He folded his arms over his chest and gave her a stubborn look. "Woman, ah've no idea what yer talkin' aboot."

She nodded her head once. "Fine."

Skye did not move from where he stood until the door closed behind her.

Inside, An found a fire waiting merrily for her and set her bag on the bench. Putting Cipín in her corner, she sat to remove her boots. She reached into her bag and pulled out the white thread she had bought and the packet of hooks, went to the table beside her chair and set them on top of it. She ran her hand over the table's polished surface, telling the house in the way it told her things, that these were all for the use of her 'little friend' if it was wanted.

She heard the sound of the kettle whistle on the stove and she looked over, saw the cup on the counter with the tea bag hanging from it. She gave a tired smile. "Not tonight. I really need to get some sleep. Yer welcome to it an' ye like. And Martha put some of her caramel apple crumble in th' pantry, help yerself to a bit o' that too. She'll be offended if none of the' crumble's missing. If she's made any sweetbreads for breakfast, I think one of those and a cup will be all I'll be wantin' in th' mornin', I just..." she sighed, heading to her room. "I'm just not in the mood, really."

She felt the house was not happy that she was not happy as the living room fire died back and the one in the bedroom sprang up. An changed into the freshly laundered gown waiting on the bed and sat at the dressing table to brush out and braid up her hair. She felt exhausted, emotionally and physically. Now that the moon was out and filling her room with its silvery glow, she felt the day weighing her down like a heavy quilt.

She turned to the bed and found a dainty, oddly shaped mug steaming fragrantly on her nightstand. She sniffed the dark liquid and smelled chamomile and vanilla and a hint of something more potent. She sat on the bed and sighed. Normally she eschewed alcohol, but in this case... perhaps it would help her to sleep better. She drank the hot toddy and found she could not complain about the flavour. Before she had finished it, there was a delightful heaviness to her limbs that told her she was more than ready for sleep.

Feeling warm, she threw open the sash to let in the cool night breezes, tucked herself under her light covers, and slept.

An woke to the sun shining in her eyes and rolled over to bury her face in the pillow. She felt as if she had just lain down. After a moment of laying there, she began to hear the kettle whistling as loudly as if it were in the room with her. Finally, she threw off the covers and rose. She checked the open faced watch on her dressing table and groaned. It was nearly eight. The car was supposed to come for her in half an hour. She hurriedly dressed, rushing into the kitchen to see if she had time for a cup of strong tea. She did not bother to pack, knowing that once she got back to her little garret, she would be activating the door to here.

There was a single cup of tea waiting on the counter, which she was grateful for, but said nothing. She did not want to insult the brownie. She had worried that the gift of the thread and needles might have been taken the wrong way and driven her off, but the waiting tea set her at ease over that.

She swallowed down the tea and rushed to the front door, pulling on her freshly brushed and cleaned boots and lacing them up. She heard the car pull up in front of her gate and grabbed the black bag where it sat beside her on the bench, threw on her shawl and held out her hand. Cipín jumped into it and she trotted down the path to the open gate, only slowing when she crossed that threshold and could no longer see what was in front of her. She proceeded at a more sedate pace, holding out her hand for the driver to take and help her into the car.

Once inside, she felt the stimulation of the tea and running late start to fade. She reached into the bag to pull out the threads, feeling her way through them, to find the one she had been working on and felt something hard and small in a side pocket she had not known was there. Putting her hand in it, she found her hooks neatly organised and a small bottle of sweet coltsfoot oil and smiled.

She arrived at the house as Mrs Tallow was leaving for work. Sharon paused long enough to welcome her back and let her into the house. "I hope you had as wonderful a time as we did," she beamed. "Elizabeth's already off to school, but she'll probably talk your ear off when she gets home."

"I'm sure. I'm glad ye enjoyed it. Ye deserved th' time off."

She went into the house as Sharon left, locking the door behind her and going straight into the kitchen to find something for the breakfast she'd missed. She made herself another cup of tea without much difficulty until she reached to the back of the counter where the canisters of sugar and flour were kept. The tender underside of her wrist brushed against a ceramic pot that was not normally there and was extremely hot. She pulled back as she felt the burn begin. She gasped as it didn't stop, but instead continued to swell as the burning filled her until it was the sum of her existence.

When she reached the tempering of the ocean, she fell back, cracking her head on the counter behind her and collapsing to the floor in a puddle, gasping for air and bleeding from a cut on her scalp. The flashback was as vivid as the first vision and left her weak and sobbing in a heap. She tried to rise, reaching up the cupboard looking for some support and failing. Her head swam when she sat up. She had to get off the floor, had to remember where there was a telephone in the house.

She remembered Sharon spending time on the phone in the kitchen, remembered running into a long cord between Sharon and the wall by the fridge. She dragged herself closer to the humming cold she could feel. She scraped the burn on the linoleum and set off another repeat of the whole vision.

As soon as she could breathe again, still suffering through little corpse after little corpse, she reached up, flailing for the long, curling cord she knew was there somewhere. Her fingers caught the rubbery spring coil and pulled, begging the phone to drop to her. The old Bakelite handset landed with a crack next to her other fingers, missing them by millimetres. An grabbed it and pulled it close, fumbling for the buttons, to remember the number she had been told to use.

After a few seconds that seemed like minutes, Roulet's voice came sleepily through her ear. "Hello?" she yawned.

It was all An could do to choke out, "Roulet... help me... make it stop... please. Don't tell Skye."

She felt something happening and pushed the phone away from her just in time, as a burst of lightning emerged from the handset and solidified into Roulet. She stood there, wearing only a long t-shirt and panties and looking wild with her hair writhing as if alive. She looked around for the trouble, saw the blood and An curled in on herself, and dropped beside her. "Baby, what happened?" she asked, even as she was checking to see how bad An was hurt.

"I... burned myself. I had th' vision again. I hit m'head and... I get dizzy when I sit up. I'm... hurt, and I didn't... know what else t' do. I can't clean up what I can't see."

Roulet looked around the kitchen, took everything in. "Ok. Looks like you burned yourself on the crock-pot." She checked her over. "The burn's not bad, and... neither is your head. I can fix both, just hold still."

An felt like a thousand ants were creeping over her body, nibbling without real pain, just tingling all over. It sank into her burned arm and the back of her head, and the headache and dizziness began to subside. She breathed a sigh of relief as the pressure eased off.

"All this was caused by the vision?" Roulet asked, helping An to her feet.

"Well, the burn caused all the rest. The first when I touched th' pot; the second when I scraped th' burn on th' floor. I hit m' head when I started drownin'."

Roulet guided her around the smeared puddles of blood, checked to make sure she wasn't leaving bloody footprints. "All right. First things first. Let's get you cleaned up. I'll get your clothes to the laundress before the blood dries."

"Blood is a hard thing..." she protested.

Roulet laughed. "The laundress is a *Bean Nighe*. She's an expert at blood. Working with the Family, she has a lot of experience. Once I have you in the shower, I'll come back down and clean the kitchen up, then come up to do the bathroom. Ok?"

"Aye," she sighed, hating that she had to ask, but grateful there was someone she could.

It did not take long. An showered, getting the blood out of her hair and wrapping up in towels. Roulet found her room and brought her a change of clothes, let her dress while she got all traces of blood from the shower walls where it had splattered with the water. An finally settled on the bed in her garret and breathed deeply. While Roulet pulled up the chair and straddled it, An reached over to the nightstand and pulled out the cell phone, slipping it into a pocket in her skirt. "I think I'll be keepin' this on me at all times from now on."

"Probably a good idea," Roulet commented. She watched An twist up her hair again, never minding that it was wet. "This the first time this has happened? That you've seen that vision since you touched the ring?"

An nodded. "As far as I know." She shook her head suddenly, "No, I had it once the mornin' after, when I was in the bath, but I don't remember ought else. ...Though I haven't been sleeping as well as I should."

"Hmm. I might be able to fix that. There are things you can take."

"Laudanum," An nodded.

Roulet chuckled. "Can't really get that these days, but they have these little pills that will help you sleep. I can run to the drugstore and get you some if you like."

"I need to do something," she sighed.

Roulet vanished in a flash and An got up, remembering she needed to open the door to the cottage. She crossed to the closet door and stroked the wood, placing a small, inconsequential glamour on it as she hummed a particular melody. She felt the magic flare beneath her hand

and turned the knob. It opened into the living room of her cottage and she sighed, taking a deep breath. She hadn't realised until that moment how stale the air in the garret was, filled with the musty smell of old wood and wallpaper, or how alive was her new home.

Roulet was back five minutes later. She handed An a small bottle, showed her how to open it. "I've already pulled the damned cotton out of it, so it'll be easy for you tonight. Just put it in your nightstand and take one before bed. Should put you right out."

"I hate resorting to this," she began. "What if something happens while I'm out?"

"Hon, you have to sleep sometime. You've got, what, at least four hours until Elizabeth gets home? Why don't you take half a one now and get some rest before she does? Sleep during the day so you can watch at night?"

"There's a thought to that."

"Here," she said, and flashed for a moment. Then she was back, pressed a glass of water into An's hand. "Go ahead. I'm going to head back to the apartment over Courtz and catch some shut-eye myself." She guided An back towards her small bed. "Now, don't hesitate to call me if you need anything."

An nodded, surrendering. She sat down, slipping out of her boots and swallowing half of one of the tiny pills. She laid down on the coverlet fully clothed, pulling the side of it over her, and tried to sleep as Roulet zipped out of the house as quickly as she had arrived. Only a trace of ozone in the air proclaimed that she had even been there.

An lay there, trying to feel the drift of on-coming sleep, and found herself thinking of her little house, and how dead this room suddenly felt.

An was once more trapped in the cycle, repeating it over and over without end until suddenly there was a break in it. A hot flash in the middle of her forehead in the midst of the eternal, cold sea, and she opened her eyes to a hand in front of her face and a small finger pressed to her brow. She gasped, blinking, and the hand withdrew and she found herself looking into Elizabeth's concerned blue eyes, which were slightly more violet at the moment.

The girl said nothing, just moved her hand and sat back, watching her warily with that look that mothers get when they're determining just how sick their child really is. An met that gaze unflinching as she ran her own assessment. Finally, An whispered. "That is not going to work."

"What isn't?" The child's voice was flat.

"These," she said, pulling the bottle out of the drawer and handing them to Elizabeth. "Get rid of them, please."

Elizabeth turned them over in her hand. "Why'd you take these? In the middle of the day?"

An sighed, started to explain, then stopped and looked at her. "What did you do to me?"

Elizabeth shrugged, slipping the pills in the pocket of her wind-breaker, intending to put them in her mother's medicine cabinet later. "I came home and couldn't find you, but the house was giving me a headache. I wanted to ask you about it, but you weren't downstairs, so I came up here to see. You were sweating and thrashing, but like you were held down. You weren't breathing. I tried to wake you up and you wouldn't,... so I poked your third eye."

An frowned. "I only have two," she said.

Elizabeth smiled. "No, you have three. Everyone does. It's a chakra point, and an important one. It's a metaphysical thing. I looked it up once, trying to figure out what was different about me."

An rubbed her forehead. "Well, I'm glad ye did... whatever it was."

"What was wrong with you? Your body... read differently. Like it wasn't you but was, or like someone else was wrapped up inside you."

An started to evade the question, then realised there was a lesson here. She gestured for Elizabeth to shift so she could sit up. "I did something for a friend without thinking this weekend. I used some of those magics that I have, to learn about a magical thing that turned out to be very dangerous. This is th' backlash. I will have to find a way to cope until it lessens. I was hoping to sleep during th' day, so I might remain vigilant tonight but..."

Another thought occurred to her. There was no way she could bring herself to sleep in this room again, and if something happened in the house, this was a clear route for Elizabeth to escape out of their reach. She slipped her arm around the girl's shoulders and pulled her close.

"Do you remember those books we read that first fortnight of school? The ones by C. S. Lewis?"

"'The Lion, the Witch and the Wardrobe'?" she grinned. "Yeah, I loved those. 'The Last Battle' was kinda sad though."

"Well, 'Further up and further in,' I tell ye. But ye have to promise me ye'll not use this frivolously. Ye will not wander beyond because this is a real place with real dangers, very different from here. If I tell ye a place is forbidden ye, it is because, for *you* especially, there are terrible things that could happen to ye there. It is pastime I took ye to a friend of mine."

"Who?" her eyes lit up.

"You've met him. His name is Sean. Now, do you have homework?"

Elizabeth tipped her head. "Yes, but it's really easy and not due 'til Wednesday. I can do it tomorrow without any trouble. Also, Mom's not going to be home 'til Dad is, after eight. Because she took Friday off, she has a ton of extra stuff to do. She left a note for me to microwave us something."

"Well, that will not do at all," An said, standing. She straightened her vest and held out her hand for Cipín. "Now, from now on, if ye need me in the night, this is where ye will find me. Ye must promise me never to say thank ye for anything done for ye where we are going. I happen to like my little friend and do not want them to leave, nor must ye try to catch sight of him or her."

Elizabeth's eyes glittered as she looked up at her governess. "All right."

An led her to the closet door, running her fingers lightly down the wood before her and quietly hummed the refrain to "Red is the Rose". The door clicked, and An gestured for the girl to open it. She paused a moment to look at An with a suspicious excitement, but then pulled open the door and gasped with delight at the little house which loomed beyond the portal.

An took her hand and led her through, pausing just past the threshold to introduce her. "House, this is my ward, Elizabeth Tallow. She is to be allowed through the door if she needs me, and if she knocks, please let me hear it no matter the hour."

She put out her hand to the wall to feel the response and smiled. "It says that yer welcome here. But I am going to ask ye to be on yer best behaviour, and once ye have activated the door, and heard the click, that ye knock first. Ye will know whether or not 'tis all right to enter."

She nodded, swallowing as she tried to take it all in, to read the house as she sometimes read people. It overwhelmed her. "You... live here?"

"I do now. Danny built it fer me. I can see everything in it. I will be sleeping just through that door," she said, pointing to her bedchamber, "from now on."

"I can see why you'd rather."

"It is no slight to yer mother's delightful accommodations. Had this place not existed, I would be more than content there. Now, you and I have a visit to pay."

She led her through the living room to the front door, which opened for them and out into the garden. An stopped on the front step, thinking about where they should go from here. Then she saw Liberty coming around the side of her house with an arm full of something and smiled. "Liberty!" she called.

The woman paused, looked over and grinned. "Hello, An, love. Who's yer friend?"

"Liberty, this is Elizabeth Tallow. Elizabeth, this is Miss O'Keefe, a close friend of mine."

Liberty's eyebrow went up as the name clicked. "Pleased to meet ye, Miss Tallow. An, what can I do fer ye?" she asked in that pointed tone that said the things her words didn't.

"I need to take her to see Sean and... well, I thought letting my house make a decent supper was better than sommat from that infernal microwave. Her mother's working late t'night."

"It happens enough I know what to do," Elizabeth chirruped. "More now that she knows An will take care of things." An gave her a glare. "Well, not more, but Mom worries less when it does."

An cleared her throat and finally the child got it. She politely straightened up and said, "Afternoon, Miss O'Keefe."

Liberty smiled and continued to the front of the house. "Let me take care of these and I'll be right there. I'll see where Sean's at."

"Thank ye, luv," An sighed. She turned back to the house and set her hand on the lintel, silently telling it that Elizabeth would be staying for dinner.

Moments later, Liberty had come over, phone to her ear, and clicked off as she came through the gate. Liberty paused to shake Elizabeth's hand, meeting her more formerly. She then turned to An. "All right, Skye's said we can use th' Mead Hall. He's got no classes today. Sean's meeting us round here very shortly. When do ye have t' have her back?"

"Eight, I think. I figured we'd dine here about seven afore I take her home." She looked down at the girl. "If I am ever not at home and something's happened... that is where Liberty lives, and that," she pointed to the other side of the garden wall, "large buildin' there is where ye'll find Skye. He's an enormous Scotsman, but he'll protect ye. Across the way in the gypsy wagon is Solitaire and Roulet, two other friends of mine, one of whom ye met once. If no one is home, tell the house to have Ian told. Then stay put here and someone will be around."

"Ok. This is all a little... strange."

"It's about to get weirder," came Sean's warm tenor as he appeared at the door to the Mead Hall. He waved the group over.

An took Elizabeth's hand and brought her around to where Sean waited. "This is Sean O'Keefe. He will be yer... McGonagall," An added with a smile.

The girl's eyes lit up. "Really?" She looked back at him, suddenly recognising him. "You're one of the ones who got rid of the stick woman. You were in the yard last week, too."

"Aye, I was," he said as she shook his hand. "Are ye willin' to trust me? T' let me test ye and teach ye things Miss An here canna?"

Elizabeth actually blushed. "Yes, sir."

"Good, we can get started then. Miss O'Keefe, will ye be watchin' or will ye be back when we're done?"

"Is Skye home?"

"Aye."

She stepped forward. "Then I'll be at my own lessons."

He nodded with approval. "Very well then."

Elizabeth was wide eyed when she was introduced to Skye. She had walked in, looking around and turned right into him. She found herself staring at a broad buckle and a thick leather belt above a dark plaid. She looked up, found her neck craned as far as it would go and just let it hang there, open-mouthed.

Skye arched an eyebrow as he looked down at her. The girl's mouth barely twitched as she gaped, "Hi."

He chuckled, the sound occurring deep in his chest and coming out a rumble. "Ye must be Elizabeth." He held down his hand to her. "Ah'm Skye."

When her hand went into his, she spent more time comparing their sizes than actually shaking it. Skye let her, amused by the magic child. He gave An a grin over her head. Finally, he stepped back and gestured to the room. Elizabeth left off gawking at the tall Scot and proceeded to Ooo and Ahh as the Mead Hall arranged itself to suit their needs. From her half of the large hall, she could see An at fighting practice, but not hear it, so the sounds would not disturb her concentration as Sean tried to figure out what kinds of things she was capable of learning.

Skye, meanwhile, put An through her paces and began to notice that her reaction times were down. He frowned. He could see her skill, and that she was not in top form. He was about to ask her about it when she stepped back and called a halt.

The ringing of his weapon against Cipín, the vibrations going up her arm, were starting to have a familiar ring to them and she suddenly feared another attack and backed off. "I think this a bad idea."

"Ye need t' learn. Yer slower than..."

She held up her hand, cutting him off. "I know," she snapped. "But that's not why. It's starting t'... we should hold off on that kinda poundin' fer a while. It's startin' t' sound like a hammer on an anvil," she growled pointedly as he began to puff up to argue the point.

That deflated him, though it took a second for it to filter through.

"Perhaps right now we should concentrate on defence that doesna require ye t'be armed like a knight and more like a thug?"

He tossed aside the practice sword immediately. "Aye. Well, let's start wi' th' common muggin'." He then proceeded to show her the kinds of ways she could be attacked and various means to escape them.

Two hours later, An was sore but feeling tired, which she counted a good thing. Elizabeth was wrapping up at about the same time, and the two of them said their goodbyes and returned to the cottage. Elizabeth was delighted to find a table for two set up in front of the fireplace with all kinds of good things she had never eaten, but that smelled delicious. As An took her seat opposite the child, she gave her an indulgent smile. "Now, no sneaking in here for supper just because you do not desire your mother's spinach loaf."

There came a sigh at that which told An that had been exactly the child's plan. She laughed, and they ate while she listened to the girl going on about the things she had learned.

15

An was not getting any rest. Not even sleeping in the cottage. The week after the sleeping pill incident, it was bad enough that Sharon commented on it. It was then that An decided something must be done. The brownie had been giving her hot toddies nightly, but they weren't doing anything more than helping her fall asleep. That wasn't her problem anymore. It was staying asleep or avoiding the dreams.

Finally, Wednesday night after the family had gone to bed, she stepped out into the night, locking the door with the magical key and turning on the alarms. The last time they had gone to Skye's for her and Elizabeth's lessons, Sean had given her what he called a remote; said if the perimeter was breached, it would go off no matter where she was. She slipped this into her pocket with the key and retraced her steps down the block to Courtz.

It was hard not to think of Jonny on the walk. The only time she had traversed this path had been with him, and every step reminded her of that. She chastised herself for pining after a man like a love-sick maid and forced herself to concentrate on the walk and avoiding the dangerous street.

At that corner, she paused, hearing both people and cars nearby, and finally broke down and asked someone to help her with the street. They were kind enough to show her the crosswalk sign button and how to listen for it. An thanked them and crossed the street on her own with a small amount of pride.

She found Courtz the same way, by the sound.

An entered the first room and stepped out of the way, trying to get a feel for the chamber. There was music playing, though not nearly as loud as the last time she had been here. There was the sound of billiards and the distinct thunk of darts into corkboard. She remembered the path the waiter had guided her through and attempted it slowly, finding only the occasional obstacle of people in the way. When she found the door and entered the main room, she was surprised to find it almost quiet, save for the people. There was the sound of dining and drinking, some softer music, and that painful squeal of the microphone as someone fumbled with it, rustling papers.

An tread slowly to where she remembered the bar being, following the sound of foamy liquids pouring into pints. She felt for an empty space and stood there, waiting for the ghost girl down the way to notice her.

Tori came over with a smile. "What can I do for you, miss?" she said with genuine cheer in her voice.

"Well, I... I think I would like a table, but I despair of finding one on my own."

She grinned. "Oh, I think we can accommodate you." She turned and yelled down at the other bartender. "Brad! I'm going out on the floor for a bit!"

Brad grumbled, but apparently either nodded or really had no say in the matter.

Tori lifted the end of the bar up and stepped out, taking An's arm. She led her to the aisle that ran between the tables and the bar and looked over the crowd. "Ok, I've got the perfect table for you. If you decide to come back more regularly, then you should be able to remember this path."

She began to lead her five strides to the right, parallel to the bar, then made a left. "Now," she said, "You'll always want to keep your right hand out to the side like this," she added, holding An's arm out beside her, in front of Tori's own body with the palm facing the stage. She set the hand back at her elbow, "The dance floor is on your right and this will keep people from backing into you as much. Then you can use your tap stick in the left to make sure no ass has left a chair out." She counted out another six strides before turning left again and settling An at an empty table at the front of the dance floor.

"It's kinda empty on Wednesdays, not so much with the dancing, but Open Mike is popular with the poets. Some of the local musicians will occasionally try out new pieces, too. We even had a dancer once." She set a menu that An could plainly see in front of her and smiled. "Liberty has assured me you can see this," she said quietly. "Though ye might want to 'braille' read it for appearances. Our menu changes too much to be able to actually print one up for you. So, can I get you a drink while you decide?"

She smiled up at Tori. "Ye are a right dear, ye know that? I would like some tea, but... I need..." She could feel her face flush with embarrassment. "I need somethin' strong. I'm... havin' trouble sleepin' and mother always recommended..."

Tori laughed softly. "Nightcaps. Mine always went for the brandy. Swore by it for teething. I've got something that might do. How much you want?"

"The bottle?" She sighed. "Slip a healthy bit in my tea, please and be discreet. 'Tis embarrassin' enough, my need."

Tori gave her shoulder a pat and headed back to the bar.

An ran her fingers over the slick paper of the menu, her eyes following her fingertips, though her head was up enough to make it appear she was facing the stage. She had learned to take advantage of the inability of people to tell where she was looking. She saw scotch eggs near the bottom and immediately closed the menu.

Sharon's meal tonight had been wholly unappetising and so unfamiliar her stomach had complained. She had not eaten a lot. She had discovered that Wednesday and Friday nights were the nights Sharon had designated 'health food' nights, and cooked things with a meat that wasn't from any animal. She had no idea what a Tofurkey was, but it was certainly not fowl.

She was beginning to tune in the poet on stage when Tori returned with a tea tray. She set it down in the centre of the table and verbally guided An's hand to it, telling her where and what everything was. "Full teapot here at twelve o'clock, your cup at two," she said, directing An's fingertips to the delicate overturned cup, "sugar bowl and tongs, a few... biscuits," she grinned, using the British term for cookie, "fresh from Lafayette. And the milk," she added, setting a spouted cream server which was not cold enough to protect milk in An's hand. "I'd go easy on the 'milk'." There was something in Tori's eye that warned her it wasn't remotely dairy. An smiled, blessing the woman for her discretion. "Have you decided on anything to eat?"

"Aside from the fact that I believe I'll be dining here or at home on Wednesday's and Friday's?" she sighed. "Aye. I'd like a plate of Scotch Eggs and a conversation with Roulet if she's here."

Tori laughed, taking the menu. "She's at Depravity tonight, working with her sister. She'll be here this weekend most certainly, though. Would you like to talk to Liberty, maybe?"

"That would be nice, thank ye."

Tori left her and An prepared herself a cup of tea, taking a discreet whiff of the 'milk' and discovering the potent perfume of alcohol. She added it to the tea and tried her best not to make a face as she sipped. One of the biscuits helped to cut the bite. They were drizzled with the chocolate Elizabeth had introduced her to, and she found it a nice balance between the flavours.

The current poet left the stage to a smattering of applause. When the next person took his place, the audience began to clap louder in anticipation. There came the sound of guitar strings and An looked up in curiosity, felt her heart stop to see Jonny sitting there, tuning the strings on the instrument resting on his thigh. His hair fell across his face as he worked, though it did not fall from his shoulder. He tossed it back and began to sing.

The melody was passing familiar, though the words were new, and An quickly gathered that this was the song she had been told to request of him months ago and never got around to.

Lady of the Mist

From beneath a cloudy sky,
I heard a young girl calling...
"Bonny Jack, they've taken you away
You stole the giant's harp and gold
Like a hero young and bold
And he's taken you a changeling for to stay."

High rise the fields above the sky
Where fear of falling teaches us to fly
He tried to bring you down
That damn giant with his crown
But you leapt from the clouds for to be free.

From above a cloudy sky,
I heard a young man calling...
"Jenny, all I did, I did for thee.
I stole the giant's golden crown
For to save Old London Town,
Now you must go back to Arthur without me."

From beneath a cloudy sky
I heard a young girl calling...
"Bonny Jack, I'd die to set you free.
For though Arthur is my love,
still I swear to God above
It's dear indeed your friendship is to me."

High rise the fields above the sky
Where fear of falling teaches us to fly
He tried to bring you down
That damn giant with his crown
But you leapt from the clouds for to be free.

From above a cloudy sky
I heard a young man crying,
"Jenny, you must never die for me.

By your honour I implore,
For the kingdom needs you more,
You must hie back to Arthur without me."

From beneath a cloudy sky
I heard a young maid crying
"Bonny Jack, you break my heart in two.
It's an awful choice you bring
twixt my lover and my king,
but I'll go back to Arthur without you."

High rise the fields above the sky
Where fear of falling teaches us to fly
He tried to bring you down
That damn giant with his crown
But you leapt from the clouds for to be free."

When he was done, his eyes cast over the audience as he bowed, caught An's and gave her his sad smile. It wasn't until he left the stage and An raised her tea back to her lips that she realised her eggs had come and she was no longer alone at the table. Liberty was watching her with a nearly hidden look of amusement. "When...?" An began.

"Second verse." Liberty set her hand on hers as An blushed. "It happens around him. See," she pointed out the small cluster of fangirls swarming him near the end of the bar.

An's cheeks darkened even further. "That does not help."

"Ye wanted t' see me?" she asked.

"Aye," she said, setting down her cup and cutting into a crusted, sausage wrapped, boiled egg. She was grateful for the change of subject. "I've been thinkin' about coming more often. Well... I need a few hours away and I don't always want to eat at home, alone... this," she gestured to the room, "sounds like the table I'm used to. I'm alone but in company."

"Mrs Tallow's cooking not to yer likin'?"

An groaned. "She's on a tear about healthier eatin'. I understand about no meat on Fridays, but she's trading it fer sommat... I don't know what it is, but 'tis awful." She took a bite of her egg and sighed with

266

contentment. "'Tis been more'n a century since I've had one o' these. Anyway, I was wonderin', since that street yon is a bit... rough, might I link my door to one o'th' one's upstairs?"

There was a brief moment of chill heralding his approach, then Jonny was standing there with a bottle in hand. "Lookin' t' avoid my walkin' ye home again?" he commented dryly.

An was beginning to think her cheeks would never return to their normal colour. "'Tis not that... I... once in a bit it would be nice. Just.... Several reasons. Would ye like a seat, some tea perhaps?"

He pulled out a chair and sat, shook his head about the tea. "Mayhap later."

She continued her reasoning. "One, comin' here is dangerous and more than just that street. There's th' risk of someone seein' me leave th' house."

Jonny nodded. "Good point."

"Two, I've begun takin' Elizabeth to lessons with Sean every Tuesday and Thursday and if her mother comes home afore we get back, I can just take us here and walk home. There's a park nearby I take her to, and there is plenty here by way of excuse without havin' t' explain t' her mother th' lessons. Lessons which she'll eventually want to see demonstrations of, which is th' only reason I haven't told her." She took a breath. "I hate keepin' it from her, but it's fer th' best and she has granted me a great deal of autonomy with her daughter over th' last month. I think she likes th' improvements; now that she's not gettin' in trouble at school for things nae her fault. Well, they were, but not under her control."

She slowly ate her egg and drank her tea.

"I don't see a problem with it at all," Liberty said. "I'd recommend the third door, though. That's Roulet's. Occasionally there are small gatherin's up there, private parties, and that door is far enough back they'll not see sommat odd when th' door opens from yer cottage an' not a bedroom."

An nodded. "Wise. Thank ye. That and if Elizabeth has to escape and no one's home..."

Liberty gave her hand a squeeze, rose. "I'll leave ye two be. I've got sommat t' deal with," she said, eyeing something happening at the bar.

"Oh, and An, if ye kin think of it, ye kin order it. Lafayette's good that way. If it'll take more than a half hour to cook, just call ahead." She rose, paused behind Jonny's chair with a hand on his shoulder, her voice lowered. "Stay with her. If anything happens, keep her calm and everything should be fine."

"Aye." He glanced over at the bar, eyes following Liberty as she slipped through the crowd.

"What is going on?" An asked calmly as she cut up the second egg and fixed herself another cup of tea.

"Mundane trouble. Just a pair of cops. Not a full raid." He drank his beer and changed seats, taking the one Liberty had vacated so he could watch the goings on.

"Raid? Like a cattle raid?"

He chuckled at that. "No. It's what they call it when the police come into a place and start looking for illegal things, like drugs or people too young to be drinking, etc. There's only two, so likely it's not one. They're prob'ly checking on a complaint. If they find anything, more will come and we will leave discreetly."

She nodded, unable to keep from worrying. She sipped more of her tea. She found herself wanting to ask if she could get a bottle of the 'milk' to go home. This stuff was potent. Perhaps she should just ask her brownie.

She fidgeted with her biscuit, sipping occasionally of her tea, neither of them really saying anything, and that was perfectly fine with her. Sitting in silence was kind of nice, too. At least, this kind of silence.

They listened to other poets read their work, and two other singers, one with a song of their own crafting and moderately good. Jonny excused himself for a moment after the performance and drew the artist aside, offering them some advice which An assumed they took well by Jonny's attitude. He did not sit down when he returned, but reached out and took up her hand, pulling her to her feet. "It is time to go." Something in his voice said it was not wise to debate the matter.

She reached down for Cipín. "I have t' pay m'tab," she insisted, pulling the plastic card from her pocket that Liberty had shown her how to use.

He slipped it back into her pocket, pulled her close and smiled, "If

Liberty will even take yer money, ye can give it to her tomorrow. I promised I'd keep ye safe and 'tis now time to leave," his voice was a near purr, so soft that if it had not been meant for her, she would not have heard it. It sent a chill down her spine for multiple reasons.

"Fine," she gasped, swaying a bit from both the alcohol and his nearness. She let him put his arm around her waist, pulling her close as they meandered out the door like a pair of lovers.

Once out in the cool night air, they began to walk down the pavement with her still wrapped in his arms. They had not gotten as far as the next store-front when several cops pulled up to the curb and got out, heading into the club. Jonny stopped, turning back to look like everyone else, drawing An back against the building and out of the way. Once the gawkers began to move on, he loosened his grasp on her and turned to walk her home.

He saw her to the door, watching her with concern. "I am certain ye can go to Courtz tomorrow and fix th' door. 'Tis a good idea."

"What time do they open?"

"I'm sure if you called they will be open when you get there. Miss O'Keefe and Roulet both have taken a shine to ye." There was a sparkle in his eyes when he said it, and An got the feeling there was more to the statement than the words.

"Thank ye for walking me home and avoidin' that.... That."

He smiled, bending over her hand. "My pleasure, Ceobhránach. Call Roulet. Liberty may be busy in the morn."

She blushed as his lips touched her skin. "I... I can wait. A few days more will make no difference."

"Do not wait too long," he smiled and stepped back, watching her get out her magic key and open the door, going inside. Once the door closed, he shifted and flew away.

An slipped upstairs on silent feet, paused to check in on Elizabeth, saw her sleeping soundly and headed to her own room. Her own bed was neatly made. She never slept there any more. The room was dead to her. She went to her closet and opened the door to the cottage. The fire was not even on in the front room, though the bedroom door stood open, waiting for her, and she could see the fire gleaming from in there. Silently grateful, she let Cipín go to her corner and sat to draw off her boots, setting them beside the bench, and drifted to her room.

Her gown was laying out on the bed as usual and the fire blazing away at just the right level to keep out the increasing chill of the night. On the nightstand was another toddy, but somehow she did not think it was enough any more. She sighed. "'Tis not that I'm ungrateful, but I don't think this will do tonight. Have we anything stronger?"

She felt the question between her toes and sighed. "The strongest can be found. I need sleep beyond dreams."

The house warned her to be careful as she slipped into the bathroom to attend her needs. She took a little longer than necessary before coming out and slipping into her gown. She tucked herself up into the bed before she turned to the small tumbler resting beside the lit lamp. She smiled, took a sip of the incredibly potent liquor. She could taste the honey that had been swirled in to kill the bitter, dry alcohol taste. She felt the languor creeping into her limbs immediately and sank back against the pillows. Her last thought before she slept was that she needed to be up and to the other house by eight.

An found the poitín worked to a small extent. The liquor tasted like rubbing alcohol smelled, but the honey stirred into it helped. A rose and headed back to the Tallows to get Elizabeth off to school. Over the last month, Sharon had begun leaving earlier for work, since she did not have to stay to get Elizabeth ready in the mornings, staying only long enough to kiss her tow-headed curls as the girl ate her breakfast.

Once the school bus had left, An locked up and walked to Courtz. Whatever had gone down the night before had been over by morning. Liberty took An to lunch when she arrived to enchant the door and explained over Chinese food. "Apparently someone had called in a complaint that they saw Brad selling coke from th' bar."

An frowned, gestured to the glass she only knew Liberty had because of how she held her hand. "Ye mean what ye ordered to drink?"

Liberty laughed. "No. Tha's Coca-Cola, a legal drink. 'Coke' for short. They were talkin' about cocaine, a potent and highly illegal drug. Also 'coke' for short. Same root word, same nickname. Anywho, they came t' check it out an' found a box behind th' bar he was supposedly distributin' out of. I made them run finger prints. Th' box was half empty an' there were no prints on it a'tall. Therefore, it was planted. And there were no evidence of th' little baggies they were packaged in anywhere in th' club, so they're lookin' inta who'd want t' frame us. Da's lookin' too, and will likely find 'em first. He's some ideas."

An nodded. "I was hoping it was nothin'."

"Dukes and Torres, th' cops what came last night, are good people, but they've got their jobs t' do. They were actually relieved when things failed to add up. I think they'll look fer th' culprit just cause they don' like bein' used t' hurt th' innocent."

"Or made to look foolish," An added.

Liberty shook her head. "That I don't think has a lot to do with it. Maybe for Dukes, but not Torres. Anywho, glad ye plan t' come regular. Ye should read or sing one night. Not just eat an' run."

An blushed. "I'll think about it."

An did think about it, and decided against it. Then one night when she entered the cottage about a week later, she found a large envelope on the table addressed to her. She went to it, curious. "Mail fer me?"

The papers inside had been handwritten in glamoured ink so she could read them. It was sheet music.

She laid them out on the table, sorting the different songs together, and smiled. "I think he's tryin' t' tell me somethin'. Trouble is, I don't read music."

She was reading through a page of one song when she heard music coming from the pantry. She rose, opening the door, and saw a place where nothing was, essentially a hole in the shelf. She closed her hand over the object and felt the music between her fingers. She carried it back to the table.

The sounds coming from the device matched the lyrics at least. There were modern songs and some of folkish bent. Most were not Irish at all. She spoke to the device, asking it to play one of the other songs on the table, and it immediately obliged. She smiled. Her reading music problem was solved. Now she just had to get up the courage to get on the stage.

It was just over a week after she had received the music that Jonny approached her at karaoke. She had come early that Friday, not even pretending to stay for supper, and ordered real food. She found the concept of karaoke very curious. The folk who got up to sing ranged from excellent to out-right caterwauling. What interested her was that most seemed to feel little embarrassment at how badly they had done. An was just finishing her dinner when Jonny appeared at her elbow, his hand out. "Come. Sing wi' me, Ceobhránach," he said in his soft voice.

"I...," she started to refuse, then realised that she had best get in practice. The next funeral she would likely be asked again and far better to be horrible among strangers. "Which? Is it one I know?"

He gave her a tip of the head that was as close to a shrug as he ever came. "I sent ye the piece. Yer part's easy. Mine may come across somewhat hard for ye, but there's meanin' here I'd have said."

She reached up and set her small, warm hand in his slim, cool one and he noted the purple, iridescent paint on her nails and smiled at her. "Indulgin' in a wee bit of modern vanity, Mistress?" he teased. "An interestin' choice of colour."

An blushed and tried to reclaim her hand, but he used it to draw her to her feet instead. "Elizabeth... wanted practice. An' this week t'was the on'y way I could get her t' sit still long enough t' take in th' Lewis and Clark expedition. I was goin' t' remove it, but... I smelled supper and felt th' need t' escape."

"'Tisn't bad, though I'd ask her for sommat more pale." He drew her along to the stage, expertly dodging patrons. "Do ye remember 'Love Th' Way You Lie'?"

She thought a moment, trying to run the melody through her head. Then she realised it was only the female part that was sung. The rest had been an aggressive staccato. She nodded. "I can manage. I liked the melody."

"Good. Follow th' lyric and don't let me throw you off." Then they were on stage and he set her in front of the mike, leaving her for a moment to tell Roulet what he wanted.

There was no lead-in to warn her and only the visual on the monitor, which was lost on her. She started a beat late, but caught up, finding herself quickly lost in the melody. Her voice wasn't as high as the version she had listened to, but it was haunting none-the-less. Then Jonny launched into the rap, shouldering her out of the way more gently than he appeared to. He was angry. He was passionate. He was frustration incarnate. When he turned on her, she took a step back, unconsciously bowing up in the face of his aggression. It sent chills down her spine in a way she had never felt before. When he grabbed her arms, she gasped, then threw him off the way Skye had shown her and began to sing again.

She poured more of herself than she knew she had into the performance. When they were done, she was exhilarated and wrung out, and too full of alien emotions. She had stood in the face of his anger, and it was real anger, if not aimed at her, and held her own; felt the surge of that tide like weathering a storm in a stone barn, able to stand back and appreciate beauty of nature's wrath from safety.

He did not touch her again when they were done, was turned away from her, staring into the back of the audience at someone. An felt the air beginning to seep out of her high slowly as her eyes caught the figure of a frosty blonde back by the front door, leaning against the frame in something scandalous, arms crossed over her ample chest and scowling. Catching the look traded between the woman and Jonny, the rest of her elation flooded from her.

She took a step back, turned and felt for the rail of the short stairs, half stumbling down them without Cipín to guide her footing. She went to the bar, calling the shillelagh to her and damned who saw. She ordered a double of poitín and slammed it back. She did not even try to pay for it. She had already been refused. She winced at the taste and left the glass on the bar, headed upstairs to the door to her cottage.

Skye was at the far end of the bar and watched the whole thing. He had been impressed by the performance, but scowled when he realised Jonny had used her to send a message to someone else. There were too many people for him to see who, but it was enough that Jonny had left her on stage to fend for herself without her stick. He drank the last of his Guinness and started back towards the bathroom when Jonny staggered out of the crowded dance floor, looking around, he assumed, for An. His suspicion was confirmed as the man's eyes went to the stairs and headed in that direction.

Skye placed himself in the way, blocking off the stairwell. He glared down into the elven man's eyes. "Ah think no'," he rumbled. "Ah believe she's had her fill o' ye t'noight, ye numpty keech."

Jonny was taken a little aback by the insult, but Skye took more than a little pride in the confusion on his face that said he wasn't sure what he had just been called. But the man did not push the matter.

Skye remained by the stairs, watching him move through the crowd, eventually hooking up with a slight young woman with short blue hair. He scowled as the two wandered out of the club arm in arm in such a way as to leave no doubt what would be happening when they got wherever they were going. He clenched his fists, cracking his knuckles in the process. A tilt of his head cracked his neck, and he turned and headed up the stairs, using the same door An had, but to a different location.

16

Samhain dawned clear and cold, and An had managed to get permission from Elizabeth's parents to take her to her 'Uncle's' house for a big party with trick or treating in a nice, safe neighbourhood. She promised to have her home by ten, and as it was not a school night, this was accepted. This time it was Skye who pulled up to collect her in an SUV, which apparently impressed George and made him more comfortable with the whole deal. He was also impressed with Skye, as An introduced him as her brother.

This caused Skye to raise a brow, but he did not contradict her.

Elizabeth was dressed as Hermione Granger caught mid-polyjuice potion and Sean had helped her fashion a very convincing glamour. She carried a small cauldron for her treats. She had also convinced An to dress for the occasion, though she chose Mary Poppins, which let her carry Cipín without clashing with the costume.

Skye laughed when the pair came down the walk. He was dressed as Shrek, not that An had any clue who he was supposed to be, but it made

Elizabeth laugh.

Skye didn't drive all the way out to the Rest, but down to Courtz, parking the vehicle in the back alley. The three of them went up the back stairs to Roulet's door, and An took them through her cottage and down the back garden gate to the path. Elizabeth held both of their hands going through the woods, as the wind rattled eerily through the branches, and the fading sunlight cast odd shadows through the trees.

As they walked by the rath, Elizabeth turned, watching it. They were almost past, and she was twisted between them, trying to keep it in sight. "What is that?" she asked when she finally turned back around.

"That is the faery fort, and one of those places you will avoid as if your life depends on it. Because your freedom certainly does," An said shortly. "That place opens onto a trod in the borderlands of Faery, and on nights like this the Wild Hunt rides with the Northerner at their head."

"Northerner?"

An took a breath, "The Morrigan. The Red Queen. Head of the Unseelie court. If ye want t' know more, ye might ask the Bard."

There was no time to say anything more as they left the wooded path and came out to the green and saw swarms of people in various costumes. There were kids everywhere, gathering together in clusters.

They brought Elizabeth over to Bethany's group and introduced her around. Skye counted out the children in the group and looked over at Liberty, who was coordinating the clusters. "Ah got ten little heathens here! This moi group?"

Liberty looked over, nodded and signalled him to head out.

An waved to Elizabeth as she set off with Bethany and Skye to go trick or treating with a horde of new friends.

An smiled and turned back towards the veranda, intending to spend a moment in a rocking chair to watch what she could see and enjoy the smells and the crisp chill of the air.

Night fell while she rocked, catching fragments of sleep, but not enough to slip into the dream state where the nightmares waited, which meant not deep enough for sustaining rest. When she opened her eyes, she took in first the orange and black streamers which marked everything for her; then the figure leaning against the post across from her, watching her as a fox watches a rabbit's den. It was not a friendly over-watch. An suppressed a shiver.

Serephina waited until it was clear An was awake before speaking. Her voice was full of cold venom, beautiful but deadly. "So you're Jonny's new conquest."

An remained calm. Truthfully, she hadn't the energy to get worked up. "I am not his conquest. He has been th' perfect gentleman and friend."

"Ooo, he must *really* like you then."

An ignored the barb.

Serephina shifted, rolling her back off the post sensuously. "He'll get around to it," she added. "Always does. And a few others while he's at you."

"A man's prerogative." An was unfazed, and it clearly irritated the woman. An let her rant with her body and simply adjusted the wrist of one glove where it had got twisted. Her face was looking down at her hand, but her eyes were on the succubus before her, for there was no better way to describe the woman. "Should ye be out here chasin' other men whilst yer husband lies on his deathbed, Mrs Morelle?"

If An knowing her name fazed Serephina, she did not show it. Instead she smiled, an expression which came across as unquestionably evil. "My husband lies in his grave, my dear."

"Well, ye'll not find yer next one out here," An said, thinking of Roulet, Bethany and Solitaire's conversation about her a few months back.

To her surprise, Serephina scoffed. "Like I'd bother to look out here." Something in the way she looked out over the peopled fields made An think she had already tried and been brushed off by the only ones of any interest to her. Suddenly the woman looked back at An. "Wait. Ye think...?" She laughed. "I'd not have Jonny to wed for all the jewels in Araby. I know how that tale ends and I'm no love-sick fool. Best watch your step with Sorrow, lass. He'll break your blind heart as soon as look at you." With that, she strode off the veranda and out into the dark. She brushed past an old woman carrying a basket, upsetting its contents and nearly knocking her over. She never looked back.

An got up, went to the woman to make sure she was all right. Up close she was hideous, and An could tell the hag look was no costume or glamour. She maintained her stoic demeanour, determined not to be rude, and bent to pick up the apple which she saw had fallen from her basket. As she turned to hand it to her, she saw the old woman going through the motions of picking up other things.

The old woman looked at the apple in An's hand and the others on the ground, then at her eyes and grinned, wide and toothless. Her face scrunched up like one of those dried apple-headed dolls from An's childhood. "Should tek you to goblin market vit me," she grinned, her accent thick and Russian.

An gave her a sad smile. "Would do ye no good, Grandmother. Over there I see everythin'. Once it's here..." she tipped her head in a shrug.

"Misty Poppins," she cackled, eyeing An's costume. "Might ask you, vhen come home. Sometime goblin cheet."

She gathered the rest of her apples, and An made an attempt to help. When they stood, and An gave her a nod and started to move away, the old hand shot out and locked, claw-like, on her arm with a strength that surprised her. "Whatch dat one," she nodded in the direction Serephina had taken. "Silver snake is trouble, for you, for me, for all of us. Bard too." She looked off into the night. "Dough she is not de won whe must whatch tonight."

She pressed an ordinary apple into An's hand, patted her cheek and shuffled off into the thick of the people, cackling. An stood watching her go, handing out apples as she went. She had a peculiar habit of shaking them and holding them to her ear before she gave them over. None of the apples she gave away were visible to An's fey sight.

An smiled tiredly, stifled a yawn.

Some of the groups of children were coming back from their rounds with tons of candy, and An turned to look for the ones she could see, which were thankfully few, when her pocket began to buzz annoyingly. She pulled the phone from her skirt and opened it. "Hello?"

It was George, and he sounded stressed. There were unpleasant sounds in the background. "Um... Miss O'Keefe?"

"Aye," she said, confused and getting more worried.

"Is there... any way you and Elizabeth can... stay out at your uncle's tonight?"

There was a cold feeling in the pit of her stomach. "What happened?" she demanded.

"Well, Sharon and I took advantage of the empty house for a night out. Haven't had one in a while and… while we were gone, someone broke in. Or tried to. Doesn't look like they did more than vandalise the outside but… Elizabeth's window is broken and I can't do more than put up paper until tomorrow."

An frantically patted all her pockets for the remote, sank onto the veranda steps, weak in the knees, when she did not find it. "I… It will be fine, Mister Tallow. My uncle would be delighted, and she's having fun with th' cousins her age. It will be a grand adventure for her. I'll… hang on to her 'til tomorrow afternoon, as I think they've something planned for All Saint's Day. There usually is with this crowd. We'll be home by evening if that will suffice?"

"Sure. Sure. As long as she's having fun. …And is safe," he added. His tone did not sound like her safety was an after-thought, but a reluctance to actually voice it. "I'll… call if there is any other trouble. The cops are still here checking things out."

Someone spoke to him on his end, and he rang off without another word. An closed the phone and just sat there, stunned. How could she have failed so badly? If Elizabeth had been home….

Someone large loomed behind her and she looked up, saw Ian standing on the top step, lighting a cigarette. "Somethin' the matter, An?" he asked with deceptive casualness.

"I… I failed ye."

"Oh?" he asked, sitting down beside her. "How so. I see th' young miss over yon havin' th' time o' her life," he said, pointing out the tow-headed girl with the cat ears amid the small swarm around the old lady getting some kind of treat from her basket. "Though yeh might want t' warn her about Baba. She's safe enough t'night so long as yer polite. But there are times…" He left it hanging and turned back to An. "So tell me how yeh've failed."

"Some… someone tried to get into the house tonight."

"Tried or succeeded?"

"I don't know yet," she said softly, her eyes on the girl she was responsible for. "They broke her window. I don't even know if the alarms went off as I left the damned remote... at home, I think."

Ian smoked quietly for a moment, contemplating her. "She was here with you, so yeh did yer duty by her. She is safe, e'en though her house isn't. If yeh'd had th' remote, nothing would have been different."

"But I wasn't paying enough attention..." she did not add why that was.

He cleared his throat. "Was everythin' golden with th' gilded trio? Over yon?"

"Well..."

"Any o' 'em ever run off? Get lost?"

"Lion turned th' youngest into a fish once and lost him in th' moat. We searched for hours until th' Prince realised what we were looking for and remembered where he had tossed him. Sorting th' lad out took all night," she admitted. "And there was th' time th' princess was missing a whole fortnight..."

"And none of that was marked against yeh fer not takin' fair enough care. That child is fine. Though yer not. We'll get it all squared away. I'll get someone over there to replace th' windows in th' mornin'. They'll look like whatever workmen he's hired *and* give him a better price," he added, silencing the protest she had started to make. "And they'll double check th' house for plants. Yeh see anythin' out o' place when yeh get back, yeh call me immediately."

"Can Elizabeth stay up here at th' big house tonight? I'd let her stay at my cottage, but I don't want her gettin' too used to it. I already am spoiled t' th' point I couldn't sleep anywhere else, I think," she said with a soft laugh. "I can only imagine how quickly it would affect her."

He laughed easily, dragging the last of his cigarette down and rolling it out with his fingers, slipping the butt into his pocket. "I think Bet'any and Kellain are plannin' on takin' over th' barn t'night. All th' kids are sleepin' there, if they sleep at all. Ghost stories and whatever else they come up with. Th' barn's well out o' th' path o' th' Wild Hunt should th' Bitch escape th' hedge."

"The maze Fox put up at midsummer?"

"Aye. It only lasts 'til dawn, but 'tis usually enough. More than once in th' last... oh, hundred years or so, though, she's managed t' find her way through."

280

He rose, stretching. It sounded like every bone in his body cracked. He laughed. "Old man body to go with old man brain." He held out his hand to help her up. "Don't be so hard on yerself. Yer doin' right well, even for a woman with full sight."

He lifted his head as she got to her feet, hearing something off nearer the bonfires. With a nod to her, he headed off in that direction to find out what the yelling was about.

An, a little curious herself, drifted in that direction. Elizabeth found her, running up breathless with a half-eaten cookie in hand. She was grinning broadly and obviously enjoying herself. "Look!" she beamed, showing An her small cauldron, which An could tell was filled with all kinds of treats to just under the brim.

"I see you managed to make th' cauldron bottomless after all," she smiled.

Her cat whiskers twitched at that as she wrinkled her nose. "Nah, just deepern' it should be. Still cool! But, I meant the cookie!"

An suddenly realised she could see the confection. "Did you get that from..."

"Baba Yani, yes!" she crowed. "She's a nice old lady. Scary, but cool. She said all the children had to have one, and we had to eat it all tonight. It's to protect us. Make us invisible to the fey. At least until dawn. Isn't it cool?" she added, taking another bite. An was a little dismayed to watch her fade a little before her eyes. Though, even when she ate the last of the cookie, she never faded completely from view.

"It works. Well, I hope ye thanked that one."

Elizabeth stopped moving and stared wide-eyed. "You said not to."

An sighed. "It is hard sometimes to tell. But th' *people* ye kin thank. Ye never thank a fey thing, not directly. And I meant my house. Thanking a brownie is a terrible insult, and to fey... it signifies a debt they'll expect to be repaid. Baba... if she's a Baba Yaga, you have to be really polite to her. She eats rude children. And does terrible things if adults fail her tests. I'll have to read you some of th' Russian faery tales about her. She's dangerous."

"She's not Baba Yaga," she laughed, then imitated the old woman's accent and gruff manner, "Baba Yani. Baba Yaga Mama!" She devolved into giggles. "She's one of the daughters of Baba Yaga."

An looked off to where the old woman was listening to an apple in front of a tall, lithe, beautiful man with cat-like accents about him. "They were all impossibly beautiful. She can't be."

"Oh, but she is!" Elizabeth was taking a great deal of delight in teaching her teacher. "She was the youngest. Then Katchi the Dying..."

An corrected her, "Katchei th' Deathless."

"Katchei the Deathless," she repeated, "came to the Yaga for a promised bride and took the youngest and most beautiful. She did not please him, so he turned her into the likeness of her mother and sold her to the Northerner."

"Hmmm. Still. Ye should beware of witches, this night especially. So go thank her and be careful with your words. Remember, your choice of words matter. Magic doesn't always follow th' spirit of what you say, but th' letter. And Magic always listens."

Elizabeth nodded, handing An her cauldron to hold. An watched her run up to the old woman as she walked away from the confused man beginning to eat the apple she had pressed on him. The woman listened carefully and smiled.

"I'm sorry," Elizabeth began with a small curtsey. "My governess told me not to thank anything over here cause of faery precautions, and I thought she meant 'everything' but she only meant her house and... I wanted you to know I liked the cookie and thank you for trying to protect us. Best medicine I've ever had to take!" she grinned.

An watched the old woman light up. She beamed at the child, muttering something An could not make out between the softness, the distance, the lack of teeth and the accent. But she watched her reach up and pat Elizabeth's cheek fondly and wander off, singing an off-key song in Russian, with a lighter step than she had. Elizabeth trotted back to her, flush with happiness.

"She said I was a good girl!"

"What else?"

"Something about it being rare. ...I think. I couldn't really tell. But she liked me." She seemed to suddenly realise how late it was and began to deflate. "What time is it? Please tell me it's not ten o'clock yet."

An chuckled softly, ruffling the girl's hair and scratching behind her almost real cat ears. "'Tis no matter even were it midnight. Yer t' stay here t'night."

Elizabeth nearly exploded with glee. "Really!?"

"Aye. Bethany and Kellain are campin' out with th' rest o' th' children in th' barn t'night. Yer stayin' with them. Now," she said more loudly as Elizabeth began dancing around in her joy. "Ye'll obey any adult what tells ye t' do sommat... unless they creep ye out, and some will. If they make ye uncomfortable, be polite, but seek another adult immediately fer confirmation. Yer not to go into th' woods or near th' rath. Ye stay with th' other children or Kellain or Bethany or any of th' others I've introduced ye to. I'll find ye in th' barn in th' mornin'. Yer not to come out t' th' cottage by yerself. Th' woods might not be safe."

"All right!" she squealed. "Wait 'til I tell the others!" She stopped long enough to kiss An on the cheek before she ran off, yelling after a group of the girls who stopped for her, leaving An holding her cauldron.

An smiled and turned back to the main house, slipping into the kitchen quietly. She set the cauldron on an empty shelf in the pantry, spoke softly for whatever of the brownies might be listening. "If ye would be so kind as t' slip this inta me own pantry? Feel free t' sample an' ye like."

She turned and walked out of the kitchen, confident her request would be carried out. She headed back outside to mingle with the others, enjoying the festivities as best she could. She still avoided the alcohol tables, got herself some plain cider and a mincemeat pastry.

There was music of a sort being played as she approached the bandstand. The band was taking a break, and a stereo was playing something she was unfamiliar with, but there were a great deal of people on the floor. From the handful of dancers she could see, she could only describe it as a zombie dance. Every one was having fun and enjoying the spooky music so she moved on.

She caught a glimpse of Jonny over where she had first met him. He was surrounded by what she assumed were children sitting in a circle around him, and he seemed very animated tonight, telling a story that brought cries of fright and delight in equal turns. She smiled dimly, feeling her heart ache, but walked on.

She was near the bonfires when she heard the argument. It had apparently escalated from the heated discussion of earlier into a full-blown screaming match. She drifted nearer. There was a dark red-headed woman with flashing green eyes and a bestial mien pacing between Mikey and Henry in a fury. Her shoulder-length hair was wild and puffed up, like an animal with its hackles up.

"You shouldn't have killed him, Raigne!" Mikey growled.

"He pissed me off. You 'just shoot' people all the time," she snapped, rounding on him.

"Not like that, I don't. That wasn't enough provocation. That wasn't business. That was a personal slight in a BAR, Raigne!"

"Ye ran from de scene, so obviously ye realised ye'd fucked up," Henry stamped. His antlers were fully prominent, as was the crown of holly between them.

"I was feeling claustrophobic!" she turned on him. "I would think you, of all beasts, would understand that."

"I understand dere are odder ways of dealing wit' yer problems dan pullin' out magical pistols and shootin' a man dead in fronta witnesses jus' fer touching yer arse!"

"He did more than fondle my fanny, Henry," she snarled, getting in his face.

"Yeah, well, dere are ways t' deal wit dat, too. Quiet-like."

She laughed, high and scornful. "No wonder the Russians are moving in on us. They have no respect for the O'Keefe's cause we haven't given them a reason to."

"It's not yer call how to handle our reputation," Henry replied, with a stag-like snort of anger. An watched his left foot unconsciously pawing at the ground. "Dat's de chief's call and we are not dat kinda mob, Raigne. Yer not to go out again, not until we're sure ye're stable."

She got up into his face, her heels seeming to stretch farther from the balls of her feet, making her taller. Her face wrinkled up even as it began to get more wolf like. "You don't get to put a collar on me, buck-boy. You're just a prey animal with a ritual title and no power at all."

"That's enOUGH, Raigne," bellowed Ian, suddenly looming among the rest of those who had begun to gather near, drawn by the conflict. He was nearly half-gryphon, larger than normal, and his feathers raised in anger. "*I can,* and I say yeh'll do as yer told. Yeh'll not leave th' Rest until we can get this straightened out. We have to see how much they have on yeh, whether they can identify yeh enough. If I have to put yeh under house arrest, I will. What yeh did was foolish and puts all of this in jeopardy!" he growled, sweeping a wing-like arm out to indicate the whole community.

Raigne spun, started to bow up at Ian and thought better of it. "So many damned restrictions, Ian! Do this! Don't do that! I want to rip out throats and I don't cause you asked me not to," she screamed. "But there are some things I can't tolerate. I won't. I won't be locked up again. At least with Her I could run free and drink the blood of my enemies!"

There was a collective gasp at that shout as she shifted fully, running at the crowd as a huge blood-red wolf. When the crowd did not yield to her an opening, she turned and ran at the bonfire, leaping high and over it, tearing off into the night. There was a snarl and cry from Ian's eagle's throat as he called for pursuit. Henry pulled a horn from his hip and blew it, calling for others to join the chase to stop the maddened wolf.

Beyond the fire, from the direction Raigne had run, An heard someone scream and the wolf howl as she ran. Ian launched himself into the air and flew after her. The resultant wind and the rush of folk to join the hunt and stop her before she could get to the fort knocked An about, buffeting her one way and then another as the pursuers were less than careful. She was pushed nearer to the bonfire than she would have liked, where she eventually fell.

The centaur ran at her, leaping over her head and the bonfire, clipping the top logs with his back hoof and sending it falling behind him. It landed near enough to An that she rolled out of the way, recoiling from the sudden heat that swiftly escalated until she felt the full effects of being in the fire and melting down into a lump of white-hot metal to be pounded into shape.

Skye had pulled his sword and answered the call, running between the fires to join the chase when he saw Coach And Four go over the left bonfire and dislodge some of the embers. He heard An scream before he saw her thrashing form on the bare ground, too close to the flames for safety. He changed course immediately, letting go of his sword and snatching her up, pulling her away from the danger zone. His touch made her scream all the more, her blind eyes open wide and the mists full of fire and pain. He held her down, trying to convince himself he wasn't hurting her more this way, that it was all phantom pain.

Out of the corner of his eye he saw a blonde woman of incredible beauty in a slinky, iridescent cocktail dress and highly impractical heels for walking on the Green. She was watching the scene with amusement and no small amount of malice. But Skye did not have time to say anything or react before An had slipped into the ocean and begun to drown, gasping for air that would not come.

He nearly crushed her against his body, trying to still the thrashing; ignoring the pounding of her fists against him or the claws that eventually dug in when rescue came. When she dissolved into sobs, he lifted her up in his arms, turned to say something to the woman and found her gone. Writing it off for now, he ran back to the main house, looking for the small side door that led down to the basement that he had linked to the Mead Hall. He was not going to risk the path through the woods tonight.

He passed from the basement door to the training hall and back out again, crossing to the gate at the front of her house. It swung open for him, as did the door. She was clinging to him, sobbing her heart out as he carried her into her bedroom and laid her on the bed. She did not want to let go, so he sat on the edge and just held her.

An was shaking. Her sorrow was no longer just at the loss of the endless string of unfaithful girls, but for all her sleepless nights, and the bouts of pain that woke her whenever she did manage. It was all too much, and she feared she was losing her mind.

Skye held her until they heard the sound of fey horns bellowing from the woods and the answering howl of the hounds of the Wild Hunt. An shuddered, looking up and out the window in a panic, and the sash on the window dropped and the shutters slammed closed. The jarring sound was abruptly cut off.

"Is Elizabeth safe? I heard the hunt," she insisted, clutching Skye's jerkin, still trying to see out.

"She eat th' witch's biscuit?" he countered. An nodded. "Then she's foin. Ah left her wit' th' other bairns by th' barn. They're locked up safe an' tight. Though how th' red-coated Bitch got pas' th' heidge...."

An took a ragged breath, getting herself under control. "Raigne, likely. When she went in. I don' know if she's th' power t' unmake it, but if naught else she could have lead them through."

"That mingin' cow," he swore. "Ah git m' mits on her ah'll rip her throat out like th' other o'them Northerner cú."

When she let go of him and sat back, (pried herself off, more accurately,) he let her compose herself before he began to ask the questions that had been brewing for about a month now. "What t' devil is goin' on, An? What have ye doon to yersel'?"

"It's the ring," she sighed, leaning back against the headboard.

"Still?"

"Aye, still," she snapped. "'Tis not lettin' me rest. I sleep fer a little an' then th' dreams come an' I can't get out o' them. I've tried drinkin', but it only makes me sleep when I can't. It doesna protect me from th' dreams. I need.... I need sleep beyond dreams an' I can't manage!"

He looked down at the small bin beside the nightstand, saw it full of empty bottles. He picked one up, read the label: Quad-distilled poitín 180 proof. He frowned. "Ye've drunk all these?"

She looked over the side of the bed and groaned when her head swam. "That's been since... since the week or so after it happened. It's been a progressive thing, tryin' to get rest."

"Ye try sleepin' pills?"

She shuddered. "Aye. It just trapped me in th' dreams and kept me from escapin'. Elizabeth found me, woke me up. The house, she said, was givin' her a headache. I don't know how much o' that was my fault."

"Then we need t' try sommat else."

He got up off the bed and her hand shot out, seizing his wrist. "No one must know. I... couldn't bear it."

He looked at her, thinking of that silvery blonde near the fire and the malice that had come off of her. "Ah'll do what ah can. But there's at least one soul ah'll hav' ta tell. Get ready fer bed. Ah'll be back."

Skye left the same way he came, going back to the Mead Hall to return to the manor and the Green. There were fewer people milling about now that the Wild Hunt had ridden through. Very few were timidly beginning to come back out, in fear of when the Hunt would return to the mound, as she surely had to do. This night there was nothing they could do for the mortals out and about. They had done what they could and failed.

Most of the people out were coming from the Manor itself, furtively slipping out to gather up the food and drink and other things left unattended, and all were in masks. The barn was still locked up tight with the children inside, safe and sound with iron horseshoes over the door.

It was over by the barn, slipping out and darting for the safety of the woods, that Skye saw his target. He ran to meet her, slowing as he neared so as not to alarm her.

"Ah'll walk ye where ye need to git, gran'muther, if ye'll spare me a bit o' yer time."

Baba Yani looked him over critically. Finally she nodded, walking towards the wood path, looking left and right as if expecting the Hunt or some lurking ambush at any moment.

Skye started to talk to her, but she held up one ancient claw. "Not yit," she snapped.

Skye obeyed and followed her. She was especially skittish around the knoll, hurrying past as if afraid it might swallow her up. Just past it, she hung a left, away from the mound and into the deep woods where the path was little more than a deer trail. It took nearly twenty minutes before they came out into a small clearing where a little house shone in the scant moonlight. It looked like it was made of gingerbread.

When Baba saw this, she scowled, lifting the twisted cane she carried, and struck the little gingerbread man fence with it, swearing at it in Russian. The whole house shuddered and shifted, becoming something more in keeping with a witch. The fence became more pickety, and there were skulls with flaming eyes on each post where a gingerbread head had been. She humphed, satisfied, as the house stood up on a pair of gnarled chicken legs and turned around, managing somehow to look sheepish.

She started forward and then stopped, squinting under the house. Even Skye had to do a double take. Baba groaned, then sighed. Hidden under the house like a hen keeping an egg warm, was a large, blueish-grey wolf curled up and sleeping. "I'll test him later. Kip him slipink," she growled and the house obediently settled down on it again. The front door opened and let them into the tiny hut.

Skye started to ask if that had been Raigne, then stopped. She had said 'he'. He ducked and followed her into the house.

It was tiny and cramped and smelled of God only knew what herbs and unguents and brews. The house did not seem big enough to have more than this small room, but there were several doors. Baba came in, set her basket on the beat up old chop-block table and dropped herself into the only seat, a rickety rocking chair. She groaned, glad to be off her feet. She let go of her cane and it flew into a troll's foot umbrella stand.

Skye kept his thoughts to himself and stood respectfully, hunching to keep from hitting his head on the ceiling, waiting for her.

After several minutes, she opened an eye and glared up at him. "Still here?" she grumbled. "Ah, best spit out, boy. And tek off dose awful ears. Dey're disgrace to real ogre." Skye sheepishly pulled the band from his head and slipped them into his pocket. "Let's see if vhat you vant is vorth valk home."

Skye only arched an eyebrow at that. "A walk home on a noight th' Hunt be abroad. Worth more than other noights."

She sighed, leaning her head back on the chair and nodding. "Point. Lucky you, I lik vay you talk."

When she fell silent, Skye guessed it was time for him to 'spit out'. "M' sister..." Her eye reopened at that, the eyeball glaring accusingly at him.

"She's called me brother," he protested. "An' truth told, she feels loik a sister. At least ah think this be what a sister feels loik." This seemed to satisfy her, and the disturbing eye closed again. "Well, she read Raven's ring.."

Skye did not get any further. The old lady shot up, claws on the ends of the chair's arms and her eyes pinning him where he stood.

Skye had never felt fear before, not like this. This was something he could not fight.

"Who did vhat?"

"An... Th' blind lass wit' foggy eyes," he said, willing to answer even though he felt compelled to do so. "She touched Raven's ring, t' talk to it."

He could see the thoughts flying rapid-fire through her ancient brain. "And vhat did she learn?"

"Th' ring were a person, melted doon an' hammered inta a ring; tossed into an ocean then put on th' finger o' not jest one lass but a bunch."

She ruminated on this; the information seeming to confirm something for her. She got up from the chair, began moving around the room poking into baskets and jars, looking for something with a spryer step than she had affected all night. "And you are here because deese has done vhat?"

"She canna sleep, been havin' noightmares. Sometime she'll see sommat or hear sommat what sends her inta th' vision. She burns, she drowns, she watches them die like she was th' bloody ring," he growled. "Ah came hopin' ye'd have somethin' would put her t' sleep past dreams. But let her wake come morn," he added. "She needs rest, but she's a charge depends on her."

She paused in her search, regarded him again. "So ye risk vitch for deese voman you niver knew 'til you rescue an' King say 'tek home'?"

Skye started, and the old woman cackled. "I know t'ings, boy. Pitch vorries out vit bathvater, tovarish. I help. But only cause you valk home, an' girl may be of use in future... and vas nice to me vhen angel bitch vat's no angel vas rude. Oooo, but dat one gonna get..." her words became unintelligible at that. "I'll eat her one day and not in vay she used to."

Skye was confused at that, especially because it caused him to blush without really knowing why.

Suddenly the old woman shouted in triumph and came out from under a cupboard with a basket which she struggled to put on the table. Skye moved to help, taking it gently from her and putting it on the table for her. She grunted and took off the cloth hiding a mound of ripe, peach-like fruits. The aroma that wafted up from the basket was soporific and made him light-headed. The old woman carefully picked one out and put it into a sealed jar. She quickly covered the basket with the cloth and gestured for him to put it away where she'd gotten it.

When he stood again, she handed him the jar. "Theese is you need. Von bite and is out, slip beyond drems. Is good. Trouble is, you bite and you no get to chew. Stays in mout'. Vhich mean no vaykink. Trick is to find vay get down t'roat. Von bite vort' is enough for night slip. Must be careful dough. Too much no dremink mean girl go mad."

Skye thanked her and started to leave when her voice stopped him, rooting him to the spot. "Deese is dengerous magik, deese memories.

Dey will not fade or 'go vay vit' time'. She vill haf to see somevon. Soon."

"Who?"

She shrugged, waving him off. "Don't know. But dere are piples. She vill find whon. Dreamer she needs. Go. Hunt come back soon. Should be gone before. Here," she pressed a small animal skull into his other hand. "Light from gete, vill lead home. Just set on vall vhen get home, he vill come back on own."

With that, she shooed him out the door with a broom and turned to go deal with the wolf sleeping under her house.

Skye felt awkward at the gate. He held the two skulls a few inches apart, facing each other as he examined them, trying to fathom what he was supposed to do. The question became moot when the human skull flared and the animal skull's eyes lit up. He turned, facing the woods, and noticed the eyes grew dimmer and brighter depending on which way he faced. He turned to where it was brightest and followed its lead back to the cul-de-sac.

He was just stepping out of the woods into the field behind An's garden when he heard the sound of the returning horns. He hurried to the back gate, which would not open for him. He tried to force it, and it stubbornly wouldn't budge. The skull in his hand started to get a little warmer, and he looked down, suddenly remembering Baba's instructions. He set the skull on the low wall beside the gate and saw the fire go out with a disappointed gleam, and then the skull flew off into the night, back into the wood.

The gate now opened easily, and Skye hurried up to the waiting house. An was in the kitchen, sitting at the table in her dressing gown, sipping an herbal tea.

She looked up as the door opened, hope in her exhausted eyes. "Well?" she asked.

In answer, he set the jar on the table beside her cup. She frowned, opened the locking lid, and took a deep breath of the aromatic fruit. She wavered, immediately feeling the ether-like effects, and Skye moved the jar away from her, closing it with one hand while using the other to make sure she didn't fall out of her chair.

He pulled out the second chair and sat down once he was sure she was steady. He set the closed jar between them. "One bite, she seid. But findin' a way to swallow it.... Ye bite, yer out 'til it's removed."

She sighed. "Snow White's apple."

"Apparently. Though this be more peachy," he frowned.

She nodded.

He folded his arms on the table and rest his chin on them, staring into the jar at the perplexing fruit. "How do ye swallow sommat what knocks ye ballywhomped th' moment it touches yer tongue?"

An took a sip of her tea, thinking. Suddenly she looked into the teacup. "Ye drink it."

His head came up. "Mash an' blend."

She shook her head. "Too thick. Harder t' swallow. Has t' be thin enough t' slip down even as one passes out."

"Poitín," he grinned.

She frowned. "That's just too risky. Though it might act preserver. Somethin' less potent, perhaps?"

He laughed suddenly. "Got any vodka?"

An raised an eyebrow even as the house gave her an answer. "Third press from th' door."

He got up and went to the cupboard, chuckled when he saw not only a bottle of vodka with a few inches missing, but a funnel and a blender. He set the bottle on the counter and found a nose-and-mouth-only gas mask behind it. He set that with the bottle, and took down the blender, found the cord caught on something inside the cabinet.

As he reached in, looking to unhook it, An spoke up. "House says to leave it. There's no electricity in the cottage. Likely it's plugged in at the manor."

Skye shrugged and put on the mask, fetching the jar from the table and dropping the 'peach' into the blender. He'd seen the bartenders use this at both the Hedge Gate, (which he preferred,) and at Courtz, (which he had been frequenting more lately for entirely different reasons,) so it did not take him long to figure the machine out. He thought, too late, that the fruit might have a stone, but if it did, it was soft and pulped with the rest of it.

He set the funnel in the neck of the vodka bottle and poured the yellow slurry into the clear liquid, which instantly went cloudy. He rinsed the blender pitcher immediately, and the funnel, then closed the bottle and shook it up.

He set the mask, funnel and blender back in the cupboard and took down the single shot glass that was sitting on the shelf. He poured what he estimated to be a 'bite' for her into it and turned around. An was slumped on the table. He frowned, then realised he could smell the sweet sleepiness in the air and chuckled. "Glad ah wore th' mask."

He set the glass down and drew her back to pick her up. He had just lifted her from the chair when she roused.

"Huh?" she moaned, finding herself carried once more.

"Dunna worry yer pretty heid none. Th' fumes got ye. Ah'll get ye t' bed, then get yer medicine."

He wasn't really surprised when he got her into the bedroom and saw the tiny glass sitting on her nightstand and the bed turned down. He tucked her in and handed her the shot. She accepted it, looking worriedly up at him. "Goo on," he encouraged. "It'll help fer nao. Ah'll handle Elizabeth in th' marnin'. Loik as not, she'll sleep as late as ye t'morra."

"Ye might want t' put the rest in the fridge," she sighed. "Alcohol or no, 'tis still fruit. Do I want t' know where ye got it?"

"Drink!" he growled. An tossed back the shot and held out the glass. It took a second as the alcohol delayed the fruit's bite, suffusing her limbs with a tingling heaviness that felt as if she were being dragged down through a sea of cotton.

Skye grabbed her before she slumped, easing her back onto the pillow and setting the glass on the nightstand. He tucked her in, checking first to make sure she was still breathing. It was deep and slow. She was perfect stillness, like the girls in the stories, though she was obviously still alive. He slipped quietly from the room, even though he knew subconsciously he didn't have to be.

As he closed the door, he turned to find the fire crackling away in front of a pallet made up on the floor before it, big enough for him, and on the small table by An's chair was a half pint of a dark beer and a plate with a thick sandwich on it. He stopped himself before he thanked the house and sank into her chair to eat before falling into the bed.

17

The next morning found An waking to a good deal of light pouring through the window and a bath waiting for her in the bedroom before the fireplace. She rose slowly, uncertain of her body yet. She seemed all right, even clear-headed. She picked up her watch as she slipped out of her dressing gown, which she had apparently fallen asleep in. It was just after noon, but understandable considering how late she had taken her new medicine.

She undressed, pinned up her hair and slid into the bath, careful not to submerge her face. As she washed, she tried to remember anything of the night, and found that everything after the shot glass of sickly sweet yet bitter brew was a blissful blank. Without asking, the house told her she slept like the dead, unlike previous nights.

Thankfully, it didn't elaborate on 'previous nights'. It would explain the increasing doses of the poitín. She understood why all the bottles had been in the bin when Skye had asked. It was the brownie' way of getting her help. An's half-thought question of why the tub was in the bedroom was answered by an image of the stubborn Scotsman from next door sleeping on a pallet in the front room, then by a more current image of him and Elizabeth sitting at the table eating a lunch of grilled cheese sandwiches which, the house proudly informed her, the child had made herself.

With this information, she rushed through her bath and dressed. There was a sandwich waiting for her and An kissed the top of Elizabeth's head, whispering, "Thank ye, my wee brownie," to her.

Elizabeth looked shocked for all of a second, then put on her indignant face. "How rude!" An laughed softly and Elizabeth giggled. "How did you know I made them?"

An ignored the question smoothly and picked up the teapot. She glanced inside and saw there was enough for maybe a cup and a half. She poured less than a full cup for herself, getting up to set the remainder in the press while it was still warm, and closed the press door.

Elizabeth frowned. "You aren't going to wash that first?"

An added a lump of sugar to her own tea and slowly stirred as she answered. "One, the brownie will wash it when she's done. Two, normally I'd put it on th' counter and leave it for her, but I thought she might like it while it's hot. This way she can."

Skye rose to put his dishes in the sink. "So yer sure it's female?"

An gave him her shrugging nod. "Fairly certain. She's taken no offence to my calling her so, and there have been clues." That was all she would say on the matter as she ate her sandwich.

Elizabeth watched Skye come back to the table, and the way he watched An as she ate gave her the feeling she shouldn't be here. "May I be excused? I'm done, and I'd like to go down and play in the garden."

An nodded. "Ye may, if ye open the pantry an' take th' little bowls of milk and honey down to th' back wall, by th' lilly of th' valley. Tuck it inta th' flowers for me."

Elizabeth's eyes sparkled at the thought of feeding faeries and jumped at the chance. She put her dishes with Skye's and opened the pantry. "There's a little white roll here, too," she announced.

An tipped her head. "Take it too, then. ...Ah, apparently Martha makes faery rolls on All Saint's Day. That is also for the pixies," she added as she was informed of the tradition by the table.

Once the child was out the back door, Skye spoke up. "How'd it work?" he asked.

"Fair fine, I think," she smiled. "I feel actually rested. Thank ye."

Skye seemed only a little relieved. "Good. But there's sommat else tha' witch seid. Ye cannae take it too long. No dreams apparently makes ye mad. An' they won't fade on their oon."

"I'll be fine, thank ye."

He growled, but didn't push the matter further. There was something about her this morning that made him think it would have the opposite effect. He got up from the table. "Well, ah doubt she'll gi' me another. She seid ye'd find yerself a dreamer. Ah've got t' go. Got a few thin's t' do afore ah get th' SUV agin t' take ye an' th' wee lass home."

She nodded. "Again, thank ye. Fer everythin'."

He growled again. "Ah think ah'd be more comfortable an' ye treated me accordin' yer brownie lass regardin' th' thanks, thanks."

"Very well," she breathed. "We'll be ready t' leave at four if that gives ye enough time?"

"Aye."

Skye took his leave, and An finished her brunch and headed out into the garden to check on the yellow rose, which was still doing poorly.

Life seemed to speed by. Between the nightly potion and the cottage, An finally began to feel rested and more herself again, able to function. She found she still had to watch out for certain stimuli or she would get caught up and spiral into the vision-trap, but her sleep was no longer dangerous. Elizabeth's lessons with Sean were going well and An's skills with her stick were improving.

Ian had been true to his word about Juan. The small Filipino man had a great deal of disdain for weapons, but once he had met An, he was more than happy to teach her an entire style of fighting for her shillelagh. He said it was from his country, though he taught her some fencing moves to go with it.

When she sparred with Skye after those lessons, he found her growing more and more dangerous. He noticed nothing in her behaviour that caused him to worry about her and eventually put matters from his mind and concentrated on her skills.

An continued to go to Courtz on Friday and Wednesday nights for her dinner, and even to The Hedge Gate at least twice a month, usually with Skye and the others after Sunday dinner at the manor. Jonny was not always there, but often enough that she was no longer surprised when he either appeared at her table or seemed to have been there the whole time.

One night, when he gave her another batch of sheet music, she explained that all she could read was the lyrics, that reading music was not a skill she had ever learned. She handed him the small music device, "This thing lets me hear th' music. I just tell it what I need t' hear."

"How do ye operate it?" he asked with a soft laugh, turning the smart phone over in his hands. There were no buttons, just a touch screen.

An tipped her head. "I ask it. Things talk t' me, remember?"

His eyebrow arched at that. "Bit risky, isn't it? After that last..."

She smiled. "I... I was hasty wit' that thing. An' it was eager to be understood, known. Things... just want t' talk t' me, it seems. I suspect it was th' little prince's doing. He was always more of a child than th' other two. Lingered in that stage where everything was real and could talk. By th' way, it said that if you send it th' songs ye want me to hear, it'll play them whenever I ask."

Jonny handed it back to her. "I don't know how t' operate those infernal things any more than you do. An' I can see it."

"Ask Bethany?"

He nodded. "There might be a plan in that. Make sure she has th' phone number."

"Phone number? No. That's a different device..."

He laughed softly. "No, Ceobhránach. That there is a phone. One of those 'smart phones'. I personally object to an object that's smarter than it's user. I'll just send ye lyric sheets then, easier to get and modify, an' have Bethany send ye th' music."

"Thank ye for going through th' effort," she said, putting away the secondary phone, which was happily telling her that it was a 'very smart' phone. "I'm woefully behind on modern music. And I've missed a fair bit, it seems, of traditional."

He sipped his beer with a gesture of it being no matter. "Ye've an interest, an' it pleases me t' hear ye sing. Ye've a good voice that shouldna be wasted."

She blushed. "'Tis barely suitable fer lullabies an' laments. I've no trainin'."

"Thank God fer that," he said, perhaps a bit more curtly than he had intended. "Yer voice has power for all th' rough edges. Its beauty is in its raw state. I know too many technically perfect singers who can't emote their way out o' a broken jar. Yer voice has soul. Don't put it down."

He said little more that night, having spotted Serephina in the crowd on the dance floor, and his mood soured quickly after that.

Nor was that the only night Serephina made her presence known. There were times An would catch glimpses of her watching. Occasionally Serephina would get up on stage and sing something whose lyrics An could tell were aimed at her, or Jonny if he was obviously present. And An got the feeling Jonny's earlier remark about technically perfect but soulless had been about her.

The woman seemed to be feeling An out, trying to get a reaction. An ignored her as best she could, which was impressive until the woman started getting others to go up and sing things for her, things with very rhythmic, sharp beats that slowly began to sound like hammers ringing on metal. An would have to leave shortly into that.

By the end of November, the bottle was nearly empty, and she began to short her doses, making it last. She began getting less sleep as a result. The night after she took the last dose, sleep refused to come at all, and not even the poitín could coax it out of hiding. She started sitting up and reading, then writing, but nothing helped. For a few days, alcohol in excessive amounts would make her fall asleep, but she always woke screaming within an hour or two and would be unable to sleep again.

Early December saw her four days awake and visibly worn to the point that Sharon insisted she take some time off to rest. An got the impression she was worried An was either coming down with something serious or 'on something' as Elizabeth put it.

The child was the one who told An what her mother was thinking. She had convinced her mother that it was 'exhaustion', and that was why Sharon wanted her to take some time off. "Besides," Elizabeth added as she sat on the bed, watching An sitting in the rocking chair with her crochet, "we're going up to Virginia to Granma's for Christmas. You at least should go home to your family, too." The child lowered her brows and glared at her governess in a fair imitation of her own stern looks. "You should have that looked at, anyway. See Baba Yani. Something."

An sighed, knowing the girl was right. Perhaps she could go see the young prince. He was a dreamer, she remembered, though she was loath to let him know that one of his gifts had turned against her. "I'll see what I can do. Just ye remember to do what Sean taught ye about protectin' yerself, keepin' things from noticing ye." She handed her the original cell phone, the one with the buttons. "Here, keep this with ye while yer there. Roulet's number is the fourth button on the bottom row and then one. If somethin' happens, call her an' drop th' phone. She'll be with ye shortly."

"You mean the first number on the speed dial?"

"If ye say so."

Wednesday night, though she had intended to stay home and sleep, she went to Courtz, out of boredom and the need to do something. The silence in the cottage was making her see things, small animals or insects out of the corners of her eyes. She knew it was the lack of sleep, as the brownie would never have allowed such things, but there was little she could do about it. And with Elizabeth gone, she was not risking the sleeping pills again. She was working on day five of straight wakefulness and nothing was working. She figured if she kept going, eventually she would just pass out.

When she came in, it was a little quieter than normal. She noticed the new bartender immediately. He was Touched. He was a gorgeous man: perfect, creamy skin, thick dark curls and the bluest eyes she had ever seen on a cat. There was no denying there was something of the feline about him. It took An longer than it should have to realise he was the man who had been given the special apple by the witch on Samhain. He was different now, no longer a man who was made to resemble a beast, but a beast who occasionally looked like a man.

"Um," she began, not sure how to approach the subject politely. "I remember ye from th' Rest. Samhain, wasn't it?"

He smiled. "Yeah," he beamed. "Best night of my life."

"Really?" she asked. She introduced herself.

He reached over the bar to shake her hand. "Silhouette. That's all I got right now. Memory and all," he said with a chuckle, as if she would understand, which she did.

"When'd ye get out?" An was aware the moment the words left her lips that it sounded like he had just got out of prison. In a way it was likely true, but still rude.

Before she could apologise, he laughed. "About three weeks before Halloween. If I see you out that way one night, I'll tell you about it. Hell of a story."

She nodded. "Ye'll have t' forgive me. I live at th' Rest, but work out... here," she indicated the world beyond the bar. "I don't get in much."

He shrugged. "It happens. Not like we do a mass get-together more than eight times a year," he laughed. "I'll likely see you around. I like it here. Roulet was nice enough to give me a job. Get me settled. Brad's on vacation, so they needed help. That and business is picking up. They wanted extra help ready before New Year's."

"If business is pickin up, why's th' place dead, then?" she asked with a ghost of a smile.

"Holidays. It'll start jumpin' closer to Christmas and after. Can I get you something, beautiful?"

She blushed. "Och, flattery, sir."

He shook his head, resting his powerful, bare arms on the bar. "Flattery is when you don't mean it and you want something. I find your eyes fascinating. And," he added, standing straighter, as if pulling himself away from her eyes with effort, "I don't want something. ...Well, I do. I want you to tell me what you want to drink."

"Tea. To my table yon. Kaley, knows. I don't usually come t' th' bar. I wanted to ask ye... but it would be rude."

He grinned, very catlike. "So, let's be barbarians and dare."

She blushed again, but allowed his charm to put her at ease. "I was concerned, because I see a change in ye, since th' apple an' all and... I wondered what she did to ye. I... got something from her m'self an' was worried..."

"There might be side effects?" He nodded. "Entirely possible and wise of you, Miss An. But I couldn't be happier with what that apple did to me. Find me at Yule and I'll show you." When she flushed crimson and started to take a step back, he moved back, putting up his hands, "Nothing improper, I assure you."

There was no lie in him and she relaxed, her blush fading a little.

"So, you sure I can't get you something a bit stronger than tea. I'm usually pretty good at figuring out what folks will like. It's a gift," he enticed.

She hesitated. Finally, she gave in. It could not hurt at this point. "Aye. I'll tell ye, though, I'm not fond of beers or Jameson's."

He looked her over critically. "How do you take your tea?"

"Preferred? Honey, just a touch. Th' tea itself, strong side. Though occasionally I like a delicate brew fer flavour."

He began to putter around behind the bar. Thought about mixing several things, but his hands stopped before he grabbed anything. Finally, he latched onto a bottle of American Honey and seemed satisfied, poured her a measure in a chilled glass. He slid it in front of her with quiet purpose.

An watched him, assessing his manner. He was confident, even though she wasn't and picked up the drink. The cold glass felt good in her hand. The liquid smelled slightly sweet and enticing. She remembered the honeyed poitín the brownie had been making her and took a sip. The amber liquid felt thick and silky. It was sweet and heavy with just enough burn to make her feel it. It made the honey flavour come alive on the tongue as the alcohol evaporated in her mouth.

She smiled. "Perfect." He relaxed completely and grinned, pouring a little more into the glass before putting the bottle away. "I'll still take m' tea, though. At m' table. Thank ye. Oh, an' tell Lafayette t' go light on th' sweets. Some fruit perhaps?" He nodded and turned back to the order screen as she headed to her table. It was not until she walked away, using her shillelagh as a tap stick, that he realised she was blind.

An sat at her table alone. She ate little, sipping her whiskey and listening to poets she could barely follow and the few singers trying out new renditions of Christmas carols, getting fancy or simplifying. She felt the urge to get up there herself for once, and ran through her mind for a poem to recite, among her own, or the ones of others more famous that she could remember.

She did recall one she was rather fond of that her Grandfather used to recite by Charles Wolfe and got up, intending to recite it. She stood by the steps, waiting her turn, struggling to run the words through her mind to freshen them. She was debating asking her new phone to help her remember the poem, when other things began to press against her skull, other words, other thoughts, other memories. She found herself on the stage, not quite in front of the mike, but the hollow insistence of her voice made the device unnecessary. There was no corner of the quiet bar that could not hear her, or feel her. Her pain and incumbent madness were plain. A weak mist began to gather at the hem of her skirts and spill out over the blackened wood of the stage.

"Lost,
Lost in my own mind
Pressed for space by my own memories
Trapped by thoughts without end

None of this is mine.
All of it.
Spilling out, boiling over into my life
Taking over
Killing all possibility of normal

A song heard on the wind
Voice of lost soul
Luring me into danger
Trying to make me fall
Cost me everything

Can't sleep
Drinking oblivion to steal an hour
Seeking solace in the nothing
And then I burn
Fire eating my soul, making me
What I'm not

And the voice
In my heart
Filling the hole."

The applause startled her, a rapid, distant and high-pitched enough a sound to mimic the crackling of fire and the answering heat began to rise in her body. Suddenly, a cold hand touched her, dropping her temperature sharply in an instant, and she jumped, panicking. Jonny was there, hands on her arms, making her look him in the face.

"Ceobhránach," he said firmly.

"Jon?" she almost sighed his name, clutching at straws in the dark. Her vision swam even in the dark fog that was everything but the beautiful, elven face before her. She could feel herself losing the battle to remain conscious, could feel the forge fire lapping at the air below her, eager to devour her, waiting for her to fall. She wouldn't wake up from this, she knew it. She clung to the cold limbs holding her above the abyss. *"Get me out of here,"* she whispered.

No one else would have heard her.

Thankfully, he did not sweep her off her feet and carry her out. He slipped Cipín's knob discreetly into her hand and set one arm around her back, the other taking her arm and sheltering her against his body as he guided her off the stage and down the steps.

It seemed only the space of a breath before they were outside in the cold night air and she could breathe. He drew her aside from the café traffic, away from lingering people, and stepped into a recessed doorway of a closed shop. "Breathe," he said softly. "Slow an' deep." She leaned back against the wall and obeyed, struggling to hold the vision at bay, to keep out of the jaws of sleep. "This from the ring?" She nodded.

There was a rueful laugh in his voice. "I was going to ask how ye were farin' after... well, after; but I see I have m' answer."

"I was all right for a while," she began.

"Aye, for a bit," he admitted. "Had even me fooled. But yer not, are ye?"

She shook her head, hating to admit it, and paid for the gesture. Her world swam, and she lurched forward. He grabbed her again. "I've na' slept in days. I can't. M' body won't let me. I think...," the truth began to dawn even as she spoke the words, "I think it's tryin' t' protect me from th' visions. Th' Nightmare. It comes every time I close my eyes more than a moment; any time I feel too hot or hear th' wrong sounds. I'm afraid I won't wake up this time. ...I'm terrified and I'm slippin'." She clung to him, growling to herself. "I don't want t' be th' kind o' woman needin' rescue every time ye turn."

"Well, if ye'd ask fer help afore ye reach the point o' rescue..." he commented dryly.

Jonny leaned her back, bracing himself against the wall so that if she fell, she would fall onto him and not out onto the pavement. He pulled a small penny whistle out of his vest pocket and played a short tune, and suddenly she could see the shop door as it flared into view. He opened it inward, looking carefully through it as he put the whistle away. There was only darkness on the other side. He seemed satisfied, turned and gathered her up, carrying her through.

She gasped at the sudden drop in temperature. It was colder here than the December weather on the outside; which in her experience was more like September. The cold was welcome. It kept her awake. "How did ye...? Ye kin make doors of nothing?"

He chuckled. "No, just doors of doorways. 'Tis a wee complicated, but good fer emergencies. Trouble is, 'tis not like connectin' two known doors. There's no tellin' where ye end up. Luckily, I know this stretch of road."

She accepted this, but protested being carried. "I'll walk, thank ye. I'll not have ye carryin' me home twice in a row."

He set her down, but did not let go. "Very well, but I'm not takin' ye home." He watched her to make sure she was steady enough before he let go.

She looked up at him in the dim light she was only now beginning to register, a little shocked. "Then where?"

"Some place safe. Where we can fix this," he said tenderly, brushing calloused fingertips across her forehead. The touch was as light as rose petals. "If ye'll let me."

It took the resultant blush threatening to overheat her to the burning point to throw caution to the wind. "Aye," she sighed. "I can't let m' pride... or m' propriety..."

His voice was snow-on-silk soft, "Pride can get ye killed. Propriety... well, that can just stifle yer life."

An could just begin to make out his eyes and saw the self-depreciating humour in their dark depths. Had anyone else said those words, she might have taken them for warning.

He took her arm and began walking her down the cold, dark road before them.

Without thinking about what she was doing, she thought about her own home and Cipín answered her. She could get her there, but it would not be a straight road, nor would it be exactly safe. Then Jonny was leading her off the path and towards an archway of branches which flared as they neared, opening to yet another location.

This one was a snow-covered wood. There was more light, though she could not see a sun through the clouded sky. It was beautiful and delicate, like a sigh. The snow crunched pleasantly underfoot and what little wind there was made wind-chimes of the icicles hanging from the branches. There were a few evergreens that whispered against each other in that wind.

This place was what Winter meant to her, peaceful, sleeping; that breath the world takes between harvest and rebirth.

They followed a little path around a stand of birch and a snow-covered holly thicket, and as the path rounded the bushes it revealed a small, dark house. It was not much different from her own in style, except, on closer inspection, it seemed made of snow. There was a great deal of earth mixed in, making it a mottled brown and white that made it hard to see unless you knew what you were looking for.

She glanced back on the path and found it gone. There were no tracks in the snow, nothing to mark their passing or existence. She heard him open the door and allowed him to lead her inside.

The outside was less of a shock than the interior. It looked more like a snow cave than a house. There was a chest near a rough wood table with a single chair. There was a recessed shelf carved into the wall with neither pillow nor blanket, but she knew, none-the-less, it was his bed. There were instrument cases of various types stored on shelves of their own and a beautifully carved Celtic harp set in a place of prominence. There were garlands of some plant she did not know off-hand draped through the snow rafters, and an ambient light whose source she could not find. In all, the single room smelled of snow and earth and cold. She should have been freezing, but wasn't quite.

Jonny sat her in the only chair, setting it sideways so she could lean against the table if she felt faint. He began to busy himself at the windowless walls, doing something that left behind light trails to her sight.

"Is this like my house?" she asked, trying to keep herself awake even as she noted the similarities. This house, however, felt neither awake under her hand, nor dead like the Tallows'.

"Not quite," he answered, still working. "It was a hunting lodge. I found it, took pains to hide it. I've fortified it over th' years. I use it as a dream fortress. It is a safe place to dream, and it enhances my ability to work with them."

"Are all yer instruments magical?" she wondered aloud, noticing belatedly that was able to see them.

He gave a half smile as he worked. "Not a'tall. They've just been in here too long. It happens even t' mundane things in th' borderlands."

She fell silent, watching him lock the place down. When he was done, he crossed to the chest. It was then that she realised there were seven latches on it. He chose the fourth, flipping it up, and opened the lid. He pulled out a bundle of fur blankets and carried them to the bed, arranging them for ground and top cover.

It was then that An realised he intended her to sleep here. Words Serephina had spat at her at Halloween drifted back through her mind, but there was nothing in Jonny's manner that spoke of seduction. At this moment, it was fairly... clinical.

She started to relax and then realised it was a bad idea. She stood, began pacing to stay awake. Soon he was guiding her over to the bed, sitting her on the edge of it. He tipped her chin up to look at him.

"Ceobhránach," he began. "I need ye to trust me. Do ye? This will be difficult at best, and dangerous an' ye fight me ...fer both of us."

She nodded, strangely on the verge of tears, she was so tired and so scared.

He knelt, taking her foot gently in hand and deftly unlacing her boot. An was privately glad she had chosen to wear full, thick hose instead of the shorter, modern socks she had been wearing lately. There was a terrible intimacy in his taking off her boots, but she knew she should read nothing into it. It was not as if she could have done it herself in her current condition.

When the second boot joined the first, he lifted her feet and swung her around onto the bed, helping her to lay back and make herself comfortable. She unfastened the buttons on her vest, but nothing more, let herself sink into the furs. He drew the one of them over her, brushing her hair from her face as she looked up at him, still fighting the descent into the darkness. He gave her a wan smile and fetched his harp.

He sat on the foot of the bed, his back against one wall and his feet tucked up next to hers, taking up little room. The harp was deeply carved in knotwork, with raven heads in the corners and the suggestions of wings in the honey-gold willow. The harp's voice was sweet and hung in the air, heavy like drops of honey. His voice joined them, light and soft, singing a lullaby that was ancient when Cú Chulainn was young. The words were so old, even An did not recognise some of them, but they had the desired effect.

She felt as if large, strong hands were easing her down into the dark waters that so wanted to devour her. She could feel the tears run down her cheeks as she surrendered, letting those hands take her deep into the abyss to fight the forging.

18

An faced the terrible woman before her. Her eyes blazed green like living emeralds, and Her hair was so red it seemed to drip blood. She was beautiful as angels are beautiful, painfully perfect and terrible to behold. The kind of woman who makes you tremble in fear that She might notice you, but fear you might die if She does not. An loved Her, knelt before Her swearing she would do anything for Her 'but say the word, thy will be done'. The woman smiled, wringing An's heart with terror and elation, and then Her white arms gathered her to Her breast and lifted her as one would a child. She carried An to the forge and laid her on the bed of coals and raked them over her as gently as one would tuck in a child. Indeed, An felt childlike and that thought hurt her more than knowing what was to come.

The coals were hot, and they hurt. The pain blossomed around her body like flowers bursting from bud to full flower in a moment and felt so good, comforting. But it grew, swelling past bearable into the realms of hell-fire and damnation, and she began to wonder the wisdom of her choice. She tried to scream, but there were no lungs any more to gather air to make the sound. When it reached past the point of endurance, when she thought she should have been dead a hundred times over, that white hand reached in and gathered her up like so much loose floss and set her on the anvil, and took up the hammer, and began to make.

There was Love in that hand. With every stroke of that awful hammer, every burst of pain forcing her body into an unnatural form, she felt Her love. The terrible woman loved the work of making, loved her enough to make her perfect, loved who she was being made for. In the end, everything but love was melted away and pounded out of her, 'til there was nothing left but the ultimate expression of the Queen's love. When she was perfect, and thought she could bear Her touch no more, she was cast away, thrown into the sea and forgotten.

That sea was terrible and battering. There was no light, no air, no love, no emotion, no anything but the leviathan and the salt and the current and the darkness and eternity. She wasn't drowning, she couldn't drown. One had to need breath to drown; but it was lonely. Bone-crushingly lonely. All that sustained her was the love which had made her and the promise that there would be more.

Just when she thought she had been forgotten and had begun to grow dim, the white hand gathered her up and took her to Her breast, polished her with Her own hand. Life had purpose again. She waited to be slipped upon that white hand and was disappointed once more. She was placed upon the finger of a child. It was a bizarre, marriage-like ceremony; the taking of this child as a daughter as one would take a man to wed. She was the symbol of that promise. Her purpose was to remind the child to love.

But something went wrong, and the child disobeyed, rebelled; had the audacity to love another, to choose another over her mother. Then there was another little girl, killing the first. The ring knew what she had been up to, had made sure her mother knew where she was, if not what she was doing. She could only pass on the depth of the child's love. Then the second girl took her from the first, put her on and loved her mother, made the same promise. But always, always something happened, and the love lessened, felt suffocating as the girls grew up.

The Queen began to realise what the problem was and fixed it. As the next girl grew up, She made her a child again. And again. And again. A hundred years of growing up and love slipped. Not so much, but the beginning. The child ran away. She loved, but needed space to breathe. She loved still, but there were questions, other loves creeping in and beginning to outweigh Her. The child would die soon.

It started over again. She stood before the Red Queen in all Her glory; was reforged while a pale raven watched; languished at the bottom of the cold deep with that dark eye still somehow upon her. It was not until the first runaway that the raven did more than watch. It attacked. Before the new child could slip the ring onto her finger, the raven snatched up the ring and flew.

Something followed.

There was a man in the road, hair as white and wild as the snow that fell around them. He pulled her from the ring, ripping her body from the golden form to cast her, gasping and drenched, onto the snow-covered ground. The gold he threw from them, standing over her and drawing a pair of axes and facing what the ring became.

An turned her head, saw a serpent so red it was almost black rising up, lunging for her. Her mind substituted something else for that serpent's head as it came down, a fomoire, clawed and similarly fanged, spitting the poison that burned away her eyes.

She rolled out from between the man's feet and found herself facing a snow-bank, saw a knob of wood buried in the snow. Her initial panic became anger, and she seized the knob and pulled it from its grave. It was not Cipín, not here, but it was a shillelagh and it would suffice. She got up, turning to the man standing in only trousers and an open vest holding the axes. He put her in mind of a Native American brave wielding tomahawks, and an ancient Celtic warrior with war axes all at once. She strode to his side, and as he ducked beneath the serpent's strike, cutting for the lower coils, An swung the shillelagh over his back at the monster's eye.

As he spun up and out of the way, he seemed surprised to see her fighting, but did not allow it to affect him beyond adjusting his style to work with her. Without a word, the two of them harried the beast. An quickly learned that her stick did less actual damage than the axes, yet almost always caused the snake to strike at her, annoyed. She began to time this, hitting it whenever it was about to attack her partner and twisting out of the way in time, leaving him the opening to hack at the thing's neck. Between the two of them, the thing eventually lay in pieces in the snow. Then, even that turned to smoke and evaporated.

They looked across the road at each other. They were bloody, only a little of it their own. They were tired, and they were laughing. He cleaned his axes, putting them away. "Ye fight like a right Fianna wi' that thing."

She looked down at the stick in her hand. It had taken some damage, and would probably not last another fight, but then, it wasn't Cipín. "It got me Irish up," she growled, forcing herself to calm down. She tossed the stick aside. "I could be better."

"Ye need t' learn a better style, though. That one... it's good, but there's a few things ye do with a shillelagh ye don't learn wit' Escrima."

"Escrima?"

"That fightin' style. It's called Escrima. It's Philippine stick-fighting. Dangerous, don't mistake me. But ye wield a true shillelagh, ye should know the true style. Ian can teach ye."

An sounded indignant as she stood straighter, having finally begun to catch her breath. "He's th' one sent me to Juan."

Jonny laughed, shrugged. "Ah, well, ask him anyway. Ye've proved yer ready for it."

An looked down at the stained road where the snake had been. "That why I kept havin' that nightmare?"

"Aye," he nodded. "If only it were a nightmare. I was hopin' that's all it were. But... I saw it watchin', waitin'. It was feedin' off th' pain, tryin' t' eat into yer heart and draw ye closer to Her. It hadn't a good hold yet."

"That last... these were more...detailed," she began. "They started earlier, lasted longer. I lost my sense of self almost completely. Another few repetitions and I think I would have."

He nodded, "That's how I saw it, watchin' it sink its fangs in ye. Yer not going to want to sit up yet though," he added.

She frowned. What he'd said made no sense. But somehow she was feeling warmer than she should have, and the beginning spiral of dizziness in the back of her head. The edges of the world were blurring a little.

"What it did do to ye's goin' to take some rest and treatment."

"What'd it do?" She felt herself growing weak and light-headed. She blinked. He wasn't standing in front of her any more. It took her a moment to realise she was still lying under the furs, and he was sitting at the foot of the bed in the niche with her, watching her with his harp on his lap.

"Poisoned ye. That ye fought for yerself will help with recovery. Means yer strong. But now ye've a different sort o' fightin' t' do." He gave her his sad smile, "If yer pride can stand a bit o' nursin'?"

She gave a dry chuckle at that, laying her head back to stare up at the ceiling. "It don' need nursin'. It just resents it." She took a deep breath, closing her eyes against the dizziness. "I hate bein' a burden."

She heard him move from the bed. "Yer not a burden. Yer lettin' me fill my purpose. ...Well, one o' them."

She opened her eyes and looked over at him. He was doing something at the chest again, flipping open a different latch. She sighed. "Then I suppose I shall have t' submit. Ye bring many here?" she asked.

He gave her a shrugging tip of his head, "As have th' extreme need. Thankfully, that's not many. I like this place bein' a secret. It's my bastion."

She watched him bring out a loaf of bread and the makings for a small meal. It was interesting to watch the bard at domestic activities. He sliced cheese and some type of large sausage. He cut four slices off the loaf of bread and made fairly thick sandwiches for them. He brought hers over with a skin of water and helped her to sit up to eat it.

She learned very quickly why he had warned her not to sit up yet. The room went crazy. He propped her up against the wall, helped her to drink a little water at first. He made her eat, though it was the last thing she wanted at the moment. She had to admit she felt better when she had. He settled her back down after he was satisfied she had eaten enough. "Now ye need to sleep, an' can do so without fear."

She didn't want to. She was in his bed, and her sense of propriety was beginning to rear its stubborn head. But she found she had little choice. Her body betrayed her and began to suck her down into that soft, fluffy oblivion where dreams are safe and pleasant and meaningful. And her own. The last thing she was aware of was his fingers brushing against her temple, and the sound of his voice tipping her over the brink back into sleep.

It was nearly evening when An finally got home, feeling better than she had in some time. The lights came on in the house, welcoming her before she got in the door. She laughed as she felt the joyous vibrations beneath the soles of her boots even as she hurried to get them off. She was just slipping out of her stockings when there came an insistent knocking on the door. She set her hose in her boots, out of sight, and opened it.

Skye stood there, scowling. He looked wild.

"Aye?" she asked, completely dispensing with the proprieties.

"Where th' devil ye bin?" he growled.

That got her Irish up. The fist not holding the door went to her hip. "An' what th' devil be it yer business t' know, might I ask?"

"Ye know what business," he snapped. "Ah bin worri'd sick!"

That was too much. "I'm gone one bloody night an' ye git yer kilt in a wad? Yer takin' a step too far, ye highland ninny."

He looked like he was about to choke. "One night? Lass, it's been three since ah've seen th' winda's glow!"

An paled as the house confirmed how long it had been. She had thought the house was happy she was cured, not that it had missed her.

Skye took in her reaction and backed off a bit, but only a little. "Aye, three days. Ah know ah've been busy, but it damn it, lass. A word woulda been nice. The Tallows called an' everythin'."

"Wait, called who? They don't know about Ian."

He shook his head. "Canna no' have this conversation on yer stoop?"

She suddenly remembered her manners and stepped out of his way. He came into the house and waited for her to indicate if she wanted to sit at the table or the fire. She closed the door and headed into the kitchen to make the tea the brownie apparently didn't have enough warning to make. She busied herself getting the kettle while Skye took a place at the table. "Who'd they call?"

"The lawyer. Said ye were missin' Thursday mornin' an' they were worried cause ye'd been... ill."

An opened the pantry to get the tea things and saw a steaming plate of food that had to be fresh from Martha's table. She closed the door again, looked back at Skye. "Have ye had yer supper?"

Skye's stomach growled in response and An waited a moment before opening the pantry again and fetching both plates that now waited inside. She set the largest servings before him and the smaller portion at her chair and turned back to the fridge to fetch something for them to drink, needing something more than tea for a meal. She pulled out her phone, realised belatedly that she had the smart one, the one without the buttons, and had to ask it to call the manor.

The phone rang directly to Ian's office. When he answered, he sounded a little harried. "An?" he said immediately, without preamble. She wondered how he had known it was her.

"Aye, I'm fine," she replied.

She heard his breath of relief. She also heard him pull the phone away from his mouth and let loose a string of obscenities, then bellow out the door about calling off the hounds.

An blushed.

Skye held out his hand. "Let me see th' phone a mo'."

Reluctantly, she handed it over, not relishing Ian's voice raised in anger at her. Skye did something to it and set it on the table between them. A few seconds later Ian's voice came from the phone much louder than before. "Tell me what happened?" he asked, calmer than he had before. "Are yeh all right? Where were yeh?"

She started to pick it up to answer, but Skye shook his head. "Yer on speaker. Don't ask, just talk. Ah don't ken it much either."

"I'm better than I have been, an' I can't tell ye where I was as I don't rightly know."

"Were yeh taken?" Ian asked.

An gave a little laugh. "In a manner o' speakin', just not how yer thinkin'."

"Silhouette said yeh left Wednesday night wit' Jonny," Ian said. Skye's eyes went hard at that. "We didn't know if yeh made it home or not, as yeh don't usually let th' Tallows know when yeh get in, or often when yeh leave," he added, a hint of annoyance in his voice. "When we couldn't find Jonny to ask..."

She sighed. "Ye feared the worst. No, I... I had some issues t' deal with and... he was affectin' a healin' Liberty can't," she said, reluctant to explain. "I'd have let someone know if I'd have known it was goin' t' take three days. If ye'll tell th' Tallows... or have them told, that I...," she sighed. "Tell them I had a spell o' exhaustion and ended up in hospital. They'll believe that. An' it's not far from true. 'Tweren't a traditional hospital, but it'll serve. Tell 'em I was bein' treated fer insomnia."

There was a noise from Ian's end as a door opened and a soft voice sent a chill down her back, even though she had no idea what had been said. Jonny had apparently wasted no time.

Ian came back on the line. "I'll get back wit' yeh on this. You rest. I'll have Tisiphone inform th' Tallows."

"Tell them I'll be home in the mornin'," she sighed. "Thank ye, chief. Uncle," she corrected quickly.

"I'll have Tis tell them yeh'll be at yer Uncle's recoupin' an' yeh'll be home Mond'y," he insisted. "And I'll expect a full story tomorrow after dinner." With that he hung up and An was left sitting there being glared at by Skye.

She stabbed her pot roast with her fork. "What?" she snapped. She suddenly realised she was incredibly hungry.

"So," he scowled. "Ye went home wit' th' bard?"

She flushed. "If ye weren't sittin' across m' table, Skye O'Keefe, I'd slap ye silly fer yer insinuation," she snarled. "Nothin' illicit happened. I... was gettin' worse. I couldna sleep. I think my body had enough o' th' nightmares and wouldn't let me sleep to save me. Th' ring... attached somethin' to me is th' best way I can describe it. Once I'd spent so long out of its reach, it attacked full force. Jonny was there when I reached th' ends of my limits. I'd been up four days. I was seein' things; writin' poetry on the fly. Which reminds me, I need t' write that down. It was ...good."

Skye ate in silence, not taking his eyes from her, not letting her stop talking.

"He figured out it were a dreamin' issue and took me to his... what'd he call it... dream fortress? A bastion? A haven, really. He sealed it and went into my dream. He watched it, saw th' thing, and we battled it. That is all there were. He helped me through th' weakness after. Apparently th' thing had been poisonin' me in a manner o' speakin'. I left th' very next mornin', well, after only one sleep. I guess it was a long one, though time

316

often flows differently twixt there and here. Nothin' untoward happened."

He growled through his potatoes, angry with himself and Jonny.

An aimed a fork at him. "No. Ye stop whatever thoughts are in yer fool head, right there. I don't care what happens. I don't care what he does or doesn't do. Unless I tell ye ye kin thump him, yer not to lay a hand on him over me. Ye ken?"

He opened his mouth to argue. Her fork lashed out and struck the back of his hand right across the tendon. He yelped and pulled it back, giving her the same look he'd likely given his mother after getting popped by a wooden spoon with equally impossible swiftness. In spite of the fog banks that made up her eyes, he could feel the threat behind them and quailed. There was no fighting it. "Foin."

She went back to eating as if nothing had happened. When she spoke again, her voice was casual, but hiding a very real threat. "Hurt him and I'll never fergive ye."

That was why he'd given in. He sighed, nodding.

"Besides. If I'm of a mind t' have him hurt, I'll do it my bloody self," she finished, putting a bite of carrot into her mouth as if she had been talking about rain this afternoon. Skye nearly choked.

19

The morning of Yule found An and Skye at the rath, slipping into the borderlands in the wee hours before dawn. Just beyond the gate, a carriage waited. It was gold with green trim and had the Gryphon King's sigil emblazoned on the door. The driver had four handsome bays hitched up and the page boy in green livery held open the door with high formality. She paused before stepping in. "I think ye can let me go from here, Skye. I thank ye fer what ye've done, but ye've things of yer own t' do. I'll see ye at dusk. Oh..." she added, suddenly worried. "The hedge! Are they goin' t' lock us in t'night?"

At this the page spoke up, "No, Mistress," he smiled. "Tonight no one rides out in force, and if we choose, we are welcome to come to the Masque. We have to abide by Hospitality, though. The King's gone once, a long time ago. They'll not put up the hedge tonight. And you'll not be late. ...So long as you arrive in time to the palace," he added pointedly.

An nodded and let him hand her up into the coach. She waved to Skye as he watched them ride off. Skye did not turn back to the gate until the carriage had entered the tree-lined avenue and faded from sight. Even so, he barely made it through before the door closed as the sun peered over the horizon.

She was right, though. He had a lot of preparation to do.

Most of the festivals and rituals occurred outside, on the green behind the manor. Not so the Yule Masque. After twelve noon everyone was run out of the house, even Shannon and Martha. Ian did something with his keys.

Skye stood back and watched as Ian, Henry, Sorrow, Liberty, Gabrielle and a woman named Magdelena, all gathered around the house. He had felt the expenditure of magic. It had a rippling effect throughout the gardens, and when Ian reopened the doors from one of the skeleton keys on his ring, the interior was no longer his house.

Skye walked through, gaping like a wonder-struck tourist. The outside of the house looked the same, except for maybe the garlands that draped the walls and windows and the absence of the roof on the veranda. The inside was one large ballroom with tall windows that glinted with frost at the edges. The floor glittered in whites and blues, and garlands of holly and evergreen draped the walls. The chandelier was made of icicles, and the fireplace at one end of the ballroom was large enough to have roasted an entire bull whole.

Ian strode across the tiled floor with Mikey, Skye and several others in his wake and threw open the French doors on the far side. "Well, gents," he began, "time t' fetch th' firewood."

They each grabbed an axe from where they gleamed against the wall and marched off into the wood to find a Yule log.

By the time they had returned, dragging the enormous section of tree trunk behind them, the greensward and the surrounding grounds had undergone a transformation. There was a light dusting of snow on the ground, making the trees pretty as a painting and the log easier to drag to the house. Sean and the others had been hard at work. Coach And Four followed the woodsmen, pulling the wagon with the rest of the wood by himself.

It seemed no time at all before it was time for everyone to get ready.

Skye had chosen his costume carefully, portraying something he most certainly did not see himself as: Prince Charming. He had acquired a glamour that made his hair fall in golden ringlets to his shoulder and a dashing black coat with gold braiding and the trousers with the red stripe of satin down the seam. His mask was black with a gleaming red and gold sunburst erupting from one temple, stretching across the bridge of his nose. He looked in the mirror and adjusted himself, very pleased with the results.

He stepped outside, not trusting the fey door to the manor at the moment. He had asked Ian if he might borrow a horse for the evening and waiting at his doorstep was a spirited white charger held by a rather short little grooms-man in green. As the groom handed up the reins once Skye was mounted, he gave him last-minute instructions. "Ride up in style. He likes showin' off. When ye dismount, toss th' reins o'er his neck an' he'll trot himself on home."

"Will doo," he said with a nod.

"An' lose th' accent, me bucko," the groom grinned. "That is unless ye want t' be known."

Skye nodded again, groaning to himself as he turned the horse's head. That would be the hardest part of all of this.

Skye's arrival was everything he had wanted. He rode up, the horse prancing and high stepping up to the front door. He dismounted with flair and strode in, basking in the attention of those who were already present. He came off as dashing and devil-may-care.

The dancing lessons he had taken from Liberty had paid off. He had no shortage of dance partners as the sun began to set and more people drifted in. Very few arrived in pairs, but this did not confuse Skye. He knew why. There were a few couples: a Sonny and Cher, a knight and his horse, and Jack and Jill, the bucket dangling from Jill's hand.

Even the musicians were costumed. The entire small orchestra was dressed as Goblins in tuxedos. There were only a few servants, mostly to hold the reins of those who, like Skye, had chosen to ride, to help folk from sleighs and to hold the door. Food and drink was set up along one wall in one massive, unending buffet.

Skye was more than a little surprised when 'Jack' asked him to dance. "Um... but... ye...you," he said, catching himself.

'Jack' laughed. "Tonight? Of all nights, one never knows what lies beneath. You could be a woman for all I know, or a goblin, a member of the Gentry. Or, more importantly, the Queen."

That made Skye stifle whatever objections he had been trying to articulate. If this was Henry, then dancing with him would delay his finding the real Liberty. He bowed over 'Jack's' hand, stopped short of kissing the air above his fingers. "So, who shall lead?"

'Jack' grinned. "Since you asked," he said, taking the lead and trying to sweep Skye out onto the floor.

The dancing was a little more awkward after that, as Skye kept unconsciously trying to lead and kept tangling them up. "And here I had thought you graceful as I watched you," 'Jack' commented dryly.

"Perhaps it is my partner," he growled with a tight smile.

He was saved from a retort by the sight of a carriage riding past the tall windows. They turned, wandered over to the closest window and watched the arrival of a carriage made from spun ice. More impressive than the graceful swirls and delicate filigree which graced the vehicle were the four polar bears pulling it. When the carriage stopped at the front door, an Arctic fox boy in pale blue livery jumped off the back and ran over to fold down the steps and open the door.

Skye could feel others pressing to the windows behind him, trying to see. He nearly missed the lion-man that descended the carriage in his attempt to keep from being jostled too much by a small otter in a ballet dress who slipped between him and 'Jack' to get a better view. He did see the lion extend his hand into the vehicle and draw out a woman in flowing white.

There were gasps all around him at the sight of her. Even he had to admit the dress was beautiful and flattering. It clung to her waist and belled to the floor, slightly longer in the back. The neckline was swept across her chest, just to the edges of her ivory shoulders, and the bodice presented her feminine assets perfectly without being brazen. Pinned to the centre of the band was a huge diamond encrusted flower pin, and her throat was circled by a glittering, jewelled vine with snowflowers. Her mask was elaborate. It had white feathers that swept up and back, and small branches of silver leaves on the sides that followed the upswept line of her pale golden curls. The mask itself, which seemed to be made from pressed snow, caught the light and fragmented it. There was a line of ice crystals that dangled against her white cheeks. The red lips smiled up at her escort and suddenly Skye knew her, in spite of the perfectly normal eyes he saw within the mask. He smiled, kept his mouth shut, and turned to watch her entrance into the ballroom proper.

An felt her heart beating a rapid tattoo in her breast as Lion set her hand on his arm and led her to the now open doors. He purred a soft word of comfort and a reminder which caused her to draw herself up as the Snow Queen she was meant to be.

She almost lost it again when they stepped through the door into the ballroom. It looked every inch a fey place, and she could see all of it. She closed her eyes, turned to look up at him as she opened them slowly. He smiled, his pride apparent. She strode into the room as if she owned it. She had seen this act before, enough to be able to imitate it and felt herself sinking into the spirit of the Masque and the purpose that had drawn her here.

Lion let them gaze at her in awe for a moment more before he signalled the orchestra and led her across the dance floor. The dance was beautiful in its apparent simplicity, though it was as complex as it was serene. Others joined them on the floor, but none could follow the steps, and so dissolved into an easy waltz around them. The final flourish of the music came, and he spun her out and she sank into a deep curtsey before him. He kissed her hand and drew her up, whispered words to her in his rumbling voice. Those near enough heard only purring, but she heard the words he intended her to. "For one night," he said. "May it be all you hoped. It ends at midnight, 'Cinderella'. Use your hours well."

With that he turned and strode towards the veranda doors, which for this evening only led to an uncovered patio at the foot of which waited his golden horse. He leapt from the top step to the saddle and, rearing, the horse spun on his heels and galloped off down the trod into the woods.

Left behind and feeling his absence sorely, An turned slowly, surveying the room. As she spun and the hem of her skirts swirled across the floor, snow began to fall from the ceiling. She looked up, watched the delicate, glittering flakes float down, evaporating before they hit the floor, and laughed.

As if this were some sort of cue, the goblin orchestra struck up a whirling, spinning melody that put one immediately in mind of swirling eddies of snowfall. She began to wheel into the stately steps, managing to put a more regal twist on what was essentially a peasant dance. One by one, the women took the floor, slowly spinning out to orbit around her, all of them snowflake sprites dancing in the wind. Later, the men stepped in, one by one as they found the courage, floating up to a woman and joining her if she allowed it.

The first to so approach An was 'Jack'. An smiled, allowed Liberty to take her hand and lead her into the graceful steps of the partnered portion, far less complex than the one the prince had put her through. Even her voice was slightly different, deeper. "Evenin', my Queen," 'Jack'/Liberty grinned. "You've outdone yourself."

An conceded. "I had help."

"Who? The witch said..."

"I found a 'fairy godmother'."

Liberty's eyes danced, flitting through all the things that could mean. "I wish ye luck of it then, luv." The dance came to an end, and she kissed the back of An's hand, bowing out and moving to another young woman, cutting in and sweeping off with the girl as the music restarted.

About halfway through, An noticed that the music was modern, something she had heard at Courtz, but, played by a full orchestra, it sounded far more high-culture. An found herself, for the moment, standing in the middle of the dancers without a partner, watching them move around her.

She was not the only singlet on the floor, but that one was a spritely young thing in a ballet version of a milkmaid costume. She was cavorting about the couples, taunting, encouraging, in a manner Liberty would have said reminded her of ballet, though An had never seen it performed, only knew it from the paintings by Degas. It did not take An long to realise that while the milkmaid was flitting about everyone, herself included, she had her eyes on one individual in particular.

The song ended, and An began to move off the floor now that it was safe to do so. She saw the woman pounce on her target and begin flirting in a shameful way which sent his current partner off blushing. Before An could reach the safety of the resting area, 'Prince Charming' was looming before her and bowed, held out his hand.

"My Queen? Will you honour me?" he asked.

There was something deliberate in the way he spoke, as though he were trying very hard to cover an accent. She accepted and let him lead her back out onto the floor. He did not say much, just watched her with a smug look in his blue eye.

Finally, she could stand it no more. "Is there something which amuses you, Your Highness?" she asked him, using his costume's title.

He laughed, spun her around and bent his mouth to her ear. "Th' Prince out-did himself t'night. Or did his sister have more t' do wi' yer glamour?"

She gasped, pulled back and only with a great deal of effort resisted popping him. She put on her cold, Snow Queen demeanour, raised an eyebrow with convincing hauteur. "Cheat," she said flatly.

He just laughed at that. "Worry not, your Majesty. Your secret is safe with me." He sent her out into a spin, pulled her back in. "Hell, I might be convinced to run a little interference. Trip Henry in your direction. Though it seems to me, someone else has landed him... for a little while at least."

An followed his gaze, saw the milkmaid with her hand on the backside of a man with long black curls in a bright red pirate coat and hat. They were headed out the patio door into the night.

Skye escorted An over to the buffet tables, offered to get her something to eat or drink, and seemed surprised when she smiled secretively. "No need."

She reached across to a fountain of chocolate and picked up a strawberry, running it under the stream, and ate it delicately.

A raised eyebrow was his only response. He was thinking of saying something else, but whatever he had to say was cut off by the approach of a tall woman in a slinky silver evening gown patterned with snowflakes in tiny crystals. Her hair was the colour of a raven's wing and fell in ringlets beside her deeply exposed and heavily corseted bust. Behind the black and silver feathered mask were eyes the colour of ice.

She slithered up and wrapped her arms around his arm and pressed her breast against him, looking up into his eyes with an easy grace. "Ooo, Prince Charming. I have been looking all over for you," she purred.

She was beautiful, and she smelled like heaven, but the eyes were wrong. Skye knew they could be just a glamour, but still…. Something in his gut recoiled. Skye turned to An only to find her gone along with any excuse he might have had. He decided to do the polite thing, in case this was the witch for instance, and offer her a single dance.

"My lady," he said with deliberate formality. "May I have this dance?"

She flashed him a smile that would have melted most men and pulled back enough to curtsey and let him go through the rest of the little ritual. As he took her out onto the dance floor, he examined what he could see of her. Her jawline hinted at a perfect oval face and an aquiline nose. Her lips were full and pouty, perfect for kissing even though that was the last thing he wanted to do to them at the moment. Her breasts were bounteous over a slim waist, though she did not have much in the way of hips. She was most men's definition of beauty.

He glanced over at An, dancing again, this time with a tall, lean young man in a green suit. He had never thought her plain as he had heard her described at the camp, but tonight she was radiant. She truly was the most beautiful woman in the room. Even the beauty he danced with looked more like a goose than a swan compared to her tonight. It did not change his heart, however. His eyes did a sweep of the room, looking for someone with the dancing skills he knew Liberty possessed. So far the only women showing that kind of skill were the milkmaid, Jill, and someone who looked like she might be the Lady of the Lake.

He sighed, returned his attention to the viper he was partnered with. She made attempts at conversation, trying to draw out of him clues as to who he might be. He deflected them back at her, perhaps leading her on to believing he was someone he was not. When the dance was over, he bowed, excused himself and ducked out quickly as someone else came up to vie for the woman's attentions.

An spent nearly as much time sitting watching the world dance by as she spent dancing herself. Occasionally someone, usually one of the women, would sit and talk for a while and then move on. Most of the conversations were about how their significant others were absolutely clueless. An watched the crowd, looking for someone herself, seeking some sign that might mark him from the others.

The pirate returned, looking very self-satisfied, and the milkmaid moved on to riper pastures. He spied An sitting across the room, looking every inch the regal queen of winter, chatting quietly with 'Jack', and strode purposefully over. 'Jack' leaned back in the chair, crossing his legs in a manly manner and trying his best to look lazy.

The pirate bowed flamboyantly to An. "Captain Henry Morgan, at your service, My Queen."

An smiled coldly, nodding. "Your obeisance is accepted."

This threw him off a bit, and he straightened, eyeing 'Jack' warily as if fearing he might be a rival. "Might this humble servant have the honour of this dance?"

An stood. "He might. Though he is anything but humble."

The Captain laughed, taking her hand. "I would be less effective if I were."

As he drew her to the floor and swung her into position, she maintained her cool smile and aloof demeanour. "And what exactly would it be that you do for me?"

He pulled her uncomfortably close. "Keep your majesty safe from marauding Englishmen."

"And who is to keep me safe from marauding privateers?"

He laughed at that and loosened his grip, trotting her across the floor in what he thought was fancy footwork. "Ah, my queen, I protect you even now. You see that other pirate over there, the one in black, the Dread Pirate Roberts?"

An glanced in the direction he aimed their joined hands. There was a man there in a black pirate shirt, black pants tucked into tall, suede boots. There was a pouch slung at his belt and a strap across his unlaced chest. His hair and face were hidden by a scarf with an eye mask sewn into it, completely obscuring the upper half of his head accept for the piercing brown eyes that seemed to watch her as if she were an enemy ship on the horizon.

"That one, yes," he said, turning her away from him, blocking the man's view. "He's been stalking you. Circling you like a shark," he said, turning the pair of them in circles as if to illustrate his point. "I can't have that. I won't have gryphon boy beating me to the punch. I must say though, my dear, you have led me a merry chase and damn near had me fooled. But I have found you, my queen."

"What makes you think…"

He bent to her ear, giving her once more a view of the other man. "Your crown is showing." He leaned back. "Metaphorically speaking, of course."

The man in black put An more in mind of a highwayman than a pirate, whoever this 'Dread Roberts' was. He was watching the milkmaid, was about to approach her when she grabbed someone's rear and he veered away, choosing instead fair little Jill. There was something about him which frightened her a little. She turned back to Henry, for she knew it to be him now, aware he had said something but not aware of what.

"Are we not?" he repeated.

She returned his leering grin with her coldest smile. "We are not."

He looked indignant. "Yer not even going to tell me I'm roight?" His eyes narrowed, and she began to see hints of holly beneath the rim of his hat. His accent of a British Gentleman-turned-privateer slipped. "Yer just doing dis because ye found out about de betting pool, making me lose. Well, I've already lost my slot, cousin dear. Ye could at least throw me dat bone."

She heard the song come to an end and tried to step back from him. He did not let her. "The only bone We are likely to throw you will be your own, if you do not unhand Us."

"Royal We's?" he asked, wide-eyed. "Really?"

She stiffened in his grasp, her expression ice. She did not raise her voice, but there was all the more threat for its softness. "Unhand Us, pirate, or We shall revoke your letters of Marque and ye shall find thy next dance partner to be the Ropemaker's Daughter."

He let go immediately.

She took a single step back. "Come midnight ye shall learn if thy bet is won or lost. Not before." She then turned and walked away. She decided she needed a little air and went out onto the patio.

The sky was alive with stars and she set her hands on the low marble rail to look up at them. They were not quite the ones she remembered, but they were real and she could see them and they were beautiful. There were tiny fey lights woven into the garlands of holly and evergreen that decorated the patio rails, and more scattered out among the low lover's maze she could see off to her left. From the flickering patterns of some of those lights, she guessed it was in use tonight. No doubt that was where the milkmaid had taken Henry.

She was aware of a few other people nearby, at least one couple cozying up in a corner of the patio behind her, and a few others walking not far away. Therefore, she was surprised to notice another presence, one with a bit more menace. She stood straighter, wishing she had her shillelagh, and slowly turned. The highwayman was there, by the door, watching her. It seemed the more he watched her, the angrier he got.

She decided it was time to go inside, remembering what she had been told, that sometimes the Gentry came. There was a chance.... As she passed him by, he reached out, stopping her without touching her. She turned, fixing him with what she hoped was a quailing stare. He seemed unaffected. "Dance with me, my queen?" he asked, though it sounded more a venomous demand than a polite request.

"I think it would not be wise," she began.

He cut her off, rolling off the wall and slinking up to her. He loomed behind her, close enough she could feel the heat of his breath on her neck, see it in the air between them. "Ye've a waltz for a filthy pirate, but not so much as a minuet for a lowly highwayman?" he accused.

She took a single step and stopped, unable to walk away from him. She was terrified, but there was something... something she couldn't put her finger on. He took that for ascent and slipped up behind her, one hand circling her waist to pin her back against his chest, and the other capturing her slender wrist. He guided her forward, out onto the floor to a fiery music that seemed to suit his mood. He was breathing down her neck and An was suddenly aware of the view he had. She flushed from the edge of her mask all the way into her dress-line, and she felt his anger grow. He turned her suddenly, a move full of suppressed violence as he swept her across the floor.

"When is a queen not a queen?" he asked.

She was determined not to allow this man to terrorize her, tried to maintain her cool. "When she takes off her mask."

"And when this mask of ice comes off, what will you be? Queen or tart?"

"Neither," she snapped, harder than she'd intended. This anger was beginning to ring familiar, though the last time she had seen it, it had not been aimed at her. Now it was. "Why have you been watching me? Stalking me?"

He scoffed. "Stalking? That the pirate's word? You didn't notice me until he pointed me out."

"You were skulking, and I was enjoying conversation. Answer the question."

"I was looking for someone. I was hoping you weren't she, but I fear I may be mistaken. If I am, then she is not the woman I thought her to be."

Her heart skipped, threatened to not start again. "And why would that be?"

"The woman I thought her would never be this shallow. This cold and heartless."

"Because she wanted for one night to be beautiful? What little girl would not want to be a princess for a single night given the choice?"

As their tongues sparred, the moves he guided her feet through also became combative, each of them fighting for hard won ground, and An feared she was losing and suddenly realised she wanted more than anything not to lose this one. He pulled her close, crushingly close. "I am no prince," he said in her ear.

Her temple was pressed to his cheek, and she whispered, her heart caught in her throat, "No, you are a Bard, and that is just as out of reach."

Skye was dancing with 'Jack' again. They had finally sussed out who was leading, and Skye was dancing much better. "I take it back, you actually are a fairly good dancer," 'Jack' said teasingly.

Skye smiled, remembering who'd taught him. "I had a good teacher."

'Jack' suddenly smiled with his whole face, "Awww."

Skye knew instantly who it was. "Gotcha!" he grinned.

"Oh, you're a right bastard," Liberty growled, but she was smiling. "Keep it under yer hat."

"What hat?"

His attention was suddenly diverted by bumping into another couple. He turned to apologise and saw it was An with the Highwayman who'd been lurking most of the evening. They did not even acknowledge the collision and danced off, and Skye thought he saw a tear glistening in the corner of An's eye.

He watched the pair, growing angrier the more he did, until Liberty had to snap him out of it. "Don't do whatever you are thinking," she growled.

An and her partner had stopped, even though the music had not. The highwayman started to walk away, and she reached out, touched him. Skye's sword almost dropped into his fist as the man in black whirled on her, backing her up as he approached. They stopped, their voices drowned out by the music and the chatter of the oblivious. She set her hands on his chest, pleading or explaining. He seized both wrists, driving her back again, turned her so that he was pulling instead.

"So you chose to be th' Snow Queen?" he was saying. "A cold-hearted bitch who collects hearts like trophies? I expected this of Serephina. Not you."

She gave a rueful laugh, tried weakly to free her hands from his iron grip. "It is a winter ball, a come-as-you-aren't. I chose something I was not, that would attract Henry."

His grip tightened. "Henry? You *want* his kind of attentions?"

"No! I wanted to help Liberty, to distract him so he couldn't find her. And I've done it. He's stopped looking for her. He thinks I'm..."

He growled suddenly and let her go, thrusting her hands away from him as if their touch burned. He was still frighteningly close. "Ye thought this layer of ice and snow would protect ye from those kinds of attentions? Foolish girl. You see this?" he snarled, indicating his costume. "This I so very nearly was, but that She heard me sing first. Something like this..." he indicated her exposed shoulders, "would have attracted my attentions, all right. As prey."

An felt her throat growing tight, fought back her tears with anger. "You can have any woman you want. How can I compete with that? Just once I wanted to be worthy of your attention."

He softened suddenly, a terrible sadness in his eyes as he reached out and brushed her cheek with the back of his fingers. "What ye fail to understand, Ceobhránach, is that ye already had my attention. Ye were already worthy. It was this," he stroked her cheek again as she flushed as he knew she would. "This blush of innocence."

"Innocence is lost," she said softly.

He continued as if she hadn't spoken. "...And yer high collars and yer hidden ankles... all of it, true modesty hiding such strength, such self-sacrifice. Aye, I have women throwing themselves at m'feet." His arm went out in a sweeping gesture to encompass the whole room. "I want none o' them. Nothing of them. Their beauty is only outward and inside they are shallow and still, or if there is any depth, it's either rotten and foul or an empty void. You..." he stepped closer, and this time she did not back away. "Yer pleasant enough to look on, but yer beauty lies here," his hand on the bare skin over her heart was so cold it burned, "and here," fingertips brushed her temple around the silver leaves of her mask. "Yer a well, Ceobhránach. Strong and steady to last, fresh enough to slack any thirst, and deep enough for a man to lose himself forever. Yer heat is buried deep and heaven help any man what finds it."

He pressed his forehead to hers, closed his eyes, breathing deep of the scent of her. An felt a single tear run down her cheek, down her throat to her breast. Tonight he smelled of the open road, a snow-covered, blood-splattered road. "Ye don't deserve me. 'Tis I who are not worthy. Ye deserve better, more. I'll only break yer heart, Ceobhránach."

They were interrupted by two things. One, the sound of a church bell beginning to toll midnight in the distance. Two, Henry.

He approached, laid his hand on Jonny's shoulder and pulled him off An. "Here now, Roberts," he snorted. "I'm claimin' my queen. Ye've had more dan enough time wit' her."

Jonny's lips narrowed, tightened, but he did not argue. He stepped back and allowed Henry to take his place before the Snow Queen, bowing sarcastically. "All yours, Morgan. Though ye may not find her all ye expect. And for th' record, yer majesty," he added to An. "That one's less worthy than any of them."

Henry started to growl something else, but the Highway-man turned and walked away. An wanted to go after him, but she could feel the magic fading with every stroke of the bell and her limbs weakening in response.

Her vision was beginning to cloud over. The next thing she knew, Henry was untying the silk ribbons that held her mask in place and she reached up to catch it and lift it out of her hair.

Around them, everyone was unmasking with gasps of shock and gales of laughter and more than one wife smacking her husband. Henry stared down at An stupefied that he had been so wrong. He looked up, saw Liberty standing next to Skye waving at him. Then his eyes lit on the milkmaid who, as she took off her mask and the last peal of the bell rolled away, became bent and haggard; her once lustrous dark brown hair becoming stringy, grey and coarse. Henry's eyes popped and his mouth dropped open in horror and revulsion even as the old woman cackled in true wicked witch fashion.

More than one person, An half-noticed, was having moments of horrified regret. At least one, though, had only a few seconds of 'eww' before contemplating the matter, then seemed all right, even impressed.

An's eyes cast about, looking for Jonny. He was by the French doors, walking out, his mask still on. She ran, stopping in the door-frame, called after him.

He paused, slowly turned. He took her in, from her honey-brown hair, still elaborately dressed in a cascade of curls and sprays of crystals, to the faery damask gown that she still filled rather nicely, even though the artificial beauty had faded. Her eyes were once more dark voids swirling with mist and fog, and tears glittered in their corners. He crossed back to her, regarding her with a tip of his head, a very raven-like gesture. He looked up to the lintel of the door above their heads. Then, without warning or preamble, he seized her, crushing her against him and kissed her.

It was long and deep and passionate, full of his temper and his fire and something she dared not name. She was startled, shocked, and had no time to melt or stiffen or react. The kiss was a volcano erupting, and it took her breath away, devoured her. Everything stopped in the wake of that first kiss: the world, time, her heart, all thought. Then, just as suddenly, it ended and, with a rush of white feathers against her cheeks, he was gone and she was cold and alone in the doorway without a thought in her head. Quite reasonably, she slipped to the floor in a dead faint.

There was a roar from behind her as Skye rushed forward, pushing Mikey aside. He checked her over, glaring off into the night at the white raven winging away. Liberty was there, the voice of reason and control, ordering someone to fetch a couch and telling Skye to pick her up.

Skye obeyed, gathering her up easily, and growled. "Ah'll break his manky wings fer this."

Liberty popped his arm. "Ye'll leave him be is what ye'll do," she snapped, shooing people out of the way as they brought her to the fainting couch Mikey carried in.

"After what he just did?"

"All he did was kiss her under th' mistletoe, ye Highland Ass!" she snapped, began to rub An's wrist.

"Ah may not be experienced in th' arts, but a kiss shouldna have that effect!"

Liberty put her hands on her hips and glared up at him, held up her fingers, counting off her points. "One, that was prob'ly her first kiss. Ever. Two, that was intense... passionate. Hell, it'd have curled even MY toes. Three, it happened suddenly and in public and she's Victorian. Add those up and faintin's a perfectly reasonable response. Now th' lot o' ye back off! She's goin' ta be mortified enough when she comes to."

Most began to move away, though Roulet trotted up, handed Liberty a small vial which she broke and wafted under An's nose.

An came to with a start, trying to escape the foul stench. She sat up slowly. Her vision was foggy. Not even Liberty was coming in clearly. It was like walking from bright sunlight into a darkened room. It was getting better, but slowly.

Roulet was leaning over the back of the couch, smiling down at her. "Your coach melted, I'm afraid."

"What?" she asked, looking over her shoulder, confused.

"Your coach. It was out front all night. It just melted, polar bears and all." She glanced down at the 'ice' at her breast and on her throat. "Luckily, that's the only thing. You still got yer bling, girl."

Liberty fingered the pendant. "That is lovely. How do ye feel?"

"Embarrassed, heart-broken, tired and blind," she sighed. "I'll be fine."

Liberty laughed softly, elbowing Skye as he loomed too close. "After that, I imagine it will be a bit before yer 'fine'. Either way, we have to go outside shortly. Even th' orchestra is packing up."

Skye looked over at the band, was surprised to see they were still what they had seemed to be earlier: goblins in tuxedos. The man who had been dressed as a djinni, complete with blue skin and Arab clothing, was handing the conductor a bag. He turned around after the exchange and began to cross the floor, telling various groups to grab what food they wanted and head out to the Green. It was Ian.

Henry was suddenly there, glaring at Liberty. "You planned alla dis, didn't ye?" he accused.

"Well, I didn't plan on the Highwayman or have aught to do with what Baba did to you," she began, though a faint twinge told An this was not entirely true. She laughed as Henry shuddered at that. "But that's not to say I didn't enjoy it. Ye brought it on yerself. If ye'd not been braggin' ye'd know who I was by cheatin', I'd never have got th' idea to go to th' witch in th' first place."

Henry started to say something, reaching for Liberty's hand, but Ian's voice stopped him. "Not so fast, Henry. Yer forgettin' sommat."

He turned, glared over at him. "She's mine 'til ye win her, Green Man."

Ian laughed. "What yer forgettin', Holly King," he said deliberately, "is that neither of us found her, so... neither of us starts with her. 'Tis on even ground, we are, boi. No early spring, no long winter."

Henry growled, but dropped his hand. "Shall we battle, den?" he asked sarcastically.

Ian nodded. He took a moment to check on An. "Yeh all right, lass?"

"I will be. I can walk out on m' own," she said, standing. She was still flush, but managing. He nodded again as the group began to head for the door.

Liberty took An's arm, remembering she did not have her shillelagh with her for a guide. "What'd ye pay them with this year?" she asked her father.

He chuckled. "A handful of gold coin and a brace of Rubik's cubes. That ought to keep them happy some while."

As the others laughed at the joke which Skye did not get, he stripped off his jacket, and tossed it along with his shirt over the back of a rocking chair on the newly restored veranda. "Oi, Chief," he said. "Havya any paint?"

Ian looked back at him. "No, I've no woad. Not a real war."

Skye sighed. "Had to ask."

As he stretched, his naked chest rippling in the light of the newly kindled fires, he heard several whistles and calls of appreciation. The loudest was from the old woman who trailed behind, looking like the cat that ate the canary. She winked at Henry who could not suppress a shudder and he hurried out to the field to round up his side.

Someone brought Skye the wooden claymore.

"Try not to break any heads with tha'," Ian called as he strode out onto the field.

Liberty led An and a handful of others, mostly women but not all, over to the bandstand to sit and watch the battle. One of the fires was near enough to provide sufficient heat, even though the night was warm for December as far as An was concerned. She found herself seated between Liberty and Solitaire, as Roulet had gone out onto the battlefield.

Henry came over to them as the final groups were lining up and got himself a kiss from Solitaire.

Liberty scowled at him, teasing, "Oi, gettin' kisses from someone other than yer queen in front of yer queen's bad form. Bad luck for you."

He growled at her, peeling off his coat and hat to allow his antlers free rein, "Takin' the kiss of an unwillin' woman inta battle's worse luck, wench."

The women in the pavilion laughed at that, and Solitaire shooed him off.

An could begin to see some of the combatants. Ian had gone full gryphon and, as he trotted up to square off against him, Henry went full stag. Ian was enormous. Even Skye standing near him seemed small.

Ian's voice was loud, and clear as it rang out over the battlefield. "I, Ian gryphon O'Keefe, the Oak King, challenge fer sovereignty. The days are growin' long an' warm and yer time on this earth is done. Lay aside yer crown or I'll break it from yer head."

"And 'tis welcome ye are t' try, ye nut-headed antique!"

With that, both armies rushed forward, and the melee began.

An was still too absorbed in recent events to watch the battle with any interest. She was only just beginning to see more than the strongest magics, everything else was still a blur.

Something did click with her, distracting her thankfully from her moody ruminations. "Ye lied to Henry... sort of. Ye did have aught t' do with Baba and he..." she blushed, and didn't finish her sentence.

Liberty and Solitaire both laughed, and Solitaire leaned in. "Well, she made the agreement, but I had more to do with that bit of embarrassment. You see, her price for the charms was a bit of Henry."

"A button, a hair, anythin' from his person," Liberty grinned.

"So I got him alone in the maze and... got a ...hair," she said, leaving a great deal unsaid to preserve An's dignity. It had been bruised enough that night.

"So she used it t' cheat th' magics and find him?" An asked.

Liberty nodded. "He's been a mite rude of late, and she felt he needed some takin' down. Poor ol' girl doesn't get laid that often. She takes it where she can get it."

"Here here!" Solitaire crowed, raising her glass in toast. An found herself blushing nonetheless.

Someone in the back cringed and made a sound of sympathetic pain at something that happened on the battlefield.

"You did a brilliant job with Henry though," Solitaire added, laughing. "That touch about removing his 'letters of marque' had him convinced. He thought you were referring to his gonads."

Liberty laughed. "That would seal th' deal."

"It was not what I meant," An blushed.

"Just as well. Not that he'd ever have considered I'd be dressed as a man," she chuckled.

They watched the war below for a bit, the only noise the sounds of battle and the cheering on of the people watching. An found her fingertips brushing her lips thoughtfully. Remembrance left her warm inside as she pondered what it could have meant.

"That was some kiss though, huh?" Solitaire's voice drifted in through An's reverie.

Liberty glared over An's head at her friend as An began to blush again. Solitaire put up her hands in surrender. "I wish I had a man would kiss me like that, just sayin'."

"Still not a conquest?" came the snide voice of the woman in silver.

An looked up to see Serephina lurking in the corner, watching her. She was surprised by the calmness of her answer. "Conquest implies seduction, not courtship. A 'love them and leave them'. One does not waste a great deal of time or effort on 'conquests'."

"So how long is long enough? Before you give him your other cherry?"

"Serephina!" Liberty snapped. "That is quite enough. Either comport yerself with some decorum or get off elsewhere. Woman's done naught to ye to warrant that kinda venom."

"You can't banish me from the Rest, Liberty, for all you're the ritual Queen and the Chief's daughter."

Liberty stood, every inch both of the things the woman had just accused her of being. "Oh, can't I? Th' ritual is in full swing, and I hold all power in matters of my court. As fer th' other, with yer reputation ye really think Da will even ask fer a reason should I ask?" She didn't wait for the woman's response before she continued. "And don't even think about bringin' that shite inta m' bar. I know what ye were tryin' t' do all last month. I even suspect yer goadin' her or any other o' my patrons an' I'll have ye thrown out like th' trash ye are."

An saw something flash in the woman's eyes and reached up, setting her hand on Liberty's arm to warn her. "Not on my account," she whispered.

Serephina humphed and stormed off, disappearing into the night back towards the carriage house.

Anything more was interrupted by a bellow like that of an elk being taken down and the cry of an eagle in triumph. Then the crowd was parting as Ian strode forth to claim his prize, filling in his wake. The wreath on his brow grew into a shining crown of Oak branches, the leaves a verdant green and subtle hints of mistletoe interwoven. He stood before the bandstand, mostly man again and looked up to his daughter who stood on the top step looking down at him. Vines of winter flowers and greenery had grown down around her Jack costume and formed a rough gown. The coronet on her shining brow was made of fir with bright holly berries and edelweiss.

"I am th' Oak King, and th' lightening year is mine," Ian announced, his voice deep and loud enough for all to hear.

She nodded her head regally, looking out over the two armies made whole, beaten and sore. "I am yours, my king, I and all my gifts."

Ian knelt before her, as Henry had six months past, arms spread. "Yer blessing, I beg, Bright May. For we are tired o' th' cold and th' dark and long fer Spring."

She descended the steps, stopping on the last, and placed the healing kiss upon her father's forehead. For extra measure, she plucked a snowdrop from her gown over her heart and tucked it into his crown.

Ian grinned up at her, even as the collective sigh of relief flowed out of the crowd as the healing flowed in.

Skye stood just back from Ian and Mikey, looking up at Liberty, his eyes bright. He could not help but notice the two women at the top of the steps flanking her: Solitaire, in her watery gown of the Lady of the Lake, and An as the now crownless Snow Queen. Both women were shining as the moon peeked through a hole in the clouds.

When Liberty stood again, and Ian took his place beside her, she was radiant and the fields began to smell more like flowers than sweat and churned earth. All around them, the magically placed snow began to melt, though the night remained near forty degrees.

Ian raised his arms and shouted for the after party to begin, and people began to stream towards the tables of food that had been brought out while they'd been fighting. Drink was more popular, as was the dancing area once it was cleared, and the Rest's handful of musicians brought out their instruments and began to play rousing country music.

An was not surprised when Cipín found her, slipping into her hand with a wooden sigh. She was grateful, having missed her once the masks had come off. She wandered around the gathering party for a little while, looking and hoping, but not at all surprised when she found no sign of Jonny. Well before two, she found herself passing through the woods back home, a quiet joy battling an incredible sadness in her heart.

20

The Tallow's home was lonely with the folk gone, so An only came by once in a while to make her rounds to check on things, making sure nothing had been tampered with. All remained quiet. She spent most of her time at her cottage, making her lace before the fire, working on the cobweb gloves for Elizabeth. She noticed that other lace things had started to crop up, delicate cobwebby patterns gracing the arms and headrest of her chair. New lace to some of her plainer blouses. An did not mind. She would find something to do with all of it, when there became too much.

An had it in mind to make an Irish lace dress, a wedding dress. She knew *she* would never need it, but was certain that eventually Elizabeth, or Kellain, or Bethany would. She and the brownie began making the little motifs of the lace thread and adding them to a basket under the table. It kept idle hands busy and happy and would come together eventually into something truly wonderful.

Wednesday she was at Courtz, hoping for a glimpse of Jonny, for a chance to talk, but he was not there that she could see. She briefly saw Serephina, but after a glare from Silhouette she simply sat there, drinking her Martini, and eventually went home. An went on as she always did, enjoying the poets or the singers, ate her dinner and drank her tea.

Sil convinced her to try a new honey whiskey, but she did not like this one quite as much.

Eventually, An got up to recite something she'd written in her little book. She was nervous, but there were precious few in the bar she could see and so took courage from it and found her way to the stage and spoke.

> Your touch like frost against my skin
> My cheek flares with heat
> Your voice like bells upon my ear
> I cannot breathe, my heart is still
> In darkness I wait
> You come like the breath of winter
> To cool my soul from summer's fire
> I cannot fathom why
> Soft like snow your hand on mine
> Like the stillness after a fall
> White blanket and quiet and peace
> Even your silence is a song to my soul

She drifted back to her seat, blushing from the applause. There was something on her table, resting delicately across her plate. It was a rose fashioned of snow. She could see the individual crystals pressed together to an icy hardness. It looked as if someone had taken the rose and stabbed someone with it and recently, each petal's edge sharp as razors and kissed by blood.

At first she didn't know what to make of it. She sat, picked it up by the stem and examined it. It did not speak to her, nor did she really ask it beyond wondering who had left it for her. She smelled snow and earth and rosin and smiled, knowing. She had not seen him since the kiss, but he was here none-the-less. She pondered what it could mean, what he could be telling her, but found it difficult. There were too many possibilities.

She thought to wait for the blood to dry and knew immediately that it never would. Lifting it from the plate, she noticed it had left no trace on the china, did not drip though it should have. She ran a finger along one petal, and though the blood felt wet, what came away on her fingertip was her own blood where she had cut herself on the edge. She rubbed it, feeling the cut less than a paper-cut. She put the blossom to her nose to smell it. It was cold, smelled like a rose with faint fragrance, like breathing snow.

She kept it with her the rest of the night, got more than a few comments on it before she left. The mortals saw it as being cut from crystal. The only Touched who saw it that night, Silhouette, merely raised his eyebrow as An held it as if it were the most precious of gifts.

She set it on her nightstand as she slept and dreamed of kisses.

In the morning, she braided her hair up for working in the garden and looked over at the rose in the mirror, thinking how it would look. She crossed to it, picked it up by the long, icy stem and found it more flexible than the night before. She returned to the mirror and set it against the side of the bun she had twisted her braid into. It wrapped itself around and through the plait to hold it in place.

She smiled. It wasn't made to do that, but somehow it did so to please her. She ran a finger along the rounded tops of the petals, managed to do so without cutting herself. She rose and headed into the kitchen for her breakfast, humming happily to herself.

She started in the lower garden, checking the state of the roses and whether they were ready for pruning, taking up the empty bowls from the pixies. There were tiny footprints everywhere, and this pleased her. Her garden would have none of the usual pests, and her winter cabbages were doing nicely. The footprints put her in mind of the yellow rose and the fact that she had never seen footprints around it. Perhaps this was why it wasn't flourishing.

The morning air was suddenly rent by a screech from up by the house. It was high-pitched and terrified and ...cursing in Gaelic. An got up, running to see what was the matter, and saw the yellow rose bush struggling to wrap up and hold on to a long, white and black, dragon-like creature. She tried to pry some of the branches away, but the rose retaliated, taking a swipe at her, savagely tightening around the creature. The line of blood across the back of her hand angered her and she held it out, calling Cipín from where she rested against the back door. Why she had been there never crossed An's mind to ask.

She wielded the shillelagh against the rose bush, battering it back until it recoiled, letting the dragon go. The silvery-white creature limped quickly behind An's skirts, clinging to her desperately. An aimed the shillelagh at the rosebush, glaring. She noticed, however, that the yellow blossoms were singed with a great deal of red. They were beautiful and fragrant, filling the garden with their perfume.

It dawned on her in an instant, "Ye drink blood?" she growled at it. "Why'd ye not let me know somehow! No wonder th' pixies won't tend ye."

It occurred to An then that a rosebush was a living plant and not subject to the gift she had been given. She sighed. "Fine. I'll find ye something I can feed ye. But ye leave this poor wee beastie alone!"

It started to reach a vine out for her and she waved the shillelagh at it and it withdrew. At her ankle, the little thing hissed at the bush, breathing out a puff of ice and frost. An knelt, held out her hand to the creature and let it limp into her grasp. "Och, ye poor wee thing. Yer wing's ripped t' shreds and scratched t' pieces. If yer of a mind, I'll take ye t' someone I know can maybe manage some mendin'," she said, beginning to carry it around the side of the house towards Liberty's.

The creature stretched out along the cradle of her arm, adjusting itself so that it hurt less.

An used Cipín to guide her from her own gate to Liberty's front door, using the knob to knock so she did not disturb what rest in her arms. After a few minutes, Liberty answered the door, obviously still in her pyjamas. "What's... that?" Liberty said, changing her question mid-sentence.

"I don't rightly know, but I found out what th' yellow rose eats," An said ruefully.

"It tried to eat that?" she asked, horrified.

"Aye, can ye help? I can dress th' scratches but that wing..."

Liberty threw the door open wider and beckoned them into the house. She closed the door and stepped in front of An. "Follow me." She led her to the back of the house into the large kitchen. "Set it on the table. I want to take a look before I start mending."

An laid it gently down, watching it stretch out, taking great pains to spread and lay its wings flat so they could be examined better. The scales were tiny, a pearlescent white, with black horns and nails and minor accents. The membrane of its wings was almost opal-like, shifting colours subtly as the light moved across them.

Liberty looked it over, tsking over the damage. "The body's nothin'," she sighed. "But that one wing. Ye were smart t' tuck th' other up when ye did," she surmised. "This is going to get a mite uncomfy," she warned, and began straightening out the larger shreds of the membrane. She used a cotton swab and water to manipulate the tinier fragments, making them stick slightly to one another until they formed a mostly cohesive whole. Throughout the procedure, the creature made no sound beyond the occasional whimper or clenching of its tiny fist.

When she had it as whole as she could, Liberty exerted her magic on it, watching it knit itself back together. With a soft, damp cloth, she began wiping off the blood. There wasn't much.

"Well, now I know what th' long red thorns are for," An sighed.

The dragonling turned its head at that, and in a very feminine voice spoke in Gaelic, "*And who was the daft ninny what put a Vamprick Rose in your garden in the first place?*"

Both women gasped, then laughed. "*We didn't,*" An said.

Liberty shook her head. "*It sort of appeared just before the wall went up when we were buildin'. I wouldn't put it past Danny to've seen it, liked it and said, 'Why not? She'll love it'.*"

"*I didn't know it was a Vamprick Rose,*" An explained, suddenly remembering having read about them once while in service. "*I've spent months trying to figure out why it wasn't thriving.*"

"*And the fact that your garden pixies avoided it like the plague didn't clue you in?*"

"*No. I've... had other things happening to keep me from noticing.*" An looked a little sheepish at that, sighed, then narrowed her eyes. "*If ye know so much about them, why'd you go near it?*"

She simpered, licking one ebony talon. "*Hard to tell what they are when they're dormant. Besides, I wasn't expecting to find flesh-eating plants outside of*"

Faery, now was I?"

An remembered her manners. *"First of all, would ye like something to refresh yerself? Something to eat or drink?"*

She thought about it a moment. *"A drop of whiskey would do my parched throat fine. And a bite of,"* she paused to sniff the air, *"that strawberry something I smell if ye can spare it."*

Liberty laughed and turned. *"Comin' right up."*

"I'm An, and that's Liberty," An said, introducing them. *"Have ye a name or something we can call you?"*

The creature tipped her head, regarding An with a narrowed eye. *"I don't know whether you're giving me 'use' names or if your naming practices are indeed that inane."*

"Now that's a mite rude," Liberty quipped in English without thinking, returning with a small shot glass half-full of Jameson's and a saucer with a bit of the strawberry pie and a cocktail fork.

The creature picked up the tiny fork delicately and cut off a bite, nibbled it. She nodded and gathered up another. "It is what it is. Ye tell me yer names are 'Of' and 'Freedom' and what else am I supposed to think," she responded in kind.

Another moment of stunned silence and a grin. An rest her arms on the table as she watched the creature eat. "Well, we're sorry to disappoint ye, but I don't remember my name. I was called *Bean an Ceobhrán* while in service and have just taken An Ceobhrán to name. Well, I've added O'Keefe to it."

"And I grew up in New York," Liberty said. "My mother had a twisted sense of humour."

The creature thought this over, sipping the whiskey daintily, shifting back to Gaelic which seemed more comfortable for her. *"Very well, then. My name is Aislynn. And I'm a petty drake, in case ye were wondrin'."*

An smiled, nodding, *"It would have been a rude question t' ask."*

"So would askin' ye where ye served, but since ye brought it up..." she said, arching one eye pointedly at An.

"I served as governess for th' Gryphon King."

The dragonling made a little face of being impressed, finishing her pie. *"So, assuming ye do something about that Vamprick Rose, ...can I live with you?"*

"*And why would ye want to live with me?*" An asked as Liberty got the drake another piece of pie. "*Ye don't even know what kind of person I am.*"

"*Oh, I have a pretty good idea what kind of person ye are. One, ye saved me. Ye've been trying to cultivate that rose, by yer own admission, since ye moved in, but ye were willing to beat it to a pulp to rescue me. Two, ye have a brownie in yer house. A very happy one unless I miss my guess, too. Three,*" she paused to ooo over the second bit of pie. "*Two... wait, I was on three. Three, ye have a garden full of pixies in spite of having a Vamprick Rose and they haven't tried to kill it, all because ye've been trying to save it. That says a lot about ye.*"

An was stunned to silence.

"*A lot,*" she reiterated, taking a huge bite of strawberry and munching happily.

Liberty grinned. "*That is a hell of an endorsement, An, luv.*"

"*I... never really gave it thought. I've just lived ...over There... so long I guessed I just knew how to live with them. Never thought.... They really would have killed it if I hadn't been trying to...*"

The dragon nodded. "*In fact, they were getting ready to deal with it when ye started fertilizing it. They were waiting for it to attack ye, but it didn't. That perplexed them. They're kinda interested in seeing what ye do with it.*"

"*And how d' ye know so much of this if ye didn't know it was a Vamprick?*" Liberty asked shrewdly, setting down pie and tea for An and herself.

The dragon gave a little snort, and a tiny puff of condensation rose from her nostril. "*They told me after I got caught. Ye didn't hear all the buzzing? It weren't bees, let me tell ye. They were apologizing.*"

"*So ye get along with pixies?*"

She nodded. "*And some sprites. Have one or two boggart friends, but we don't usually talk about them.*"

"*Well, I don't see a problem with it, but,*" An began, picking at her own pie. "*I don't stay at home much. I'm a governess and have a child t' care for in the afternoons and evenings. And while she would be absolutely delighted with ye... her mother might find yer appearance somewhat... shocking.*"

Aislynn gave her wings an experimental snap, flipping them open and then closed like a pair of fans. "*That's fixable. I can look like anything I want... to humans. They see what they expect to see.*"

Liberty nodded. "*That's how it is with most of us. Humans by and large just don't want to see magic, so they don't.*" Liberty thought a moment. "*This, however, might solve one of yer little problems."*

"*What problem might that be?*" An asked with a frown.

Liberty chose her words carefully. "*Yer need fer a service animal.*" She turned from An to the dragon. "*Ye see, the shillelagh can only help her so much, keep her from runnin' inta things. But finding the day-to-day mundane is a chore. She has to feel her way around on the table to find her cup, but with you helping her, most of that's a non-issue.*"

Aislynn cocked her head the other way. "*But she sees fine. She found me with no trouble.*"

"*I have a gift that allows me to see all things magical,*" An answered. "*And my house itself is magic. But this teacup in my hand is only so much fog. It shows up only as a hole in m'hand, a place I cannae see. I am in all senses, outside of magical places, blind. And I've already burned myself in the Tallows' kitchen because I didn't know there was a pot ye could cook in off the stove.*"

Liberty winced. "*Ooo, a crock-pot. They're a time-saver, but a bear trap if ye don't know it's there and on. So, will ya?*" she asked, turning back to the petty drake.

"*What must I do?*" she asked, nibbling another bite of her pie.

"*Just stay with her, ride on her shoulder mostly, warn her when she's about to hit something or someone or get hurt. Also, make sure she knows where her plate and cups are. That sort of thing. Oh, and I don't recommend flying in public. Out here at the Rest, no one's going to look at ye in askance, but beyond... best they take ye fer a service monkey.*"

"*Monkey?*" she hissed, insulted.

"*'Tis the most common service animal fer what ye'll be doin'. If ye accept.*"

"*Ye don't have to,*" An added. "*I'll manage on as I have.*"

"*Dodgin' traffic and hopin' no one runs a red light?*" Liberty snapped. "*Ye think I don't know what ye face comin' ta Courtz every Wednesday and Friday?*"

An blushed a little. "*I can stop comin',*" she said quietly, knowing the reaction she'd get.

Liberty nearly exploded. "*Like hell! I'll install a bouncer at that corner waitin' fer ya if I have ta!*"

An laughed as Aislynn squealed and swore in Gaelic.

"*All right, I'll do it. Easy work anyway. Plus, there'll be snuggling and warm places and more pie... right? There* will *be more pie?*"

"*There will more of a lot of things. The brownie and Martha both are excellent cooks. So's Lafayette."*

"Well, that's all right then," she simpered, curling her tail around herself as she sipped her whiskey.

Liberty settled down, turned to An. *"So, yer goin' t' be at the Christmas Party at Courtz, right?"*

"Well,... I wasn't plannin'..."

"I'd like ye t' come. I throw a party every year for underprivileged children, and I'd like yer help."

"What do ye need me to do? That I can."

Liberty's eyes lit up. *"Tell stories."*

She smiled. *"Well, I know a few."*

21

Christmas Eve dawned cold and clear and An slipped into the dark green skirt and vest the brownie had laid out for her. She tucked her rose behind her ear to hold her hair off that side of her face. She could feel the light pricking of the near invisible thorns and the petals, but did not mind them in the slightest.

Aislynn watched her from the bed as she dressed. The dragon had made herself quite at home fairly quickly, even got along with the brownie which she claimed to have seen. She eyed the rose warily as An put it in her hair.

"*Why do ye wear that thing? I've seen it cut you.*" While Aislynn understood and could speak English fairly well, she preferred old Gaelic.

"*It was a gift.*"

"*Do ye even know what it means? This gift?*"

An paused. She knew fragments of the language of flowers, but knew that it changed over the years. "*Well, I know white is innocence and purity. We've already discussed that's how he sees me. The red...*"

"*The blood*," Aislynn corrected.

"*Red means passion, but from blood it could mean anything.*"

Aislynn sighed when she realised that this changed nothing. "*Makes me wonder about the gift giver.*"

An only smiled shyly at that.

Before they left for Courtz, An placed a letter in the box for the children, though she could hardly call them children any more. It contained her usual greetings, let Lion know how the 'prank' had gone over, especially about the witch's own little joke, knowing he would be pleased. It also asked Eagle if she would loan her a couple of books on petty drakes and vamprick roses.

They took the door directly to Courtz and went downstairs. The children for the party had not yet arrived. Liberty hurried over dressed as Mrs Claus, took time to show An how the layout of the club had changed. There was a place near the foot of the stage where a wing-back chair had been set up for her, with plenty of room on a new red carpet for children to gather and sit to listen. There was a buffet table with all kinds of cookies and treats with juices and other childish drinks. An could smell dinner cooking in the kitchens more than usual. There was a Christmas tree in the middle of the stage and plenty of room for the kids to dance if they wanted. Roulet had the speakers turned down to more reasonable levels and was playing a variety of children's favourites.

It was not long before the children, and their parents arrived, and the chaos began. The children were fascinated by the little monkey that curled up on the back of An's chair, happily sucking on a candy cane. An told her stories, including the "Night Before Christmas" poem and Dickens's "A Christmas Carol", as well as a few lesser known but highly entertaining tales, and held the children rapt. She knew some of them came and went, some kids getting bored and going for sweets or to dance, others coming to listen. She was aware some of the parents were also near.

After a little while Santa Claus came downstairs, ho-ho-hoing and carrying a sack over his shoulder he really shouldn't have been able to, and all the children swarmed him. As he began calling names and passing things out, An studied this Father Christmas. It took her a few minutes before she realised she could see him because it was Skye. She laughed, and Aislynn climbed down and draped herself around her shoulders. "*What's so funny?*" she whispered.

"Nothing, luv," she answered, stroking her throat scales gently. "I just realised I know Father Christmas."

An also knew that in the other half of the room, the parents were receiving other gifts: quilts and jackets, warm socks and shoes without holes in them, all in decorative shopping bags so that they wouldn't look like charity. An smiled and sank back against the chair, sipping her tea. Liberty had thought of everything.

She was a little startled when Father Christmas appeared in front of her, holding out his hand. "Miss An, ah believe this is fer you," he said, his accent only barely managed.

She flushed a little. "I... don't have..."

"Ah'm bloody Santa Claus," he growled lowly. "Ah gi'e th' gifts t'noight."

Aislynn bristled at the growl, her dainty, angular head coming out from under An's hair on the side away from the snow rose.

"What th' wee devil is that?" he exclaimed.

An chuckled, taking the present before he dropped it. "Aislynn, this is my brother, Skye. Skye, my petty drake friend, Aislynn. I rescued her from th' rose bush."

He frowned. "Flew into it, did she?" he asked.

Aislynn snorted. "*No, I was looking for rose hips and it... tried to eat me.*"

An laughed as Skye jumped back, startled that it had spoken. "*Apparently, it is a vamprick rose. I've asked th' princess for a book on it, so hopefully...*"

"*Yer keeping it?*" he exclaimed. "*A blood drinking rose?*"

An shrugged, "We shall see."

Knowing better than to continue the argument, he changed the subject. "Well, are ye goin' ta open it?" he said, pointing at the box.

Remembering it, she felt for the ribbon, pulling it loose and lifting the lid. She felt inside and found a metal whiskey flask, just the perfect size for the small bag she always had on her. She smiled. "Caterin' to my newfound vice, are we?" As she pulled it from the box, she discovered it was not empty. She opened it, took a sniff. It was one of the honey whiskeys Sil had been giving her, her favourite so far. Aislynn crawled off her shoulder and stuck her nose to the mouth, dipped her long skinny tongue into it, tasting it. She purred as An closed it up and put it away.

"Thank you," An said, slipping it into the bag with her book. She was about to say something else when 'Mrs Claus' came up and drew him away, excusing them first. An laughed and sat back, watching the two of them take a turn on the dance floor to the delight of the children who began to sing "I Saw Mommy Kissing Santa Claus".

The Christmas party at the manor that night was a very different affair. The tree stood where the rose and lily bouquet always had and nearly brushed the ceiling. An could not see the tree itself, but a good many of the decorations glittered in the air in the centre of the room. There were more children and more presents and more people. Ian handed out the gifts, though he was not dressed as Father Christmas.

An had enough warning this time to bring some of the presents she and her brownie had been making: lace things for the ladies, Liberty, the twins, Martha and Shannon, and Bethany and Kellain. She had made lambswool gloves for the men.

Ian noticed the petty drake right off, even though she tried to hide from him in An's hair. He chuckled. "I'll not eat yeh, little one. Yer hardly a mouthful."

Aislynn poked her head out, "*Promise?*"

"Aye."

An affected introductions. Ian pulled something off the Christmas tree, one of the things An could not see, and held it out to Aislynn. She hesitated, sniffing it. "*Is that...*"

"Aye. Silver. I'm sure An can get yeh more when yeh want. It's not like she's spendin' her money," he said, giving her a look at that last.

"It's not like I need it for much," she countered. "I'm housed on yer lands, though ye'll take no rent. I eat out o' yer larders. For all I know*, my laundry's done by th' Bean Nighe.*"

He nodded. "Point taken."

"I do buy the Princess books, though."

He laughed as Aislynn took the object, began sucking on it as if it were a lollipop. An looked at her. "Ye eat metal?"

"*Only precious and only occasionally.*"

"Good to know." Her hand drifted to the pendant around her neck and the diamond brooch she had taken to wearing all the time since the Masque.

Aislynn snorted. "*I don't eat worked... unless it's just... bad art. Those are pretty.*"

Ian was distracted by others and An moved on, wandering out onto the veranda to listen to the children playing.

Skye came up, offered a miniature cupcake to Aislynn, who popped out from An's hair and took it happily. It was then that he noticed the rose in her hair and frowned. "Tell me tha's paint."

An's hand went to it unconsciously. "I can't. I don't know rightly. I doubt it."

"Where'd ye come by it?"

"It was left on my table," she said, moving over to the rail, feeling defensive suddenly.

"So ye don't know who left it ye? It could have been that blonde cow, what's been raggin' ye."

An looked over at him, surprised he knew about Serephina. "She's not blonde. Not really. An' there's no call fer that kinda language. I may not be Scot, but I know what ye intend by callin' her that. And no, it's not from her."

"So ye know."

"Aye."

"An' yer defendin' it, so it must be from that white-haired, girly-boy yer moonin' over."

Cipín cracked across his calf before he was aware she'd turned. She was glaring at him, her lips tight.

"Ah don' trust th' bugger," he growled, hopping sideways, his hand to his leg. "Ah've seen him go off with other women."

"So?"

"So he's unfaithful. He's just after..." he stopped there, seeing the shift of her grip on the shillelagh. "Ah'm concerned fer yer heart."

"I'll tend to that m'sel', thank ye kind. Yer warnin's fair taken." Her voice was cold, sending a chill down his back.

"He'll break yer heart," he insisted.

"He's told me as much. Doesn't change anything. Men... are permitted to do as they like so long as they come home."

"Hardly fair, ye think?"

"Is anything in love ever fair?" she countered.

Aislynn had moved to the rail to eat her cupcake, tinsel paper wrapping and all, watching the exchange with interest, frosting on the tip of her nose.

An turned away, arms folded, watching Coach And Four out on the green playing with the children, the centaur kicking up his heels like a colt. Everyone was enjoying themselves. "It may all come to naught anyway, so what does it matter?"

"It matters cause ye deserve happiness."

She shrugged. "I'll be content with whatever I can find. It is my way. I'd be foolish to look fer more."

Skye sighed, realizing the battle was hopeless.

"Th' heart wants what th' heart wants, Skye. Ye should know that by now."

Skye didn't know what to say to that, or what she meant by it, and just stood there, watching her. Eventually he turned and left her, disturbed to the core but uncertain what he could do about it.

After a while, An went back into the house to the solar. As she passed the Christmas tree, she heard Ian's footsteps from the east hallway where his office was. He was not alone. She turned to look without thinking, the smile for Ian frozen on her face. Jonny was beside him, slipping a flat, black box into an inner pocket of his open vest.

His hair was loose, flowing over his shoulders like snowfall. He looked a little tired, was nodding at something Ian said, accepting the hand on his shoulder. As they stepped into the atrium, An suddenly realised she was staring and turned, continuing her walk to the solar. She changed her mind at the last moment and headed to the front door, which was closed due to the weather.

As her fingers touched the ancient wood, feeling for the handle, he was there, opening it for her. She did not look at him, unsure how exactly to face him. Jonny watched her as she nodded her thanks and crossed the front porch to the steps carefully.

She stopped on the top step, Cipín clutched in her hand, telling her where the drop was. She turned her head back to him, over her shoulder, but not far enough she could actually see him. "Happy Christmas," she said, unable to think of anything else to say and feeling she should say something.

Aislynn flew through the open door before Jonny closed it, landing on her shoulder. She coiled around her neck and looked back over An's shoulder at Jonny. She looked up at the rose over An's ear, then back at him and her eyes narrowed. She muttered something in Gaelic and tucked herself away under An's hair.

"Happy Christmas," he said. Then he was beside her. "May I walk ye home?"

She nodded, not trusting herself to say anything else.

He took her arm and guided her down the steps and onto the path that would eventually lead back to her cottage.

"Thank ye," she eventually said.

"Fer walkin' ye home?" he asked.

"The rose."

"Ah," he replied. The silence became awkward. Finally, Aislynn left her neck and flew on ahead, leaving them a little privacy, but not much.

"I..." she began, clammed up, reluctant to ask. "I want to ask... what it means?"

They stopped beneath the spreading branches of an oak tree and he turned to face her, holding her hand between them in both his own. "Ye've no idea?" he asked, surprised.

She blushed. "Oh, I've plenty of ideas, that's th' problem. Th' colours say one thing... th' substances... confuse th' matter. I never needed to know th' language of flowers. It was above my class. A girl in my situation would get wild daisies and be thrilled."

He gave a soft chuckle, stroked her cool cheek with his colder hand, touched her hair, fingering the single leaf which lay against her temple. "I must say, I like what ye've convinced it to do for ye."

"Well, it refuses to talk, so... it compensates." She suppressed a shiver of delight at his touch. She was terrified he'd kiss her again and hoping fiercely that he would.

He smiled, took the rose from her hair, rolling it delicately in his fingers, ignoring the thorns. "Well, white..."

"Is for innocence," she supplied when he hesitated. "Purity. I know that."

"The snow, because, for all its pristine beauty, snow can kill. The red,... that's for all th' usual things. The blood..." his eyes locked with hers, his voice softer than his touch, "*my blood,* blood I'd spill fer ye. The edges..." he said, drawing the blossom gently across her cheek, making several shallow cuts there that she barely felt, "are my warnin', Ceobhránach. I *will* hurt you."

An's hand covered his, tender.

"I hurt everything my heart touches," he breathed, gazing at the blood lines across her cheek.

"Love is a risk," she whispered. "And its own reward."

He gave a tiny laugh, "Livin' is a risk." He slipped the rose back into her hair. "But we do it, anyway." He looked up into the tree above them at the moonlight shining through the bare branches and the outline of the drake glaring down at them with glowing, opaline eyes. He sighed. "Would ye faint again were I t' take advantage of yon mistletoe?"

She blushed. "That was... circumstantial."

"Unexpected?" he asked, whisper soft. He tipped her chin up with one long finger, tilting her face so that the moonlight fell on it.

"And public," she breathed. "I... I'd never... been..."

His lips touched hers, feather light, and she felt everything from her chest down drop away. The spinning she felt was not a threat to faint, but something else entirely. She felt lighter than air, held aloft by the touch of his hand cradling her head and the contact of his mouth. There was passion in this kiss, but it was restrained, not the crushing blow of the other one. This kiss was almost a plea, a request for forgiveness instead of the punishing demand of the first. Neither was better than the other. They were just... different.

When he pulled back, she felt bereft, though he did not let her go, uncertain of her equilibrium. She looked up at him, saw his hair glowing in the moonlight, casting his face in shadow as the light wind lifted the loose strands and held them aloft. She looked into his eyes until she couldn't bear it any longer, and the sound of a branch snapping above made her look down. She drew her shawl up closer around her shoulders.

The silence dragged on for a moment, as she listened to the wind in the bare trees, the beat of her heart and the rhythm of his breathing. His lips had been warm.

"The masque..." she said.

He sighed. "Shattered expectations," he said flatly, self-accusing. "I should know better by now."

"I didn't want to..."

He stopped her with a cold finger to her burning lips. "I was only a shade of myself. It happens. I have... so many lives trapped inside me and I don't know which one is me and they all have their say. I looked for ye. When I could not find ye and began t' suspect.... I grew angry. I... am sorry. For what it's worth." He brushed a tendril of hair from her face, smiling at the fog rising around them.

"It's worth a great deal." She started to say something else, to apologise or explain her choices, and thought better of it. "Expectations," she said, leaving it at that.

"I don't know why ye want this. I will hurt ye... again."

She looked away once more. "Ye don't get a say in what th' heart wants."

He turned her to look at him. "I *will* hurt ye. I can't help it. It's what I was, what I was made. I damn near was the Heartless Highwayman. I left...," she could see him struggle for a name, a face, "her," he said instead, "for a thing of beauty. She prob'ly never knew what became of me. Mayhap she thought I'd abandoned her as some Bards will do, and hated me th' rest of her days, for all I know. In a way, I did abandon her. I can't be faithful, An. I can't promise ye that." There was pain in his voice.

She set her fingers on his lips, silencing him this time. "I am not askin' fer promises. I'll take what I can get. However, I can get it. I never thought I'd have anyone, much less..." she stopped, glancing away. She set her hand on his chest, over his heart without thinking about it. His hand rose up to capture hers. "If I am not careful, I'll find myself..." she laughed, embarrassed, "daring things I shouldn't. Things have already been said..."

"Like what?"

She shook her head. "It doesn't matter."

"If it bothers ye, it matters." He was so close, his breath so cool and sweet, and those soft, fair lips so tempting.

Then Jonny's head came up, eyes darting, raven-like, across the wood around them. Aislynn suddenly dropped from the oak onto An's shoulder and buried herself in her hair, never minding the rose. Her slim, white body was trembling.

From further in the forest, a howl shattered the night. Jonny's eyes darted to the road they had come down and grabbed An, pulling her behind the tree and shielding her, drawing one of his two axes. An's hand slipped down Cipín's throat, getting a fighting grip.

Something came skittering up the road, something small and dark, cackling like a mad hen. It was followed by the thunder of hooves as Henry galloped after the boggart, mad as hell. An could hear others following after him, yelling at him to come back.

Henry had nearly reached them when he reared to a stop, transforming half to man. Jonny shifted, putting himself between An and the woman who now stood on the moonlit forest road. Her hair was wild, and she smelled of blood and gunpowder. Her smile was malicious.

"Merry Christmas, Henry," Raigne said. Then there were two pistols firing in her hands. Henry's sword never left its sheath.

An stifled the scream that wanted out as part of Henry's head went one way even as his body continued forward, trying to charge Raigne.

Skye roared, his open run up the road shifting to a full charge as the claymore dropped into his hand. There was a crack and a sound like something in a fire exploding, and the length of the sword erupted into flames as he lunged for Raigne.

Jonny shifted yet again, letting go of her and drawing his other ax, moving behind her, his back to hers. An watched, horrified as Raigne fired again, nowhere near as accurate or effective as before, and lost her head in a single stroke. Then An heard the low growl of the hounds and felt her blood turn to ice.

Others ran up, following Skye in time to head off the massive black cú hounds coming out of the woods on the left. An had no time to cry out or think, as she became aware of other beasts on her side of the road. She turned.

Jonny was already swinging his axes with all the effectiveness of his dream-self, and An forced back her panic and faced down a second hound coming at them from the side. All the skills Juan had been teaching her came into play as she swung and counter-struck. She led with the knob end, rattling its jaw and deflecting the teeth that only grazed her, tearing her sleeve. She finished with a stab to its shoulder with the iron end and was pleased to hear the yelp and sizzle.

She smelled a puff of ozone just as something lunged at her from behind and felt a burst of frost from the back of her neck. She half-turned, resetting her back to Jonny's, saw Roulet tackling a hound with its face iced over. She swung again at the one on her side, narrowly avoiding getting bitten, swung and stabbed again. It howled and then Jonny's axes bit into its neck and it collapsed.

Aislynn jumped from her neck and tackled a nearby bush with a curse and another burst of frost-breath. From the shrub came what sounded very like a cat-fight. An flinched as overhead she heard the cawing cough of a makar, followed by the sound of a very angry gryphon.

There was a gurgling snarl, and An turned, saw the beast Jonny had put down rise and lunge at him. Instinctively, she stepped in the way, taking the full weight of the beast and the crush of that bloody maw even as she drove Cipín's iron tip through its chest. She went down beneath it.

Just as quickly as it began, it was over.

Skye turned, looking over the battlefield. Mikey and some of the boys were collecting the bodies of the hounds, dragging the enormous carcasses just out of the woods where Fox was setting them on fire. Occasional flares of lightning through the trees showed where Roulet was finishing another off. Henry lay in the road twenty feet from the headless body of the traitor, Raigne. From the corner of his eye, he saw something coming out of the brush beside the narrow road and turned. He saw Aislynn walking backwards in small jerks, dragging the body of the boggart who had started the whole thing.

He felt a stab of panic. If Aislynn were here, that meant An was not far off. He looked around wildly, stepped towards the wood on that side and caught the flash of moonlight on white. Behind the broad trunk of a spreading oak whose barren branches were thick with mistletoe, An lay in the bard's arms, her face buried in his chest, the man's cheek pressed to the top of her head and Cipín's bloody knob lying on the ground beside her.

An Oeireadh
(The End)

*The quote at the end of chapter 6 is the opening line of David Copperfield by Charles Dickens

Acknowledgements

Some books are gardens. This one has had so many tenders that to mention them all would read like film credits. So to all of my gardeners and hedgemen, thank you. I hope you are happy with the results, and not too mad at what I had to omit. But some, I have to mention by name:

Jack Kellum for providing the land and allowing us to cultivate it, as well as for sending the storms and the molehills we made into mountains, not to mention the hurricanes we stood in the middle of and said 'it's just a light drizzle, it'll be over in a minute'. The poem 'Above a Cloudy Sky', the ballad of Jenny and Jack, is his work. All other poetry, good or bad, is my fault. Thank you also for the research.

Tré and Laura, whose names I sincerely hope to see on future gryphon's Rest novels as authors, for working with me on this massive community and for letting me tell my story first and set the world up. I just hope I've left you enough room to work in when you finally tell the stories of Liberty and Skye and Roulet. I know I cannot do them justice.

For Chris, who put up with my going on about another man; was able to argue with me 'in character' and still maintain a Scottish accent in the face of me with my Irish up and on; and helped me write the insufferable big brother and plot fight scenes, even when I was obsessing over a certain elven bard...

So many people helped with this, with the circus-sized cast, that I could not use all of your ideas. Perhaps those stories will be told in other volumes. There will be more... if my readers are rabid enough.

For Amy Moore, who gave me the idea for the cover, though due to the interference of Life, was unable to give me what I needed. Thank you for trying in spite of everything else.

For my patient and thorough editors: Stephanie Kellum and Laura Dees. Thank you, for everything.

For my Mother, who didn't have a teddy bear this time (she'll know what that means) but none-the-less devoured every chapter and asked the pertinent questions. ...And got mad at me for the ending. Sorry, blame Murphy for that. It was all his idea to leave it there. But fear not. The next book should not be too far behind. I'd give you a sample, a taste of the first pages, but...

...Spoilers!

Other Books By
S.L.Thorne

Love In Ruins
The Speaker
Mercy's Ransom
The Gryphon's Rest Series:
Lady of the Mist
The Gloaming

SHIFT Books 1 & 2
Stag's Heart
Dragon's Bride

All Available in both paperback and ebook
at:
Thornewoodstudios.com/books

Made in the USA
Columbia, SC
10 October 2023